THE CELTIC SERPENT

by S. Robertson

CCB Publishing
British Columbia, Canada

The Celtic Serpent

Copyright ©2012, 2019 by S. Robertson
ISBN-13 978-1-77143-027-2
First Edition, Revised

Library and Archives Canada Cataloguing in Publication
Robertson, S. (Sally), 1943-
The Celtic Serpent / by Sally Robertson – 1st ed.
ISBN 978-1-77143-027-2
Also available in electronic format.
Additional cataloguing data available from Library and Archives Canada

Book cover designed by Megan Simpson, Victoria, British Columbia, Canada.

This work has been registered with the Canadian Intellectual Property Office:
Copyright Registration #1094327

Disclaimer: This is a work of fiction. Names, characters, and incidents are the products of the author's imagination or are used fictitiously. Any resemblance to actual events and persons, living or dead, is entirely coincidental.

Extreme care has been taken by the author to ensure that all information presented in this book is accurate and up to date at the time of publishing. Neither the author nor the publisher can be held responsible for any errors or omissions. Additionally, neither is any liability assumed for damages resulting from the use of the information contained herein.

Publisher: CCB Publishing
               British Columbia, Canada
               www.ccbpublishing.com

To Bill and Gregory

PROLOGUE

Ireland 60 C.E.

Dawn broke, the stillness punctured by a flock of birds as they rose in unison, their high pitched cries heralding a preordained disaster.

Out of the morning mist a Roman army stealthily moved onto the Island of Mora off the west coast of Wales. Under Imperial orders, General Suetonius Plautius was ready to strike a lethal blow against the Druids by attacking their college center and the residence of the Arch-Druid. By day's end every soul would be slaughtered and the sacred groves of Britain hacked to the ground. Fearing the power of the Druids, the Roman Emperor had decreed their extinction, a campaign which would last for centuries. That evening, as a heavy mist shrouded the Sacred Isle, it was said that some could hear the ancient gods weeping.

Days later, a Druidic Seer walked slowly up the Hill of Tara in Erin. At the halfway point he stopped to gaze on a cherished scene, likely for the last time. He envied the freedom of a lonely hawk as it soared on a gust of wind. While his premonitions foretold of danger it did not speak of such savagery. Menacing clouds were everywhere. Continuing his journey he headed towards a small group of students at the top of the hill.

The Druidic students, dressed in white, their colored sashes depicting their degree, stood near an oak tree, their accustomed meeting place.

"Thank you, for being here, we have much to talk about and little time," said the Seer, Imergin, as he joined them. "The attack on Mora is but the beginning of a dreadful campaign against our Order which will last for generations."

"Why did the Romans attack us, Master?" asked one of the younger students unable to restrain his anxiety.

Imergin carefully chose his words, "I'm sure the Romans will give many excuses; maybe their condemnation of our beliefs, our way of life, or our magic, but perhaps their greatest fear is that we may have a greater legitimacy to rule than they do. Power-mongers fear competition and grow more strident when they command armies."

"But Master, why now? What changed?" asked an older student.

"That, my son, is the key question. Obviously, certain Roman leaders decided that by eliminating our Order, it would be easier to conquer our people. The severity of this attack was intended to undermine our confidence.

Only time will tell if it achieved its purpose."

"Master, what do you mean; we have a more legitimate right to rule?"

"That, my son, is something you need to know. It will be important to your descendants. As you know, our Order has very ancient roots. From boyhood, I was taught that the Druids existed from before the Great Flood. When Atlantis was hit by comets, a small remnant of our Order survived and made their way to this Sacred Isle, a remaining piece of their homeland."

"Master, do you actually believe we are standing on a piece of Atlantis?"

"Yes," replied the Seer, "and other cultures hold similar beliefs. Even today, people living in distant lands cherish the sound of the Atlantic waves as an echo of their departed forefathers and, disperse their kings and heroes to rest in the Western Land of the Blest. Across the great ocean, other cultures tell of foreign gods dispersing knowledge after the comet attack, stating their homeland was slipping beneath the ice. It was also rumored these ancient teachers wore a snake symbol on their robes."

"Just like ours?" asked a young student.

"The same," responded the Seer. "The serpent has always been connected with wisdom and healing. You have been taught that 'The Swan,' a snake coiled around the Tree of Knowledge and Wisdom, is an ancient emblem of a fully enlightened being. Many societies recognize the serpent's power in their ritual vestments. The ancient Egyptian scepter of rejuvenation is a rod topped with a brass serpent."

"Master, if the Druidic Order existed for centuries, why do they say it is a recent creation?" asked a more inquisitive student.

"What they say may hold some truth," replied Imergin. "Around 3150 B.C.E. the Druids, fearing another comet impact, deserted these lands. Prior to leaving they decided to preserve their knowledge by sharing it with a chosen group of people from different cultures, some from as far away as the Mediterranean. Their prediction of a comet was correct but it landed in the Mediterranean with less destruction than feared and spared the Atlantic coast. Over time, waves of former inhabitants began to return, a sign of the sacredness of this land. The earliest returnees reestablished the Druidic Order."

"As for our connections with royal families, over the centuries, Ireland has been strengthened by input from three ancient, powerful, royal lines; the Scythians, Egyptians and the Israelites. In 1360 B.C.E. the first Scythian-Egyptian marriage occurred between Niul, Prince of Scythia, and the daughter of Pharaoh Smenkhkare of the Eighteenth Egyptian Dynasty. Merytaten-tasherit, in becoming a Princess of Scythia, was called Scota. Coming to Ireland their descendants would become the High Kings of the Picts, Irish, and Scots."

"The second Scythian-Egyptian marriage was about 600 B.C.E between the daughter of another Egyptian Pharaoh, Nekau (Nechonibus) and Prince Galamn of Scythia. They also came to Ireland and their son, Eire Ahmon, became the forbear of the Kings of Ireland, and later of Scotland."

"Links with Israel's royal family occurred in 585 B.C.E. when the prophet, Jeremiah, came to Ireland following the destruction of Jerusalem by Nebuchadnezzar of Babylon. Accompanying him was the only surviving member of the House of David, a princess named Tamar (Teamhair) Tephi who married Eochaidh, the High King of Ireland. For centuries Eochaid's successors were crowned in the presence of the sacred Stone of Destiny. Jeremiah also brought the temple treasures. Some say it was Jeremiah who established the Druidic colleges."

"About three hundred years later, the Tautha De Danann (Tuadhe d'Anu), known as the Dragon Lords of Anu, or the Royal Scyths, arrived in Ireland. Considered one of the most ancient races on earth, they were tall blond or red haired people with green eyes. These ancient people brought with them several magical items or talismans including oval balls of crystal, called Serpent Stones, and the Serpent's Medallion, a powerful amulet which was worn by the Arch-Druid. The Romans were likely also after these magical talismans."

"Master, what happened to all these treasures?"

"Long ago, all but the Serpent Stones and the Serpent's Medallion were secreted behind a magical veil, a power of the Ancients which our Order still possesses. It is prophesized that these items will remain behind this veil until the *'coming times'* in the future when a prophet or prophetess of Tara will release them. As you know, my dear students, the sacred duty of our Order is to protect the *'times beforehand'* and the *'coming times'*. We have had centuries protecting the *'times beforehand'*. The attack on Mora signaled the closure of the *'times beforehand'*. We now face centuries of preparation before the *'coming times'*."

Realizing the impact of the Mora attack a student asked, "Master, what happened to the Arch-Druid's Serpent's Medallion, for its powers alone could be catastrophic in the wrong hands?"

"Do not be alarmed, it is safe. Prior to being assaulted, the Arch-Druid secured it within a magical spell which only another Arch-Druid could break."

"Are the Serpent Stones now in danger as well?" asked another.

"The Serpent Stones, which all Master Druids possess, are being rounded up and will be placed behind the magical veil. But the Serpent's Medallion has to remain in this dimension, awaiting the signal of the return of magic to this arid world. However, since this is centuries away, to stifle its powers and prevent it falling into the wrong hands, the medallion is being dismantled as we speak. The crystals are being dispersed to the female Druids, a group the Romans do not recognize."

Hesitantly, a student inquired. "Master, are we going to be killed?"

"That's possible, my son, unless you are very clever. Understand your life as a Druid is over. From this day, you must remove all Druidic insignia and blend into the communities for, I can assure you, this persecution will not cease in your lifetime or in that of many of your descendants. You will be fortunate to escape its wrath."

Sensing their discomfort, Imergin talked on, "Until this attack on our sacred college, we thought we were safe, as Druidic leaders were renowned for their knowledge in religion, philosophy, jurisprudence, education, astronomy, and medicine. Our magical powers astounded our enemies. Many royal families and elite Romans sent their children to our sixty colleges. But none of these matter now as the Romans intend to destroy us."

Grasping the ramifications of the danger their Master was imparting, the students sat restlessly looking at each other, a few stared into the distance.

To soften the blow, Imergin decided to share his vision of the future. "Stay concealed for many years. In time, some of you and/or your descendants will find a home in Celtic Christianity. These Nazarene Christians, followers of James, the brother of the prophet Jesus, will have familiar views on mysticism, nature, creation and family. Life will still be precarious as the Romans will decree that membership in either the Druidic or Nazarene communities to be a capital offence, punishable by death. Nevertheless, here your descendants will find a haven for almost five hundred years. In the seventh century the Church of Rome, a relic of the Roman Empire, will send a person to Britain to stamp out the Celtic way. Nevertheless, Druidic ideas will continue in Ireland, Scotland and Wales for another ten centuries hidden in the folds of the remnant of the Celtic faith and an order of monks called the Culdee. Since Celtic priests and Culdee monks marry, their children will eventually become members of a select number of leading Irish, Scots and Welsh families, identified secretly as the 'sacred gentry'. Throughout the centuries the Serpent's Medallion will remain dormant, protected by your descendants for, even up to the 1500s, the Church of Rome will denounce all magic. By the mid-1600s, life which had been precarious in previous centuries, will become intolerable for the Guardians."

Pleased his diversionary tactic was working, he continued, "After many centuries, names of lands, as we know them, will change. Much of the Pictish land will be known as Scotland, and much of the land south of it, will be called England. By the mid-1600s the English will have occupied part of Scotland by force, establishing troop garrisons along its entire east coast. English ships will patrol the coast. The conquered will require passes for any travel, and gatherings greater than three will be condemned. The English campaign against the Irish, this Sacred Isle, will devastate the country. Forty percent of the population will be reduced due to war, famine and disease, with countless numbers transported to other countries as slaves. Irish troops will be forced to leave and will serve in foreign armies. Religious trials will terrify the remaining citizens, who will be forced to report anyone or anything. Despite these dangers, a small courageous group of your descendants will risk a secret rendezvous to protect the medallion."

"Eight Guardians will travel by boat to a clandestine meeting at the Palace of Birsay, a residence of the Earls of Orkney on the extreme north-west of the Mainland of the Orkney Islands. The two-storey, stately palace with its central courtyard and large stone towers overlooking the great ocean will offer a safe haven for this auspicious meeting. Fearful of the ramification should the Serpent's Medallion fall into the hands of ruthless political or religious leaders, the Guardians will establish a plan which, they hope, will protect the medallion for the next three hundred and fifty years, until the prophesied *'coming times'*. But the plan will impose a major sacrifice on some of them."

Caught up in the story, one student enquired, "What kind of sacrifice, Master?"

"Four of the younger couples will be asked to leave their homeland forever to live in a newly discovered continent, called America. They will make this sacrifice out of family duty, not because of our ancient Order, for by then, we will be little more than myth."

Realizing the enormity of what the seer was saying, one student wondered aloud, "But Master, if the crystals are removed and some sent to distant lands how will our descendants know how to reconstruct the medallion, activate its powers or even know how to safely use such powers in some distant time?"

With a gentle smile, Imergin replied, "As guardians of the *'coming times'* it is our duty to make sure there is some secret knowledge retained for such an event. Your spirit must be so strong that once triggered, your descendants will understand where to go and what to do. Our task will certainly be complicated by the passage of time and the lack of magical skills of our descendants, but it will come to pass."

Knowing their white robes were now conspicuous targets for their enemies, Imergin beckoned his students to quickly follow him down the Hill of Tara. Leading the robed group, the seer continued to reassure them, "Come, I will teach you how to become invisible, how to specifically strengthen your spiritual skills and together we will create a system that will survive centuries of magical darkness. Be assured, our spirits will be there to help our descendants awaken the Serpent's Medallion in the *'coming times'*, for that is our destiny."

Chapter 1

Canada: Halifax Health Science Centre, 2012

A golden snake slithered out of her grandmother's trunk. Angi knew this thrice-repeated dream was a cosmic harbinger but she couldn't interpret its message. "If I even mentioned such a dream," she thought, "a psychologist would spend days tramping through my sexual fantasies." But Angi knew otherwise. From childhood her grandmother had taught her that such dreams held fateful prophecies.

How well she knew that old trunk which sat beneath the bay window in her grandmother's bedroom. A family heirloom, passed down through the centuries. The wooden, rectangular box with its oval lid and black metal straps and hinges looked ancient, its mystery enhanced by a worn brass lock, opened with a skeleton key kept hidden by her grandmother. While the exterior had faded over time, the interior retained much of its original texture. Angi's only access to this mysterious box was in the presence of her grandmother, a stipulation which remained even when she grew up.

The dream haunted her. "Why a golden snake? Damn," she thought, "Gran would have this translated before my first sip of morning tea. Thankfully, my vacation begins in a few days and she can enlighten me." Running late, she shifted to more practical matters. Dressed in a white lab coat over operating room greens, Angi moved rapidly along the hospital corridor heading for security.

"Hi Gus," said Angi, "always good to see you on a holiday weekend."

"Yah," replied Gus, a middle-aged, heavy set, ex-policeman, "it should be a lively one. I bet you are looking forward to your holidays?"

"Just five more days," said Angi "and I'll be back on my precious Island for some R&R. I need it; the past weeks have been hellish."

Gus pushed the electronic sign-in slate towards her as he handed her a managerial electronic tablet called Airmid.

"Don't know what I would do without this baby, Gus. It is a God-send. In an instant, I can access the status of patients, beds, staff, supplies; get information on medications, treatments and the latest medical news. In addition, I can call up those darling robotic porters. How did they ever do it in the past? It must have been a nightmare."

As she signed in she noted the large warning at the top of the slate; a penalty of $300 for forgetting to return the tablet at the end of the shift. Few managers made the first mistake, fewer still a second.

About to leave, she recognized a familiar voice. Marcy, an old classmate, now the Director of the operating and intensive care areas, was signing in. Slightly built, with blond streaked hair and piercing black eyes, Marcy had been the chatty one of their student group.

Completing the sign-in routine, Marcy turned to Angi with a quick wink said; "Another day, another dollar, heh Angi? By the way, did you know that Airmid is the name of a Celtic goddess?"

"Fascinating, who was she?" asked Angi, knowing that Marcy was always a wizard when it came to such trivia.

"Well, the other day a patient told me that Airmid was the healing goddess of the Tuatha de Danaan who existed in Ireland before the Celts. She was a goddess of medicinal plants and brought the dead to life." Smiling, Marcy continued, "Now this electronic tool has a personality. I occasionally chat with her. Enough already, I believe your vacation is almost due?"

"A few more days and I am off," replied Angi. Then she remembered their last meeting and asked, "How are you doing, Marcy? When we last talked you were really down. Any change?" They began to walk along together.

"You know, Angi, except for the increased salary, this managerial life leaves much to be desired. I'm tired of the 'prima donna' doctors, the shortage of staff and supplies, unions blocking me at every turn and the never-ending automation being forced on us. So, in answer to your question, nothing has changed. I need a vacation, a change, or both. Actually, Angi, I didn't become a nurse to be a referee. I like caring for patients. Perhaps its time I rethink my career. Angi, is it any better in your area?"

"Well, I don't have the variety of doctors you have to contend with, but I have the shortages and similar issues. However, I like the automation, particularly the robots. But, like you, I prefer direct care for its immediate rewards. This managerial world is a far cry from our student expectations. I'm still a neophyte in management after ten months but so far, it is OK and I have even introduced a few changes."

Reaching the elevators, Marcy pressed the button, "God that takes guts. Good for you! Hope it works. Must run..... Have a great night old buddy. Let's have coffee before you slip off to that Island of yours."

"Great, I'll send you an e-mail later tonight. 3am is usually quiet."

Finding an alcove near the elevator Angi took a quick glance at the ER day report checking on the beds, staff and key issues.

Walking on, she thought again of Marcy's dilemma. Marcy was not alone. For years, cracks were appearing in a system plagued with excessive expectations, ongoing shortages and no limits. After forty years the idealistic, publically funded health system in Canada was beginning to show its age. Few solutions achieved much. Politicians and senior managers feared risk, and entrenched health groups were determined to hold on to their sacred turf. Introducing change was hellishly risky.

Graduating with her nursing degree from Dalhousie University at 21, Angi took a fast-track promotional route. By 25, she had become the Director of the city's main emergency department for adult care in a 1,000 bed Health Science Centre serving a population of a million people. Halifax, the capital of Nova Scotia, was the largest city on the east coast. This being Friday evening of a long weekend, it would be busy as, in addition to routine health issues, the weekend offered a melee of sports, arts and other events augmented with the arrival of four American navy ships.

Greeting people en route, Angi moved lithely along the corridor, her athletic movements the result of early ballet training and years as a runner. While she might have described herself as somewhat ordinary, others found her platinum blond hair and emerald green eyes stunning. Glancing at her watch, she increased her stride aiming for her first official stop.

Outside the ambulance receiving area, she encountered one of the fleet of robotic porters with supplies for some unit. Like miniature forklift trucks, the robots followed a pre-programmed route using sensors and beacons guided by a floor laser beam. On board communication devices allowed automated doors to open and close along corridors and the robots could even summon an elevator. Angi thought, "I rather like these little workaholics. They've improved infection control, deliver supplies and meals, clean rooms and remove waste and dirty linen. There are even rumors they might be used to dispense drugs. More sophisticated ones are already in the works for doctors. Wait till they see what the Japanese are developing, they even have nurses." Then she chuckled, "I'll likely be obsolete in a few years, best make the best of this while I can."

Angi chose the Emergency Department as her career option because she liked its energy, excitement and constant change. She also liked Halifax. It was a lively city with lots of social offerings. "I know I should be thinking about returning to the Island to help Gran ....maybe later," she thought.

Arriving at the ambulance area Angi spotted a commanding figure vigorously giving instructions to the crew of an incoming ambulance. Dr. Graham Greene, the Medical Director of the Emergency Department, stood head and shoulders above his staff at six foot four, a strongly built individual with a wicked sense of humor. His Newfoundland accent was still evident after years in Nova Scotia. Recognizing Angi, he smiled and signaled he needed to talk to her, pointing to his office and waving both hands to indicate 10 minutes.

Angi nodded and proceeded to make her rounds.

Graham watched her while he waited for a response to his telephone instructions to an incoming ambulance attendant. He liked working with Angi for her quickness, cool headedness and her ability to work with different staff. He was glad she chose the ER after graduating and not surprised when she got promoted. While he wished her well he was not happy at losing a valuable professional to management. "There are few exceptional ones these days," he thought. He was not looking forward to his chat with her for he would be the bearer of bad news. "Life really sucks," he mumbled to himself, as he replied to another question from an incoming ambulance crew.

The ten entrance ambulance bays were already busy; four ambulances had just arrived, the overhead electronic board indicating five more were en route and word had just been received of a bad car accident near the airport. It would be a busy night.

Noting the time she quickened her steps towards Graham's office.

Bursting into the room on Angi's heels, Graham greeted her with a somewhat over enthusiastic, "How are you feeling, Angi?"

Sensing a medical inflection in his question, she replied, "A bit tired, but otherwise OK. I'm glad my vacation's in a few days. Why, is there a reason for your question?"

"Remember the blood test you asked me to take a few days ago?"

"Yes, any results?"

"Perhaps you should sit down," he said, pushing his office chair towards her.

"That's not a good sign," she thought. She had assumed anemia, but, perhaps she had picked up some infection. "I've had no temperature but there have been bouts of nausea." Accepting his advice, she eased herself gently into the chair.

"Well," Graham continuing, "I had the blood test repeated and got a confirmation this morning. Angi, there is no easy way to say this. I'm sorry to inform you the test results indicate you have chronic lymphocytic leukemia," the diagnostic bombshell exploding in the small office air. He concentrated on her reaction.

Stunned, Angi went silent. "My God," she thought, "the lights are being turned out before my life has begun." Scrambling, she tried to remember former patients she had nursed with the disease. All seemed older, and died even with chemotherapy.

As if reading her thoughts, Graham continued, "Now Angi, you know the prognosis for this disease has greatly improved in recent years. The disease may progress slowly and you are young and fit. I suggest you get a second opinion.........immediately. I would recommend Dr. David Wong, the best hematologist in the city. I'll be glad to make the referral, if you wish."

Wanting the world to stop spinning, Angi slowly replied, "Just.....wait, I need time to get my head around this, I..........." and the words ceased.

"Yes, by all means give yourself a few days, come and chat with me if that helps. Above all, don't carry this burden alone."

Before she could comment her electronic tablet came alive and she responded. "I have to go, there's a problem with a patient in the psych ER. ......have to run."

Graham wanted to say more but instead placed a hand on her shoulder, "Very well, remember my door is always open. Angi, I'm truly sorry. Let me know what I can do for you when you are ready." He watched her scurry from his office.

She couldn't remember if she replied.

Stoically, she headed towards the psych ER. "O God," she cried, "how will I tell Gran? She was relying on me to help her in her senior years. Damn.... damn this world.....damn fate.....damn, damn, damn........I'm going to fight this!" And moments later she thought, "Is that what that stupid golden snake was trying to tell me? Strange."

Ireland, Dublin: Trinity College

Torrential rain accompanied the rolling thunder, as a lone figure, under a green golf umbrella, zigzagged through the semi-darkened streets of Dublin. Reaching the front door of Trinity College, he stepped aside to let an elderly woman pass, glancing briefly at her flowing white hair and long gray dress and cape. "What a hell of a night for a costume party," he thought. Then, spying the open elevator, he dashed across the lobby, jumped aboard and pressed 'three.'

Entering his office, he deposited his umbrella against the doorframe, swung his jacket over the back of a wooden chair, and flicked on some Irish music and then his computer. Waiting for the computer to warm up, he watched the rain forming long streams on the windowpanes.

The overhead illumination gave the bland décor of his academic retreat a certain glow. With no order to the books, papers and ancient bits and pieces resting on several bookshelves, the only open space was at his computer desk. The aroma was a unique blend of books, dust, mold, and human occupation which only centuries could create. The lone token of nature was a plant near the window which flourished on neglect.

The storm reminded him of Sundays with his grandmother and Irish tales of the ancient gods and goddesses, ghosts and leprechauns. This likely led to his professional interest in Ireland's past before the Anglo-Norman invasion, a lost heritage he loved to unearth. He chuckled as he remembered how her Banshee warning upset his little brother. She kept insisting that the O'Gratteney's were one of the Irish families sometimes visited by an old woman of the fairy mounds as an omen of death.

Kevyn O'Gratteney at 35 was an intensely competitive and intelligent Assistant Professor of History at Trinity College. Recently, he found himself running into problems with the pro-Roman Catholic members of faculty because of his popular lectures on Celtic Christianity and the Druids and his antagonism to centuries of church domination made worse by recent child abuse allegations. Restless, he needed a distraction and one appeared.

In 2012, with Ireland's economic downturn ensnaring everyone, Kevyn jumped at a chance to augment his salary with a private contract from a Boston colleague. The straightforward project asked him to search the Trinity College's well-known library and archives to determine if and why, in the 17th Century, for some unknown reason, valuable crystals were removed from a piece of Celtic or ancient jewelry to be guarded for centuries by select Irish/Scots families.

After months of research Kevyn had little to report. Then, one evening, a random computer search elicited a faint whisper of a secret cryptic code blocking access to something. More progress was made when he solicited the help of colleagues familiar with 17th century codes and secrets. He also contacted his brother in Cork, a computer specialist, to help penetrate restricted files. More time elapsed as he chased one clue after another, the labyrinth growing more frustrating with each discovery. Unfortunately, Kevyn's activities also attracted unwanted attention.

Antonino Borgiano had been exiled to Trinity College under a shroud of secrecy after his well-orchestrated career in the Vatican had collapsed following an incident at a boy's school. But after years of privilege, remaining invisible was out of the question for Borgiano, however strongly it had been ordered. Instead, he adopted a lavish lifestyle, arriving daily in a red Maserati, dressed in the latest Italian fashion to aimlessly strut about the campus.

Rumors circulated that he was under some cloud. Yet, despite his apparent wealth, he had few friends after nine months.

Trapped, Borgiano needed an escape. A chance comment focused his gaze on Kevyn. Maybe he could find something lucrative in Kevyn's contract. So, unbeknownst to Kevyn, Borgiano began tracking his activities, bribing library and other staff and hiring an outside computer hacker. Weeks of frustration finally paid off when he accessed an unencrypted e-mail. This scant clue gave him enough to solicit the help of two cousins at the Vatican library and call an ancient history professor in Italy.

As was his habit, the friendly voice of Dr. Marcus Camisso answered the phone on the third ring. Slipping quickly past the preliminaries, Marcus asked, "Antonino, I heard you were out of the country on sabbatical leave, is that true?"

Avoiding any discussion on the reason for his exile, Borgiano casually stated, "Yes, I'm here in Ireland doing some research. I'm calling to see if you might be able to help me."

"If I can," was the cautious reply.

"Have you ever heard of a secret Celtic piece of jewelry or gemstones which may have existed in the 17th century or earlier?" requested Borgiano.

"Interesting," stated Marcus, "you are the second person seeking this information. As I told the last person, there were vague rumors of such an item at the time of the Inquisition, but nothing was ever found. As you well know, the church took a dim view of pagan magic."

"But Marcus, if such an item surfaced, what, in your opinion, might be its value in today's antique market?"

"Well, that's hard to judge without seeing it." Marcus continued, "Anything Celtic these days is popular, but one with supposed magical properties, however remote, might be worth millions."

Satisfied, Borgiano thanked Marcus, mumbling something about including him should anything develop, a promise he never intended to keep.

"This may be my resurrection," he thought, "but two e-mails, one of a 17th century witch and the second a sentence in a Roman legionnaire's report about the Druids owning some magical device, were insufficient." Still, unable to penetrate Kevyn's files, he devised another tactic.

One morning, Borgiano, unannounced, arrived at Kevyn's office with a provocative salutation. "Well, O'Gratteney, I hear you've hooked yourself a lucrative American contract?"

Irritated, Kevyn responded, "I don't believe that's any of your business." Looking up he saw an impeccably dressed stranger, whose staged smile belied the deadness of his eyes, "Who are you, anyway?"

Borgiano stepped across the threshold and commandeered a chair, making sure not to upset the crease in his pants, replied, "I am Antonino Zailo Borgiano," each name pronounced precisely, "You should be nice to me, O'Gratteney, I come bearing a gift." Dropping a document on his desk, he stood up and abruptly departed.

The name registered. Kevyn did not like unsolicited material from strangers. Perplexed and intrigued, he reached for the document dated 1650. It was the testimony of a young Irish kitchen maid, Maggie Omrie, who was charged with having killed a farmer's goose, rendering his hens sterile, of being involved in magical healing and talking to the Devil. At her trial one man swore under oath that she had two witch marks on her right shoulder. Terrified, Maggie began boasting she could give the council information about a great treasure. Encouraged, she told of being hired for a grand party of visiting Irish/Scots lords and ladies. During the event she overheard another maid talking about a Scottish lady who owned a magical gemstone. Unable to substantiate the story, Maggie was labeled a liar and a witch and executed.

After reading the case Kevyn thought, "Another case of communal madness. Unable to explain environmental disasters at the time due to a mini-ice age, community policies were enacted against witches, mainly women, for all the woes. The old blame game. It still haunts mankind."

Uncomfortable as to how Borgiano had stumbled on to what he was doing, he dismissed any threat but saw a benefit in using the material in his next report. What he had not calculated was in accepting the document he gave Borgiano confirmation of the treasure's possible existence.

Days later, Kevyn had arrived at the college to work on course work and complete his contract report. Bringing up his private file, he was alarmed to discover the security encryptions his brother installed had been breached. "Damn it!" thought Kevyn, "It has got to be Borgiano! What the hell is he up to?"

Unsuccessful in reaching anyone by phone on a Sunday evening, Kevyn opted for an e-mail to both his Boston colleague and his brother in Cork, sending both his critical files and alerting them to the computer hacking, Borgiano and his concerns. Making two back-up DVDs, he placed one in a secure slot in his desk and slipped the other into his jacket pocket vowing to talk to security in the morning.

It was another stormy night. Lost in thought, Kevyn exited the building, sloshing through the growing puddles heading in the direction of his parked car a few blocks away. At the edge of campus, he raised the umbrella, thinking he heard a cry, but, attributing it to the storm, walked on.

Stepping out onto a quiet side street he did not hear a car engine rev up. In a flash, he looked up to see car lights barreling down on him. Unable to scream, Kevyn was thrown up into the air and landed on a nearby parked car.

A witness would describe the deliberateness of the accident and that Dr. O'Gratteney didn't have a chance.

Borgiano sat coldly monitoring the accident. In his rise to power, he learned how to remove obstacles. A distant relative had found him a capable assistant, one he would use again.

℞

United States, Boston: Sword & Anchor Bar & Grill

A hybrid cab screeched to a stop. A tall male figure stepped out, his limp becoming more pronounced as he strolled along the upscale street in the Back Bay area of Boston. Hesitating in front of the Sword and Anchor, Bar & Grill signage Wolfram smiled, "The old place has had a face lift. Amazing what a bit of paint and renovations can do. This was once my second home. I wonder if it is under new management?" Wolfram Stark opened the door.

A familiar voice rang out, "Well, I'll be damned," the comments coming from a jovial, well proportioned figure who stepped out of the back shadows. "Hey everyone looks who's here," yelled Dillon Clancy, the owner, as he barged forward to enclose Wolfram in a bear hug. Wolfram winced. "It has been too long my dear Wolf, or have you dropped your old musician's name?"

"Some still remember," replied Wolfram disengaging himself from the bighearted welcome. "I actually like it."

"That was one hell of an accident you had. How are you doing?" Dillon stepped back to assess his new arrival. "Your hair has a distinguished white streak now wandering through that black mop and I see you're hobbling."

"Dillon, it has been a long hard road. I'm still in therapy." Shifting position and leaning against the counter, he continued, "This left leg is still a problem but according to my doctors it is a miracle I'm walking at all. Changing the subject, I see you've gone uptown?"

"De ya like it, me boy?" Dillon said with a wink. "I had to keep up with the Jones. The community went upscale a year ago with expensive condos and boutiques. It is good for business but I would do even better with some great music. I don't suppose you, Morgan and company have any plans for a come back? Celtic music is all the rage."

"Not likely, Dillon, the old gang has scattered. The last I heard from Jake and Zoe was that they were heading west for new jobs. But Morgan should be along shortly. He's now fulltime in the Boston University history department. He'll be taking the 'T' commuter rail as parking around here is a nightmare. I took a cab as I need to travel carefully these days."

"I expect you left the police force after the accident? So, are you doing anything except healing these days?" asked Dillon, with genuine concern.

"Isn't it ironic, Dillon, I fought against joining my grandfather's antique business for years and here I am doing investigations into fraudulent antiques. I'm even getting referrals from other cities. Been at this for over a year and business is picking up."

"Crooks are everywhere," said Dillon with a grin, "which, in your case is good for business. I think it is a perfect match, your police training with your family's business. As I recall, didn't you also get your law degree from Boston University?"

"Yes, through part-time studies. I had just obtained my degree and had one more week at the police station when the accident happened. I got a small disability pension which helps."

"While you are waiting for Morgan can I get you something?" asked Dillon, "It is on the house for old times' sake."

"A burger, fries and salad would hit the spot or is that too plebian for your high class joint?"

"For you, it has been reinstated," said Dillon as he patted Wolfram on the shoulder and headed for the kitchen. "Your old booth awaits you by the window."

"Dillon, light on the fries and generous with the salad," called Wolf, who, grown weary from standing, moved to sit down. Looking out the old familiar window onto the street, he began reminiscing over former days, a past musical world. Several staff came to welcome him back.

In the kitchen Dillon thought to himself. "The boy has aged. That accident took a toll on him. I wonder if he can even play the guitar. What a shame. He's spunky. There's lots of steel in those pale blue eyes under the glasses. I wonder how Morgan, the old Red Fox is doing. I haven't seen him in some time. That group had magic in their music. The modern stuff gives people indigestion."

Wolfram had spent most of his 36 years with his grandparents, Gracelyn and Tyloar Harrison, who owned a high-end antique business in the city. He had little contact with his parents. His mother, the Harrison's only child, became a flower child in the post Woodstock era and spent her life floating in and out of mental health and drug addiction clinics. Mentally frail, she now lived in Arizona. He never met his father who was from a Texan family. He played lead guitar in a Rock band for years and, it was rumored, ended up on drugs somewhere in Los Angeles. Perhaps his parent's broken lives led Wolfram into the police force.

Growing up in his grandparent's antique business, it was assumed he would follow that course after high school. To their chagrin, at 21, he decided to enter the Boston Police Academy. After a few years, he grew restless doing routine police work, and, at 30, enrolled in a combination business/law degree program at Boston University. He chose courses with an emphasis on the identification and prosecution of fraud cases, especially those with international connections. The benefits of his studies came to the fore when he was recovering from his accident. His grandparents helped him in setting up an investigative business; referring clients to help him get started. As his expertise spread, his clientele increased.

During his rehabilitation, his grandmother took him aside and told him about the family legacy. Going to their home safe, Gracelyn brought out a small gold and silver engraved box containing a marquis cut sapphire. She indicated that the guardianship of this stone would be his after her death, even though the usual recipient should be female. She explained that the female line was used to ensure safety as tracing women was more complex in male dominated societies. She then informed him that, to her knowledge, there were eight gemstones belonging to some ancient medallion. Each family knew the names of only two guardians of the gemstones. Gracelyn had one contact in Canada and another in Australia. Because this guardianship had existed for over three hundred years, Gracelyn assumed the gemstones had been globally scattered by now, if they still existed. To substantiate the story, Wolfram discreetly had the sapphire examined and found that it was of exquisite quality, likely very old, and had been customized for some piece of jewelry. However, his search for a secret 1600s medallion hit a dead end. For this reason he contacted his old friend, Morgan Mandelthrope.

Eventually, Morgan barged through the door, oblivious of any changes to the bar.

As he passed the front desk, Dillon called after him, "Morgan do you want something to eat?"

"Just coffee," mumbled Morgan, making a bee line for Wolfram.

"That's a first" said Dillon to himself. "The old Morgan had a hollow leg."

As he approached, Wolfram looked up and asked, "Fox, old buddy, I've never seen you so upset. What's wrong? You were rambling on the phone."

Morgan, two years older than Wolfram, was a short, wiry individual known for his sing-song manner of speaking, and a fascination, bordering on fanaticism, about anything Celtic. His rumpled attire, and red bushy hair and beard gave him a badge of nonconformity at Boston University, features which endeared him to his students but not to the university elite. He loved telling stories and would burst into an Irish/Scots folk song at the drop of a hat. Taught to play the fiddle by his maternal grandfather at the age of six, he had become a gifted musician, a skill which made him irreplaceable in the "Animals" musical group. It was not surprising that some labeled him

11

Boston's own leprechaun, a title he relished. But today there was little joviality in his manner as he plunked himself down on the bench facing Wolfram.

Morgan's father wanted him to become an accountant to follow him into the corporate world. Morgan hated numbers and rebelled after the first year of studies. He shifted to history where he excelled. His Celtic bent had propelled him to being one of the country's noteworthy scholars. So, when Wolfram approached him with a Celtic mystery he plunged into the research. But much to his angst, time dragged on with little to show for his effort.

Morgan, forcing himself to be calm, began, "Months ago you asked me to look into whether that 17th century medallion your grandmother mentioned was real or not."

"Yeh, when I didn't hear from you I thought you likely reached the same dead end as I had," as he watched his friend closely.

"Well, like you, I found nothing in the university archives and, as we agreed, I contacted two colleagues, one in Ireland and the other in Scotland, both experts in Celtic history. They also seemed to be hitting blanks until a few weeks ago my Irish contact, Kevyn O'Gratteney, e-mailed me to say he had found and deciphered a seventeenth century code which mentioned a secret. He was going to dig further."

"That should have been good news, right?" replied Wolfram, still trying to grasp the problem.

"Wrong," snapped Morgan, "investigating this secret medallion may have awakened ancient demons." Pausing to catch his breath, he continued. "I was away at a conference this past weekend and did not pick up my e-mails until this morning." Pulling papers from a nylon case he dropped them on the table. "Read the last four paragraphs of O'Gratteney's e-mail!" Unable to wait he continued, "See where O'Gratteney says his computer, particularly our contact file, had been hacked............ He even names the culprit."

Wolfram, noting the rising tension in his friend's voice, sought to calm him by saying, "Just a minute, give me a chance to read this. ....All right, so his computer was hacked, it happens. He admits that he has little information on the secret let alone a medallion or gemstones. What's the problem?"

Fox's voice rose an octave "When I called to talk to O'Gratteney, I discovered he was dead.......... a car accident!"

"Dead," Wolfram was startled by the news. "What happened?"

"Apparently, on a rainy night going to his parked car some distance from the university he stepped out onto a side road and was hit by a car. The driver didn't stop."

"It sounds like a hit and run, so?" Wolfram was still unruffled.

"A student witness said the car deliberately aimed at O'Gratteney. The

Dublin police force, the Gardai, is investigating the accident as a homicide."

"Fox, even if it is a homicide, it may have nothing to do with the medallion. After all, you don't know everything about this guy, do you?" Wolfram continued to downplay the event but his police instincts had been stimulated.

Dillon brought Wolfram's food and again, looking at Morgan asked "You sure you don't want something?"

"On second thought, I'm starving. I'll have the same, but more fries," replied Morgan, feeling better now that he had someone to talk to.

"That's the old Red Fox. I'll be back in a jiffy," said Dillon half way across the room.

Morgan continued, "I guess I'm overreacting. Your right, there could be another explanation. To tell you the truth Wolfram, I was heart sick with worry that I might have caused someone's death."

"Morgan is there anything you are not telling me?" asked Wolfram, knowing his old friend well and recognizing his hesitancy.

"Well.......... maybe," replied Morgan, then taking his time ...."I'm afraid in one of my relaxed meanderings I may have given O'Gratteney the name of the Canadian woman on Prince Edward Island who has one of the gemstones."

Alarmed and angry, I replied, "What! You idiot! You promised me you would not divulge any names. Did you also slip my name or my grandmother's in one of your meanderings?"

"No, no other names. So help me. Just one slip," replied Morgan, seeing his friend's anger.

"OK, let's reassess the situation. Assuming the most positive scenario, perhaps O'Gratteney overplayed his suspicions, as this was the first time anyone hacked into his computer. And let's say, the car accident was, however horrendous, a straight forward hit and run. This means that your concerns are likely needless. Nevertheless, let's err on the side of caution. I'll contact Josh Alder. He's the best guy I know on electronic issues. Let's get the medallion files off your computers. How many are we talking about?" Wolfram's noble efforts at reducing his friend's anxiety had increased his own. His immediate reaction was to block access to further information, although by now he knew that Antonino had O'Gratteney's material, whatever it contained. Next he had to get a handle on this Antonino by contacting some old law enforcement colleagues.

"Just one, my office computer; the lap top I use for research. These days I do very little work at home," replied Morgan, feeling sheepish at his indiscretion.

Wolfram pulled out his cell phone, "I'll see if I can get Josh to meet us today." While Morgan dove into the food, Dillon had delivered; Wolfram contacted Josh giving him a brief explanation for his call. A meeting was possible and in closing he turned to Morgan and asked, "What's your office address again?"

"226 Bay State Road, 3rd floor," replied Morgan, finishing his lunch.

"OK Josh, we'll meet you about 4 at Morgan's office." Wolfram closed his cell phone and continued. "There, we'll get Josh's help and seal this matter until we find out more about this Antonino. Right now, we have some free time, so let's relax and chat with Dillon about happier times. I'll get a cab about 3."

Morgan, relieved, replied, "Your right, I'm magnifying the whole thing. My lips are sealed. No one knows it was you who asked for this research. It is so good to have a friend like you Wolfram. I may know the frailties' and oddities of university life but criminals are totally out of my league."

"Unless they are Celtic rogues," Wolfram said with a chuckle.

"Well that's another matter. But they existed in another century. That's easier," replied Morgan with a smile, the first since he arrived.

Dillon joined them for a chat. While Morgan and Dillon rambled on about their glory days as musicians Wolfram began thinking, "The worst case scenario is equally possible. This Antonino could already be en route to North America and, if that hit and run is a sample of his tactics, then trouble is heading our way. Time is of the essence. Investigating this 1600s secret may have opened a Pandora's Box."

Escape from Britain

The catalyst to Antonino's behavior arrived weeks before. By registered mail, he received an official letter from the church stating he had been dismissed as a priest because of his abusive tactics in a Roman Catholic boy's school in Italy. He was furious. Pacing up and down waving the letter, he ranted, "Bureaucratic baboons. Stupid, sanctimonious idiots! Who are they to judge me? I could write books on some of their activities. Twenty years down the drain. Wasted time......Wasted money......... Wasted energy. Years of bending to church rules, ingratiating myself to superiors, and collecting favors, all for nothing. My father was right. He had scant regard for priests and thought I'd do better in business. At least by now I'd have something to show for my efforts. Instead, here I am, middle aged with no livelihood, no future and no pension. May they all burn in hell." This event sent Antonino on the prowl.

Using his intellect and cunning, Antonino had set a trap. Kevyn revealed his hand in accepting a free document but his electronic data only hinted at the medallion's existence." Kevyn's electronic data had one name, a slip in an e-mail from his Boston colleague. It was the name of an elderly woman living on a small Canadian island. "A beginning," thought Antonino. "A small city will make it easier to find her. But it is risky. A wrong move could spook both the police and my prey."

Antonino, the oldest of eight children, was born into a small Calabria farming community. His father, a sergeant in command of the local Carabineer, was known for his ruthless flogging of offenders. His mother also bullied the slave children on their farm. Slave children were at the bottom of the social roster. For centuries they came from parts of Calabria and Sicily, parents selling their children to make ends meet, a dark secret ignored by the Italian press. Brought up in this atmosphere, Antonino had no qualms in using the same tactics on children under his care. He enjoyed inflicting pain on defenseless small boys, and for years, under an umbrella of fear, he was able to hide his actions. But the church's growing intolerance of abuse gave his enemies ammunition against him. His abuse was documented and reported to the hierarchy. A trial of sorts was held with witnesses coming forth to describe their ordeal, some threatening to go to the media and sue the church, an intolerable situation for a church trying to mend its record.

To get him away from his accusers and the press, Antonino was expelled to Ireland for an indefinite period of time while church lawyers considered his fate. As months passed Antonino knew his future was becoming more and more precarious no matter how many favors he called in for support.

His new companion, Rudolfo Marquis, was a 45 year old petty criminal with an Italian police record. Suspected of fraud and murder in a recent gang roundup, he was on the run and grateful to have an escape. With the help of Antonino's relatives, Rudolfo arrived in Britain under a false passport and would be leaving under another.

Rudolfo grew up on the streets of Calabria leaving him with an unquenchable desire for money, and a blank conscious in acquiring it. Having killed a man at 20, he had spent over twenty years in trouble with the law, including five years incarceration, a situation he never wanted repeated. He thought himself debonair, but his overall rough demeanor made him uncomfortable away from his own kind. The bargain was that in payment for doing Antonino's dirty work he would be introduced to important American underworld contacts. Before leaving Italy, Rudolfo learned that Antonino was one of those individuals who had contacts on both sides of the law. Antonino floated easily back and forth, depending on his needs. Thus he had little difficulty in acquiring a false passport for Rudolfo.

Antonino calculated the police would assume O'Gratteney's death was an accident, unless someone raised too many questions. Still, he had time, for in his opinion, "Cops take ages to deal with a case." He also reasoned a few adjustments to his Vatican passport would facilitate his exit from Ireland. The plan was to pass off Rudolfo as another priest, a convenient cover, but Antonino wasn't sure it would work. A dress rehearsal before their international flight revealed the problems.

"Those ugly tattoos on your forearms will have to be hidden. They're a dead giveaway," said Antonino, irritated at the discovery. "You will have to wear a heavy, long-sleeved shirt and never expose your forearm for the whole trip."

Annoyed at the criticism, Rudolfo sarcastically replied, "Fine, I'll sweat like a pig. Is there anything else? I want you to know that being a priest was never one of my ambitions."

"Next, you'll only speak Italian until we land in Halifax, your vocabulary is too rough for a priest." Antonino stepped back to inspect his travelling companion, all the while tapping nervously on his black notebook. "How far can I trust this imbecile," he thought, "he's stupid, sly and unscrupulous, a toxic mix. I'll get a better candidate in America to do my skut work. For now, I'll have to keep this one on a tight chain."

"Great," said Rudolfo, mumbling to himself. "Just like prison. The damn guards criticized me for everything. I didn't like it then and I don't like it now. I need to rid myself of this pompous ass as soon as I reach the USA."

Days before their flight Antonino insisted on a rehearsal. Telling Rudolfo as little as possible, he laid out a number of maps and Internet sheets on his bed.

"Our flight from Dublin to Halifax is just over five hours. We arrive in the early morning. Our cover will be that we are two priests attending a conference in Halifax and doing some sight-seeing. Let me do the talking. I'll rent a car at the Halifax International airport." Pointing to the maps, he continued, "We then drive north about 83 kilometers to Truro, then on to Amherst to a Best Western Motel. The rooms will be booked in my name. In Amherst, you will rent a second car in your passport name. Then, while I remain at the motel, you will go across the Confederation Bridge into Charlottetown, the capital city of this small island."

Rudolfo, pointing to one of the Internet documents, and asked "It says here there is a bridge toll, will we have any Canadian cash?"

"Yes, you will be carrying about three hundred Canadian dollars. We'll use cash only, credit cards can be traced."

"Heh, note this, it says here this is the longest bridge in the world to span ice covered waters."

"Concentrate! This is not a holiday," Antonino snapped. "It is 56 kilometers from the Bridge to Charlottetown, straight roads, estimate an hour. You will likely get there after lunch, so park near this government building which seems to be within walking distance of the Gordon B&B. Look at this Google street map printout of the house, memorize it. Your job is to get in, grab the gemstone, and get out. I want you to call me on your cell phone on your return, just at or near the Island entrance to the Confederation Bridge. I'll plan on meeting you near the car rental agency in Amherst. Once we get rid of your rental, we will head straight back to the Halifax airport and fly on to Boston. Do you have any questions?"

"Fine, except I hate small communities. Everyone knows each other and outsiders stand out."

"True," replied Antonino, "but we're in luck. The Internet says that in July and August the place is swarming with tourists."

"What's the back up plan should anything go wrong?" asked Rudolfo, uncomfortable venturing into a North American small community for the first time.

"Such as......?"

"I can think of a few. What if the old woman refuses to tell me, or has forgotten where she hid the thing? Old people forget, you know. How hard do you want me to press this?"

"No rough stuff. If you run into too much resistance, get out of there. We'll try another angle in Boston. At this stage, I want time on my side."

"What's the timing again?"

"Assuming everything goes as planned; you should get into Charlottetown just after lunch, retrieve the gemstone by late afternoon and be back across the Confederation Bridge by 5. This gets us back into Halifax and onto Boston before midnight. How does that sound?"

"There're a lot of ifs and unknowns. We are on unfamiliar roads in the middle of summer; anything could mess up the plan. But assuming everything goes as planned, I should be calling you no later than 5:15."

"Good, we're set. You have a speed dial to my cell phone. Any problems, ditch that cell phone. Now, let's get some rest, we leave in three hours." What Rudolfo didn't know was that Antonino had his own back up plan which he wasn't sharing.

No alarms sounded as two Roman Catholic priests eased their way through the Dublin airport security system. In fact, security and air flight attendants were extra courteous when it was discovered one carried Vatican credentials. One security officer mentally questioned the shady appearance of the second priest, but in the crush of passengers he dismissed his gut instinct.

After an uneventful flight, the two priests landed at the Halifax Stanfield

THE CELTIC SERPENT

International Airport. They breezed through Canadian customs. The customs official quickly checked the passports and faces and waved them along.

In Nova Scotia, Rudolfo drove while Antonino sat thinking. "I can only hope the old woman will be compliant. We don't have the time, nor is it possible to tear the place apart. I detest old women; they can be so damned stubborn. She's likely hid it in some ungodly place or, as Rudolfo says, has forgotten where it is all together. My chance of success may be infinitesimal. But by God I'm going to try. It is my only chance at a fortune."

Chapter 2

Canada, Charlottetown: The Gordon B&B

Something was about to happen. Nellie sensed it in every fiber of her being but could not identify the recipient. "Whatever it is," she reckoned, "it draws near." She rarely spoke of her psychic ability as scientists had negated its existence and religious organizations labeled it pagan. Restless, she forced herself to stay focused, expecting the next phone call or knock on the door to herald the event. Today, she had baking to do for her B&B guests and a church funeral.

She placed the final baking, a pan of brownies, next to the muffins and cookies, on the kitchen counter in front of the window to cool, the warm blend of chocolate, cinnamon and nutmeg capturing the attention of each passerby. Wiping her brow, she eased into her favorite kitchen chair, remarking to herself, "There was a time when I could do this baking and clean the entire house in a day, but no more. Maybe it's time to retire. But what would I do? I've worked all my life." The thought of change brought a flood of memories.

Except for one trip to New York and a few sojourns to local provinces, Nellie had spent her entire life on the Island, the '*land cradled on the waves*' according to the Mi'kmaq Indians. She loved the idea of a wee cradle bobbing on the waves. The red soil and white sandy beaches had attracted wayfarers for centuries, the current throng of summer tourists being the latest. Nellie's Island roots went back to the early 1800s, but with sadness, she wondered if she might be the last. Reminiscing she thought, "I came to Charlottetown for a year and stayed a lifetime, a life I couldn't have envisioned."

An economic downturn in the 1950s had forced her and her oldest brother to seek temporary employment in Charlottetown, the capital of Canada's smallest province. Elizabeth Cameron, called Nellie, was the eldest of two children, the only girl, of a well-known farming family near Montague. When her brother returned home, she found herself living with strangers in a rough boarding house with poor food and unpleasant company. For months her life revolved around her job at the Gordon Hardware Store on Queen Street and little social life, as most of her earnings were sent home. Life improved when John, the only child of the store owner, returned from his studies in Halifax. John took an immediate interest in Nellie and before long they were 'an item'. After a year's courtship, she and John were married at St. James Presbyterian Church, called 'The Kirk'. Bending to social mores, Nellie quit her job as, at that time, it was unacceptable for a married woman to be working. She resigned herself to being a dutiful wife, and trying, however unsuccessfully, to endear herself to her mother-in-law.

The arrival of Catherine two years later, their first child, healed the family, the Gordons relishing their role as grandparents. When Catherine was four, John's mid-winter flu complicated into meningitis and within days he was dead. A small allowance was created for Nellie and Catherine, which over time needed to be supplemented. Fortunately, by the 1960s, Nellie was able to negotiate a deal with a nearby motel to take overflow guests. She established a B&B, minimal signage being a stipulation of the Gordons, who were sensitive to public opinion.

Catherine grew into a fine young woman, and at twenty shortened her name to 'Cathy', the same year she graduated as a Registered Nurse from the PEI School of Nursing. With a scarcity of nursing jobs on the Island, Cathy one day arrived home to announce that she and three other nurses had been offered jobs at Mount Sinai Hospital in New York with excellent pay and benefits. Beaming with enthusiasm Cathy referred to it as 'a great adventure', just one year and she would return. Nellie tried to dissuade her but finally consented with "one year and you'll be home again," to which Cathy, hugging her, whispered, "Yes, Mom, I promise!" But it was not to be.

Within the year, Cathy fell in love with a young doctor, David Talismann, and in 1983 they were married at 'The Kirk', returning to their jobs in New York. A year later, Nellie travelled to New York, her first trip out of Canada, to hold her granddaughter, Angela, a beautiful baby with wispy white hair and emerald eyes. She resigned herself to being alone and grateful Cathy and her family visited each summer. But life held more surprises.

By 1988, David and Cathy were divorced, Cathy returning to the Island with Angela. When Angela was seven, Cathy died from a medication reaction leaving Nellie, to bring up another child, one very different from her own.

Like her mother, at sixteen, Angela announced that her new name was 'Angi', and it stuck. When she graduated from high school, her American grandparents offered to pay for her university education and proposed she might board with friends of theirs, the Perlmans, when Angi chose a nursing degree program at Dalhousie University in Halifax. And so, once again Nellie watched another child leave the Island.

Nellie knew each sad episode in her life had been preceded by a similar haunting premonition. This was no different. Out loud she pleaded, "Dear God let it be me this time, not my darling Angi. I'm an old woman. I've had a full life." With that her eyes fell on the kitchen clock. "Oh my, it's almost three and Margo said she would pick up the brownies on her way home." The thought had barely registered when the doorbell rang. Nellie walked through the living room to the locked front door.

Opening the door, she greeted her old friend, "Thanks Margo, with B&B guests, it will be impossible for me to get to the church tomorrow morning. I expect it will be a big funeral, George Fraser was well known." Closing the door she failed to notice a thin, male figure skulking near the corner. Running late, Rudolfo was about to pounce when Margo arrived. He retreated and waited.

The twenty year friendship of Nellie and Margo Foster rested on their mutual involvement in church activities, but it had other benefits. Margo, in her mid-60s, seven years younger than Nellie, was a short, plump, well dressed woman. She had been a high school teacher, later dabbled in real estate and was now into civic politics. Money was plentiful. Her cell phone, never disconnected, kept her abreast of city life; news and gossip. Nellie enjoyed Margo's effervescent personality, and was grateful for her business sense and contacts. In return, Nellie helped Margo with a number of family issues, particularly dealing with a difficult daughter.

They were an odd pair. Nellie was a tall, slender woman with a reserved personality who had little interest in gossip and less in politics. With meager funds she barely kept up with the fashions. Over the years, as an Elder and chair of several committees, she had become a formidable presence in the church and in the community. She was also known for her knowledge of herbs and healing methods which she dispensed freely.

Relocking the door the two women headed towards their favorite chat room, the kitchen. "I do hope you have time for a wee cup of tea?" asked Nellie.

"How could I resist, with a house impregnated with such aromas." As she pulled out her usual chair, Margo asked, "By the way, Nellie, will you be taking in guests when Angi comes home?"

"No, this time I've told the motel I'll be unavailable for three weeks. They understood, but I know it's difficult, it's the peak of the tourist season."

"About time," replied Margo, "that heart of yours is not indestructible, you know. Have you given any thought to selling this place? You and I know that Angi, like her mother, will likely find a husband in Halifax and settle there."

Nellie hesitated. "Margo, I know you're right. I guess I'm fated never to have children nearby, the heartache of so many Island parents. It will be difficult to leave this old house with its fifty years of memories."

"I understand, but Nellie its best you do it when you're able. By the way, I never asked before, do you know the history of this place?"

Replenishing their tea, Nellie replied, "This place is over a hundred years old. It was built around 1892 for a sailing ship owner, a long forgotten era for many Islanders. In its day, this must have been a costly undertaking. Just look at the stonework and stained glass windows."

"That's the point, Nellie; the maintenance costs for this historic relic will continue to mount. Just the other day you mentioned the roof needed to be replaced. That could cost thousands. Why not give such headaches to someone else. I'm sure it would be snapped up by someone interested in heritage property and its location. You are sitting on prime land here at the corner of West and Kent Street within walking distance of the city center and Victoria Park. Whenever you're ready, I'll put you in touch with someone that will do justice to the sale. In the meantime, I'll keep my ears open for a nice one or two bedroom condo. I expect you'd like to live in this area?"

"A two bedroom condo overlooking the harbor would be nice," replied Nellie, growing more receptive to the idea. "I'll talk to Angi; after all it's her heritage."

"Nellie, you seem worried? We've known each other for years, and I know when something is bothering you. I hope it's nothing I've said. Is there anything I can do?"

"Oh Margo, you know me too well. As a matter of fact, I've been having one of my premonitions. It's been years since this has occurred. It's upsetting this time because I cannot identify the recipient."

"Has Angi mentioned anything in her phone calls that would give you an inkling something was wrong?"

"No, we chatted Sunday. She gave me her travel schedule and stated she was looking forward to some rest. Everyone else on the Island is fine. I know outside events can play their part. You haven't heard anything?"

"As you know, Nellie, July and August are vacation months around here, a poor time for news or gossip. But if I hear anything, I'll phone. I must be off. I've got company for supper." She picked up the covered brownie pan on the counter and got up to leave.

Margo, Nellie and the two B&B guests all reached the front door in unison. Dave MacLean, a robust, slightly overweight, ruddy faced farmer, had spent his youth as a Peacekeeper in the Canadian military, greeted both women with a cherry, "Well, hello, Margo. Nellie, the aroma is intoxicating. Smells like home." Looking at Margo, "It's one of the reasons we always pick Nellie's place when we're here on government work. We eat like kings.

Nellie, James and I will be off to the Old Dublin Pub for supper. We should be back in a couple of hours." Nellie nodded.

James Ross, his smaller, quieter partner, then stepped forward. He usually let Dave do most of the talking. James, also a farmer, was a volunteer ambulance attendant in Montague, a role he thoroughly enjoyed. Smiling the two men entered the house and proceeded up the stairs to their rooms.

Nellie bid her friend good bye, returned to the house, locked the door, and went into the kitchen.

Later, she heard the front door lock click as Dave and James left. Not expecting their return until later, she warmed her supper and turned on the small kitchen TV. After the evening news she proceeded to clean up and prepare for the next morning. In the midst of drying dishes she heard a sound in the living room. "Too soon for the boys," she thought, and went to investigate.

Standing in the living room shadows was the silhouette of a stranger. Rudolfo stepped towards Nellie. He knew she was alone; he overheard the heavy set guy say they wouldn't be back until later. He calculated this old woman would be easy; all he had to do was frighten her enough to tell him where the gemstone was hidden.

Thinking Rudolfo a common thief, Nellie reacted in a commanding voice, "Leave this house at once or I'll call the police."

In a foreign accent, he replied, "Never mind, old woman. Just tell me where you've stashed the gemstone, the one your family has been guarding for centuries? Get it and I'll leave."

"My God," she thought, "the premonition is true. After all these centuries the *'coming times'* has arrived." Thinking quickly she noted that he said a gemstone ....not medallion....... "I'll play for time......... Maybe Dave and James will return early."

Still in a commanding voice, Nellie replied, "What gemstone? I have no idea what you are talking about. You must have the wrong house." She eased towards the portable telephone on the side table, grabbed the receiver and pressed the key for 911.

"You bitch!" cried Rudolfo. He lunged at her, throwing the receiver onto the floor. Infuriated, he grabbed her left arm and pinned it behind her. Nellie winced with the pain. "No more tricks. I want the gemstone. I know it's in this house."

"I don't know what you're talking about," whispered Nellie, the pain now radiating down her left arm. She felt faint.

"All right, be stubborn, perhaps a little persuasion is needed." Rudolfo released her arm, swung her around and slapped her hard across the face, causing a fine trickle of blood to appear at the corner of her mouth. "Believe me, you old witch, I've crippled men bigger than you, so start talking or my next tap will be more lethal."

For some unknown reason, as Dave and James finished their meal, instead of relaxing for a chat as was their custom, Dave asked for the bill, and with little comment, stood up to leave.

Startled by his colleague's sudden move, James asked, "What's wrong?"

By the time he completed the question; Dave had paid their bill and was out the door, James in close pursuit.

Dave, walking rapidly towards their B&B said, "I don't know. I just know we have to get back ....don't ask why.........hurry!" The two men were practically running as they crossed the street.

Stepping quietly onto the porch they saw the door ajar, heard Nellie moan as her assailant struck a second blow followed by a loud demand.

Dave signaled James and both barged through the door.

Rudolfo had little time to react.

Dave's well trained military skills came into action. He pinned Rudolfo to the ground in seconds. Trapped, Rudolfo's black eyes searched the room for an escape.

James rushed to Nellie, noting her shocked symptoms. He wrapped his jacket and available throws around her. Hearing the 911 operator he picked up the receiver, explained the situation, and returned to Nellie. Her pulse was weak, there was a bluish tint to her lips and she was not responding to questions.

Within minutes the ambulance attendants arrived. They bundled Nellie onto the stretcher and exited. James called to Dave as he followed the stretcher, "I'll go with Nellie to the hospital. Contact Dr. MacAndrew. It's best if he gets in touch with Angi."

On the heels of the ambulance the police arrived.

Dave stated to the first officer, "I thought I heard a foreign accent in this bastard's demands. He's been silent ever since. He certainly doesn't look like an Islander."

"Noted," said the stocky policeman as he handcuffed Rudolfo, yanked him to his feet and escorted him out the door.

"The younger female officer turned to question Dave. "Have you any idea what he was after?"

Dave thought he heard 'gemstone' but wasn't sure. "No, I can't help you. Somehow he doesn't look like a petty criminal. Check that accent. I'd like to know why a foreigner is after Nellie. He would likely have killed her if we hadn't returned early."

"We'll need to talk to you both later," said the police officer who turned to leave.

"Sure," replied Dave, as he sat down in a living room chair. "James and I have been here often, we're practically relatives. We're here for the night. I'll call the Royal Motel and fill them in. I expect Angi, her granddaughter who is a nurse in Halifax, will be here by morning."

Sitting alone in the empty house, Dave pondered. "Surely it's a mistake. What could Nellie have that would be of interest to a foreigner? This Island has few secrets .... or does it? ....My God, is Angi in danger? If the Gordons are the target, there could be others bent on some thievery. I must phone Dad, he might know." He pulled out his cell phone.

When no call came by their deadline, Antonino moved to his back-up plan. Cursing to himself as he checked out of the motel, he turned the rental car towards Halifax. "I don't need this aggravation. I should never have trusted that idiot. Thankfully, he knew little about the gemstone but that's bad enough. I'll have to act fast." He gunned the gas peddle.

&

Canada: The Charlottetown General Hospital

The diagnosis haunted her days. Other than a referral to Dr. Wong nothing had been discussed with anyone except Graham. "If, or when, this news hits the gossip channels my career will be dead in the water," she thought. "It is only a matter of time. Do I want chemotherapy or not? If not, I'll be at loggerheads with the medical establishment. Can I live with that? I know patients who have survived without it. I'll boost my immune system with meditation, exercise, a better diet, more rest and positive thinking..... I'll do more research. Sooner or later I must face the cold reality of my diagnosis." In her usual way, Angi's work provided the perfect distraction.

At three in the morning of another shift, Angi took her usual break. Before she had time to place her coffee and sandwich on the snack room table, she received an urgent call that a nurse had been assaulted in the ER walk-in.

Racing through the hospital she found one of the triage nurses laying on the floor, dazed, with Ann, a senior volunteer at her side. Two security guards held a heavy set male who was babbling incoherently as he struggled to free himself.

"Thank heavens you were nearby, Ann. What happened?" Angi asked as she surveyed the scene. Ann, in her early sixties, was one of a newly created volunteer group of retired nurses enticed back into the workforce with a lucrative stipend. She had been an ER supervisor in the old hospital and was Angi's mentor.

Sara, the triage nurse, holding her right jaw, tried to speak "When I went around the desk to put on his hospital bracelet and check his blood pressure, he sprang out of the chair screaming something about being attacked, and socked me in the jaw. He showed no signs of mental illness, drugs or anything, otherwise I would have redirected him to the Psych ER."

As Angi took photos of the scene with her Airmid, she continued to listen. Confirming Sara's description, Ann continued, "Angi, I was nearby. The man sat quietly. There was nothing to indicate or precipitate this attack. Unfortunately, this is happening all too frequently. So many walk-ins appear normal, and then something triggers this violent reaction. It's getting worse. There are too many mentally ill and addicted people walking the streets."

Helping Sara to her feet, Angi responded, "You know Ann, no matter what we do, nurses are being abused like this on a regular basis. Nurses take self defense courses to protect themselves but even this doesn't help. No wonder we're short of professional staff. With so many choices today, why would anyone willingly take this path? Ann, I need you to stay with Sara while I readjust the staffing. You know what's needed, she must be examined and the Workman Compensation forms filled out tonight."

"Sure, Angi, I know the drill," replied Ann.

Rubbing her chin, Sara interceded, "I'm OK Angi, you're short-handed and it's a busy one."

"Not on your life, Sara. If anything turns up later you'll have nothing to fall back on. You've had a hard blow to your chin and I note your protecting your right arm. Did you hit your arm in the fall?"

"I guess so. I was off balance and got propelled against the wall. Just a bruise," replied Sara, still rubbing her arm.

"Ann, I'll check with you later on the medical report. I also need to send a report to administration." Angi hesitated, as she observed the evening administrator walking towards her.

Maryln MacDonald, was a forty plus, thin individual with a crusty personality. Coming from a technical background, with a post-graduate business degree, she was better at numbers than people. Recent media attention to health centre problems made her irritable, as she blamed hospital problems on incompetent staff looking for time off, a position which left her at loggerheads with the unions.

Angi thought as she watched her approach, "I don't need a battle with Maryln tonight. How did she hear about this incident so quickly?"

"Good evening, Maryln, I expect you want a report on the assault?"

"No, that's not why I'm here," was her abrupt reply. "There's a long distance call from the Island for you. Come, I've left the party on hold."

Alarmed, Angi turned and followed, as her thoughts quickly shifted to home, "It must be Gran.......her heart."

A familiar voice responded to her "Hello" as she reached the office phone.

"Angi, its Jock MacAndrew. I need you to get home at once."

"It's Gran?" asked Angi.

"Yes, she's in hospital. I won't waste time on the phone. I've already talked to your administrator. It's serious."

Without asking for details, Angi replied, "I understand. I'll sort things out here and I'll be en route ASAP."

"Angi, jot down my cell number and call me from the Halifax airport, whatever the time. I'll meet you at the Charlottetown airport and take you directly to the hospital."

"What is he not telling me?" thought Angi. "No time........" Jotting down the telephone number she replied "I'll give you mine as well, just in case." Placing the receiver in its cradle she turned to the administrator who was lingering nearby.

"Maryln, I need to leave at once, it's my grandmother." Angi stated, preparing herself for the usual argument about staff coverage and taking early leave.

"I understand Angi. Give me an hour. We'll manage."

Surprised by the mild reaction, Angi said to herself, "Wow, she's almost human. Too bad this doesn't show up more often." Without assessing the reason, she sped off to alert her staff to the expected change.

What Maryln wasn't saying was that Dr. MacAndrew had explained the situation to her on the phone and the vital need for Angi's quick departure.

By 5, Angi was free. She raced to her condo, packed, and got a taxi to the airport where she phoned Jock, saying that she was booked on the Air Canada morning flight to the Island.

It was a short trip. As the plane approached the Island Angi recognized the familiar cradle with its emerald fields, red soil, white beaches and the sun glittering off the water. "My precious Island home" she thought, "Every lane, shore, street and the warmth of its people are imprinted on my soul. While I love the excitement of Halifax, my soul belongs here."

As she reached for her suitcase at the airport carousel a familiar voice greeted her, "Welcome home, Angi, I wish it was under better circumstances."

She turned to greet Dr. Jock MacAndrew, an old family friend. She noted that he was a bit older with more gray hair, but the same old open, kindly face.....but today it seemed much more somber."

"How's Gran?" asked Angi, focusing on the main topic.

"She's holding her own but we had to move her to the Coronary Care Unit," replied Jock.

"That serious, heh?" said Angi, still thinking it was a heart attack.

Their conversation was brief as they walked to his car. Jock dropped Angi's suitcase into the trunk and, when settled inside, turned and said, "Angi, I didn't want to alarm you over the phone, but the truth is that your grandmother was attacked in her home." He then proceeded to tell her what he knew of the incident.

"My God!" replied a shocked Angi. "Why? Who would want to attack my dear grandmother? There's nothing of value in the house. Do the police have any answers?"

"Not at this stage," replied Jock. "I've been mainly concerned about Nellie. There is some rumor the perpetrator had a foreign accent. He's in jail and will remain there. That's why we are heading directly to the hospital. It's imperative you see Nellie at once. Then, after a brief visit, I'll drive you home."

Struggling to grasp the enormity of the situation and what this might mean to her Grandmother, Angi replied in short sentences, "Thanks. That's very kind of you. I must see Gran." Angi said little else as they drove.

At the hospital she went straight to the Coronary Care Unit with Jock and was startled to see the degree of facial bruising on her grandmother. While her grandmother slept, a cardiac monitor and an Intravenous were the only visible signs of monitoring and therapy. A sickening feeling engulfed her as she pulled up a chair and reached for her grandmother's free hand. Jock left on rounds. Angi eyed the monitor. "This kind of shock could be devastating. I know she's had a weak heart for the past decade."

Moments later, Nellie awoke, and in a faint whisper said, "Angi, you're here." Gripping Angi's hand she tried to go on.

"Don't talk, Gran, save your energy," replied Angi, her nursing instincts taking command. "There's plenty of time for us to talk. I'm home for my holidays."

"No, I must tell you now," her grandmother insisted. "Angi, he was after the medallion."

"What medallion?" asked Angi, thinking her grandmother delirious from the attack.

Irritated, Nellie went on in a whisper, "Remember the summer you were twenty-one, I told you of our family legacy?"

Angi suddenly remembered. "Oh....... yes..... I had almost forgotten." At twenty-one she had dismissed it as some fading link to their British roots. "Surely this couldn't be the target of the attack," she thought. Then feeling a slight twinge of guilt she thought, "Am I just like the rest, dismissing critical family matters that generations have held dear. God, forgive my flippancy."

Struggling, Nellie continued, "Yes, Angi, this family duty now falls to you........you must be careful!" There was alarm in her grandmother's voice. "I never thought the '*coming times*' would happen in my day or that I would be the trigger."

"Gran, what are the '*coming times*?" asked Angi, not recognizing the term.

Nellie, ignoring the question pressed on, "Angi, when you get home I want you to call Gracelyn Harrison in Boston and Brigit O'Keefe in Ireland. Promise me you'll do that before you go to bed!"

Not wanting to upset her grandmother she replied, "Sure Gran, I'll do it. The phone numbers are in the plastic cardex on your desk.

"Yes," her grandmother's voice growing faint, her grip eased as she closed her eyes.

Realizing her grandmother needed rest, Angi released her hand saying, "Gran, we'll both get some sleep and I'll be back." Troubled, Angi mulled over what her grandmother had been saying. "I should have paid more attention. I didn't ask enough questions. It just looked like an old piece of jewelry with missing stones. And what does this '*coming times*' mean? Gran will tell me later."

As she opened the front door of her grandmother's house, Dave greeted her from the kitchen "Hi Angi, how's Nellie?" Dave and James had decided to have some coffee and muffins while they waited.

"She's in the Coronary Care Unit and managing, but I'm worried. This attack has complicated her underlying heart condition," replied Angi as she pulled out a kitchen chair and sat down, the events and her illness beginning to register.

James, noting the tiredness, responded, "Have some coffee. You must be weary. Dave and I stayed the night thinking you might need company this morning. Everyone understands. The assault is all over the TV and Guardian newspaper."

"Thanks," said Angi as she sipped her coffee and nibbled on a warmed muffin. "I really appreciate the company. I've been up all night and need some sleep." She was now weary. Directing her question to the two men, "I wonder if one of you might handle the telephone and visitors, as Islanders will certainly start responding. I'll have a rest and get back to the hospital. How long were you booked for?"

"Another two days," replied Dave as he refilled their coffee cups.

"I wonder if you could stay for the next two days while I tend to Gran. No cost."

"No problem," replied Dave. James and I will work out something. We will be glad to help. Nellie means a lot to us. We've been coming here for years. This has been our home away from home. We only wish we had been

29

here earlier to stop that bastard before he got near Nellie."

"I am grateful," replied Angi. "I heard from Jock that if it wasn't for you Gran might have been killed outright." Angi took steps to retire.

"Your suitcase is already in your room, Angi. Let us know if there's anything else you need. We'll hold the fort," said Dave, assuming charge duty.

Remembering her grandmother's request, Angi went to the kitchen desk, picked up the circular cardex container, "I'll use the phone in my room to make these long distance calls. Perhaps these two women can enlighten me on why this medallion is so unique."

&

Canada, Charlottetown: The City Jail

Alone and caged, for hours Rudolfo paced back and forth in his cell like a captured beast, the sweat pouring down his face and tattooed arms. Furious, he kept mumbling Italian curses on everyone and everything. On Antonino for getting him into this mess, chasing after a nonexistent gemstone owned by some dimwit who likely lost it decades ago and on this damnable foreign town and its inhabitants who dared to incarcerate him. Finally exhausted, he collapsed onto his cot and stared at the blank ceiling. His thoughts rambling, he reviewed his situation. "I should have stayed in Italy and taken my chances. Now I'm trapped here with no contacts, dependent on a man I barely know, who might just as easily have me eliminated if I become a handicap. I heard rumors in Italy about this one. Cold and ruthless, that's him. Yet, he can't leave me here for any length of time in case I spill the beans. So, he's likely working to get me out of here PDQ." With that ray of hope he contemplated his legal predicament.

"What's the big deal? I hardly touched her.....just wanted to scare the old bitch. I hate old people.......some of them are just plain ornery It's likely an assault charge, something Antonino should be able to bribe his way out of especially in this hick town. He's got lots of money and connections. I'll be out in no time. Antonino will be pleased when he hears that I have remained stone silent since being arrested. The false name on my passport and personal papers will confuse the polizia for awhile but my fingerprints will soon bring up my Italian record and name. I'll play for time."

Hours passed.

About nine in the evening, a loud, boisterous man, a lawyer, arrived at the jail demanding his right to see his client. After some negotiations, the evening administrator agreed to give him fifteen minutes in a lounge adjacent to the Guard Room.

Rodolfo was relieved when a guard appeared at his cell to say that his big-wig Halifax lawyer had arrived and wanted to see him. Rudolfo smiled saying to himself, "Good old Antonino, he came through. That clever brain had a back up plan after all." Confident of release, Rudolfo strutted beside the guard to the interview room.

He entered a semi-dark lounge to greet an aging, overweight, balding man dressed in an expensive dark suit, standing with a small box in his hand and a rather odd smile. As he stepped forward to greet his client for the first time he said in a friendly manner, "Well, its' good to see you. How are you being treated? Is everything OK?" Providing no time for a reply, he continued, "I've brought some personal items and that Turkish candy you like." Without missing a beat he passed the box to the guard, "This officer needs to check the contents while you and I chat. It's a bit late and we have little time." Looking at the guard he asked "May I speak with my client at the far table?" Getting a positive nod, he maneuvered Rudolfo to a table the farthest distance from the seated guard.

Rudolfo noted the lawyer's clever avoidance of names.

As they sat down the lawyer proceeded in whispered tones. "My name is Fred Simpson from the Halifax law firm of Quinn, Graham and Green. Your friend from Italy contacted our firm but I had no discussion with him. So let's get started. Your arrest record states you assaulted an elderly woman in this community, a woman you didn't know. So, just answer quickly the following questions.

"Did you plan this attack?"

"Not me, but it was planned."

"How did you get access to the house?"

"I picked the front door lock. It was easy."

"How many times did you hit her?"

"Maybe four to five times.....light taps. I just wanted to scare her."

"I don't suppose there's any point in asking why you were here in Canada. Never mind, it's not my job to know such details. Have you made any written or verbal statement to the police since you were arrested?"

"No, I've been silent," Rudolfo replied triumphantly.

"Absolutely nothing?" the lawyer asked with a slight note of disbelief.

"Absolutely zip," replied Rudolfo running his fingers across his lips. "But, you'll have to work fast for it's just a matter of time before my past catches up to me."

Confidently, Fred responded. "No rush, everything's in hand. I have already contacted an Island lawyer and tomorrow we shall work on your bail.

Remember, in the meantime, it's imperative you continue this silence. Talk to no one and say nothing. Is that clear?" the last phrase came as a command.

"You can count on me," Rudolfo winked. He never questioned the proceedings, all he saw was escape. His mind was focused on how easy he could slip out of Canada into the USA.

The guard noted Rudolfo had been speaking English to his lawyer, approached the table. "Everything's OK, just basics and some candy," and slid the box towards Rudolfo.

Rudolfo briefly examined the contents, thinking, "I'll need a change of underwear for tomorrow. The candy's a plus."

Fred, noting his time was up, stood to leave. He turned to the guard with a gracious farewell, "Thank you for letting me see my client. This is all for tonight. I'll be back tomorrow." Nothing seemed amiss.

As the three moved towards the doorway, Fred slapped Rodolfo on the back with a cheery farewell. "Have a good night's sleep, my boy, everything will be settled in the morning."

Rudolfo returned to his cell, placed the box on his side table, had two pieces of the candy and prepared for bed. Just before dozing off he thought, "Odd, that lawyer never took a note and that sickening smile..... Where have I seen it before? Who cares, tomorrow I'll be free." He drifted off to sleep.

The next morning when there was no response from the cell occupant the morning guard opened the cell to discover the cold lifeless body of Rudolfo, his appearance indicating he had been dead for hours. All hell broke loose as the jail exploded with the news.

Shortly after 10:30am an urgent meeting was held at the jail with Conrad Burke, the city Chief of Police, Stuart Baxter, an RCMP Superintendent, and Mike Fraser, the Jail Administrator.

Conrad's fury was palpable as he began, "This is the worst God awful mess I've ever encountered and likely one with painful consequences for all of us. A leading citizen of this city, Nellie Gordon, is attacked in her home by an outsider and, just fifteen minutes ago, I received word that she has died in hospital. Her assailant is an international, petty crook, identified through Interpol as Rudolfo Marquis of Calabria. This international criminal arrives on the Island with a precise target. We have no idea why. He gets arrested in the act of assaulting Nellie. We get little out of him on admission and he gets killed while a guest of the city jail. The coroner is certain it is poison and has already ruled out the candy delivered by his so-called lawyer. He's still investigating. His lawyer, a Fred Simpson, does not exist. The Halifax law firm of Quinn, Graham and Green has never heard of him nor is he listed in any legal firm anywhere in the Maritimes. So, we must assume this was a false identity however well informed he was on our legal system. In summary, on this fair Island for the first time in its history we are facing an international crime spree in which we have two dead bodies, one a leading citizen and the other an Italian, who we can assume was eliminated by a hired hit man. Who organized and paid for all this we have no idea nor do we have any leads. Within hours, we will need a reasonable explanation behind these two deaths and what we are doing about it or otherwise we're going to look like a pack of idiots. Does that pretty well sum up the hell we're in?"

Mike, looking weary and feeling the brunt of the fury, responded. "I can assure you that everything was properly carried out. The so-called lawyer had all the right credentials, and knew the names of key Island lawyers. He was given fifteen minutes under guard to talk to his client. They did not drink anything and, as observed, nothing except this small box containing underwear, toiletries and candy, passed between them."

Stuart stepped in, "Have they been able to get any fingerprints off the box?"

"No," replied John." It was rough material and before you ask, this guy cleverly managed to avoid touching anything."

Conrad, reducing his anger, went on, "I'm not making any insinuations of mismanagement, Mike, someone has cleverly manipulated this whole scenario. A very fine woman is dead and the citizens of this city will be up in arms about this. The fact that an outsider has slipped onto the Island to perpetrate such a deed will threaten the security of many. Irrespective of a criminal nature of this case we are standing here with our trousers down with no information. That's why I'm upset. Stuart, do you have anything to add?"

Stuart now began to give his assessment, "This has the markings of organized crime, but why? Surely, our upstanding citizen, Nellie Gordon, has nothing of value to attract such criminals nor is there any evidence that she or any member of her family has been involved in criminal activity. Yet, she was definitely the target. This wasn't a mistake. Marquis had a printout of her B&B in his belongings. We have to get into Nellie's house and find out what they are after, as it's clear there is more than one party involved. The situation has just got more complicated as, I understand, Nellie's granddaughter arrived home from Halifax to be with her grandmother. She is living in the house and could well be the next target. Whatever these criminals are after they may try again. Let me talk to Jock MacAndrew, he's the family doctor and may have some answers. Leave it to me. I'll get back to you later today if I learn anything. In the meantime, I think Nellie's residence and her granddaughter need our attention. Conrad can you increase your patrols and I'll see what I can do behind the scene. This wave of killings may not be over. Talk to you both later."

33

Days later the coroner would identify the rare poison as that of the Golden Poison Frog and discovered a fine pin prick on Rudolfo's upper back, the location of Fred's final farewell.

Chapter 3

Canada, Charlottetown: A Secret Revealed

Angi woke from a dreamless sleep. "One o'clock. My God, I've overslept! I must get back to the hospital," she thought, dashing into the en suite bathroom to take a shower.

Downstairs, Dave was manning the phones and door. He and James had organized a form of shift duty between Nellie's place and their usual government meetings. Busy with the inquisitive and do-gooders, Dave spent the morning storing donated baked goods from the townspeople and diplomatically fielding Margo's insistence that she had to be in charge.

After a shower, Angi slipped on a pair of pale blue slacks and light blouse. As she unpacked and was storing her suitcase in the closet, she noticed her Irish harp, the clarsach, resting elegantly on the dresser. "My old friend, how I've neglected you in the past few years," she said to herself. As if responding to the attention, the twenty-six string Brigit harp beckoned to be played. As Angi picked up the harp to tune it, old familiar memories reappeared.

Up to the age of seven, music had not been a dominant interest in her life. So it was perplexing when, out of the blue, an elderly relative on her grandmother's side arrived from Georgetown, with a small Celtic harp wrapped in a plaid woolen blanket. This boisterous, middle aged, woman, insisted that Nellie had a duty to make sure that Angi learned to play the Celtic harp. Angi, fascinated by the small harp, fell under its spell when this strange relative began to play a Celtic lullaby. With limited funds music lessons seemed an unattainable luxury. But, undaunted, this relative agreed to pay for the lessons and had already contacted a Celtic harp teacher in the western part of the Island, a rare entity in the province at the time. Thus began a nine year program of music lessons, enhanced by the strange but enchanting qualities of the teacher.

Within weeks of the harp's arrival, Albert Aucoin appeared. Angi remembered opening the front door to a small, unkempt, stooped, elderly man, with a strong French accent, and disturbingly long fingernails. Every month this strange man appeared for their three hour music lesson, usually on a Saturday morning.

In time, Angi learned that Mr. Aucoin, the last member of his family line, had come to live on the Island with distant relatives. He was a descendant of generations of harp players, his ancestor being one to the Irish gentry who were expelled to France in the 1600s. The expulsion, known as the 'Flight of the Wild Geese', involved 14,000 soldiers and 10,000 women and children, their descendants becoming French citizens, many forgetting their Irish roots. One positive outcome of this horrific event was the survival of Celtic harp music in Europe when it had practically ceased in Ireland under centuries of an English ban on its playing.

Angi's initial uneasiness with her mentor quickly evaporated under his enthusiastic love of the harp and his mysterious presence. In looking back she thought, "Mr. Aucoin, a harpist to Irish royalty, had stepped out of time."

Within months her rough musical efforts mellowed under a steady program of basic music reading, cord building, improvisation, composing and arranging. Mr. Aucoin was a stern master but each lesson was softened with his fascinating stories of the harp's ancient roots in Egypt, the Middle East, Europe and the Celtic Isles. Later he charmed her with tales of the Tuatha De Danann, the old Irish gods/goddesses, known as the fairy race of Ireland. She especially loved the story of the magic harp owned by the good god of the faeries, Dagda Mor, which flew through the air when summoned. She chuckled remembering the times she tried calling her harp from her bed, expecting it to fly through the air, but it never did. She could still hear his voice as he reverently referred to the harp as 'the voice of the gods', because its resonance could bring joy, sorrow, enchantment or healing to its listener. It was an instrument associated with magic, and these were magical memories.

In reverence, Angi picked up her own harp, wondering if her shortened fingernails might now be a handicap. Conducting a brief meditation to center herself in preparation, she began, letting the healing vibrations of the music flow through her. The music drifted out the open bedroom window, a slow, soft musical interpretation of the Secret Garden-Nocturne.

At this moment, three men approached the front door, a small man between two taller men, one in uniform. Listening to the music Alex Dumont said to his companions, "What a beautiful piece of music, almost a lament. Is that a harp? It must be Angi. You'd almost think she knew?"

Jock replied, "Well, that wouldn't be a surprise. Nellie Gordon was known to have *Second Sight* which has likely been passed on to her granddaughter. Somewhere in Angi's soul the death of her grandmother has already registered. She was a fine Celtic harp player in her youth. It is good she has not lost the gift." Pressing the door bell he continued, "Nevertheless, gentlemen, this does not make our task any easier."

Dave, opening the door, knew by the presence of the three men what was in store. Entering the living room, the four men stood in silence as they waited for the music to cease. On its completion, Dave went to the bottom of the stairs and called gently, "Angi, you have company. Can you come down?"

"I'm on my way," was the quick response. Angi stopped midway on the stairs when she saw the three men, knowing what news they brought.

Jock stepped forward and spoke, "Angi, I'm truly sorry to be the bearer of such sad news. Your grandmother passed away this morning at ten. The strain on her heart was just too great."

Angi felt the urge to scream, "No, no, not my dear Gran. It is too soon. There are too many unanswered questions!" But her professional training immediately overpowered the urge as she faced the reality before her. Without siblings, and being the last in her grandmother's line, she had to stand tall.

Jock continued, "Angi you know Alex Dumont, your grandmother's lawyer." Alex nodded. And turning he motioned to the third member of the group, "And this is Superintendent Stuart Baxter of the RCMP, an old friend of mine." Letting this register, he went on. "Angi, I hate to place more stress on you at this time, but the situation has become rather complicated. The man that attacked your grandmother has died in custody."

"What?" replied a startled Angi trying hard to grasp the enormity of the situation. "How could that happen?"

Jock replied in a steady refrain, "Somehow, we think, he was poisoned. The situation is under investigation. But this means there are others involved in this attack on your grandmother. What is troubling all of us is that we have no idea what they are after. Do you, Angi?"

Before Angi had time to respond, Alex stepped forward, "Angi, the day before Nellie was attacked, she appeared in my office with this letter, saying it was to remain sealed and given to you if anything happened to her before your scheduled summer vacation. Before I had a chance to get anything else out of her she abruptly left." He passed the letter to Angi.

Alex continued as Angi examined the letter. "Angi you know your grandmother's estate goes to you. You will need to come to my office to sign some papers. Angi, I have known your family for decades, and yet I stand here today with no idea why anyone would want to attack Nellie. As far as I know, other than this house, your grandmother possessed few assets of any value. Is that true?"

Angi opened the letter. As expected her grandmother was directing her to contact the American and Irish Guardians, indicating that Angi might have to travel to the United States as she was now one of the Guardians of the medallion. Angi returned the letter to its envelope and stared at the four men, her thoughts racing, "How much can I trust these men with this centuries-old family secret? In light of my own health I am left with few alternatives. I must trust someone, for I may not live long enough to be a Guardian to anything." Glancing upward she said to herself, "Forgive me Gran, for the first time in our family, I am the one that must break this code of silence. Whatever punishment this may entail, here goes."

"Actually, there is something. It is very old. I have no idea of its value but it was the last thing Gran talked about in the hospital and it is referred to in this letter. Come with me." The four men followed her upstairs to her grandmother's bedroom.

Finding the skeleton key in the drawer of her grandmother's bedside table, she inserted it into the timeworn bronze lock on the wooden trunk and raised the heavy oval lid revealing a cluttered interior.

"Angi, this trunk looks like something from a pirate movie," said Jock, seeing the trunk for the first time.

It is over three hundred years old," replied Angi. "It has been in the family for generations. While this old trunk may have its own mystery, it is what is inside that may be the reason for the attack." She reached in and pulled out a large triangular shaped item wrapped in a thick gray-woven material.

"What's that?" asked Dave.

Angi removed the covering to reveal a Celtic harp of exquisite beauty, the gold and jewels sparking in the sunlight. The thirty stringed harp measuring about thirty-three inches tall and eighteen inches wide, glistened with gold and silver carvings on every inch of its case. The instrument was engraved with a fantasy of animals, reptiles, and little creatures playing musical instruments flowing from the mouth of a dog's head which surmounted the sounding board. The pillar was elaborately carved with Celtic interlacing patterns of leaves, flowers and fruit. The metal strings appeared to be made of gold and silver. Colorful gems were inserted in various parts of the engravings.

The four men stared in silence. Stuart was the first to speak. "My God, if what I am looking at is genuine gold, silver and precious gems then this harp could be worth a fortune, more if it has a history."

"It has never been valued," replied Angi, having forgotten the harp's beauty. She then gave a brief account of her harp lessons and her music teacher. In closing she went on, "On my sixteenth birthday, Mr. Aucoin, then a man in his early eighties, arrived for our last lesson. He gave me this magnificent harp, his own, saying there may be only one of similar quality somewhere in Ireland. That day, he played an unknown tune he said he learned from the faeries. It truly sounded like it had come from the angels.

The metal strings produce a very different sound than my poor student harp which I normally use. As he was about to leave he said, 'Angi I am gifting this treasure to you, for one day you will be asked to play for the Lords of Anu'. Smiling he kissed me good bye. Months later he died."

Inquisitively, Jock asked, "Angi, what did he mean by the Lords of Anu?"

"I haven't a clue. It hasn't come to mind for years. Perhaps I'll look it up on the Internet."

"So, this is what the thief was after?" asked Stuart. "It is expensive enough but it needs to be properly assessed."

"While this certainly looks valuable," replied Angi, "I expect no one except Mr. Aucoin, my grandmother and me even knew it was here. I was never allowed to take it out of my grandmother's trunk. No, this is not what the thief was after."

Angi then went to her grandmother's bedside table and picked up a small knitting needle resting under a doily. She inserted a pointed end into a small, almost invisible, hole in the trunk lid. A faint click was heard, and a secret panel slid open to reveal a small box-like item wrapped in a purple velvet bag. Angi removed it from its secret chamber, undid the cord tie and pulled out a gold and silver engraved box. Taking it to her grandmother's bureau, she pressed a small leaver on the side which opened the lid to reveal a piece of antique jewelry. Angi picked up the golden medallion and chain and displayed it to the four men.

Jock examined the item carefully. "I'm no expert on antique jewelry but this certainly looks old. The center stone is most unusual. The amethyst is lovely. My wife always said the amethyst had something to do with psychic powers. It would be interesting to know what the other stones might have been; they likely fit into the empty sockets. Angi, is this really what the thief was after? It is rather innocuous. Does it have a story?"

"What I know is rather limited, I'm afraid. When I was twenty-one, Gran showed me this medallion and tried to get me interested in its history, but, I paid scant attention. I do remember something about the missing gems. The gems had been deliberately removed centuries ago in the British Isles and scattered among a number of Irish/Scots/Welsh families. As there are eight gem slots, I expect there were eight families, the Camerons being one. A number of the original eight families immigrated to North America so that the medallion could not be assembled until, the *'coming times'*. In the hospital, Gran kept mumbling the *'coming times'* had arrived. I've no idea what that means. Through the centuries each Guardian kept in touch with two other Guardians. I have the names of the two Guardians Gran contacted each year, usually at Christmas. In hospital, her last request was for me to phone these two women. I called them early this morning and will need to contact them again now that Gran has died."

"What did they say when you called?" asked Stuart.

"Both kept repeating the same '*coming times*' phrase. Obviously something has begun. They would not say anything more over the telephone except that I could be in grave danger. The Irish woman kept mumbling something about the medallion having magical powers but nothing specific. Another interesting feature of this secret, is that the medallion was to be mainly guarded by women, as they were the least likely to be traced in a masculine world. How's that for seventeenth century feminism."

"I know you are hesitant in giving out their names, Angi, but in light of recent events they may also be in danger," said Stuart.

Angi hesitated, "I will ask these women about releasing their names when I call about my grandmother's death and, if they agree, you can notify the Boston and Galway Bay, Ireland police departments on what has happened here. Is that OK for now?"

"Fine, Angi. We will at least get the police onto this before there are any further problems." Stuart was not entirely happy with this arrangement but at least he now knew the motive. "Well, the medallion's magical powers seem rather tame at present?" said Stuart as he examined the piece of jewelry, "but, your safety is a definite concern," as he glanced quickly at Jock.

Ignoring the safety issue, Angi went on, "According to Gran, the medallion only becomes activated when all the gems are in place. Considering there has been over three hundred years since these gems were scattered, there is likely little possibility of finding them at this point."

Alex, who was now quietly examining the medallion and storage box, asked "May be that's not as impossible as you think. If these Guardians have been contacting each other for centuries, they may still have a living network. Whatever this secret is, great care has been given to the design of this storage box. It looks French, maybe 1600s, and of a very costly craftsmanship. Someone went to a great deal of effort to protect something for centuries. It deserves our attention. It is your heritage, Angi, we can only advise you."

"Well, gentlemen," said Stuart looking around, "I need not stress enough the need for silence on this matter. The value of these two items, the golden harp and the medallion, is sufficient to attract any number of treasure seekers and criminals. Although our deceased thief was certainly not the brains behind this attack, he knew precisely what he was after. He was likely the pawn of a more dangerous predator. Someone definitely knows more than we do about this medallion, and that bothers me. In the meantime, Angi, I advise you to get these two items out of this house. Alex and I will make arrangements with the Royal Bank for a special safety box and we will settle this matter today if you agree."

Angi nodded her head in agreement.

Then, hesitating, Stuart glanced at Jock and continued. "In light of so many uncertainties, I suggest you have a bodyguard for the next few weeks until we can get a better handle on this whole matter. Angi, you could be the next target."

The idea of a nursemaid irritated Angi, and she responded, "I don't need a bodyguard. For heaven's sake, this is Charlottetown. The city police have been making extra rounds. That should be enough."

Stuart pressed his point. "Angi, this man had international connections and such sophisticated criminals have few scruples if they're after something of value. I insist on the bodyguard because you will be alone in this house when Dave and James return to Montague tomorrow. This bodyguard, a female, will be inconspicuous. You might introduce her as one of your nursing colleagues."

Reconsidering the practical reality of the situation, Angi's next response was more conciliatory. "Perhaps you are right. Under the circumstances being alone would not be good. I'd like the company as the days ahead could be difficult. The way my grandmother was attacked has rattled me even if I am trying to ignore it. So, when should I expect my so-called bodyguard?"

Before Stuart had time to respond, the sound of a motorcycle roared into place near the front of the house. "There she is now," said Stuart. "Let's go down and meet her."

Angi returned the two valuable items to their respective bags placed them back in her grandmother's trunk, and locked it. The party of five returned to the front room to greet their new arrival.

Dave opened the front door and in stepped a slightly built female dressed in black leather from head to toe, sporting a tousled pink and green cropped hair cut and numerous tattoos. "Hi all, I got here as quickly as I could. Slade Gallant reporting for duty," she said with a broad smile as she nodded a special greeting to Stuart.

Angi stared in disbelief. "You must be kidding. Inconspicuous, it will be extremely difficult to pass Slade off as another nurse."

"No problem, my dear," replied Slade, undaunted by the negative reaction. "Miracles can happen. Today's undercover cops have the latest training in theatrical make-up. We are experts at disguise. Give me a washroom. You'll be amazed at what a few chemicals and soap and water can do. I need to look like a nurse, heh, well, that's what it'll be." Angi pointed to the downstairs washroom. Slade disappeared clutching a small leather bag.

Stuart called after Slade, "I'll make sure the motorbike is stored at headquarters. You and Angi can use Nellie's Toyota parked in the driveway." Without waiting for the transformation, Stuart headed for the front door,

"Alex and I are off Angi. We will be back in a couple of hours." Sensing Angi's uncertainty over the new arrival he continued "You'll be glad to have Slade. She's one of the best. Her father and I trained together many years ago." When he reached his car he phoned Conrad to arrange an immediate meeting. He knew that the police in Boston and Galway Bay had to be notified.

Jock stayed, briefly discussing with Angi the arrangements for the transfer of her grandmother to a local funeral home. As he was about to depart Angi stated, "I'll contact Margo, she can help me with the arrangements."

Within the hour Slade reappeared. Angi and Dave stood in disbelief. It was an entire transformation. Her hair was now auburn, the tattoos gone and she was dressed in casual slakes and a sweat shirt embellished with a sassy pink bear.

Angi couldn't believe her eyes. "How did you get rid of all those tattoos?"

Slade smiled as she replied, "These days we have removable tattoos. Mind you, they are not easily removed but with the right chemical mixture they do come off. I'm likely poisoning myself. Now, you will have to fill me in on what kind of nurse I'm supposed to be. Before that, I'm starving. I've not stopped since I left Halifax hours ago. Stuart really convinced my dad this was urgent."

"How were you able to get off duty?" asked Dave, thinking, "I wonder who's footing the bill. Normally, it is a rare situation for police protection of this caliber. I'll not press the matter; Angi has enough on her plate."

Slade, choosing her words carefully, replied, "Actually, I'm on a sort of leave...... between assignments........" she let the sentence drift with few details.

Quickly changing the conversation, Dave replied. "Did I hear you say you were hungry? The Kirk women have been dropping off food all morning. There's plenty to eat. Angi, you decide on the menu while I make the coffee." Looking at the strained look on Angi's face, he shifted gear and asked. "Never mind, Slade and I will take care of the eats. Is there any chance, Angi, your grandmother kept some liquor in the house? This has been a rough day."

Angi, feeling the stress of recent events and a strange feeling her world was being altered by forces outside of her control, replied in a quiet voice, "Gran has some sherry in the dining room cupboard." For the first time since she arrived home a wave of nausea swept over her and she eased herself into a kitchen chair.

"I'll find it," said Dave as he moved towards the dining room.

At that moment James arrived, heading straight to Dave for an update.

In the kitchen, Angi asked Slade. "I do hope you have another name than Slade?"

"Oh yah," replied Slade. That's my working name. My family calls me Vette, short for Yvette. Will that do?"

"Better," smiled Angi. "Vette Gallant it is. I will introduce you as a Halifax nurse working with a special unit caring for the mentally ill and drug addicts. How's that for a cover?"

"Perfect! It fits my recent work. If asked, I'll soften the details. Stuart gave me some briefing over the phone and you and Dave can fill me in on today's happenings. After some food, I'll find a suitable downstairs place to sleep, and all my needs will be met."

Angi liked this practical, exuberant, stranger. "It'll be good to have someone guarding my back," she thought, "I have enough on my plate."

Within minutes sherry was made available for everyone. While Dave, James and Vette proceeded to get some lunch ready, Angi slipped into the living room, choosing a soft chair a distance from the kitchen. The kitchen voices drifted into the distance as she pondered the happy memories of this old house. The house seemed empty; her grandmother's spirit was gone. Tears blocked her vision as the impact of the emptiness engulfed her. "I'm the last of this family line," she thought. "My illness means there will likely be no descendants. Perhaps it is best, Gran never knew. Life certainly has its surprises. My comfortable life as a nurse has been turned upside down. I am now facing two life-threatening possibilities, a major illness and an international killer after an ancient medallion which I know little about but am one of its Guardians." Her thoughts were interrupted by Dave's call from the kitchen that lunch was ready. Angi picked up her sherry glass, let the liquid slip down her throat, and headed towards the life-filled voices. "It is good to have such people around at such times; a blessing of strangers."

United States: Boston Police Station

The cold reality of a predator targeting one's family registered when Wolfram learned of the attack on Nellie Gordon. Antonino had reached North America. He was after the medallion and its gemstones and had few scruples in how he obtained them. Wolfram sent out calls to former law enforcement colleagues to get a bead on this phantom. Days passed. The urgency of the information escalated at an unrelated meeting at the Boston Police Station. Wolfram was there to discuss an upcoming fraud case with global tentacles.

He sat uncomfortably in the waiting area outside the Deputy Superintendent's office. The activities and sounds of the police station were familiar, too familiar. A part of his soul was still held in its spell. "What was it," he thought, "the sense of duty or the clear purpose, perhaps both?" He stood for a few minutes, started walking, trying to find some comfort. Frustrated, he thought, "It hardly matters what I do. This leg hurts if I sit or stand for any length of time. I'm cursed. If I don't exercise I can hardly move. When I do exercise I get this throbbing pain. I have to blank it out."

At that moment the door opened and Gus, in his usual boisterous manner ushered him into his office with, "It is good to see you again, my boy, and glad you are getting about. That leg's still a problem but you seem pretty much on the mend."

"Well, almost sir. Still a lot of rehab ahead but it is improving," said Wolfram, wanting to bypass the topic. He made a bee line for the most comfortable chair in the room, which he soon discovered provided little comfort to his aching limb.

Gus Ferguson, a man nearing retirement, positioned himself into his oversized leather chair, and retrieved the case file in the midst of a stack of papers. At that moment, his secretary barged into the room to announce there was an urgent call from Atlantic Canada. Turning to Wolfram, Gus said, "This should be brief," then to his secretary, "I'll take this one and then hold my calls for the next hour."

Wolfram had known Gus for over ten years. As he waited he thought to himself, "I've missed the old codger, growl and all. He'll be hard to replace. Years of pulling the force, kicking and screaming, into the electronic age and routing out the deadwood came with a hefty price. He's aged in the past year. While some griped about Gus's management style, I discovered he had an unequaled understanding of law enforcement politics and dealing with complex cases. In several instances his mentorship proved invaluable. I suppose he felt bad that my accident occurred while I was on duty and within days of leaving. Whatever the reason, I'm the winner."

Gus picked up the receiver with a cheery, "Hello how's the Maritimes? I've a cousin near Yarmouth, Nova Scotia. Haven't seen him in years.......... Oh, you are calling from Prince Edward Island.........Never been there. Heard it is a lovely place. ...... What can I do for you, Conrad? Two deaths! Nellie Gordon, a prominent citizen of your community, how did she die?"

Alarmed at hearing Nellie's name, Wolfram squirmed. "She's dead!" He knew of the assault from his grandmother. "That certainly screws my theory of it being a random car accident in Dublin. A God-damned storm is heading this way."

Gus continued talking, "I see......The assailant was from where? .... Wanted by Interpol, you say? What was he doing in Canada? .... What? Gus noted Wolfram's unease and knew it wasn't entirely due to his injuries.

While concentrating on the call he now began to observe Wolfram. "He was killed, in your jail, by a suspected hired killer. Now that's a nasty twist......... Poisoned, heh?"

Wolfram felt a cold chill. His thoughts raced, "My God, three deaths in so many days! This Antonino is lethal. The dead jail bird was likely the Dublin driver. Antonino avoids soiling his own hands. What in God's name are we dealing with? This man has powerful contacts to arrange a hit like that. I'm sorry I ever heard of this damn medallion. It will be the death of us all. Morgan's the next target and it is just a matter of time before he zeros in on the rest of us."

The international call went on, "That's an expensive send off for a petty thief wouldn't you say? Do you have any idea of the motive or who's behind this? No? .... So, why are you calling?"

Gus kept watching Wolfram. Startled by the news from Conrad, Gus asked, "What name did you say?" ....He stared at Wolfram repeating the name out loud......... "Gracelyn Harrison. I certainly do know her," the emphasis falling on the 'do'. "You think she may be the next target? Not on my patch."

Wolfram knew his grandmother's name could only have come from Angi and she would not have revealed it without permission from his grandmother. His thoughts began to race. "Obviously, 'the *coming times*', whatever the hell that meant, had raised the curtain of silence. The Guardians knew they were now potential targets. If Antonino was able to get to one or more of the Guardians, he could possibly unravel the whole chain."

Wolfram knew the call was about to end as Gus said, "Conrad, be assured that I will definitely look into this. Thanks for the heads up. I'll get back to you if I learn anything more." He dropped the receiver into its cradle and stared at Wolfram, "OK, my boy, to hell with the fraud case, talk to me! I get irritated when one of our noted citizens becomes a target of some international killer. You know more? Start talking!"

There was no escape from the thundering voice and demand. Wolfram began. "I can't believe it has come to this. It is hard to know where to begin. This is a secret which has been kept by my family and others for centuries."

"To hell with secrets," roared Gus, "your family's very life may be at stake. This killer is heading this way. In fact he's likely already in town. Damn the secrets, talk!

"Ok, when you put it that way. Months ago when I was recovering from my accident, my grandmother informed me of this old family secret. Sometime in the 1600s the gems of a particular medallion were distributed among a number of Irish/Scots/Welsh families. Some of the families immigrated to North America, and, according to my grandmother, in later centuries one or more families went on to Australia and New Zealand. Each family was responsible for one gemstone, my family having a sapphire. I have no idea if all the stones are identical."

"Are these large stones?" asked Gus.

"No, actually the only one I've seen is relatively modest. However, according to my gem appraiser, the sapphire is very old and of exquisite quality."

"You have no idea how many families were involved; five, ten, fifteen?"

"No idea. And after so many centuries, I don't believe the Guardians of the stones know either. According to my grandmother each family had two contacts which they wrote to each year in a coded message. But, sitting here this morning, however remote the possibility after three hundred years and the global scattering of the stones, it may not be as impossible to break this chain of silence as I first thought."

"My God," said Gus, "I feel as if I've stumbled into some Scottish legend. My ancestors came from Galloway in Scotland, who, my grandfather insisted, claimed descent from Fergus of Galloway, with ties to Robert Bruce. I spent my childhood listening to Celtic stories from my grandmother. There were many secrets in the 1600s for it was a turbulent period in history. Don't dismiss such tales. There may be more behind this than you know. It must have some importance for aristocrats to take such risks and immigrate to North America, which was pretty rugged at that time. Someone out there knows more than you do, my boy, and they are willing to kill for it. There are two deaths already."

"Possibly, three," replied Wolfram hesitantly "and in just two weeks. Perhaps I better continue telling you what I know."

"You are damn right, press on," said Gus, pushing himself away from the desk relaxing into his chair and staring out the window. "This case is beginning to have legs........ legs from hell."

Wolfram went on, "I took my grandmother's sapphire to be appraised. The jeweler, a reliable fellow, felt it could be worth thousands but he wanted to see the medallion to make a full assessment. I then went to my friend Dr. Morgan Mandelthrope at Boston University to see if there was anything in the archives about a 1600s secret or some special medallion. When he failed to find anything he contacted two university colleagues; one in Ireland and another in Scotland, both with extensive Celtic history expertise."

As Wolfram talked, Gus kept nodding his head and saying nothing.

"Just the other day we got word that his friend, Dr. Kevyn O'Gratteney at Trinity College in Dublin was run down outside his university, a suspected hit and run. His last e-mail hinted at finding a seventeenth century coded secret. Days before he was run down, someone hacked into his computer and retrieved information on the medallion. This information included the name of this Canadian woman and my friend Morgan. My Grandmother's name, to the best of my knowledge, was not in any of these files. Her name has likely been provided by Nellie's granddaughter, with permission of my grandmother."

"Are the Irish police investigating the hit and run?"

"Yes, they have a witness that states he saw the car being deliberately aimed at the professor."

"Is that it," snapped Gus.

"Almost," replied Wolfram.

Gus, swinging about in his chair and confronting Wolfram said, "So far, as I understand it, we have an ancient medallion with an unknown number of precious gemstones, which was dispersed for safekeeping sometime in the 1600s. These stones and some secret have been kept by a number of elite Celtic families for over three hundred years. We know of only two families involved with this secret, your family and this Gordon lady in Canada, right?"

"Actually my grandmother may know a few more. I don't."

"OK let's leave the number for now. By any remote chance do you know who's behind these killings?"

"I believe there is only one person, his name is Antonino Borgiano. Professor O'Gratteney fingered him in his last e-mail. The little I know is that he is a recently defrocked Roman Catholic priest with powerful contacts."

Gus, in an angry voice replied, "That's all I need, a disgraced Roman Catholic cleric, possibly abusive, with powerful contacts in Rome. That's enough hell in itself but this one's also a serial killer ....my cup runneth over!!! This ex-priest likely has access to Vatican or other church archives that date back to the 1600s. That may be his trump card. He likely knows more about this medallion than either you or any of the Guardians. His ruthless tactics indicate as much. He knows precisely what he's after and why. We're handicapped without this information, and no photo or profile on this man. The hit in Canada has an underworld signature........and anyone who maneuvers easily between clerical and criminal worlds is highly dangerous in my books. This fraud case can wait, it is months away. This case is now priority one. We have to combine forces. Your grandparents and friend need protection. I've no official funds for this so we'll just be creative."

Rising from his chair he continued, "First I'll contact the Canadian authorities with this name. Then I'll get in touch with the Irish police ...... what city did you say?"

"Dublin," was Wolfram's quick reply.

Gus, still giving orders, "You contact Gritty Mahr, he's semi-retired these days but a fine detective. He's looking for work, and would be a good bodyguard for your friend Morgan. From your account, I expect he's the next target. Gritty, is quick, crafty and loves to outwit clever criminals. He'll love this case; he has a deep seated hatred for abusive priests. Do you have his number?"

"Yes, I've used him before. He'll be a good match for Morgan. But first, I'll have to convince Morgan he needs protection."

"I'll open channels to get a photo and info of this serial killer at once. He may have entered Britain on his own passport, that'll be a start. I expect he's under an assumed name here in Boston. I'm sure he's here. I need to know his contacts, which will tell me a whole lot. I'll send out a low-key alert, but will be ready to raise its status at any hint of trouble."

The moment he reached his car, Wolfram called Morgan on his cell phone. "Where are you, Morgan, we need to meet at once. How far are you from Josh's place? Good, I'll see you in about thirty minutes." His next call was to Gritty asking him to a meet at Josh's place, a location he knew well. Josh had chosen a renovated warehouse in Charlestown for his high tech business. It was north of Cambridge near the Navy Yard, Bunker Hill Monument and U.S.S. Constitution and, most importantly, with easy access to scores of hearty-fair restaurants. The building had lots of space for his equipment, but the heating was atrocious. Josh kept saying the coolness was good for his electronic computers and other devices, but Wolfram knew it had more to do with scarce resources.

Finding a parking space at the back of the building, Wolfram took the rickety elevator to the second floor, the stairs still a challenge. There he found Morgan and Josh chatting about some recent Internet find.

Avoiding a greeting, Wolfram approached the two with, "Josh, do you have a cubby hole where Morgan and I can chat in private?"

"Sure, you can use my cluttered office at the end of the hall. I'm alone today my two techies are off on a job."

Morgan turned to Wolfram with a slight annoyance "What's up? You are a bit tense."

When the door closed in Josh's office, Wolfram, with little fan fare began. "Morgan, sit down," as he pulled out a worn wooden chair. "I have bad news."

Morgan sensed the drama and sat down. "I have a feeling this is not going to make my day."

Morgan blurted out, "Nellie Gordon in Canada is dead."

Morgan slumped, sitting silently for a few minutes, in a depressed tone asked, "How did it happen?"

"She was attacked by someone, not Antonino, possibly the same man who drove the car into your Irish colleague in Dublin. I expect her age and health plus the attack contributed to her death. But this is not all. The assailant was arrested but later killed in jail by a hired hit man."

"Hell, what have we stumbled into," moaned Morgan. "This is becoming a horror show ....and it is all due to my stupid carelessness. I caused those deaths. Mark my word. Wolf, I am going to hell for this." He stopped looking at his friend and stared out the large storage building window at a brick wall.

"Stop that, Morgan; you can't blame yourself for the fanatical killing spree of this mad man. Listen to me, this situation is more serious than you think."

"More serious, I suppose you are going to say I'm the next target."

"That's exactly what I'm about to say. Remember, you are the only other name he has from O'Gratteney's files, at least that is what you told me, right?"

"Right," said Morgan almost in a whisper.

"Well, this killer is likely already in the city."

Fear gripped Morgan as he contemplated his fate. "I'm going to be killed........I can feel it in my bones. This is a righteous outcome for my foolish slippery tongue." He sat dejected, like a lost child.

"Well, that's not going to happen. Pull yourself together, Morgan. Stop being maudlin, listen to me. We are going to fight this. You are not going to die if I have anything to say about it." He reached forward and shook Morgan to get his attention. "The Boston police are on the case. I was in Gus's office when the call came in from Canada. I want you to have a bodyguard starting today."

"A what?" asked Morgan, trying hard to grasp the enormity of the situation.

"A bodyguard. I have someone in mind. You will need a cover story for the university, such as an out of town researcher or something. Can you do that?"

Still slow in responding Morgan finally replied, "Sure, it is summer, there are always researchers floating around. A short spell will not be noticed. How long are you thinking of?"

"Let's say a month, maybe more. Now your home may not be safe either. I don't suppose Kari-Ann would agree to a boarder?"

"Not likely," responded Morgan in a scowl, "We're hardly on speaking terms these days. She has her life and I mine."

"Well, we'll have to think of something else," replied Wolfram, realizing this could be the weak link in his plan. Still wanting assurance that Morgan would accept the idea he asked again, "So you'll accept a bodyguard?"

"I have little alternative. Without your help and this shadow I'm a goner. If this Antonino can wipe out three people in less than two weeks, I'll be a cinch. I was never a fan of murders, books or shows, and it is too late for a crash course."

At that moment, a light tap came on the office door glass. Wolfram waved in his old colleague, Gritty Mahr, a nondescript late fortyish man in jeans and mustard colored sweatshirt, almost emaciated, with graying hair and a wide grin. "Well, my old friend, what kind of mess do you need me for this time?"

Wolfram stepped towards the open door and turned, "He's sitting right here. This is Dr. Morgan Mandelthrope of Boston University. Morgan say hello to your bodyguard, Gritty Mahr." The two men eyed each other; one trying to assess what protection this little, wiry man could provide, the other wondering what would necessitate the need for a bodyguard for this man in front of him. Morgan stood up, said a quiet "hello" to Gritty and slumped back into his chair.

In the next half hour Wolfram filled Gritty in on the situation and his expected duties. Gritty kept nodding his head as Wolfram spoke, interjecting the occasional question for clarification. When Wolfram finished Gritty turned to Morgan.

"You and I will have to discuss my cover. I'll blend in, I always do. It would help if I had a photo and profile of this killer," looking at Wolfram.

"Gus should have something later today. I'll make sure you have it."

"What's happening at his house, I can't cover twenty-four hours?"

Wolfram, still in charge responded, "Gritty, do you have anyone that might be able to do night duty in front of Morgan's house? I was hoping that you or someone else might get inside the house, but that's a no go."

Gritty thought for a moment. "Well there's........no he's out of town. May be ....no, he's in hospital. I know I have an old army buddy. He did police duty overseas, a great guy who prefers nights. I'll get in touch with him and get back to you. How are we communicating on this?"

"We'll stick to the old fashioned methods like cell phones. This guy has used technical hackers before so let's stay away from the Internet. Morgan, are you listening?"

"Yah, I'll have Gritty to remind me. No e-mails and no calls from my office phone. This is going to be difficult."

Irritated, Wolfram replied harshly, trying to imprint on Morgan's subconscious the seriousness of the situation. "In case you need any reminding think of the three dead bodies........and then realize you could be next."

Morgan cringed, "Yah, that seals it."

Thinking again on the potential problem of coverage at Morgan's home, Wolfram made a note to himself, "I'll need to make sure that this fellow Gritty has in mind for the night shift is up to the task, for Morgan's home could be the attack zone."

"OK, let's set some parameters. We will only talk about this case here at Josh's. If, for any reason, we need to meet in a hurry, let's have an emergency communication like, "Josh, urgent." Is that workable?"

"OK by me," said Morgan.

"Nice and simple," said Gritty. "By the way Wolfram, who's footing the bill? I don't suppose the city's flush with cash."

"For now," replied Wolfram, "you'll bill me. Gus and I will work out the details later."

"Fine with me," said Gritty with a smile, "I prefer dealing with you. Gus and I don't always see eye-to-eye."

Morgan, suddenly realizing the economic implications of his protection blurted out "Heh, I can contribute something, after all it is my life you are protecting."

"Fine, Morgan," said Wolfram, "you and I can work out some arrangement once I clear this with Gus."

Just as they were about to depart Gritty added, "So this killer is a defrocked priest, likely one of those 'dears' protected by the great Vatican cover up. The whole world needs protection from that lot. Thanks for thinking of me, Wolfram. I have a special stake in this. Old wounds......... Old, deep, ugly, wounds."

Wolfram and Morgan both looked at each other wondering, but not wanting to hear anything about such 'old wounds'. Their main concern was whether it might have any implication to their newly formed partnership.

Morgan and Gritty gave Josh a quick farewell as they departed. Wolfram watched them leave noting their similarities.

He stayed to fill Josh in on as much as he felt he should know. After all his place would now become there hub for meetings for the next while.

Canada, Charlottetown: The Funeral

A black car eased gently to the curb. Angi disembarked, alone. The funeral was over. It had been a day of sadness and heart-wrenching testimonials. "Thank God," she thought, "they didn't expect me to speak." The circumstances of her grandmother's sudden death and police cautiousness were given as reasons for such leniency. It was fortuitous, for mid-way in the church service, for the first time in her life, she felt faint. Suddenly feeling cold and clammy, she drifted into a strange light where again the golden snake slithered out of her grandmother's trunk. Disoriented, she pulled herself back to reality, saying to herself, "Come on Angi, you are hallucinating ….stay focused." The church service and hall reception took hours and drained every morsel of her energy. "So many people," she thought, "I'm sure some were there because of the media hype."

The three steps to the front door seemed insurmountable. Struggling, as she reached the top step, the front door swung open.

"It is over!" said Vette "You must be exhausted," noting the weariness in Angi's face. "I expect you've had little to eat. It is hard to eat, talk and handle the emotional turmoil of these events. I'm also sure you've had enough of everyone and everything for one day."

Angi slipped past Vette oblivious of her questions. Talking to herself she mumbled, "I need to change…….. I'll feel better after a shower……… Maybe then I'll try some food……..something easy."

"Sure, you go on. I'll stand guard," replied a sympathetic Vette.

Days before, it was decided that Vette would not attend the funeral; instead she would stay at the house in case of uninvited house intruders. Even with the death of the assailant, the police still felt a second attempt might be made on the house especially during the well-publicized funeral. Undercover cops circulated at the funeral and reception in case Angi was still a possible target. Nothing happened.

Before mounting the stairs to the second floor, Angi turned, "By the way, did anything happen here during the funeral?"

In an almost disappointing tone Vette replied, "Not a peep, quiet as a mouse. If there were others in on this caper they're long gone."

Angi ventured a fatigued smile, "Maybe next time, Vette." The two of them had grown closer, after the first morning clash. Angi, determined to maintain her therapeutic routine which started about five in the morning with an hour of meditation. After that she dressed for her morning run around Victoria Park, a stepping stone from the house. Unaccustomed to having a bodyguard Angi first thought of Vette as a house guest. So the first morning, not wanting to disturb Vette, she tipped-toed to the front door. She had barely turned the door knob when a disheveled body dressed in mustard green pajamas bounced in front of her yelling, "What the hell do you think you are doing?"

Startled and defensive, Angi replied, "I'm going for my morning run. I go every morning at this time, rain or shine."

Upset, Vette responded, "Well bully for you. I'm guarding a health nut. Well, in case you forgot, I am supposed to be your bodyguard which means I'm supposed to stick to you like glue until this case is closed. Got it?"

At that moment Angi noticed the bandages on Vette's right shoulder and her nursing instincts cut in, "What happened to your shoulder? That's some pressure bandage."

"Stop changing the subject," snapped Vette, still angry at being ignored. "I got this trophy when I stumbled into some cross fire in my last assignment. That's why I'm here. Stuart thought this would be an easy cover for my rehab. I'm beginning to wonder if the word 'easy' is quite how I'd classify this assignment."

Angi continued in a concerned manner, "You should be resting. Perhaps exerting yourself is not the best therapy at this time."

Shooting back, Vette replied, "It is my wing that's injured, not my legs. Stay right there, don't move! I need to keep fit as I intend to get back to my normal life real soon. Baby-sitting is not really my forte."

So, after ruffled feathers had settled, it was agreed, each morning at six the two would go for their morning run. Angi insisted that she would dress Vette's wounds rather than exposing her to Jock's office gossipers. Within days a routine was established and a friendship began to grow, the type one finds in a common crisis.

Today, Angi was glad for Vette's company, returning to an empty house would have exaggerated the day's overall gloom.

"See you shortly," Angi said as she made her way up the stairs holding firmly to the banister for support.

Vette watched, "This death has really hit her. She's very pale, and she's starting to stagger. I know it is not liquor, as she consumes little and it would be unheard of at a Presbyterian funeral. Yet, death hits everyone differently. It is worse when it is unexpected and due to criminal activity. By all accounts Nellie was well liked, and being Angi's only family just made it worse. Perhaps that's all." She locked the front door and went to the kitchen. "Scrambled eggs and toast would be simple, and I'll prepare a big pot of Chamomile tea. I thought herbal tea was for wimps, but I'm beginning to like it. It is certainly easier on the gut than coffee. As coffee prices rise, this might be an option, but I'll miss my good old Columbian fix. I'll wait till she's ready."

Upstairs Angi moved in slow motion. She swallowed two anti-nausea tablets, and sat on the bed letting the medication take hold. Not surprising, her thoughts were on death. "Gran always said the one guarantee in life was death. It is always too soon. We talked often about her being there for my wedding and her great-grandchildren. Neither of us could have calculated this outcome and me following her so closely in death. A funeral certainly makes one face the fragility of life." Then speaking as if her grandmother was present, she went on, "Gran, it was a fine funeral. You would have been shocked at the number of people, perhaps too many. You might even have been embarrassed by the grand comments from so many leading citizens, some who hardly knew you. I remember chatting with you about the differences between the old and new ways in dealing with funerals. The old idea of giving the family privacy in their sorrow has given way to a demand for everyone to perform some tale of remembrance, irrespective of their emotional state. Under a shroud of correctness, it borders on abuse. Funerals have become even longer. Gran, Margo did you proud. She's a true friend. Sorry I found her a bit pushy. In the end she proved to be a real pro. I don't know what I would have done without her. However, Gran, when it comes to my turn, I think I'll request a quiet graveside service. I will never have your history and, on second thought, I don't want the hullaballoo."

Hanging up her dark suit and white blouse, she continued with her thoughts, "Gran, I was going to tell you about my illness when I came home for my vacation, but events took over. Nevertheless, I'm sure, if you were here, you'd tell me that this cancer diagnosis has a purpose, perhaps a message from God for me to change my life, but a change in what direction? I didn't think I was off course. If this illness progresses rapidly, I may not have enough time to do much changing, except prepare for my own demise. Speaking of that, I need to contact Mr. Dumont about my Will and funeral. I'll have to make some provision for this house. Perhaps Margo can help ......maybe later in the week." Realizing she had slipped into negative thinking she corrected herself, "That's enough of that, Angi me girl. Think positive! Cancer thrives on negativity."

After a long shower, Angi felt rejuvenated. She slipped into a pair of gray slacks and a cotton sweatshirt and proceeded down stairs. As she reached the bottom step the front door bell rang. Out loud she reacted, "Oh help, no more people today. Vette, please divert this onslaught."

"Sure, duck into the kitchen. I will say you're resting or something." Irritated, she commented to herself, "What's wrong with these people, have they no decency? Surely they must know she needs a break." She opened the door to begin a crisp confrontation only to encounter Jock MacAndrew, who was looking downright glum.

Still wanting to protect Angi she began, "Agh, Angi's resting. Can I help you Jock?" She kept holding the door, ready to close it abruptly.

"I know what you are doing, Vette. I would not have come today but I need to talk to her. I expect she's in the kitchen while her bull dog fends off visitors."

"OK, but she's really exhausted. I hope this is brief."

"I'll be quick. Just need to chat about a call I received today," said Jock as he brushed past Vette heading towards the kitchen.

Angi, sorting cups, dishes and utensils for their snack was surprised to see Jock enter the kitchen. "It must be important, Jock, what can I do for you?"

"Angi, I'm sorry to barge in, I know this has been a difficult day. But, I need to talk privately with you about a call I received. Can we talk in the living room?"

Vette, shadowing Jock, stopped at the kitchen door. "I hear you. I'll stay in the kitchen. Angi, how about some, scrambled eggs?"

"Yah, that's sounds good," replied Angi, as she followed Jock.

Vette assembled the ingredients but made no effort to start cooking. She moved closer to the kitchen door to listen. "Something's up. Jock never acts without a reason."

Jock went to the farthest chair from the kitchen, sat down and began in a quiet voice, "Angi, I got a call this afternoon from a Dr. Greene from Halifax who's very worried about you. I expect you know why?"

"Yes, with all the commotion I almost forgot about my diagnosis." Angi lied, because her nausea and tiredness couldn't be ignored. "I was coming home to tell Gran and talk to you about my illness when my life got turned upside down. I made the appointment with Dr. Wong in Halifax but missed it because of my urgent trip home."

"Very well, what do you plan on doing about this?"

"I haven't had much time to think about it since I got home. Perhaps in a few days we can get together." Angi knew she didn't want chemotherapy and was stalling for time.

"I brought Dr. Greene up to date on what has been happening here and he and I perfectly understand that your health has not been a priority. But now, you must start the treatment ......leukemia is not a disease to trifle with."

Vette gasped. "Leukemia........that's a hellish kick in the teeth after all she's been through. It explains the paleness and tiredness."

At that moment Angi reached another decision. "Jock, before I do anything about this disease, I want to finalize something for Gran, I owe her that much. You and I know that the outcome of a series of chemotherapy sessions can be unpredictable, so while I am able, I want to take the medallion to Gran's contact in Boston."

"What? Surely this can wait. Your health is the priority," argued Jock.

"No, it can't. The attack on Gran initiated something. Any delay might jeopardize the lives of others. You of all people know how allergic I am and if I react poorly to the chemotherapy it could be months before I can travel. The medallion needs to be placed in the hands of the rightful Guardians. Gracelyn Harrison in Boston has informed me that this item cannot be sent by mail or courier; it has to be delivered in person. So, this coming week, I'll take a few days to rest then I'll book a flight to Boston. What are we talking, two...... maybe three days, tops. Then my slate will be cleared for whatever treatments I need."

"I know there is little hope of changing your mind. Fine, two to three days and you are back here. By the way, Vette goes with you. I'm certain that you could be heading right into the arms of this killer. Have you thought of that?"

"In light of my diagnosis, does it matter?"

"Don't be flippant, Angi. You know there is every possibility of recovery with the right treatment. You are young and healthy." Concerned and frustrated with the outcome Jock called out "Vette, can you come in here?"

Vette bounded into the living room.

"You will need your Passport, Vette. You and Angi are heading to Boston for a few days. Angi can fill you in on the details," With that Jock turned to leave. "I want to know your travel plans. In the meantime I'll have a chat with Stuart. I'm not happy with this turn of events but will just have to live with it."

After he left Angi turned to Vette. "You deserve an explanation. While we're eating I'll try and explain why this trip is so important."

Vette didn't need an explanation. Somehow she felt that Angi wasn't going to take the chemotherapy. This was a heroic act. She would deliver the medallion and come home to die. To herself she said, "God knows what's in store for us in Boston. Jock could be right; we may be heading straight into the lion's den."

Chapter 4

United States, Boston, Rosie's Bar & Grill

Obsessively organized, before leaving Ireland, Antonino e-mailed his Vatican cousin who worked in the archives with the latest clues from O-Gratteney's file, rerouted funds from Italy to a bank in the Virgin Islands, contacted another cousin in Montreal now second in command to a powerful drug family, and obtained several underworld names in the United States. His mother's family had global roots.

Antonino's escape from Canada went smoothly. After making arrangements for the hit on Rodolfo, he reclaimed his priestly garb in an airport storage locker and traveled on to Boston. There he morphed into Tony Moretti, an up-and-coming movie and TV impresario with graying hair and glasses. His new occupation was looking for Boston talent with top dollar incentives. First, he wanted a bead on Morgan.

His paid efforts at hacking into Morgan's university and home computers came up dry. This forced Antonino to plan B. Later, on a Boston side street, an unexpected downpour forced Antonino to shelter under a Pin Oak tree. As the rain eased, he strode across the street and entered the Bay Street Road building of Boston University history department in search of Dr. Morgan Mandelthrope's office. A young female student gave him directions to the third floor. Nearing Morgan's office he was rewarded when Morgan and Gritty exited, arguing about something. Neither took notice of the nondescript middle-aged man standing in the shadows. Tony, Antonino's Boston alias, sneered. "I've got ya! But that scrawny sidekick is no academic..... maybe ex-police or military..........the obvious reason why Morgan's files are inaccessible, they've been moved." Cursing, his brain working overtime, he concluded, "Morgan either knows or can tell me the name of his client. Maybe there's more than one. Whatever, I need to get to Morgan. There's got to be an angle..........a weak link.......something." Turning, he retreated down the stairs and out the door.

It wasn't all bad news. Antonino's Vatican cousin came through. She confirmed that in the seventeenth century there were hints in several official documents about a secret code, a medallion or some kind of jewelry, with ancient roots and mystical powers. But even Inquisition torture revealed nothing further. Rumors persisted into the 1700s but then evaporated. Her e-mail assessment was that after hundreds of years and such intangible clues finding anything would be inconceivable. But Antonino wasn't buying her argument. "My gut feeling tells me there's something," he said with conviction. "The 1600s was a turbulent time in European history so someone, or a group of people, took extraordinary risks to protect something. The genius behind this secrecy created a shield of silence that lasted for generations. That speaks for itself."

He paid more individuals to search out everything they could find on Morgan. Within twenty-four hours he got a break; Morgan's wife, Kari-Ann. She was often seen at Rosie's Bar and Grill in Charleston. His documents had copies of photographs from her Twitter page, the names of her closest friends and details on her character. "The Internet is a pure goldmine," Antonino said as he kissed the documents. That evening he headed to Rosie's.

At twenty-six, Morgan married a young, blond, history student, a former high school cheer leader and beauty queen, who was charmed by his easy-going manner, his fiddle playing and his family's wealth. She worked in a part-time secretarial job at Boston University. While both incomes should have been adequate, money had become a constant battle. Unable to have children and loath to adopt, Kari-Ann became obsessed with her looks, fashion and decorating and redecorating their house. When these passions faded, she moved on to travelling, which, when Morgan's work intervened, shifted to excursions with three of her old high school friends. She never explained where they went or what they did.

Morgan wasn't oblivious. Often alone in recent years, he recognized the deteriorating signs, commenting to himself, "This marriage is doomed unless something changes. I should be talking to a divorce lawyer. Being ignored and deserted by my wife is only half the problem. Her silence, increased alcohol consumption and wild mood swings are symptoms that she's either having an affair, dabbling in drugs, or sliding into a mental breakdown, perhaps all three. She refuses to explain her numerous bank withdrawals which is crippling our finances. When I've suggested she see our family doctor or a psychiatrist, she erupts into a vicious rage and storms out of the house. I've been procras-tinating, too lazy to bother. Or am I too ashamed to discuss this with either my parents or Wolfram. Now that's he's recovering from his accident I'll find time. I can't let this drift any longer. It is intolerable. Thank God I've my work and this medallion mess to distract me." As an afterthought, he continued, "Now that says something, I'm actually stating that I'm glad some mad man is stalking me so I can avoid dealing with this marital disaster." Unknown to Morgan, the universe was about to intercede on his behalf.

Antonino, in his newly created alias as Tony Moretti, parked his red; Boxster B Porsche near Rosie's and walked. The Bar and Grill sign was conspicuous, an artistic salutation to the thirty-plus crowd. Knowing his age would be conspicuous, he decided to employ the services of a couple of key employees. Stepping inside he was engulfed by the noise and the scintillating décor of silver, mauve and white which blended perfectly with the upbeat music of the small jazz ensemble. The culinary bar in the distance held a bountiful display of seafood, meats, and vegetables, plus a side table of succulent pastries. The advertisement stated the bar had over a thousand wines in its cellar and by the looks of the Thursday night crowd; all these offerings were being thoroughly enjoyed by a boisterous clientele.

The four women arrived within minutes of each other, as was their custom, and went to their usual table. Kari-Ann, the oldest of the four, was the decided star. Her slight build and fashion sense made her a target of many male admirers. The women, in their mid to late thirties, were all married, two had young children. Bored with life, ignored by their husbands, with plenty of money, they clung to the belief that they had a God-given right for a few flings before old age assailed them in their forties. Petrified over growing old, one of the four even divulged that she wanted to die at sixty, as drugs and a good plastic surgeon could only do miracles until then.

Kari-Ann knew she was on a slippery path. On several occasions, after too many drinks, she ended up in bed with a man she hardly knew. She excused such dalliance on the premise that she deserved a life of fun with vibrant male company. To ease her guilt her friends introduced her to cocaine. Sniffing small amounts she placated herself with the comforting banter, "I can stop any time. Anyway, everyone does it."

That evening as the four women ordered their first drinks, Glen, a familiar waiter, came to their table with a new patron, a man older then the usual crowd. "Ladies, I'd like you to meet an old friend of mine, Tony Moretti. He's just arrived from California and is interested in producing a movie here in Boston." Saying no more he departed, a crisp $100 bill resting in his pocket for his services.

The foursome welcomed the stranger, and after a couple of drinks and the usual chit chat, Tony made his move. "Ladies, in assessing the clientele of this bar this evening, my eyes have been captivated by your stunning beauty and I'm here to offer you, I hope, a proposal you will find too delicious to refuse."

The four women purred at his compliments and waited.

Tony continued, "I'll get right down to business. As you heard from Glen, I'm here recruiting for my upcoming movie. I have four non-speaking roles which would be a perfect fit for the four of you." His black eyes darted from one to the other to assess their reaction. Camouflaged behind his friendly smile he assessed his prey, "Such vanity. It is like peddling candy to children." Assessing their non-verbal signals as agreement, he went on, "I'm willing to offer you $5,000 each" ....he hesitated, letting the figure register, "for one day's work." Before they had a chance to ask, he answered, "Your roles will be simple. You just have to sit in a similar type of bar being the young, beautiful and vibrant background in one of the leading scenes. What do you think?" To avoid appearing too pushy, he then stood up, "How about I give you time to discuss this while I get myself another drink." He stepped away to an explosion of chatter.

In the cacophony of words one of the women could be heard in a raised voice saying, "What an opportunity! This could be a new career." Another remarked, "The pay is terrific. Just think what we could do with $5,000 smackers." Another, in a lower voice, asked, "Do you think we need a lawyer?" The question went unanswered. Kari-Ann felt uneasy. "His eyes and those long bony tapping fingers bother me," she said to herself. But when the rest of her friends agreed to proceed, she acquiesced.

Tony joined the women to await their decision.

Kari-Ann spoke for the group. "It is agreed. We are interested. What's next?"

"I'm delighted," said Tony with a smarmy grin. "I'll come back tomorrow evening, same time, with contracts." To stifle any complications he went on, "Now these are relatively small roles so you won't need the cost of a lawyer. Tomorrow, I will clarify, in writing, your roles, confirm the payment, and give you a few screening dates." After shaking their hands to seal the agreement he turned and left the bar.

The following evening, true to his word, he arrived with four worthless contracts. The women were delighted to be assured they would be in a critical scene, the time assessed on the number of possible retakes. Tony assured them "The time might be even less if it is an easy run." The simplicity and lucrative rewards seemed almost too good to be true. Once signatures were obtained and copies distributed, Tony responded with, "Congratulations! Let's seal this with drinks." He signaled the waiter to the table.

Sipping his drink slowly he complimented himself and, showing no outward signs of his underlying disdain for these women, he contemplated, "How dumb can you get. Not one asked the title of the movie, the name of the production company, what previous movies I produced, or even who the stars are. They're either so dense or so totally self-absorbed that being conned never occurred to them. It is fortunate that everyone is not as gullible or this country could be sold to the best salesman with deep pockets. As for me, I'm doing fine. I've gained their confidence and can now make my next move."

Later, as the foursome prepared to leave, Tony asked, "I wonder, Kari-Ann if I might talk to you alone about another matter."

Unguarded after a few drinks and warming to Tony, Kari-Ann looked at her watch and replied, "Sure it is still early."

Tony escorted her to a different table, for two, in the corner and began. "Kari-Ann, I wonder if you might be interested in a small speaking role?"

Kari-Ann, flattered, hesitated, and finally responded, "I'm not sure. I've never been in a stage production even in high school."

Reassuring her, he replied, "There's nothing to it. I'll coach you. You are a shoe-in for this role of an international fashion model who the leading actor chats with while waiting for his girl friend. You'll have two to three lines. This might open doors to something else. It has happened before. I'll pay you an additional $15,000 giving you $20,000 for two days work. That's a pretty good deal. What do you say?"

The extra money registered. Kari Ann mulled over the offer, focusing on the positives, "Finally, I'll get some recognition for my looks. In addition, you never know. Look at the global response to that older UK female singer. She's raking in millions now. This could be my ticket to a new life and freedom from dull Morgan. Imagine me a star." Flashing camera lights whirled in her imagination. After a few minutes she replied, "Sure, why not." Relaxing, she continued. "Will I have to sign another contract?"

"Yes," replied Tony now seizing the opening, "I'll bring another contract tomorrow night or better still, I could drop it off at your home."

"No!" snapped Kari-Ann, startled at the possible conflict this might mean to the annoying surveillance on Morgan. "I'll meet you here. My place is not good for meetings right now," providing no further explanation.

Unruffled by the turndown, Tony continued, "No problem. I'll see you tomorrow evening here about eight." Almost as an afterthought, as he rose to leave he added, "I hear your husband is a well-known historian. I have some material in this movie which could use his expertise. I'll not only add an extra $5,000 to your contract for getting him interested but I'll pay him handsomely as a part-time movie advisor. What do you think?"

Kari-Ann didn't recall her husband's occupation had ever been discussed at Rosie's. But, nevertheless, she was adamant Morgan would have no place in her new life and replied abruptly, "My husband's too busy. I'm sure he has no interest in the movie business." Seeing the frustrated look on Tony's face, and not wanting to upset her movie debut, she became more conciliatory, "How about you give me your business card and I'll present the offer to Morgan. Don't expect much but I'll try."

Tony weighed his words carefully and casually responded, "No problem.

You can tell me tomorrow night when we sign your second contract whether he's the least bit interested. It is a big city. If it is not for him, I will look elsewhere."

Thinking of his offer, Kari-Ann interjected, "Will I get the $5,000 for trying?"

Antonino-Tony gritted his teeth, but replied with a broad grin, "Sure Kari-Ann, why not." Annoyed at her blatant greed, he contemplated, "What the hell, there's no actual money involved. This dimwit may be able to convince her academic partner to accept this scam. Better still, she might even entice him to come tomorrow night to chat about it. Then I'll make my move on Morgan."

Kari-Ann left the bar troubled, wondering how she was going to reignite her relationship with Morgan without making him suspicious. "I deserve this break," she surmised as she gunned the car engine. "I have to please Tony, he's my ticket to a glamorous life."

&

Boston: The Weston Estate

After a short flight from Charlottetown to Halifax, Angi and Vette boarded the 8:35am Air Canada flight to Montreal where they would transfer to another Air Canada flight scheduled to arrive in Boston at 12:48pm. Storing their hand luggage in the upper bins, they buckled in to begin their trip to the United States. To prevent unwanted questions at Customs in transporting an antique, Angi had removed the medallion from its container and stored it with her regular jewelry in the blue travel pouch which nestled in a pocket of her nylon handbag.

As Vette settled, she asked "By the way, Angi, how well do you know this guy, Wolfram?"

"Not well. I met him once when I was fifteen. He arrived on the Island with his grandmother to visit Gran. They stayed one day. As a teenager I didn't give it much thought. My recollection is that he was pleasant, about ten years older than me, and I think, he said he was a policeman."

"That's pretty slim. If true, I'd be happy with a few extra police on this caper. It is the mounting unknowns and the appearance of a criminal element that rattles me."

Angi continued, "Gran had so many people coming and going at the B&B that two more on a short summer stay didn't really stand out. Now that you ask I am beginning to recall some bits and pieces. Wolfram was tall, with jet black hair, a quiet manner and he asked a lot of questions. He was interested in my Celtic harp, an instrument he wasn't familiar with. We talked quite a bit about music. I sensed that he knew more but he never divulged whether he played an instrument. His grandmother was tall, elegantly dressed and spoke with a Boston accent. My recollection is that Wolfram didn't have an accent. That's it. With so little, I just hope I can recognize him when we land."

"So do I," replied Vette. "So far your description could fit thousands of men in their late thirties."

Wolfram arrived at Terminal E at Logan's International Airport heading straight for the Arrivals Hall. He checked his watch. "The Air Canada flight should have landed by now, but I've got plenty of time, they'll be held up getting through the Passport and Customs ritual." He zeroed in on a comfortable chair with a clear view of the exit gate. "For a Monday this place is hopping."

"I wonder how much she's changed in ten years." He began to recall that summer on Prince Edward Island. Out of the blue his grandmother insisted she had to visit her friend in Canada, a relationship that perplexed him because this Gordon woman had no family or business connection. Now he knew why.

Just after they arrived at Nellie's B&B, a slim teenage girl, in worn blue jeans and a faded T-shirt returned from running. With flushed cheeks she gave a quick greeting, "Hi, you must be the Americans Gran was expecting." His first impression was that she was bright, rather pretty, and definitely different. "I remember that long platinum braid down her back which was instantly forgotten when she removed her sunglasses to reveal a pair of spellbinding emerald green eyes. She acquiesced easily to her grandmother's request to give me a tour of the city while the elders talked."

"Angi spoke glowingly of her beloved town as we walked around the Charlottetown harbor and zig-zagged through quaint streets with Victorian houses and stone built churches. The city reminded me of New England. I can't remember if I even mentioned that I was a policeman. In the process of a couple of hours I learned she was born in New York but grew up in Canada. She liked school, loved running and enjoyed playing a Celtic harp, an instrument I never heard of. Back then, she was on the verge of entering university to pursue her nursing career in Halifax, a major city in another province. I later heard from my grandmother that she graduated, and became an Emergency Room Director in some teaching hospital. All that aside, she's arriving today following the tragic death of her grandmother, aware of the professional hit on the assailant and caught up in a web, as we all are, of some ancient mystery with a dangerous assassin on the loose."

When Angi gave Tyloar and Gracelyn Harrison's name and address as her contact in Boston, their Passport and Customs process suddenly changed. "Apparently, the Harrisons are well known," she thought. "I'm grateful for that."

Wolfram spotted her blond hair as she entered the Hall. He noted she stood three to four inches above her companion who was about five foot three. Momentarily, his sight fell on the second woman. Angi provided few details on her travelling companion when they made arrangements for her trip. "I thought it might be another nurse but that's no nurse," Wolfram said to himself. "That disciplined gaze and surveillance attitude means she might be police.........what's the name again...........yah, the RCMP. Well, good on them! Someone else is growing uneasy over this medallion affair. I'll be glad for some trained input. There are far too many amateurs, and some are elderly. I'll leave it to Angi to reveal her companion's credentials. They have only hand luggage, a sure sign they intend on a short stay."

Angi recognized Wolfram in the distance and waved. She then observed his labored walk as he headed their way. As he drew closer, she said to herself, "He's certainly disciplined. The only symptom of pain is his clinched jaw and those steely blue eyes." As he reached them, she spoke first, "Hi Wolfram, it has been a long time since we toured Charlottetown. A lot has changed since then."

"Welcome, Angi," said Wolfram with a firm hand shake. Then he continued. "My condolences, too bad your first visit to our fair city is under such circumstances." Turning, he acknowledged her companion with, "This must be Vette, your friend." A closer inspection confirmed his initial assessment.

"Yes," replied Angi, making no effort to provide any more information.

Vette, while shaking his hand, stared past him giving the hall a rapid sweep, displaying visible agitation on their lingering.

"I see you have little luggage, so let's head right to my car which is parked nearby. There are some advantages to being disabled these days." He led the way to the nearest entrance.

Vette wasn't happy with the speed of their departure from the airport terminal. She kept reassuring herself that likely the assailant had yet to target Angi or Wolfram. "But that's just fools thinking," she said to herself. "He could be lingering in that crowd over there, calculating his next move. I'm still assuming it is a man, these days it could just as easily be a woman with such ruthless instincts."

When they reached Wolfram's blue Ford Taurus, Angi placed her bag with Vette in the back seat and joined Wolfram in the front.

Unfamiliar with the city, Angi and Vette said little as Wolfram wove through the noonday traffic. After ten minutes he asked, certain Angi's watch dog was fully aware of the growing storm. "Angi, can I talk freely about this case?"

Without hesitation Angi, knowing what he meant, relied, "Certainly, Vette has been with me since my grandmother's death."

"Well, in that case," said Wolfram, "this afternoon I am returning to the airport to pick up two more Guardians; one from Australia, the other from New Zealand. They were contacted when you phoned to tell us your grandmother had been attacked. A decision was later made for them to travel to the USA when your grandmother died. These women, and my grandmother, keep mumbling something about the *'coming times'*. Angi, do you have any idea what that means?"

"Sorry, Wolfram, I'm as much in the dark as you. Gran kept saying the same thing in hospital before she died. Perhaps these women can help us. I'm still struggling with how something that occurred in the 1600s could be relevant today. I suspect that Gran's death triggered something and that this madman, whether he understands all the details or not, is willing to kill to possess something. As you can see I'm unclear about an awful lot and, at present, I'm still recovering from my grandmother's sudden death." She was not about to add the uncertainty over her own future.

"Angi, I wish we had more time but unfortunately this case keeps growing more complex by the day. This evening we'll pool our information, however deficient it might be. In the meantime, I'm going to drop you off where we will stay for the next week or so. I see you and Vette have planned a short stay."

Looking out the window Angi and Vette began to note the expensive district Wolfram had entered, and before they had time to comment, the car eased gently through stately stone pillars, one with 400 in expensive lettering. The single slate-colored driveway expanded into a circular parking area in front of an elegant three-storey Georgian Colonial mansion. The white trimmed windows stood out in stark contrast to the red brick facing. Four white pillars embraced the dark wooden front doors.

A quiet gasp was heard from the back seat.

"This is magnificent," was all Angi could muster, feeling suddenly impoverished with the limited clothing in her hand luggage.

Before they had time to ask, Wolfram explained, "This is not where I or my grandparents live. It was decided that a neutral location for this gathering might be prudent. So, George and Agnes Neiman, friends of the family, gave us permission to use their residence while they were off on a European trip. The place comes with many amenities including their own staff."

As the three approached the ornate wooden and crystal front entrance, the door opened and they were greeted by a casually dressed individual in a dark navy suit and white open neck shirt. "Welcome, these must be the Canadians."

Wolfram stepped forward to make the introductions. "Yes, Charles, this is Angi Talismann and Vette Gallant," and turning to his two companions, "this is Charles, the butler."

"Again, welcome," said Charles, "we've been expecting you. We're here to do everything to make your stay in Boston comfortable."

Turning briefly to Wolfram, he gave a quick order, "Wolfram, you are wanted in the kitchen."

"Thanks Charles," said Wolfram as he disappeared to the rear of the building.

Once Wolfram was gone Charles turned to the women, saying, "I will be escorting you to your bedrooms. Once you are settled, just make your way to the poolside at the back of the house for sandwiches and refreshments."

The butler made no effort to take their carry-on bags but led them up the curved stairway to their second-floor rooms. As they ascended, both women inspected their picture-perfect environment. On the way Vette whispered to Angi, "The unexpected perks of this case are amazing."

Charles took Angi to her room first. As he opened the door she was greeted by an artistic blend of white, pink and green, everything selected with the utmost care and expense right down to the fresh flowers in the vase on the table next to the window. The broad windows provided a scenic view of the entrance gardens with a squint of water in the distance. "It is like a magazine photo," she thought, "a far cry from Gran's practical B&B. I wonder if it is as cozy," as she gently placed her handbag and travel luggage on the nearest chair. Later she would discover that Vette had an adjacent bedroom in a yellow palette. Each bedroom came with an ensuite bathroom.

As Angi unpacked she wondered if her sparse attire would fit the setting. "I'm glad I took extra blouses to go with these slacks and single skirt. It'll have to do. Anyway, I'm only here to deliver this medallion to these older Guardians." She took care to return the medallion to its proper case and securely placed it in a special compartment in her hand bag. She changed into relaxing clothes and went looking for the pool. Located at the back of the mansion near the tennis court, she found herself alone, and stretched out on a lounge chair to wait. "Time for some Vitamin D, the flights tired me. The side effects of this illness seem relentless."

Twenty minutes later, Vette appeared whispering, "This place is crawling with cops."

Angi sat up, "You're kidding. Wolfram said this place came with some Neiman's staff."

"That's true," replied Vette, "but my instincts tell me there have been some add-ons to the regular staff. Take that butler. He seemed a bit casual, but then what do I know."

"Well, maybe their in relaxed clothing in the summer when the owners are away," said Angi trying to rationalize the situation.

"Sure, but I'll bet you at least one of the gardeners, the chauffeur and, I argue, the butler are not Neiman staff. The chef and housekeeper seem genuine."

"I wondered what took you so long. Did you canvas the entire house since last we met?"

"Not quite, I watched some of their actions from my window and made a detour through the kitchen. I always like to know my surrounds. It is an old habit. In addition, I'm supposed to be guarding your back, or had you forgotten?"

Smiling, "It is hard to forget with you around Vette. I am indeed grateful. Anyway, let's see if we can get a tour of the place. We might learn more. In addition, we'll likely never have another chance to stroll through such luxury."

"Good idea. We'll run it past Charles. If these are police, or hired security guards, then prepare yourself for bad news."

This sparked Angi's attention. "What kind of bad news?"

Speaking in hushed tones Vette went on, "Angi let's review what we know. Your grandmother's assailant was eliminated by a professional hit from God knows where. That means someone has links to the underworld. The Guardians of this mysterious medallion come from different countries; you are from Canada, Wolfram's family are Americans, and the two arriving this afternoon come from Australia and New Zealand. If there are eight slots in that medallion, then there have to be eight families. Some have to be in Britain. And God knows where the prime killer is from. This means this case has a global reach."

"You are right, Vette. One of Gran's contacts was in Ireland. If this started in Britain there has to be someone from Scotland and possibly Wales. Maybe these three older women, we're about to meet, may know other names. We may learn more tonight."

"Possibly," replied Vette, "but we'll have to hush for now, here comes the food." Charles had exited from a back door carrying a tray of food, followed by a woman with refreshments. Wolfram trailed the two.

Waiting, Angi thought, "While I'm curious about the medallion, my task is simple. I'll deliver the medallion for Gran's sake and catch the next flight home. I need to get on with the house sale and settling my affairs. Time is of the essence."

Wolfram's warm greeting was reassuring, "Hope you are settling in.

Enjoy the sun. After a quick snack I'm off again to the airport. You are in good hands. If you need anything just ask Charles. My grandparents will be joining us about four this afternoon, their taking time off from their antique business. The plan is to have an early dinner and time to get acquainted."

After lunch Angi approached Charles and asked, "Is there any chance Vette and I might have a tour of the house?"

"No problem," replied Charles. "I'm busy, but I'm sure Marta will be glad to take you around."

Shortly Marta, the German-born housekeeper appeared. "Charles indicated you wanted a tour of the place. Come, I've been with the Neiman's for fifteen years and at this estate for the past five years. I'll be glad to show you around."

Angi and Vette followed as Marta began in a well rehearsed tour guide manner. Periodically, Angi or Vette interjected questions. With a slight German accent she proceeded with a most interesting tale. "This 4.2 acre estate sits on Windsor Way in the upscale Weston district of Boston. The land was once owned by the Queen of England and later by several prominent citizens of Massachusetts. The original house was redesigned, expanded and redecorated in 2005. The mansion is 22,000 square feet, has eight bedrooms and nine bathrooms, and has its own tennis court, home theatre, fitness room, wine cellar, and library."

"In other words, it is a *petite* hotel," said Vette.

Marta responded in a clipped manner, "Actually, this is far more than a small hotel. It is the personal residence of a fine family who pride themselves in providing a gracious residence for many well-known politicians and celebrities in the art world. We have had a number of famous people staying here, but I digress." She returned to her tour script. "The redecorating took three years. Each room, as you may have observed already, has a precise theme. Mrs. Neiman and a top Boston decorator, recognized for her exquisite taste in gardens and color, created the elegant setting in which you now reside. There are also live-in quarters for staff over the four-car heated garage in the back of the main house."

This was Angi's cue. "How many staff do the Neiman's have to manage such a large estate as this?"

Marta made her first mistake in responding, "There are eight full-time staff; the chef, myself, Samuel the butler, two chauffeurs and three gardeners." Angi and Vette looked at each other. Marta made no effort to correct herself.

Without skipping a beat Vette made the next move, "I suppose with the Neiman's away, this is the time of year for staff holidays. Are any of the eight on holidays right now?"

Unprepared for such questions, Marta answered, "Yes, four are away; the butler, one of the chauffeurs and two of the gardeners." Angi and Vette had their answer. Others, possibly police or hired security, had taken the place of the vacationing staff.

When Angi returned to her room, she glanced out the window to see Wolfram's blue car swing round near the front entrance. Angi watched as two women disembarked, one taller than the other. Charles appeared at the car trunk to assist with their bags which had been removed by Wolfram. Once again, she heard Wolfram's introductions. "Charles, this is Moira Livingston from Australia, and Jessie Anderson from New Zealand."

Through her open window, Angi heard a phone ring. Wolfram reached into his jacket pocket to respond. Next, she heard him say, "Charles, I need to take this call. Moira and Jessie I'll see you later after you are settled." As earlier, the new arrivals followed Charles en route to their accommodations across the hall from Angi and Vette.

&

Boston: The Phone Call

The husky voice of Gus Ferguson was unmistakable. His blunt request was to find a private place for a call and get back to him ASAP. Wolfram eased the car away from the front entrance of the Weston estate, parked in the circular driveway, and picked up his cell phone. "OK Gus, what's up?"

With no preliminaries, Gus launched into an update. "That Italian predator of ours is definitely here. A Father Antonino Zailo Borgiano slipped through Logan's checkpoints three days ago. I expect he ditched the clerical garb after leaving the terminal. I've alerted the Roman Catholic diocese to contact us if he should surface in any of their establishments, but that's doubtful. They want nothing to do with a defrocked priest and it is unlikely he wants anything to do with them. However, there's a remote chance, if cornered, he might seek out an old colleague, if he has any. Right now I'm waiting for a CIA profile from an old contact. I need info on this guy's North American contacts. To arrange that hit in Canada he must have some powerful ties. I've had his photo discretely circulated. I expect you've done the same, right?"

"Definitely," acknowledged Wolfram. "Gritty and Fred have his photo and it has been indelibly imprinted on Morgan's brain. In addition, I've shown it to the security team we've hired."

"Good. How is everything going with regard to your friend Morgan?"

"Well, the protection is in place but it is beginning to develop some frayed edges."

"That sound ominous," replied Gus, "go on."

"Gritty has become Morgan's permanent shadow on the day shift. He picks him up and returns him to his home each day. Morgan has managed to explain Gritty's presence at the university as a special arrangement for an academic friend but that won't stick for long. Gritty's no academic."

"That's for sure," replied Gus with a chuckle, "he's better suited for rougher environs."

Wolfram continued, "Gritty arranged for an ex-military friend, Fred Morton, to do the night shift. Fred suspects Morgan's wife, Kari-Ann, is on drugs and could be our weak link. In addition, she wants no part of the surveillance so Fred's sitting in his car in a residential area which is a bad cover."

"Splendid. He's not only a sitting duck but anything could happen in that house and he would be none the wiser."

"Well, it is not just Kari-Ann. Morgan wavers between wanting protection, to stopping it because it is restricting his freedom. He's my friend and, I know, this whole case is spooking him. His vacillation shows how really scared he is. Morgan's world is in an academic environment of Celtic history and playing the fiddle for relaxation."

Sounding a bit sarcastic, Gus returned, "Wouldn't it be nice if life was fair. I've seen this before. Some academics get disoriented when the real world punctures their glass tower. But this unpredictability could be a problem. Gritty and Fred will need to keep a close tab on him. His wife, however, is definitely a target for Antonino. A psychopathic wolf like him takes no time in spotting the weak prey. Unfortunately, with limited manpower, we'll have to rely on Gritty and Fred to do double duty. Morgan remains our priority, as it is his name in those files. But Antonino will gladly use Kari-Ann to get to him, the question is how."

"That's Gritty and Fred's assessment. It would be helpful if this slippery eel would make a mistake in his well-orchestrated plan."

"Sure, but that's unlikely," was the loud reply. "I need to know his Boston alias, as I'm sure he's changed his identity. Knowing his underworld contacts would narrow the search. I hope the news regarding your grandparents and the Guardians is more promising."

Wolfram continued his report, "As agreed, I've arranged an undisclosed meeting place for my grandparents and the three out-of-country Guardians; one each from Canada, Australia and New Zealand. The Canadian arrived with her own protection, I suspect a member of the RCMP.

"Male or female?" snapped Gus.

"Female," replied Wolfram. "But neither woman has confirmed this."

"She should have reported in here if she's on my patch."

"They're likely keeping this quiet. She may be a friend of the Canadian woman. Whatever, I'm glad for the extra set of trained skills on this case."

"Very well, go on," ordered Gus.

"The four women arrived today and are settling in. I've also hired four security guards to replace half of the regular staff who are currently on vacation. It was agreed they would not divulge the name of the place over any communication channel."

"You used the security firm I recommended?"

"Yes, from what I hear they have a good reputation. Our plan is to allow these Guardians minimum time to get acquainted and share whatever information they possess on this item. Basically, I'm still skeptical there's much to this whole thing after three hundred years. Having said that, I'm not dismissing the danger Antonino presents. While he may be working from a flawed deck of cards, he's still lethal."

"You may be right but, he may possess something we don't."

"What's that?"

"He has access to Vatican files which, I believe, may have given him the upper hand. His ruthlessness means he's either mad, which might be true, or he knows more about this item than we do. I'd be delighted if you told me this was a seventeenth century hoax, some political ruse to upset the English. But my gut tells me this is not going to happen. Deep down in my old Scots and Irish genes I suspect that there are many mysteries lurking under the Celtic mist. My grandmother had many tales of ghosts, leprechauns, and magical devices of heroes and heroines. I thought these had been buried centuries ago.........but maybe not."

At that moment, Wolfram heard Gus's secretary enter the room saying, "Here's that information you requested from Sam Butler. It is marked 'Urgent'."

Momentarily, the phone went silent as Wolfram heard the slicing of an envelope followed by the rattle of paper. "Wolfram, hold on. This could be important to both of us," said Gus. Conversation ceased as Gus began reading the documents.

For the next few minutes all Wolfram heard was Gus's mutterings. Then breaking the silence he said, "This confirms the reason for Antonino's dismissal from the clergy. This guy's a sadist. In several private boys' schools he enjoyed inflicting pain, in one case the boy almost died. His downfall came when several families sued the Roman Catholic Church over the abuse, something that the Church can ill afford these days. The cases were settled out of court but Antonino had to go."

More silence as Gus continued reading...... "This guy has a fetish for expensive sports cars. That could help us in tracking him here in Boston." Not seeking a reply he continued reading. Then, after a few minutes came a loud response, "Christ, that's all I need!"

"What's that?" asked Wolfram.

"This could be real trouble. Antonino, through his mother, is related to the Scarpoli family, a sadistic Sicilian syndicate with roots in United States, Canada, and Europe. They are into every racket, but specialize in drugs and have a reputation of eliminating any opposition, sound familiar? If he gets their backing, he could be operating on several fronts. Get this information to Gritty, Fred and the security team at once. In the meantime, I'll circulate Antonino's photo to the gang squad in case he pops up in any of their circles. I'll also ask regular patrols to check expensive sports car stores. We might get a break yet. Wolfram, keep in touch. For God's sake, watch your back!" With that, the call ended.

Wolfram rang Gritty at the university who answered in his usual crisp manner.

"Wolfram, I expect you have news?"

When Wolfram briefed him on his call with Gus, Gritty's initial response was a low whistle. "That's a brutal twist." For a few minutes Gritty muddled over the news. "But maybe it is not as bad as we think. Wolfram, what we know of Antonino, is that he is a self-centered bastard with criminal tendencies. How he ever became a priest is beyond me. If he spills anything to these gang members that squeaks of easy money, they could eliminate him and take the spoils for themselves. He's no fool."

"But how does he explain his dismissal from the priesthood and being on the run. That alone should be suspicious?" asked Wolfram, anxious to hear Gritty's assessment.

"Maybe, but regardless of the story he tells, they will still respect his priestly status, and excuse his current troubles to bureaucratic skullduggery and bad timing. They may not demand a report from Italy, at least not yet. After all he is family and he will initially get the benefit of the doubt."

"What kind of tale would get Rudolfo killed?"

"That's easy," replied Gritty. "Rudolfo was already on the run so Antonino likely embellished the tale by saying he was about to divulge some Scarpoli family secret. That hit likely came out of Montreal. Killing a squealer comes easy to this bunch."

"Then how does Antonino justify his pursuit of Morgan?"

"It is likely shrouded in some academic battle with Antonino as the victim. To this gang this would seem valueless so they would offer him cover and freedom. However, if he creates too many waves, he could upset this cozy arrangement. So, he has to move fast and get the hell out once he gets what he's after."

"The bottom line is Antonino's here in Boston with Morgan in his gun sights."

"No argument there. I wish to hell I felt better about Morgan's wife. But, in her vulnerable state she can be easily manipulated, and Antonino is skilled at that. Morgan's also a problem. He's like a jittery rabbit that might leap into the nearest hole without looking. Fred and I have discussed a number of scenarios, and likely, this Italian will devise something entirely different. Our assessment is that Antonino will act in the next week, ten days tops. I'll not share that tidbit with Morgan, he's already too skittish. Keep your cell phone open, Wolfram, the days ahead could be rough."

Closing his cell phone Wolfram sat musing for a short spell enjoying the peaceful setting. "These carefully manicured lawns and sculptured gardens belie the pending hell which might erupt at any minute. I have to pressure my grandmother and her guests to reveal all they know, before Antonino discovers this hideout. The next few days will be critical. If the medallion is fiction, then the focus can be riveted on Antonino. If not, then I could be facing a far more daunting task." Seeing Charles heading his way, Wolfram stepped out of the car.

Chapter 5

The Weston Estate, Boston: The First Meal Together

It was a strange gathering; descendants of families sworn to a three hundred year old secret. Questions swirled like leaves caught in the wind. What dangerous secret would discipline generations to await a distant call to action? Why would Nellie Gordon's death be accepted as that call? What invisible force directed their action? Was it family duty or something else which drew them to Boston? While skepticism ran rampant there seemed little doubt '*the coming times*' had arrived.

About 4pm, Tyloar and Gracelyn Harrison, Wolfram's grandparents, arrived, met their guests, and clarified any lingering details about their accommodations. Anton, the Chef had already met with each arrival regarding their dietary preferences. Casual attire was agreed, with breakfast and lunch to be held in the breakfast nook or patio at the rear of the mansion, and the evening meal in the formal dining room.

In the interval before dinner, Angi and Vette corralled Wolfram to get access to the fitness room. Wolfram responded, "No problem, I'll be meeting you there each morning." As Angi left to prepare for dinner, Wolfram ceased the occasion to talk to Vette. "By the way, Vette, I may be mistaken, but by any chance are you working undercover protecting Angi? That wouldn't surprise me in light of recent events in Canada. Am I correct?"

Vette, guarded, replied, "It is that obvious, heh. Why do you ask?"

"To tell you the truth, this situation is growing more dangerous by the hour and I need all the trained help I can muster. Can I count on you?"

Seeing the worried look in Wolfram's eyes, Vette responded. "Somehow I'm not surprised. To answer your question, I am an off-duty RCMP officer with over eight years experience. A friend of my father's needed assistance and I was hired. I've already detected the extra security. Fill me in. I detest working in the dark."

"Thanks. Come with me. We'll find a quiet corner." They left to talk in the garden away from the mansion.

About 5:30pm the seven appeared at the dining room entrance; four Guardians plus Vette, Wolfram and Tyloar. The dining room had been the interior decorator's crown jewel. The spacious room was an exquisite blend of cream, coral and green. Four large windows overlooked the side gardens, two slightly open for a cross breeze. A soft scent of lilac filled the air. Luxurious coral drapes in Victorian folds encased the cream-curtained venetian blinds which allowed both light and privacy. The large oval table, draped in fine linen, sat in the middle of an expensive patterned carpet. The table, designed for twelve, was set for seven. A low floral arrangement graced the center of the table, flowers chosen from the estate gardens. The hazel wood chairs, padded in beige and floral fabric, matched the other furniture in the room. Plants were tastefully arranged to complement, but not overpower the space. The crystal chandelier was lit for effect, as the windows provided plenty of light.

Gracelyn guided her guests to their respective seats while Tyloar assumed his seat at one end of the long table. Once everyone was seated, Gracelyn took her seat at the other end of the table. On Tyloar's right was Vette, Angi and Moira. On his left were Wolfram and Jessie. Wolfram and Vette sat opposite each other on either side of his grandfather, leaving the other Guardians time to get acquainted.

Once seated, Anton appeared with a couple of white wine bottles and poured some in each glass. Then, he retreated to the kitchen.

When everyone was comfortable, Tyloar raised his glass in a toast. "May I take this opportunity to welcome our international guests; Guardians from families specially chosen to protect an ancient treasure. Welcome to the United States." Glasses were raised and the meal commenced. Still strangers, members began hesitantly to talk to their nearest dinner companion. A variety of breads arrived along with the first course, a Classic Caesar Salad. The evening was warm and Anton was determined to keep his guests cool and well fed. If the evening breeze failed he was ready to turn on the air conditioning. The Harrisons had given precise instructions.

Tyloar Harrison was a stocky man in his early seventies, with thinning gray hair and silver-rimmed glasses. Recognized as a community leader, he was at ease with business and fund-raising meetings, and known for getting things done. He was born and educated in Boston, going to Harvard University on a full scholarship and graduating with degrees in history and business. He was delighted in Boston's status as the "Cradle of Liberty" and proudly acknowledged his family links to the famous Boston Tea Party. In the late 1950s he met Gracelyn, an employee at his family's antique business. They were married in the early sixties. After decades of assisting in the family business, they became principle owners when his parents died. For over forty years the business thrived in a booming economy but the recent economic downturn had reduced their profits. Nevertheless, as he contemplated their lives together, "We've done well; we have a fine mansion, prominent and wealthy friends and are blessed with a fine grandson. Thank God he's recovering but it will take time. Our daughter is barely capable of managing her own life, let alone a business." With concern he looked over at Wolfram, "Will he ever fully recover or have a family? Gracelyn and I are nearing retirement and will soon have to make a decision about the business. But that's for another day."

He had chosen a 'hands off' policy with regard to the Guardians, leaving his wife and Wolfram in charge. He shared his grandson's skepticism over the authenticity of the medallion, "The next few days will settle this one way or another. While Nat Zieglar, our company gemologist assures me that Gracelyn's sapphire is genuine and very old, there is no guarantee the rest of these women have gems of equal quality. In the meantime I'll need Wolfram to keep me abreast of what's happening on the criminal front. I'll be damned if anyone is getting near my family. I've paid for extra security and will pay more if need be. Wolfram's police training has come in handy, but it was that cursed police work that caused his near-fatal accident. That was certainly one of life's cruel twists. I see that those two women from Canada are near his age."

"Strange what brings people together," thought Angi as she surveyed the setting? "Here we are from different countries, all linked by a mystery with century old roots in another country. Our ancestors once sat plotting this strategy, trusting it would survive until this century. That took courage. Think of the risk. Whatever happens, this medallion has already given me the potential of a larger family. I wonder what the days ahead will reveal. I'm glad Moira is sitting next to me; it'll give me a chance to know her better. She's about my height, and certainly fit." Angi turned to chat.

Moira, single at forty-six, lived in Sydney, had received numerous swimming awards and was now a coach for Australia's top female swimming team. She was training the next team for the 2012 Summer Olympics in London. This trip was an inconvenience. But once she received the call from Gracelyn, and talked to her mother and grandmother, she had no choice. Looking around the table she thought, "I'm amazed our crystal survived in light of the trials and tribulations of my family. It must have taken some guts not to sell this gemstone when they were nearly starving in the early days in Australia. Real rugged, that's my family line. If I hadn't taken this journey they'd start haunting me. That alone is enough to frighten the hell out of anyone. Not appearing was never an option." She smiled. "It'll be good to chat with other Guardians. Maybe they know more than I do. But wouldn't it be a real downer to discover this whole caper is nothing but a wild goose chase. But that's not the message ingrained in my family and I'm sticking to that." The thought lingered as she turned to Angi.

Gracelyn Harrison was the epitome of a well groomed professional matron accustomed to running a profitable business and entertaining fashionable guests. Elegant in her seventies, she sat regally surveying the gathering. "I never thought this day would come in my life time, and certainly not with a killer stalking us. The world hasn't changed much in the centuries, just more complicated. In the 1600s the predators were political and clerical, today it is individual. This killer that Wolfram speaks of is surely after gold déspite his previous connections with some religious organization. He cares little for the historic value of anything. Unfortunately, we've become a society which weighs everything by its material value. It is obvious we've lost our way. While wealth makes life easier, it is cold compensation for what truly ails the world. Before I die I'd like to think there was something else to life. I'd like to believe our ancestor's risked everything to save something of importance. I wonder if we'd be as courageous."

Born in Boston to an impoverished Sinclair family, Gracelyn went to work after high school. Her mother's family had known wealth, but lost it during the Depression. Her mother, ill prepared for such a drastic change, never recovered. Her only sibling, a sister, died of Polio in the fifties. Her first, and only, job was at the Harrison Antique Store where she met Tyloar. Looking down the table she reminisced, "Initially, it wasn't a great love affair but we've been together for over forty-five years. Our biggest mistake was spoiling our only child, Megan. Growing up in the seventies, Megan, like a moth to fire, flew off to join a hippy commune in California. There she married Maxwell Stark, a drummer in a Rock Band from a good family in Texas. Poster children to a lost generation consumed by mental illness and drugs. Fortunately, we learned our lesson when it came to Wolfram. He's our future but he's damaged. He still needs a lot of rehabilitation that could take years. I'll just have to hope. But this is no time for maudlin thinking, the Guardians come first." Gracelyn turned to chat with Jessie.

The second Guardian from down-under was the very opposite to Moira. Jessie, at sixty-four, was a small, frail woman, just over five feet, with a retiring personality. Married with two grown children, and one grandchild, she had spent decades as a music teacher in a private girls school in New Zealand. A gifted classical pianist she never had the money or support for outside competitions and had few awards. Music comforted her in dealing with life's hardships. As she looked around the magnificent dining room she thought of her mother and grandmother. "Nanna kept saying that the '*coming times*' might happen at the turn of the century. She was the one with the greatest knowledge of the secret which she tried to convey to me because Mama was too ill. Even with antibiotics, Mama's bout of Tuberculosis left her permanently weak. While she gave birth to two children, she died in her late forties, leaving our care to Nanna. I'm the only one living, James died a decade ago from stomach cancer. I planned to pass our gemstone on to my daughter, but *'the coming times'* arrived. I hope I can do justice to Nanna's teachings........it has been a long while." Looking around the table she contemplated the event, "For the first time in centuries four Guardians are sitting together. I wonder if there are still eight living descendants from the original families. It would be wonderful to meet them." The thought was left as she responded to a question from Gracelyn.

Tyloar kept the wine glasses filled, noting that Wolfram, Vette and Angi had hardly touched their first glass of wine. Each course arrived with precise timing and presented in an appetizing manner. The main course of Pan Seared Salmon in basal butter with summer vegetables and rice timbale was followed by a Chocolate Trilogy Mousse along with a platter of petite pastries, and plates of fruit, cheese, and chocolates plus cups of tea and coffee. After two hours the group moved to an adjacent sitting room, the patio doors set ajar to encourage the evening breeze. Wolfram directed the guests to the deep-cushioned blue and green chairs. Tyloar chose one near the hall doorway while the rest selected ones previously arranged in a semi-circle. The plan was to encourage the Guardians to share their information on the medallion. Wolfram took the lead.

"Let me begin by bringing you up-to-date with what has been happening. First, it was my request to an old colleague at Boston University which initiated an unexpected sequence of events. I asked Dr. Morgan Mandelthrope, an old friend and specialist in Celtic history, to investigate whether there was archival evidence of a special medallion, secret families or a secret with North American connections in the 1600s. Finding nothing, he asked two academic colleagues, one in Ireland, the other in Scotland, to see what they could find. After some months Dr. Kevyn O'Gratteney in Ireland uncovered a secret code which he was able to break. It had definite possibilities. But before he had time to investigate further he was killed in a hit-and-run car accident. His last e-mail to Morgan identified an Italian, an ex-Roman Catholic priest, who had shown an inordinate interest in his research. It is assumed that it was an assistant to this Italian who attacked Nellie. Shortly after Nellie's attack, her assailant was killed in the city jail."

Startled, Moira asked, "You mean to tell me there have been three deaths connected with this medallion in the past few weeks?"

"Yes," confirmed Wolfram, noting the startled reaction of several in the room.

"Where's this Italian now?" asked Angi, trying to grasp the news.

"We've tracked him to Boston where we believe he is now after Morgan. By hacking into Dr. O'Gratteney's computer he discovered Nellie's name, and, of course, the other two names being Morgan's, who initiated the research, and the Scottish professor. Getting nothing from Nellie, he focused on Morgan. To thwart him, all of Morgan's computer information has been removed and stored in a secure location. Morgan is presently under special protection."

"But if he gets to Morgan then he can easily get you or your grandparents. Now I understand why we are not meeting at your grandparent's residence, but how safe are we here?" Moira had quickly grasped the danger.

Determined to allay their fears, Wolfram continued. "Morgan doesn't know where we are, only the Boston Deputy Superintendent of Police. In addition, we've hired extra security. In light of the situation I must ask that you do not wander beyond the perimeter of the mansion grounds. No long walks. If you need to purchase anything, then Charles will drive you to and from a local store. I wish it was different but we need to be prudent."

Uneasiness gripped the room, each Guardian lost in her own analysis of the threatening events. Wolfram redirecting their thoughts broke the silence "So, now you understand why we must act quickly. For our first evening I was hoping we might share what we know of the medallion and "*the coming times*", and tomorrow evening we can concentrate on the gemstones. If you agree, Nat Zieglar, our company gemologist will join us tomorrow evening to assess the gems. The reason being, there is no point in pursuing this further if the gemstones are not genuine. No aspersions on anyone, a lot can happen in three centuries." Taking their nods as agreement he went on, "First, do you know the name of your ancestor? I believe there were only couples involved in this secret. This information could help us with further research if we need to take that route."

Angi was the first to speak. "I believe my ancestor's surname was Stewart but I don't know their other names. In recent centuries, the name was Cameron and, I believe they moved from Nova Scotia to Prince Edward Island near the end of the 1800s. I might find more in Gran's things once I get home."

Jessie spoke next "I never heard the name mentioned in my home. All I know is that my grandmother, Nanna, said four families had to immigrate to North America. At the time of the Civil War in the USA two families left for Australia. Around the First World War, my family left Australia to settle in New Zealand."

"I know my ancestors were Keegan and Charlotte Fitzgibbon," stated Moira "these names were often mentioned in whispers in our home."

"I believe my ancestors were Graeme and Elizabeth Reid," replied Gracelyn. "I learned this from my maternal grandmother."

"That's great," replied Wolfram, writing down the names. "It is a beginning."

"I recall my Nanna saying that one of the families, not ours, had the original list. If none of us possess it," getting a negative signal from the others, "then it must reside with a family in Britain."

"OK, let's leave it there," said Wolfram. "What do you know about the medallion itself?"

Jessie, in her soft New Zealand accent, began, "Nanna said the medallion was broken up long before the 1600s. Our ancestors in the 1600s were acting as Guardians just like us and their families had been doing the same thing for generations. Now before you ask, she did not know how far back. She did say that if ever the medallion was reassembled it was supposed to possess some magical power that could be dangerous in the wrong hands. What powers or how dangerous I don't know."

Wolfram inquired, "Did your grandmother speculate at all as to how far back in time the medallion might have existed?"

"No," replied Jessie. "She wasn't a woman who made assumptions. She dutifully conveyed only what she had been told by her mother."

Moira's entered the conversation, "I have even less to add. I conferred with my mother and grandmother before leaving Australia. My grandmother thought that the medallion may belong to the Druids, and was dismantled when they were being persecuted by the Romans. If correct, we may be talking centuries."

With mention of Druids Wolfram glanced at his grandfather, who winced. "I'm a bit nervous when the Druids are brought into the scenario as this could get us tangled up in new age stuff. Nevertheless, we'll let it stand."

Moira continued, "My Gran was also firm that the medallion was useless unless all the gems were in their original slots. That could mean millions of possibilities if there are eight. I am assuming there must be eight gemstones as there were eight families. In addition, she stressed that, if the medallion was assembled properly, only one person in each generation was chosen, or able, to wear it. How that person was selected I haven't the foggiest idea."

"There are a lot of ifs," replied Wolfram, realizing the diminishing probability of success.

Gracelyn then spoke, "I learned the Guardians were supposed to be female, as it was assumed it would be difficult to trace them in a masculine society. It was my understanding, the gemstone could, for a generation, be passed on to a male, but as soon as he had a daughter, she had to assume the guardianship."

"That's what Gran told me," interjected Angi.

Seeing that the group was tiring after their long journeys Wolfram was anxious to press on. "If you think of anything else, let me know. Now, lets talk about '*the coming times.*'"

Angi began, "From what I could gather, somehow Gran knew the attack on her was a signal that '*the coming times*' had begun. That's what she was saying in the hospital, but was unable to tell me more before she died. I wish I had paid more attention when she first told me about the medallion when I was younger."

Moira interjected, "My mother and grandmother were explicit that the death of Nellie was the signal for the Guardians to meet. It wasn't entirely clear why. Yet, as I sit here I do believe events are guiding us in some direction."

Jessie followed, "I'm afraid, except for understanding that it is the time when the medallion is supposed to be reassembled, I know little else."

The Guardians then proceeded to discuss related matters among themselves.

"Don't feel guilty Angi about being disinterested when this was first presented by your grandmother," said Jessie in a comforting tone. "It is hard for any of us in this modern age to grasp something centuries old. As a young woman in New Zealand I dismissed the whole idea, after all we were not flying off to other countries as easily as we do now. I'm still struggling with the fact that we are here in Boston talking about this, a sworn family secret. Angi, if your grandmother had not died, I was just about to pass our gemstone onto the next generation. I was convinced, as others, that '*the coming times*' could be decades or even another century away."

Wolfram now interjected, "In your minds, is there any correlation between "*the coming times*" and the 2012 prophecy of doom?"

"I can't speak for the rest," said Angi, "I would like to say, no, but we can't rule out anything. It is an interesting coincidence, don't you think? What about the rest of you?"

"I agree with Angi," replied Gracelyn. "Let's leave everything on the table; Druids and the 2012 prophecy. When we have more facts then we can discard whatever doesn't apply." She ignored the disapproving glance of her husband.

"Agreed," said Moira and Jessie almost in unison.

Before Wolfram could inject another question, Moira shifted the discussion with a point-blank one of her own, "The main question hanging unsaid and unanswered is what we can expect from this gathering. Our families have protected something for generations and we have few details to support such a heroic effort. This killer seems to know a hell of a lot more than we do. His presence on the scene makes it imperative we cease speculating and get down to business."

"That's right," replied Angi. "Let's move on. What happens next if all the gemstones prove to be genuine? Do we all travel to Britain to search for the rest of the stones? I'm not sure I have the time or money for such globe trotting." Angi wasn't about to divulge another, and more compelling, reason for her disinterest in travelling.

Wolfram stepped in. "Well that depends on what happens tomorrow night." He had previously toyed with the same thought, silently mulling over the possibilities, "What do we do if we discover tomorrow night that all gemstones are of the same vintage and quality, do we drop this or continue the quest, knowing there's a killer on our tail? Who has the resources for such a journey? How many should go?" Trying best to divert such thinking he replied, "Let's cross that bridge when we come to it."

But even his grandmother was not diverted, "Fine, but let's assume the gemstones are genuine. Then we will have no choice but to pursue this mystery to its end. We owe that much to our ancestors and Nellie. If we pool our contact names we must have a few from one of these countries. I'm sure the secret chain still exists in some form."

"I have a name in Ireland," said Angi

"I have one in Scotland," said Jessie.

"There, that's a start. Let's hold onto those names until tomorrow night," replied Gracelyn triumphantly. "We'll bring them up again when we are certain there is a next step."

Vette sat absorbing the conversation and thinking, "My God, this fantasy might have legs after all. If tomorrow night we discover these gemstones are genuine, more travelling is inevitable. I better get my head around the possibility. Any globe trotting for me will be stymied as I'm supposed to be back on duty in a week. Yet, this is a delicious mystery and police work can be so dull. The mind boggles as to the possibilities. I have either stumbled into the most fantastic secret of a lifetime or tomorrow it is going to fizzle and we will be on a flight home. I can hardly wait."

Wolfram let the women talk as he began to tally up the facts; four countries, four gemstones, and four women. These four exist, and we have access to two more names of the four across the pond. The last two shouldn't be hard to find. A cold chill ran up his back as the hair on the back of his neck curled. "That's what Antonino is thinking! He may know enough to realize that grasping any link in this chain get's him access to the prize. What the hell was I thinking when I regarded my grandmother's gem in such a cavalier manner. Now I'm praying that some of the gemstones are fakes. If real, we'll have to scramble to outwit Antonino. What was that Scottish professor's name? I'll have to phone Josh. Let's pray Antonino can't get to Morgan."

Wolfram's gut churned with the thought.

Angi returned to her room mulling over the evening's discussions. "What happens now? There has to be something to this. Our ancestors took enormous risks to preserve something. If the gemstones are real, will all the Guardians continue on this quest? That's not my plan." She sat by the open window for a while gazing at the distant horizon. "Tomorrow will hold the key if there is a next phase."

Setting her clock for 5am to allow time for meditation and the gym, she fluffed her pillow in preparation for sleep. At that moment she recalled something which she had earlier denied. "Odd, I could have sworn something joined us this evening. I felt a presence enter on a sea breeze. Was this due to the first gathering of the Guardians after centuries? Maybe it is just my imagination. .... I don't suppose you are listening, Gran? I could use your Celtic knowhow right now." Smiling, she drifted off as the weariness of the day finally caught up with her.

&

Boston: Morgan's House

"Remember, Morgan, anything out of the ordinary, no matter how trivial," was Gritty's parting shot as Morgan eased out of the car.

"I know," replied Morgan, irritated at being reminded. "I heard you the first time. Antonino's in town and is capable of anything. He's got bodies to prove it. The suspense is numbing. I can hardly concentrate. I'll be glad when this hell is over."

"You won't need to concentrate if he's successful," snapped Gritty, his sympathy fading. Mumbling as he backed the car out of the driveway, "This guy has two bodyguards on twenty-four hour watch and you'd think we were the criminals. I like the little ivory league bastard, but at times he needs a good swift kick in the ass. One minute he's scared out of his mind, the next he's declaring his rights. Thank God he never enlisted in the military, he'd have been crucified. Ah well, it'll soon be over. Antonino has to make a move. Let's hope we get the upper hand." Turning, he waved to Fred who was in position for the next shift.

Morgan, who normally arrived to an empty house to prepare a frozen microwave dinner, was greeted with the tantalizing odor of meat cooking and soft music. "I'm hallucinating. I'm definitely under too much stress." Hoping it wasn't a dream he ventured down the hall, noting the dining room table was set for two with special mats and wine glasses. He pushed the kitchen door with his fingers to find Kari-Ann removing a roast of beef from the oven. Not having had a cooked meal from her in months, his first unkind thought was, "I wonder if she's sober."

"I thought it was you," was the cheery response as Kari-Ann looked up to greet her husband. "Freshen up. I thought it time for an old fashioned home-cooked meal. I haven't done this in ages. I'm just about to pop the veggies into the microwave. The bread is from the bakery. Can you get the wine, something red and mellow?"

"Is this a special occasion or something?" asked Morgan, bewildered by the change in her behavior. He hesitated.

"No, just thought we deserved a decent meal. Did you hear me? The wine".......replied Kari-Ann peeved at the slowness of his response.

"Yeh, I'll get it. Are you almost ready?"

Looking at the roast, Kari-Ann replied, "Not quite, maybe twenty minutes, you like it medium to well done. We've got time for a wee cocktail, surprise me. I'll join you in the living room in a sec." She returned the pan to the oven.

Morgan, woodenly moved towards his study, dropped off his briefcase and proceeded to the liquor cabinet in the dining room. He poured two Dubonnet Cocktails; a mix of Dubonnet Rouge, Dry Gin and a dash of orange bitters. He checked his wine supply through the glass door of his state-of-the-art Sobra wine cellar. This silent unit of superconductor technology kept twelve wine bottles in a perfect state of readiness. He selected an expensive one, picked up an opener, and delivered them to the dinner table. Returning, he transported the cocktail drinks and coasters to separate tables in the living room. At that moment Gritty's parting command registered. "Gritty must be clairvoyant. Maybe he has a touch of blarney tucked in his genes. Sad to say, this is definitely odd. I wonder what's up." Feeling in control, he settled into a comfortable chair in his fashionably decorated home.

When Kari-Ann joined him he noticed she was dressed in a costly pair of mauve slacks and a shear blouse which complimented her svelte figure. "She's still beautiful and certainly doesn't show her age. Sadly, a marriage which had a romantic beginning crumbled under the onslaught of too many marital arguments, the cruel words leaving deep scars. Marriage counseling was an anathema to Kari-Ann. She's likely in trouble; financial, drugs or men. Maybe she's about to tell me she's leaving for another guy. God knows. It is serious enough that she had to fortify herself with a couple of drinks. I can never tell when she's on drugs." Morgan's thoughts were jarred by Kari-Ann's exuberant opening.

"I bet you can't imagine what happened to me last night?" she announced provocatively.

Irritated with guessing games, Morgan replied "Well, I certainly hope it surpassed my day."

Ignoring his negative response, Kari-Ann bounced back, "Last night a guy appeared and offered the four of us a walk-on role in his upcoming movie. What do you think of that?"

"Well," thought Morgan, "that shoots my theory. But it still doesn't explain the elaborate come on. There's more." Going along he replied, "That sounds like fun. Will you get paid?"

"Yes, not much but we have a contract," as Kari-Ann waved a couple of sheets in front of him, like a small child displaying her latest award.

"A contract?" said Morgan; amazed one would even be needed. "Nevertheless," he thought, "this is better than booze, drugs or another man."

"Yah, and, in addition he offered me a small speaking role. What do you think of that?" said Kari-Ann strutting around the room before dropping into a signature series chair next to her cocktail.

"Well, congratulations. Will you get paid for that as well?"

"There you go again, always harping on money. Anyway, to answer your question, yes, it is another contract and I will get paid."

"I suppose a lawyer is not needed for such small contracts."

"No. But we will have something like this, in writing, spelling out our role and payment." Checking her watch, "Woops, it is time to eat. We can talk over supper." Gulping down the remainder of her drink she headed to the kitchen.

Moving towards the dining room, Morgan kept mulling over the news. "Be happy for her, a movie career, who would have guessed. Don't burst her balloon. But is there any chance this could be a scam. After all, she's had no prior acting experience and she's much older than the usual discoveries. But what do I know. So, Morgan, me boy, go along for the ride and see what else the evening has to offer."

Kari-Ann delivered two well-portioned plates of food to the table while Morgan poured the wine. Before diving into the food, Morgan raised his glass. "Kari-Ann, congratulations, I can see this means a lot to you. All the best! " and he meant it. Momentarily, he contemplated, "Strange, she never mentioned the name of the movie or the leading actors. I suppose that comes later."

The alcohol was beginning to take hold as Kari-Ann soaked in the salutations as she contemplated future glory.

Hungry, Morgan sipped the red wine and savored the tantalizing food. As Kari-Ann talked on, hardly touching her food, he murmured pleasantries while opposing thoughts raced through his head. "She's on another fantasy trip. Life's easier when she's on a high than when she's morose. She spends an equal amount of money whatever phase she's in. Anything's possible. She might be a late bloomer. God knows she needs purpose in life. She's easily bored, and has likely tired of the bar scene. I once thought we might get this marriage back on track but that's a fairy tale. We've got nothing in common ......maybe we never did. Male hormones likely clouded the early years. A sure sign of her self interest, she's never once asked why Gritty and Fred have become my shadows. I'd likely do her a favor by dying. On her own, she'd squander the money in months. Then what? I never thought I was a great catch, but being a non-entity is a brutal blow."

His daydreaming was pierced by, "You are not listening! I suppose you are thinking about that stupid Celtic stuff. Listen to me, this is important," Kari-Ann demanded.

"I wasn't thinking of work, but you are right, I wasn't listening either. Go on."

"Well, this Tony Moretti was asking if you might be interested in being an historical consultant for the movie."

"Don't be ridiculous, Kari-Ann, I'm too busy and I have no interest in movies."

Unhindered by his negative reply, Kari-Ann pressed on, "O come on. All you have to do is meet him for a chat, no commitment. Do it for me. You don't have to be a consultant just come to Rosie's and meet him."

It finally dawned on Morgan, "God, I'm stupid. So this is what this is all about. I might have known there was some angle. Kari-Ann's likely promised this Tony guy that she'd deliver, gaining her some brownie point. She's trapped me again."

"For God sake, Kari-Ann, have you noticed I've got two bodyguards these days? I'm surprised you haven't asked why they are here."

Growing angry she struck back, "I don't care. Don't confuse me. I don't want to know," placing her hands over her ears. "That black guy sitting in his car at night gives me the creeps. He's always spying on me."

Exasperated, Morgan responded, "Kari-Ann, these guys are trying to keep me from getting killed."

"Don't be silly. Who'd want to kill a dull, unimportant university history professor? Morgan, you'll do anything to upset my plans. I don't care what these guys are doing, are you or are you not going to talk to Tony?"

His blood pressure rising, Morgan exploded, "The answer is, no!" the 'no' dragged out in a resounding high note which ignited a fire storm.

Furious at any rejection, Kari-Ann became enraged, "You are hateful ...... hateful ......hateful," as she pounded her fist on the table. "You are a selfish bastard, Morgan! You only think of yourself. For once, why not think of me. I've got a chance for a better life, and you will not even get off your ass to help me."

Exacerbated, Morgan dove in, "Wait a minute. Who the hell do you think has paid the bills for your crazy schemes over the years? You've spent a fortune on clothes, decorators, travel, drugs and God knows what else. We're on the verge of bankruptcy. If it wasn't for my salary we'd be selling this house to balance the books."

"There you go again, always groaning over money. I don't believe the house sale for a minute. You could always go to your parents, they have lots of money. I suppose you've poisoned them against me. When we didn't have children, your over-achieving parents thought I should get more education and a better job. Well, they, unlike you, might see my movie offer as a step up."

"Kari-Ann I'd be delighted if you could stick to anything. If this movie idea has any substance, then fine. But you and I know that this will likely be as shallow as the rest of your cock-eyed ideas. You certainly know how to spend money. God forbid if you were ever asked to earn a living..........you would starve to death."

"The same old boring Morgan," was the sarcastic reply. "I have no intention of starving." Then wanting to hurt him she continued, "You are not indispensable. I can get another man whenever I want."

"I expect you've already tested that theory." Morgan replied in anger. "Why don't you get one of them to support your latest fad? Maybe you could even find one to be the history consultant."

"OK I will. Just you wait and see. Once I'm a star I'll divorce you and find a better man......... a real man, not a wimp."

"Kari-Ann, these are the same old threats; do what I want or I'll leave. You have no intention of leaving the golden nest. You are great at threats but short on action. This is the same old childish antics I've listened to for years. A single 'no' sends you into a tantrum. I've got enough on my plate right now so back off. Surely you won't discard your financial security blanket over my refusal to meet this two-bit movie mogul. Get a grip. You don't need me; you have what you want so go on and enjoy this tinsel ride. You will be with people of your own ilk."

Shifting gears, Kari-Ann softened her attack. Trying to appeal to a by-gone era she found hard to recall, "OK, so I have no intention of leaving you. What would it hurt for you to pop in to Rosie's tomorrow night, say hello, and tell Tony you are not interested. Come on Morgie .....Please......Please...... Just this once for little old me. What harm would it do to come with me and have a drink? We haven't been out in ages."

The lingering threat of Antonino, the liquor, food and useless verbiage was catching up to Morgan. Longing for peace, he began to waver, "Why not.

If I don't relent she'll never shut up. The cold, sickening reality of my life stands before me. This hell is never going to change, just an endless rotation of similar scenes. My male ego held on to this marriage for years ....held on to what? I detest coming home to this sterile magazine masterpiece of a house and to a woman I can barely tolerate or converse with. I should have moved on years ago." In a tired voice Morgan replied, "Fine, I'll go. One hour, tops. A drink, a quick chat and out." Comforting himself, he said as he climbed the stairs to bed, "When this Antonino mess is resolved I'm heading to my lawyer. I've had enough. But first I'll need a plan to escape my nursemaids tomorrow night."

Kari-Ann smiled as she removed the plates. There'd be no dessert. She congratulated herself in the kitchen. "I can always get that moron to bend. I've earned that extra dough and Tony will be so grateful. I'm on my way. As soon as my career blooms, I'll ditch this drip. I deserve better!"

&

Boston: Testing the Gemstones

A moaning fog horn greeted the second day. A heavy mist kissed the trees and shrubbery of the estate gardens. Uncertainty accompanied the rolling fog.

Pulling herself up in bed, Angi tried to disentangle herself from a frustrating dream. In it, she was being sucked into a gigantic emerald tunnel, the golden snake slithering before her to provide light. Harp music played in the distance, a different rendition of Mr. Aucoin's final tune. Resisting the pull, she dug her heels into the slippery mud to little effect. Awake, a lingering uneasiness permeated her thoughts. Sitting at the side of her bed, she lamented, "What's happening to me? The stress must be catching up to me. That damn snake is becoming a pest."

Submerging the dream, the previous night's discussions surfaced. "That hovering predator is hard to dismiss in light of the dead bodies. Even if the gemstones are not genuine, it is not like we can send this killer an e-mail to cease and desist. Being stalked by a mad man is alarming, a far cry from my orderly life at the hospital." Angi moved to the window only to encounter a wall of gray. "Don't panic," she reassured herself, "you are not alone. Today, we'll settle the gemstone issue, and then we'll face tomorrow." Reassured, she found an open space and sitting cross legged on the floor proceeded with her morning meditation.

At 6am, as agreed, she and Vette headed to the fitness room. There they found Wolfram sweating and struggling with leg exercises. After a cursory

'Good Morning' the three went silent, focused on their respective tasks. Angi and Vette started on the treadmill machines. Out of the corner of her eye, Angi watched Wolfram's heroic efforts. A glance from Vette signaled similar thoughts. "He's certainly dogged," she thought. At 6:45am they all scattered for a shower and an 8 something breakfast.

The foggy day gave everyone respite, time to contemplate the previous day's revelations, get acquainted, and anticipate the next phase.

At 5:30 in the evening, everyone assembled at the dining room entrance to greet their new arrival, Nat Zieglar, the gemologist. Nat, a stocky man in his late fifties, was a head shorter than Wolfram. Businesslike, he was dressed in dark trousers, crisp shirt, and no tie, his thick, white hair contrasting sharply with his suntanned face. After brief introductions, he stacked two black cases, one larger than the other, on a side table and took the chair between Wolfram and Jessie for the evening meal.

As the fog edged closer to the house, Anton turned up the thermostat. Chandelier light was needed to offset the gloom. A New England clam chowder entrée provided culinary warmth to the setting. This was followed by Pan Roasted Chicken breast served with a leek and mushroom sauce, vegetables and buttermilk mashed potatoes. Dessert was a mixed berry tart with the accompaniments of cookies, cheese and fruit. During the meal, Tyloar, again, kept the wine glasses filled. The second dinner was more relaxed as hosts and guests had had more time together.

Unrushed, by 7:20, everyone joined in to clear the table down to its wooden surface. Prearranged, Wolfram produced a black velvet cloth which he draped over one end of the table. Nat retrieved his GemPro Portapac gemologist kit from the nearby table. He opened the case to reveal a compact assortment of field equipment; a refract meter, fine loupe, OPL spectroscope, calcite dichroscope, light base with sodium filter, polars with condensing sphere, dark field well and stone holder. From the smaller case he produced a lamp designed to simulate true north daylight with a color temperature of approximately 5000-6100° Kelvin. Placing a black notebook next to his Portapac, he nodded to Wolfram.

Upon Wolfram's signal, the Guardians departed to retrieve their gemstones, returning with handbags which they deposited next to their chairs.

Wolfram, taking the lead, began. "I realize this is difficult for you as Guardians, for generations this family secret was sacrosanct, never to be revealed to outsiders. So, we will walk gently. With no precedent, let's set an informal plan. If it is OK with you, each Guardian will present her family gemstone, share any knowledge she has about it, and pass it to Nat for examination." The nodding of heads was consent. This was also Nat's opening.

90

Nat with a warm inviting smile began, "First, I want to thank you for this privilege, for I know enough that this is a very unique gathering. As a brief history, the Harrisons and I go back decades and I bring over thirty-five years of gemology experience. Because of this I need to clarify a key point. Irrespective of the equipment present, the best I can provide this evening is my professional opinion on these gemstones. This is not a certification. A certification would require a fully equipped laboratory which I have downtown. So, as I understand it, tonight my task is to determine whether these gemstones are genuine. I can give you my professional opinion, and, if later, you need more then we can arrange that as well. This evening, I will be looking for what we refer to in the industry as the 'Four Cs'; color, clarity, cut and carat weight. I am aware of the time constraints so will try and keep the process rolling. Do you have any questions?"

"For my own understanding," asked Angi, "I suppose determining the value of any gemstone is rather complicated?"

Nat considered a brief response to her question, "The true value of a gemstone is measured on a number of properties such as its carat weight, proportion of inclusions, transparency, fluorescence, cut, shape, symmetry, finish, scintillation (or sparkle), dispersion (or fire), color coverage, and enhancement. I may touch on some of these tonight, but only with more elaborate equipment can I provide the in-depth analysis and true value. That's why the certification procedure is so costly."

"On the topic of costs, who's paying for this evening's assessment?" asked Angi.

Tyloar responded, "We've assumed the cost, as a family responsibility."

"Then, on behalf of all of us, we sincerely thank you and Gracelyn for this service and your hospitality," said Angi. "Without your generosity we would not be here this evening."

Itching to get started, Wolfram interceded, "I wonder if we could proceed as I have no idea how long this may take. Perhaps, since Nat has already examined it, we could start with our family gemstone."

From her handbag, Gracelyn pulled out a tiny, finely engraved gold and silver box, undid the clasp and laid the sapphire on the black cloth, the deep blue color glittering under the light. "All I know is that sapphires affect the mind and can enhance intuitive abilities," she said and stepped back.

Nat picked up the gem, and carried out a partial assessment, to assure himself it was the same stone he had previously examined. Assured, he spoke to the group. "As I said to Gracelyn, Tyloar, and Wolfram, this marquise cut gemstone is of exquisite quality and could be quite old. What you may not know, because of the remarkable hardness of sapphires, is that they are often used in other areas than jewelry. Today we find them in the optical components of scientific instruments, high-durability windows, wristwatch crystals, and thin electronic wafers for solid-state electronics. In jewelry, the sapphire has always been regarded as one of the most valuable of precious stones. Its coloring depicts its origin, as such; this stone may have come from the Middle East. Older societies thought gemstones bestowed various properties to the wearer. As such, the sapphire is sometimes referred to as the 'stone of prosperity' or the 'stone of encouragement.' It is supposed to reduce frustration, fulfill dreams, and strengthen your ability to achieve your ambitions." Realizing he was boring his audience, he returned the gemstone to its tiny box and placed the box to the right of his case. Keeping to Wolfram's timetable, he softly called "Next" and looked at the Guardians.

"Jessie, I wonder if you would like to go next?" asked Wolfram, taking the easiest option as Jessie was seated next to his grandmother.

"Sure," replied Jessie, as she retrieved an identical box to Gracelyn's from her travel bag and brought forth a different gemstone, green in color, and laid it on the black cloth.

"So the gemstones are not identical," Wolfram commented to Nat. A question Nat asked when first seeing the sapphire.

"I know it is jasper," said Jessie. "My grandmother told me jasper is supposed to work with the chakras in your body to balance, recalibrate and heal. Chakra is a *Sanskrit* word from India which means '*wheel.*' The body has seven wheels of energy, which run up the center of the body, parallel to the spinal column, as they spin; energy is moved up and down the body. Eastern healing methods refer to these wheels of energy."

"I'm familiar with chakras," said Angi. "Years ago, I learned meditation from a guy I dated who was from India. He taught me about chakras."

Noting some uncertainty in other faces, Moira remarked, "Later, I'll get more on chakras on the Internet."

Nat picked up the jasper gemstone. Silence prevailed as he went through a well-honed routine, all the while mumbling something to himself and jotting notes in his small black book. His audience watched and waited to hear the verdict. Upon completion Nat returned the gemstone to its tiny box, sat it next to the first gemstone box and began, "This jasper is rather unique. It is almost perfectly jade in color except for this fine artistic marking on one side. It bears a great similarity to the sapphire in cut and age. Jasper belongs to the chalcedony family and comes in a variety of colors including: red, brown, pink, yellow, green, grey/white and shades of blue and purple. The green color and patterns found in these gemstones are created by the organic material and mineral oxides. Jasper was a favorite gem in ancient times, often referenced in Hebrew, Assyrian Greek and Latin literature. The mineral is known as the 'supreme nurturer' and considered a sacred stone. For this reason, it was worn by aboriginal shaman to protect them in their magical practices." Without further fanfare Nat, completing his comments, smiled and turned to Wolfram.

"OK, we'll now move to Moira," said Wolfram.

In repetition to the two previous Guardians, Moira removed an identical box from her satchel and placed an amber gemstone on the table, its rich warm color absorbing the lamp light. "Most of you will be familiar with Amber. My knowledge of amber is somewhat limited. It is supposed to help you attain your goals and in healing it transforms negative energy into positive." Completing her say, Moira returned to her chair to await Nat's review.

Again, Nat took his time examining the gemstone. Then, as before, he returned the gemstone to its original box and placed it next to the other two. "Again, this gemstone is similar in craftsmanship, age and quality to the other two. Now that we have three, it appears that we are looking at a piece of jewelry with identical slots for a number of similar cut stones. This piece of amber is almost flawless, which in itself is unusual. As you may know, amber is a fossil resin, usually yellowish brown, but on occasion it can be deep brown to red, green, or blue. It is an amorphous hydrocarbon and may contain particles of various foreign materials, trapped insects, and even air bubbles. Its luster can run from greasy to resinous. It is said that amber stimulates the intellect and opens the crown chakra. It is a sacred stone to Native Americans and East Indians." In closing, Nat turned to the final Guardian, "Since the first three gemstones are different, I expect yours, Angi, will follow suit?"

Responding to the cue Angi reached into her travel bag and pulled out a larger box of the same intricate gold/silver engraving. She opened the clasp and laid the gold medallion on the table, an amethyst gemstone snuggly positioned in one of the slots. Relieved, she thought, "There, it is done! I've fulfilled my family's responsibility. The medallion is now in the hands of the other Guardians." Her overwhelming relief blinded her to the reaction of the others in the room.

Stunned, after centuries of silence, secrecy, and mystery, the impact of seeing the actual medallion for the first time, overwhelmed the other Guardians. Never in their lifetime did they expect to see such a wonder. The impact varied; one strained to get a better look, another held back a tear, a third let out a loud gasp. The first to speak was Moira.

"Mother of God, is that real? Are we actually looking at the medallion itself? What in God's name forced our ancestors to send this medallion to America in the 1600s? Imagine the risk......the sacrifice...... the trials they endured to protect it. It doesn't look like much sitting there, does it? This was one hell of a responsibility placed on your family Angi? What did you say your ancestor's name was?"

"Stewart," replied Angi, suddenly realizing the impact of her offering.

"Is there any chance you might be a descendant of the royal family of Scotland?" asked Moira still struggling to grasp the significance of the medallion's presence.

"I'm sure if we had any royal connections someone would have mentioned it over the years. There wasn't a peep."

Not letting go, Moira persisted. "Perhaps that's the whole point; your family line had to remain incognito to protect the medallion, and what a splendid hiding place, a wee island in Canada."

Realizing the medallion's presence had complicated matters, Wolfram hesitated, as he wanted to get the gems examined, although having this one attached to the medallion seemed to leave the topic somewhat mute. His grandmother intervened.

"Let's stay on course. Nat, can you examine Angi's gemstone without it being removed from the medallion?"

"Yes, it is a bit more complicated but we are looking at an amethyst, which is common enough." Taking another look he blurted out, "But this is no common amethyst." Turning he asked, "Angi, do you know anything about this gemstone?"

"Only from the little I've read. The amethyst is supposed to be a calming, protective stone, excellent for meditation and to accelerate the development of psychic abilities. Some say it is a stone of spirituality and contentment. It was well suited to my grandmother, who exemplified both psychic and spiritual qualities." Angi remained seated as she spoke.

Nat picked up the medallion to examine the amethyst. After his usual procedures he reported to the group. "In my opinion, the four gemstones are identical and were obviously created for this piece of jewelry. Amethyst is a violet variety of quartz; the color is due to irradiation, which causes the iron ions to rearrange themselves in the crystal lattice affecting the color. On exposure to heat, the irradiation effects can be partially cancelled and the gemstone can become yellow or even green. The ideal grade is called "Deep Siberian", and this stone is more than equal to that ideal. The amethyst is known to balance the energies of the intellectual, emotional and physical bodies by clearing the aura and stabilizing any dysfunctional energy. Now, this brings us to the end of our main objective, and I can state that these four gemstones are genuine. However, I'm afraid I am witnessing a number of anomalies which conflict with some of my current gemology knowledge."

"Nat, for clarification, you are confirming that the four gemstones are genuine. Correct?" asked Wolfram.

"Yes, in my opinion based on this field examination. A lab certification would give it official status," replied Nat.

"Understood," Wolfram responded, as he nodded to the four Guardians, amazed that they had achieved their key objective. "Now Nat, what do you mean by anomalies, and could these negate your original assessment?"

"Not likely," came Nat's hesitant reply, "the anomalies, while interesting, simply expand the mystery. Let me begin. First, in all my years as a gemologist I have never encountered a stone like that round one in the center of the medallion. It might be a rare specimen of another gemstone but it doesn't possess the usual properties I'm familiar with." Looking into the distance, he shook his head, and began slowly, "I could get drummed out of my professional organization for what I'm about to say. First, let me share with you an ancient tale that periodically surfaces in this business. Legends say that thousands of years ago there were mysterious blue stones which were protected in the temples of Sumer and Egypt."

"What was so special about the stones?" asked Vette, caught up in the evening's activities.

"That's the unknown. What little filtered through the centuries, was that they possessed some magical properties that only the high priests could control."

"Where did they come from?" asked Jessie.

"Well, that's the catch. There're supposed to have been rescued from Atlantis before it was destroyed. Some say the stones will reappear in this century. Most people scoff at such tales, but we've learned that ancient legends often hold a grain of truth."

Tyloar couldn't contain his silence. "This is pure madness! This medallion has bewitched you. I'm surprised to hear such foolishness from you Nat. Last night someone mentioned Druids and the 2012 Doomsday Prophecy, and tonight we're talking about magical blue stones from a forgotten, and non-existent, civilization which most intelligent people ignore. Don't you think we should keep to the world of reality?"

Before anyone had a chance to reply, Nat, smiling, turned to Tyloar. "Well, if you think that's a problem then the rest of my anomalies will make you even more uneasy. Gracelyn, Tyloar, and Wolfram you and I have encountered some odd things over the years, some right here in the Boston area. Well this may be the kingpin. Before you dismiss any of this, let me continue."

Lifting up the medallion, Nat went on, "The last time I saw gold workmanship of this quality and this type of rose-pink gold was in the Cairo Museum when I had the privilege of examining a few pieces of the King Tutankhamen jewelry collection. As you may, or may not know, Tut, the boy king, was one of the last pharaohs of the Eighteenth Dynasty of Egypt. He

95

died about 1352 B.C.E... At that stage, the Egyptians had large quantities of gold, and their craftsmen were capable of creating exquisite pieces of art and jewelry. Today we know that this rose-pink gold was deliberately manufactured, but we still don't know how they did it. Of importance, is that such gold was only the prerogative of the royal family."

Tyloar, in disbelief, stepped forward to examine the medallion. "Nat, you must be kidding. You are implying that this medallion might belong to some Egyptian pharaoh. I thought it belonged to a group of British aristocrats in the 1600s?"

"Tyloar, what I'm hypothesizing is that the workmanship and gold in this medallion could date to the 18th Dynasty of Egypt, or, and it is highly unlikely, someone at a later date was able to duplicate the same quality. Before we get caught up with this anomaly, let me draw your attention to the second."

"Since you are determined to challenge existing reality, go on. What else do you have up your sleeve Nat?" asked Tyloar, wondering if he was prepared for more dents in his world view.

"You will see that the design appears to be Celtic, but it could just as easily be Scythian. Now the Scythians around the time of King Tut were trading partners with the Egyptians. According to the Scottish Declaration of Arbroath of 1320, the Scythians travelled by way of Spain to Ireland. This might explain the origin of the design which is not so much Celtic as Scythian. It might also provide the Egyptian/British link."

"I've never heard of the Scythian connection to the Scots," said Jessie.

"Well, if you get a chance to dance your fingers over your Internet keyboard you will assuredly find a great deal on it," replied Nat, not wanting to take time for a history lesson. "Now let me add another wrinkle. So far the four gemstones we've examined are similar to those recorded in the breastplate of the High Priest of Israel. The other four would confirm or negate my hypothesis that there may be some correlation between this medallion and the breastplate."

"My God, what would possess you to think of that?" demanded Tyloar.

"Well, the time period and specifics about positioning stones and their protective properties. You will recall, in the book of Exodus, God gave specific instructions as to how to fashion the Breastplate of Aaron and exactly where each stone was to be placed," said Nat as if lecturing to a group of university students. "At dinner tonight, when Wolfram commented that the medallion stones had to be reinserted in their original state, it sounded familiar."

"I am not up to date on the Bible, I will take your word for it," said Wolfram. "But weren't there twelve stones in Aaron's Breastplate, and, I believe the gemstones were a square cushion cut?"

"Admittedly," said Nat, "this medallion has nine stones, if you count the center one, and the cut is definitely different. However, if the remaining four stones are similar to those in Aaron's breastplate then we might be looking at the Israelites as the point of origin for this medallion."

"Interesting," replied Wolfram, "I once read that many ancient civilizations thought the number nine symbolized a deep religious truth, and some thought it represented perfection, balance and order. The Chinese thought nine was a symbol of change. So the nine stones might have greater significance than we thought."

"I also remember reading that nine was the symbolic number for Merlin. In numerology, nine is also considered the eternal number, the optimum number of the 360 degree ring. I'm sure there's more," said Angi, fascinated by the diversion.

"Let's leave the speculation on the number nine for now. Because at this point you've theorized that this medallion might belong to the Sumerians, Egyptians, Scythians or Israelites. Of course we're not forgetting Atlantis. What else? I would think that is sufficient but I see you have a puzzled look on your face, Nat?" asked Tyloar, still struggling with the ramifications of Nat's earlier revelations.

"Until now, it was understood that the marquise cut was created at the end of the seventeenth century during the time of Louis XIV, the Sun King of France. Yet, this medallion has eight marquise sockets, meaning there are eight gemstones. We have identified four. It would be logical to argue that the gemstones and gold were created at the same time for some specific purpose, possibly religious. Someone else might argue that the stones were cut in the 1600s and placed into an existing piece of ancient jewelry. This latter argument does not hold for a number of reasons, one being that these gemstones are both old and unique. I could tell you more if I had a chance to examine them in my lab. So, it is my opinion, this medallion could originate about 1300 B.C.E... or even earlier. If true, then our history of the marquise cut needs to be revised. The Egyptians may have beaten the Europeans by centuries."

"Is it out of the question that the ancient Egyptians were capable of creating a marquise cut?" asked Wolfram.

"No. The Egyptians had centuries to improve their craft. What we do know, is that they were capable of some fantastic achievements. Just think of the treasures found in King Tut's tomb; the diadems, necklaces, pectorals, amulets, pendants, bracelets, earrings, and rings of superb quality and high degree of refinement which have rarely been surpassed or even equaled. I'll leave this theorizing for now until we have more proof, but I'd stake my reputation on the fact that the medallion was created centuries before the 1600s."

"To summarize," said Angi, having followed Nat's argument with rapped attention, "the medallion's date could be much older than these beautifully engraved storage containers?"

"Right, the boxes are seventeenth century French or Italian craftsmanship, maybe even Tuscany. Wouldn't you agree Gracelyn?"

"Yes, now that you mention it, the technique is definitely seventeenth century," replied Gracelyn.

Nat picked up one of the small boxes and continued, "A fascinating feature of these boxes, and one you may not have noticed, is a cleverly constructed mechanical mechanism to secure the gemstones and medallion. Watch this." He opened one of the boxes, turned it up-side-down and shook it, to the horror of the group. Nothing happened. The gem stayed securely in place. "I noted the pull of this mechanism when I returned the gemstones to their boxes. Considering the era of the construction, these were expensive purchases when you take into account the number and shape of the boxes. The workmanship and materials in these boxes alone could be worth a fortune."

"We could be at this all night, and the hour is growing late," interjected Wolfram. "Let's leave these puzzles for later. What still needs our consideration is whether we should or can reinsert the gemstones into the medallion. Moira's probability argument last night stands, without a blue print we're stymied."

Each member toyed with the possibilities. After a few minutes Gracelyn spoke up. "Wait, I remember an odd phrase of my great-grandmother. Before she died, she kept saying the medallion 'will recognize its own'. Do you think that has any significance?"

Angi jumped to the challenge. "O.K, I know we're grasping at straws, but let's take the statement as given. Suppose we position the three gems beside the medallion and see what happens. What can we lose?"

Nat, seeing the logic, carefully removed the gems from their tiny boxes and positioned them within inches of the medallion.

The expectation was huge; the probability one in a trillion. ....Silence engulfed the room as they sat staring at the medallion. Five minutes passed......... Then as restlessness was beginning at the end of ten minutes, Vette whispered "Look!"

The blue center stone began a pulsating rhythm of fine sparks spinning clockwise. As the spinning increased, minute sparks danced around the periphery of the stone. Before anyone had time to react, an arc of lightening shot out from the stone, engulfed the sapphire, and raising it into the air brought it down into a socket on the medallion, sealing it firmly in place. Seconds later, another arc grasped the jasper and in the same manner inserted it firmly into another slot. A third arc followed the same course retrieving the amber stone. With the fourth stone in place, half of the medallion was complete. The electrical current ceased and the stone returned to its quiet pale blue state. The electrical display left a faint burnt odor near the table.

Stunned.........bewildered.......mesmerized........speechless......the group sat frozen in their chairs. Minutes passed.......the clicking sound of the hall clock dominated the room........no one moved....... unable to put into words what they had just witnessed. Nat broke the spell.

"God forbid what power this medallion possesses when all gemstones are in place. I've never witnessed anything like this." Turning he stared at Tyloar, "All bets are off......I have no idea where this comes from or even if it belongs to this world. The date of origin is up for grabs." Staring at the medallion again he went on, "Since we have begun to use gemstones for technology, is it possible our ancient ancestors knew this as well? Archeologists would disagree. Nevertheless, it seems to be an energy source. But it begs the question, for what was it built?" Thinking....... "Wouldn't it be ironic if, in completing some cosmic cycle, we are just discovering technologies already familiar to our ancestors?" Taking a few minutes to consider his own question, he continued, "It is no wonder this medallion has been buried for centuries. But in waking it up are we bringing peace or hell to humanity?"

The small group, who had come together as strangers, for the first time, faced the frightening magnitude of the treasure their families had protected for generations.

"Now what?" said Wolfram, still struggling with his own reactions.

Jessie reacted. "I remember something else about the awaking of the medallion. My grandmother said that if I was around when it happened, and God forbid here I stand, then the medallion must have human contact until all the stones are in place. According to her, the selection of this Guardian would be clear."

Nat, still lost in his world of analysis, said, "Perhaps that's due to the power source. Maybe a particular human genetic pattern can keep this dynamo stabilized. This would confirm my earlier comment that it was only the temple priests who could control the blue stones of Atlantis."

"Good God, are we back on Atlantis," replied Tyloar, getting somewhat testy with tiredness.

"Tyloar, forget Atlantis, we must stay focused," said Gracelyn, and turning asked, "Jessie, have you any idea what your grandmother meant by the selection process?"

"No, she never elaborated. But let's resort to the simplicity we used with the gemstones. Maybe if the four of us try on the medallion there might be a sign. If that doesn't work then we'll have to think of something else." Jessie picked up the medallion, saying, "I'll go first."

Within seconds she screamed, "Take it off! It is burning me! .....Quick, it is burning my skin! Angi jumped up, released the clasp, and carefully removed the medallion noting the second degree burn mark on Jessie's neck. Gracelyn scurried off for ointment.

"Well, that's definite," said Moira. "I'll go next."

Moira and Gracelyn had identical reactions. The three then turned to Angi, the final test candidate.

Fastening the clasp, Angi waited for the expected burning thinking "It can't be me. I'm overdue for a different test. It is likely someone in Britain." Instead of a burning sensation, Angi was jolted by a bolt of nausea, followed by a blinding light, and then oblivion. Wolfram and Vette jumped to cushion her fall.

Chapter 6

Boston, Rosie's Bar and Grill

Waiting for a predator to attack is nerve racking. Fred and Gritty calculated Antonino had to make his move, and soon, the unknowns were when and how.

Bodyguard routine was becoming second-nature. Fred nodded to Gritty as he passed, acknowledging the end of his shift. Reorganizing his car for the long hours ahead, Fred contemplated the situation, "This case is like babysitting two unpredictable children. Morgan is still not convinced he's a target, and Kari-Ann keeps dancing to her own drummer; a troubling mix. Routine security work is looking better all the time." After several weeks he had created a well organized field office, equipped with the latest electronic gadgets.

At 7:30 in the evening he lazily watched Kari-Ann back her car down the driveway. "There goes Goldilocks, off to Rosie's. What a light-weight....... nearly forty and still no idea what she wants to do in life ....totally self absorbed........it is good she never had kids. She's a poster child for what ails our society; too much money and not enough responsibility. This fun brigade marches on singing and dancing." As the car slid past, he did not know what possessed him to take a second glance, but when he did he saw Morgan pull himself upright on the passenger side of the front seat.

"Morgan, you are a stupid, God-damn imbecile!" Fred yelled. As he ignited the engine and swung the car into position to follow, he pressed his car speakerphone to contact Gritty.

Gritty responded on the first ring, "What's up?"

"Morgan, against all sanity, has just left with Kari-Ann. I expect their heading to Rosie's. I'm in pursuit. I'll keep the line open. We suspected as much, but hoped for better."

"I'm on my way. Since I'm closer, I'll get there before them. Antonino's snagged her. She's a perfect pawn."

The one advantage Fred had was that neither Kari-Ann nor Morgan bothered to check to see if they were being followed. Kari-Ann was absorbed in the bright lights which lay ahead while Morgan was convinced this was his last act before contacting his lawyer.

Kari-Ann, parking the car at the rear of the restaurant, selected a table for four near the entrance for quick recognition. Being a weekday night, the place was busy but not overly crowded. Morgan ordered drinks while they waited for Tony Moretti, Antonino's Boston alias.

Gritty, preceding them used the employee entrance at the rear. Finding a table near a large plant he waited as, he thought, it was imperative that Antonino appeared before exposing his hand. There was the remote possibility that this was an innocent outing not needing rough intervention.

But within fifteen minutes Antonino appeared, in slight disguise. Recognizing Kari-Ann he headed right for their table. Gritty was close enough to see the slimy grin on his face as he shook hands with Morgan. "Now I have to act," he said to himself. Bringing out a couple of crisp bills to seal his intended negotiations, he signaled a waiter

Before Tony, Kari-Ann and Morgan had time to settle, a male waiter appeared looking at Morgan, "Sir, I'm terribly sorry, could you talk to the manager over there. It is about your credit card."

Reacting, Morgan exploded. "Damn it, Kari-Ann have you maxed out all our credit cards?" Angry and embarrassed, Morgan got up and followed the waiter saying, "I'm sorry, Tony, I'll be right back."

As he reached the counter, a firm hand grabbed him from the side and pulled him around the corner. Gritty, red with fury, whispered loudly, "Look at this photo you idiot!" pressing Antonino's photo into Morgan's face. "Does that look familiar? ……….. You have just shaken hands with the devil."

Fear engulfed Morgan, "Christ……….Kari-Ann has delivered me to my doom. God, I must be the biggest idiot in Boston."

"Let us not get into measuring your stupidity. What the hell were you thinking? I do recall saying 'anything out of the ordinary'. Did she drug you or use sex to get you into this mess? You are now in deep shit and I have to bail you out."

"I can't go back there," replied Morgan in a panic.

"Listen to me! You will go back and you'll do exactly what I say, or so help me, I'll do you in myself. We can't call in the police as, at this stage, it is only our suspicion that he orchestrated those other killings. I have no doubt he's guilty and you'll be the next corpse if you don't obey my instructions." Gritty phoned Fred who was parked outside. "Antonino's here and Morgan knows it. So, we'll go with the plan we concocted earlier."

Giving Morgan orders he went on, "You get back to that table. I haven't got time for details just do exactly as Fred says. I'm working on the premise that Antonino doesn't know Fred, but he might have fingered me at the university."

Stiff legged, Morgan returned to the table.

"Is everything OK?" asked Tony, appearing interested in his victim's welfare.

"Sure, everything's fine," replied Morgan, relaxed as he could be under the circumstances, "another card worked."

Within minutes of Tony ordering a drink, Fred barged through the restaurant door heading right for their table.

"There you are, you pipsqueak!" said Fred in a loud voice, aiming his remarks at Morgan. "You promised me you'd complete that report tonight so I would have it first thing tomorrow morning. I arrived at your place to deliver some more info just to see you drive off with your wife. I followed you here to find you living it up with your friends and will likely be too drunk to even look at a computer when you get home." Gripping Morgan firmly by the shoulder he continued, "Sorry, folks this report is critical to my survival. This guy's coming with me. These are bad economic times and I have a wife and three kids to feed." Roughly steering Morgan towards the door he went on, "Come on, you can party tomorrow."

While Fred was in full performance, Gritty snuck closer and took a number of photos of Antonino.

Antonino wasn't sure. "Was this an act? It is all feasible but still, why do I feel like I am the victim." Looking at the confused expression on Kari-Ann's face he realized whatever just happened she wasn't party to it. "I can't lose this perfect stooge. Maybe I'll slip away.......give me time to think. If it is legitimate, then I can set this up again. If not, it means the police could be closing in. I still need the name of whoever contracted Morgan for this medallion research. Kari-Ann may know more than she thinks." Standing up, speaking softly, he said, "Kari-Ann, perhaps, we could leave this for another time. There's no rush. I'll be in touch." With that he turned and made a b-line for the exit.

Kari-Ann, dazed at the unexpected outcome to her well-planned evening sat forlorn, unable to sip her drink. "What was that black bodyguard doing here, she lamented. What's this about a report.......he's not at the university." Depressed, she picked up her bag and dragged herself to the door.

As she inserted the car key, Gritty slipped into the front seat beside her, angrily blurting out. "Are you mad, or do you give a damn what happens to your husband? Maybe you are incapable of caring for anyone but yourself."

Irritated at Gritty's presence and manner, she screamed "You and that God-damn partner of yours just destroyed my movie career! Why should I care what you think? Why would anyone want to kill Morgan, he's just a stupid history professor."

Resigning himself, Gritty started giving orders. "Look here lady; you just about delivered your husband into the hands of a killer, one with a trophy of dead bodies. He's no movie producer, he's a serial killer. He'll not hesitate to kill again. But living in fantasyland you are resistant to such realities. So, I'll be specific. You are going to drive straight home. I'll be sitting on your bumper. There you will stay while Fred babysits your husband, is that clear?"

"Fine, have it your way. My evening's ruined anyway," replied Kari-Ann almost in tears.

Kari-Ann parked her car in front of their garage, and ignoring Gritty, entered her house.

Gritty assumed Fred's position across the street for the night shift. Once settled, he used his car speakerphone to contact Fred.

"How's our boy, do you have him securely grounded?" asked Gritty.

"Yah, he's fine. Nothing sobers one up faster than to realize that your own wife just about fed you to a killer and would do so again if given the chance. I almost feel sorry for him."

"Don't feel too sorry, he helped her do it. My warning slipped right through that huge brain. I'm sure he has some noble reason for his action. Anyway, tonight he'll stay with you while I keep an eye on Kari-Ann. Let's hope she's learned something. Talk to you tomorrow."

"I'll send my cousin, Alfie along with some coffee and bites," said Fred, "you weren't prepared for this."

"Thanks, I'll need lots of coffee. It is good Morgan has that bathroom near his pool or we'd have been truly screwed with this case."

Next, Gritty pressed his speed dial for Gus, who was known for working late.

"Good to catch you, Gus. I'm faxing some photos I captured this evening of our killer. He's definitely here and almost claimed another victim."

"Good, the photos will give us more ammunition. We've tracked him to his car dealer. He still needs to act on our patch before we can nail him," replied Gus. "What happened to Morgan?"

Gritty updated Gus on the evening's events, closing with an agreement to keep in touch.

His final call was to Wolfram. Waiting, he thought, "This was a close call. Antonino may already suspect Morgan is out of reach, so his next option is Kari-Ann. He'll strike again and this time it could be lethal. He's running a dangerous gambit with his criminal relatives on one side and the police and us on the other. But what can Kari-Ann divulge........if anything? I'd hate to have my fortune resting on that one. God help her.........I'll have to stay alert."

&

The Weston Estate, Boston: Revelations of the Medallion

Powerless, Angi kept falling backwards into a black pit....... down...... down...... finally landing on a hard bed. Through the darkness a gray apparition appeared beside her. The ghostlike eminence had no discernible face. Angi strained, "I cannot tell whether it is a man or a woman." Then a soothing voice, "Don't be afraid, I'm here to help you." Next, Angi saw a hand-held flashing device moving up and down her body, its final motion producing a warm sensation up her spine. The voice returned, "Now, go back, your friends are waiting."

In the distance, Angi could hear faint murmurings...........then a garbled cacophony, as she dragged her spirit through the pitch black toward the sound. Questions swirled; "What happened? Was it an electrical shock? ....What was I doing? .... Sluggishly, the puzzle unfurled ...."The medallion....... electrical arcs, like delicate fingers, grasping gemstones .... then the cool metal against her skin." Her physical body stubbornly resisted her commands. The voices grew distinct......... She could recognize Gracelyn's strained voice.

"We haven't been fair to this young woman. In the past few weeks she's gone through an awful lot; first, her grandmother's death and funeral, then this trip to Boston. Her grandmother was practically her entire family. Yet, since she's arrived we've been totally absorbed in this medallion. Tonight, was just too much."

Vette reacted silently, "Angi's no weakling. She's a Director of a large Emergency Department. Admittedly, her illness complicates things, but her reaction was more like someone being hit............perhaps it is the medallion. God knows. This has been a weird evening."

In a stupor, struggling, Angi reassured herself, "Finally, I have feeling in my hands and feet." She was lying on the dining room carpet, having been covered with a throw from the adjacent room and a pillow placed under her head by Moira. Both Wolfram and Vette, familiar with emergencies, were in charge.

Gracelyn kept mumbling "Maybe we should fetch a doctor or an ambulance," but hesitated when she saw Angi move.

Wolfram responded, "Let's hold off for now, Gran."

Angi opened her eyes to see the concerned faces. Trying to speak, she blurted out, "Wow, that was a wallop............. I'm OK.............. Just a fainting spell, something that rarely happens to me." She tried to rise.

"Would you like a snifter of Brandy," asked Tyloar, showing genuine concern for his young guest.

"Thanks," said Angi, "I'm feeling a bit wobbly." With Vette's help she made it to the nearest chair. As the warm Brandy slid down her throat, she began to get her bearings. "Now I remember," she said, out loud, "While I waited for the burning sensation of the medallion, three things happened in succession; nausea, a bright light, then blackness. It was like someone switched off the lights. I've fainted before but nothing like this." She made no reference to her invisible caregiver.

"How do you feel now," asked Wolfram, "any side effects?"

Before Angi had a chance to reply, Moira interjected, "My God, I forgot what we were doing," Pointing at Angi she exclaimed. "Look at Angi's neck. There's no burn mark!" Smiling, she continued, "Well, Angi, I guess you are it, at least for this round."

"No, wait a minute," argued Angi, "this can't be. I need to get back home. This was supposed to be a brief trip to deliver the medallion."

"Sorry, old girl," replied Moira, "the gods have spoken. Just to complicate your life, I recall, that under the present circumstances, the chosen one cannot remove the medallion until all gems are in place."

"You are kidding," replied a skeptical Angi, "even in the shower or when I go to bed?"

"No exceptions," continued Moira. "Those were the exact orders dispatched from my female relatives."

"But what if we never find the rest of the gems?" asked Angi growing somewhat irritated at the thought of being permanently tethered to the medallion.

"I honestly don't know. You have to admit, there's no script for this adventure. All I remember them saying is, if only a portion of the stones are available when the chosen one is found, it would be dangerous for her to remove the medallion until the rest of the gems are in place."

"Dangerous........Are you suggesting this device could release some kind of lethal trouble?" asked Angi growing concerned about her own safety.

It was Nat's turn. "Angi, remember what I said about the Egyptian priests. As I see it, your genetic makeup somehow stabilizes this device. You have to admit, there's no electrical sparks or burning. So, Moira may be right. If you remove the medallion you could upset some fine tuning. Seeing its electrical demonstration in the retrieval of the gems, this is one baby best kept in slumber. Come on, what we are talking about, maybe a few weeks at the outset."

His logic registered with Angi, "OK. But this begs the question. What happens when all the gems are in place? Do you think I could remove it safely then?"

"That's an excellent question to which I have no answer. As I recall the legendary snippets stated only certain Egyptian Temple Priests had the ability to control the Atlantian blue stones. This medallion has, as I expect, one of these stones plus a number of quality gemstones which likely work in sync. That's about our total knowledge. I'm sorry Angi we haven't the answers you need. What we do know is that within this group of four Guardians, you are the one with the right genetic chemistry to safely carry this medallion to the next step. That doesn't rule out others with a similar constitution. Perhaps you will find them in Britain."

Resigning herself, Angi looked at Wolfram, "I guess there's no short cut. I'm in for the long haul." Pondering the situation, she said to herself, "On the other hand, it is better to end one's days on a mystical quest than sit waiting for the grim reaper. If that's my destiny, so be it." Then, directing a question to the group, she asked, "What's our next move?"

At that moment Wolfram's cell phone rang. He flipped it out of his pocket and answered. "Hi Gritty, Oh..........." and immediately departed to the adjacent room to continue his conversation. Behind him he could hear the chatter of the group as they pondered Angi's question. Returning, Wolfram's grim face broke the spell.

"What's happened?" said Tyloar. "The news isn't good."

"I'll not mince words," said Wolfram. "This evening Antonino, our Italian predator, almost nabbed Morgan. Thanks to the two bodyguards we've hired, he's now safely under wraps. However, Antonino's getting close and desperate. We must assume it is only a matter of time before he gets my name which will lead him straight to you."

The news struck home. As the four Guardians looked at each other, the magical spell of the medallion was superseded by the cold realization that a merchant of death hovered nearby. Tyloar whispered to Nat a quick explanation of the ancillary menace.

Jessie, in her practical manner, spoke for the Guardians, "We'll just have to move faster than this killer. He's not going to win. Just think of the generations who risked their lives in protecting this medallion. There's no question, Angi has to go to Britain to get the rest of the gemstones. Let's get those two contact names and proceed with the travel arrangements. I can see no reason for all of us to make this trip to Britain."

Wolfram, glancing at Angi and Vette, responded to Jessie's logical assessment. "I agree. We could move faster if there was just the three of us; Angi, Vette and myself. I might as well tell you," nodding to Vette, "Vette is an RCMP officer, sent to protect Angi. I would like her to go with us."

The group turned momentarily to look at Vette, some already suspecting her role. There were no questions.

Wolfram continued, "We'll head to Ireland first, then Scotland. I'm assuming the four gemstones reside somewhere in Ireland, Scotland and Wales. We have the names of two Guardians and that's where we begin. I've already been in touch with Morgan's other university contact, Andrew Sinclair, a professor at Edinburgh University."

"Good," said Gracelyn. "Moira and Jessie can stay with us. We'll work on the premise that the gemstones will be retrieved in weeks not months.......if not, then we'll devise another plan. Is that workable for you both?" looking at her two guests.

Hesitantly, Moira responded "Well, my family insisted that if we got to this stage that I had to complete the journey. I can manage a few more weeks."

"I'm OK as well," said Jessie. "Like Moira, our families expect us to complete this, whatever it takes. But is there any way we could notify them without endangering anyone?"

Wolfram thought for a moment, "I could send your e-mails through my friend Josh's secure system, if that's OK with you both?"

"Fine, they will know we are with your grandparents." Looking at the three potential travelers, Moira went on, "Let's agree that once you get all the gemstones, and I feel certain this will happen, you will notify us if there is any further need of our guardianship. No one mentioned what we were supposed to do once the medallion was activated."

"Certainly, I'll communicate through Josh. He'll keep you updated. I'll contact him tonight. By seven tomorrow morning, I'll call Andrew to say we're heading his way." His thoughts racing, he went on, "As an extra precaution, I think it best for me to travel by way of Amsterdam while Angi and Vette go via Canada to Dublin. Now, Angi, we will need the name of your grandmother's Irish contact to let her know we're going to land on her doorstep within the next 48 hours."

"Fine, I've already talked to her twice in the past weeks. In light of time zones, I'll call her in the morning." Hesitating, she went on, "I've got a problem. I wasn't expecting an extended trip, so I'll need to get some clothes and supplies for the trip. I believe Vette is in the same boat."

"I'll help with that," said Gracelyn. "I know a trusted lady who buys clothes for several of my friends. She'll come to the house with a selection of items for you two, and you can choose for yourself. Just give me your measurements and what you need. We'll work out something for your personal items."

"Wow," thought Vette. "How's that for service. But, I'll have to talk to Angi. I may manage the drop off in Britain but I'll need my father's help to extract more time from the police force. Admittedly, I'm owed at least four weeks of vacation, but on short notice it'll be difficult to get approval. At best, I could end up flying back to Canada after depositing Angi, and then, if all goes well, making another trip to Britain. It is iffy." Smiling to herself she reflected, "Who'd have guessed I'd be a globetrotter."

"Then it is agreed," said Wolfram, already processing the arrangements in his head. "Let's hope this Scotsman is an agreeable fellow, as we'll need miracles to accomplish this mission and stay out of Antonino's clutches."

Nat, returning his field lab to their respective cases, turned to his hosts. "Tyloar, Gracelyn, Wolfram, this has been a night to remember. I hope, in time, you will let me know how this unfolds. Angi, Vette, Wolfram the best of luck on your quest. This rather inconspicuous piece of jewelry could be a powerful talisman." Looking at Tyloar again, he smiled, "Let me know if any of my theories bear fruit. Wouldn't it be ironic if tonight we were the midwives to a lost technology of our ancestors." Picking up his cases he headed towards the front door. "It has been a truly amazing evening..........thank you for inviting me..........truly amazing......" and with that he bid them good night. The fog was beginning to dissipate as Nat's car exited the gate in front of the mansion.

Exhausted, Tyloar prepared nightcaps for his guests but not all were ready to retire; Angi made arrangements with Gracelyn to call Ireland, Wolfram contacted Josh, and Tyloar slipped away to talk to his security team.

As the group departed, the apparition, which had lingered, smiled, saying, "Finally, the Guardians are coming home." With that she evaporated.

Boston: Morgan's House

Despondent, dejected, and desolate, Kari-Ann dragged herself up the stairs to her bedroom and threw her handbag across the room. Flopping on the bed, she started talking to the ceiling. "Damn those bastards........What do they care if my life's in shreds ....What was that scrawny bodyguard talking about. He likes giving orders. ....Morgan blew it. He'll not be asked again. I didn't want him anyway. ....I must get in touch with Tony, I can't let this opportunity slip away."

She rose and glanced out the window. The street light revealed Gritty well ensconced for the night. "Creep........he thinks he's got me caged. I'll outfox him. With my luck he likely never sleeps." Then she remembered. "Aha, but he's been with Morgan all day, and he's old. He can't hold out forever. I'll bide my time and when he drifts off, I'll slip away. Now where did I put

Tony's business card?" She frantically went through several purses, jacket pockets and notebooks. "Nothing............perhaps if I take a break, I'll remember. I stupidly hid Tony's card from Morgan. What was I thinking, Morgan would never check, not a jealous bone in that numb body. It is time I ditched him. I know I can do better, this time I'll get a richer husband."

Kari-Ann went downstairs and poured herself a drink.......then a second..... and a third. She dozed off on the den sofa watching some mundane TV show unable to follow the story or care what happened. It was four in the morning when she woke with a splitting headache. She went into the living room to check on Gritty, only to discover he was still wide awake. "He's tougher than I thought. But he can't last the night. I'll have a shower, and then I'll search again for that card."

Emerging from the shower she remembered putting something into a pant pocket and dashed into her closet. Triumphantly she emerged with the business card. In large hand writing on the back was Tony's Boston phone number.

"I can't call at this hour I'll wait until 5:30am. In the meantime I'll get some coffee and something to eat." She checked the front window. "Damn, he's still upright."

On the stroke of 5:30, she went to the phone. Hesitating, she got the courage to dial. Tony's immediate response relieved her anxiety.

"Sorry to call so early in the morning but I was wondering if we might get on with the contract, it looks like Morgan's not available," said Kari-Ann, trying to sound nonchalant.

"Where's your husband?" asked Tony, Antonino holding to his Boston alias, wondering how she could be calling if Morgan was in the house.

"Likely at the university where he usually stays if he has an all-nighter. He'll likely be back later today." Kari-Ann did not think this unusual.

Tony couldn't believe his good fortune. He had already dismissed Morgan but he could pump Kari-Ann. In a voice dripping with charm, he responded, "Kari-Ann, I do indeed have your contract and we should get this settled today."

Ecstatic, Kari-Ann, anxious to seal the deal blurted out, "How about this morning?" She couldn't believe her boldness.

Responding to her enthusiasm, Tony replied, "How about breakfast at seven."

"Where are you located?" asked Kari-Ann.

"I'm staying at the Back Bay 920 Hotel downtown, on Portland Street near the West End Recreational Complex and Haymarket Station. You can't miss it. It has a huge sign as you turn the corner, and there's underground parking, essential in Boston these days."

Happily Kari-Ann replied, "Oh, I know it, I went to a wedding there a couple of years ago. No problem. See you about 6:45am."

Making full use of his time, Tony contacted a cousin. He needed a favor. After the call he continued packing his suitcase.

At 6, Kari-Ann checked on her bodyguard. "Eureka! He's asleep. He's one tough hombre." She grabbed her purse, pulled on her jacket and ran to the car. Not a minute to spare. She eased the car down the driveway, turned gently and drove off.

&

The screech of the garbage truck brakes woke Gritty. "Damn it......." He jerked awake, knocking items off his lap. "What time is it.?" He checked his watch. "Seven." At that moment he spied the vacant driveway and cursed.

"Shit, she's done it now! Nothing I said registered. She's still chasing rainbows." Wasting no time, he needed help and dialed Gus, hoping he'd be in early.

"Gus, no time to chat, any chance your guys got a tag on our assailant; maybe the name of a local hotel or something? Kari-Ann's skipped, and I am certain it is a fatal mistake."

"They've traced his car to the Haymarket area, another day, we'd have him," answered Gus, recognizing the urgency in Gritty's voice.

"That's close enough. I'm off. I'll check the hotels in the area". Gritty threw a few loose items into the back seat, and aimed the car down town. He had little time to lose.

&

Tony was waiting in the lobby when Kari Ann arrived. Instead of heading towards the restaurant, he redirected her towards the elevator with an apology. "Sorry, Kari-Ann the restaurant doesn't open until 7:30am. So, while we're waiting we can get those papers signed."

"That sounds good." said Kari Ann, seeing the logic of his comments.

In the room, Tony brought out the familiar documents and signed them, handing a copy to Kari-Ann. Next, he cleverly manipulated the discussion to extract the information he sought. "Just curious, does Morgan do research outside of his academic responsibilities? A lot of academics do these days for the extra cash."

111

"What do you mean?" asked Kari-Ann unprepared for the shift in conversation.

"Well, do people contract him to look up historical information on old items, let's say an old manuscript or book they might have found in their family attic? Morgan might do this as a private contract for which he would be paid."

"If he did, he never told me," replied Kari-Ann, now wondering what else Morgan might have kept secret.

Undeterred, Tony tried again. "Maybe he might do research for a friend?"

"The only one he'd do that for is his university buddy, Wolfram. They've been friends for decades. Years ago they had their own band," replied Kari-Ann happy that she could contribute something.

Tony pressed on, "What's Wolfram's last name?"

"Stark," was the immediate reply. Then Kari-Ann, seeking recognition, embellished her comments. "He's had a bad car accident which left him disabled. Now he's into some kind of fraud investigation stuff. He used to be a policeman."

"That's it!" said Tony to himself. "Someone hired this Stark guy to authenticate an antique. He goes to his friend, Morgan, for help. It all fits. So, it is Stark I am after. I'll get my relatives to get the goods on this guy." No longer needing Kari-Ann, Tony moved to the next phase of his plan.

"Kari-Ann, let's seal this contract, the beginning of what I know will be a great movie career with some 'happy dust'. It is what all stars do these days. How about it, are you game?"

"It is a bit early, for me," said Kari Ann, overwhelmed with the occasion.

"Who cares about time........in the movie business every hour is the right one. You are in the movie world now, it is time to celebrate," said Tony, trying to exude an enthusiastic attitude.

Realizing her success at finalizing the contract, with a sly smile, she replied, "Why not. You only live once."

Tony was ready. A cocaine packet and nose straws suddenly appeared.

Feeling euphoric after the first fix, Kari-Ann didn't resist when Tony suggested a second. She watched as he shared the first but never checked on the second. Unknown to her, the second batch was spiked with recreational drugs and levamisole, a livestock de-worming medication known for its fatal results. Tony's 'happy dust' was free of any negative properties.

Time passed. Still high, Kari-Ann did not demur when Tony said he would be right back and left the suite. Enthralled with her new life she drifted in and out of wild and sometimes frightening images.

About 11am, Gritty reached the Back Bay 920 Hotel. He showed the photo of Antonino and Kari-Ann to the desk clerk and got an immediate response.

"I haven't seen the woman but that guy checked out this morning around seven."

"Are you sure? What room was he in?" asked Gritty, not accepting the news as he was certain Kari-Ann was in the hotel. He knew Antonino, once he had what he wanted, he'd discard his latest pawn, using the hotel routine to aid his escape.

"Rm 460" replied the desk clerk.

"By any chance has that room been cleaned yet?" Gritty persisted in his quest.

"I can check. It has been busy we have a full house with a national convention in town. It looks like it is not done yet."

Pressing his point Gritty argued, "This could be a security matter. Get your manager. We may already be too late." Noting the clerk's hesitancy he raised his voice. "For God sake man, you do not want a homicide on your premises, do you?"

That registered. "Hell no!" replied the clerk as he buzzed the manager and security.

Within minutes Gritty was leading the way to the elevator with the hotel manager, and a security guard, one he knew.

From the opened #460 doorway, Gritty spied Kari-Ann sprawled on the floor. Checking her pulse he demanded, "Call an ambulance, there's still some life. Chances are slim but we have to try."

"Drugs, that's all I need. An overdose," was the manager's unsympathetic response. Closing the door, he went to the telephone to order the ambulance and to get the room sealed off knowing a police investigation would follow if this woman died.

"Not exactly," said Gritty. "I believe this is a homicide" and to himself "but it'll take a miracle to prove." Seeing the white powder on the table, Gritty used his pocket knife to flip a small sample into a plastic bag which he carried for such purposes. Glancing at the security guard he went on, "Old habits die hard. I'll get this to Gus for analysis." The guard nodded.

The guard knelt down beside the body, "Gritty, have you noticed these purple blotches on her ears, mouth and cheeks? I haven't seen them before. Any idea what might have caused these? They're ugly."

"Yes, I saw them. That's why I need this powder tested. It is likely contaminated, and done deliberately. It is the hallmark of this guy I am chasing."

At that moment gritty noticed a piece of torn paper near Kari-Ann's extended right hand. Turning the paper over he saw, in a badly scribbled hand, "Help Wolf". Silently he thought, "God help her. With a brain fogged with drugs my warning finally registered. She had given Wolfram's name to the devil. I must act swiftly."

The Ambulance appeared and one attendant informed the three that they were transporting Kari-Ann to the Boston Medical Center.

As the manager alerted his team to seal off the room, Gritty called Fred. "I've got bad news. Kari-Ann's en route to the Boston Medical Centre. Her chances are not good. I suspect she's been poisoned with contaminated cocaine. I'll follow the ambulance and meet you and Morgan there."

Next he called Wolfram. "Kari-Ann has become Antonino's latest victim. She's headed to the Boston Medical Center." He then briefed Wolfram of what had happened, including Kari-Ann's note. "Sorry old friend but it looks like you are next. My advice, get to hell out of Boston. Leave this clean up to Gus, Fred, and myself. I'll explain to Morgan. Let's hope we can stop this madman here in Boston or he will be haunting your every move in Britain."

Concerned, Wolfram asked, "What do you think her chances are, Gritty?"

"Not good. I'm not even sure she will make it to the hospital. What a waste. She didn't deserve this." Gritty replied, "I may not have liked her, but I hoped to prevent an ending like this."

Understanding the gravity of the situation, Wolfram reassured Gritty, "We'll take the first flights we can get tonight. I'll keep in touch through Josh. Tell Morgan how sorry I am that Kari-Ann got caught up in this terrible mess."

&

Boston: Antonino Leaves for Britain

His ruthless philosophy of leaving no incriminating baggage meant that Antonino needed a new hideout for a few days to rearrange his plans. His cousin had the answer.

There was little regret in eliminating Kari-Ann. His only concern was whether he had erased any incriminating evidence that he supplied the drugs. Detached, he reviewed his steps, and then reassured himself "Even, if she lives, her brain will be so scrambled that she won't be making sense for ages. That gives me plenty of time to get on with my quest. My gut tells me I'm on the right track. All sources indicate that whatever this is, it could be worth millions. Stark is the key."

As he followed his cousin's directions, the quality of housing deteriorated. Finally, locating the address, his heart dropped. His new accommodation was a run down, non-descript stucco, ranch style house, with two vehicles parked in the driveway; a half-ton pick-up truck and a Jeep. His expensive sport's car would be a thief's delight, except everyone knew a crime family owned the property. Thievery was the least of his worries. His cousin appeared and introduced him to another hoodlum and a middle-aged woman; fat, tough and humorless. "A few days in this dump and I can ditch America. That will suit me fine," were his comforting words as he unpacked his suitcase in a small bedroom.

Within twenty-four hours, through another relative in the tourist business, Antonino learned that Stark was booked on a flight to Dublin via Amsterdam. In assessing this news, Antonino calculated, "Dublin, I suppose he's checking out another antique. Is this to do with one item or several? Ignore Ireland I'm sure he's heading to Scotland, after all that's Morgan's other university contact. While O'Gratteney's files said little about Scotland, that doesn't mean Dr. Sinclair isn't in on this. I'll need to check. What was the name of that Edinburgh University faculty member I met at a conference in Dublin? I'll get the name in the faculty listing on the Internet, if I can find a computer in this hell hole."

That evening, he found his contact, and called Scotland the following morning. Offering a substantial incentive, he received a quick turn-around call to say that Sinclair was expecting two Americans as house guests, one being Wolfram Stark. Smiling, Antonino hung up the phone saying out loud, "I'm an absolute genius. I'll head to Scotland and get there ahead of Stark." There would be little time for celebrating. At that moment his cousin appeared to say that there were two men in the living room, his cousin's uneasiness signaled trouble.

Antonino entered the living room to greet two heavy set men, well-known as Cosmo Scarpoli's enforcers. Marco, the oldest, spoke, "Come, the Boss wants to talk to you." Resistance was pointless.

Silence filled the car as they drove. Arriving at the luxurious, well guarded Scarpoli estate, Antonino was escorted directly to poolside. There, sitting alone reading the paper was Cosmo, a thin, muscular man in his late fifties drinking coffee. He folded the paper and looked up as Antonino approached. Seizing the opportunity, Antonino, stepped forward with an outstretched hand saying, "It is an honor, sir, to meet you. I want to thank you for all the help I've received since coming to America."

Making no effort to respond, Cosmo stated in a commanding voice, "Sit down, priest." In a gravelly voice, he continued, "It is only because of a debt owed to your mother's family that I have tolerated you on my turf. You have a strange way of honoring my hospitality."

Antonino felt it was in his best interests to remain silent. He could feel the riveting malice of Cosmo's eyes from beneath his sunglasses.

Cosmo then proceeded to lay out the reasons of his discontent, "Antonino, you have been lying to us since you arrived, not a commendable quality in a priest. I have just learned of the hit you arranged in Canada, which exposed our Montreal family to unwanted police attention. Then, within the last week I discovered the Boston Police are looking for your car, and in the last twenty-four hours, they've fingered you as a suspect in the case of a professor's wife who overdosed at a local hotel. I also know you obtained cocaine from your cousin. These nasty incidents are troubling, and certainly do not fit your initial tale of having some academic argument with a university colleague. Do you wish to comment or clarify any details?"

For the first time in his life Antonino felt a cold, sickening feeling in the pit of his stomach. He had always prided himself at being able to slide easily between the law and his criminal connections. He had learned early in life that it was foolhardy to cross crime bosses. Yet, in his lust for gold he had ignored this basic survival tenet to his own peril. He had no defense, so said nothing.

"Your silence reveals a lot. You've strutted through America with little regard for anyone or any rules. In addition, bringing extra police attention on our family at this time is most unfortunate, for both of us. It is only because of your family that you continue to live," the threatening statement hanging in the air. "You are no longer welcome. You will be taken back to your place, pack your bags and these two will drive you to the harbor. There you will board a yacht heading to Miami this afternoon. I wanted to make sure you understood my reasons and that your expulsion from Boston is under my orders. I will contact your family accordingly."

With sweat dripping down his back and lip, Antonino, not wanting to add any more fuel to the fire, had but one response, " What about my car, it is a rental."

"We'll deal with that. Give me your car keys." Antonino obliged on command.

As Antonino got up to leave, Cosmo added, "If I hear you are one of those priests who have been abusing children, so help me I will take out a contract on you myself .... Do I make myself clear?" Cosmo sealed the end of the meeting by picking up his newspaper.

"Yes, sir" came the quiet reply, as Antonino joined his escorts. In the car he thought to himself, "What a hypocrite. A guy who makes his living on every illegal business including prostitution is passing insinuations on my life. But under the circumstances, I'll not argue, or offer any flip comments. That would be fatal."

Without fanfare, Antonino's Boston exit was decided for him. His reception at the yacht was frosty. For the entire trip his stomach churned expecting a blow to the back of his head and a watery burial. For courage he kept repeating to himself, "If I make it to Miami, I'm taking the first taxi to the nearest airport and getting the hell out of this country. It is only a matter of time before my Vatican record reaches Cosmo. Then I'll need eyes in the back of my head."

Chapter 7

Ireland, Galway Bay

Unable to sleep, Brigit dressed, took her mug of tea out to the sundeck, and sank into a deep-cushioned lounge chair. Sipping the warm brew, she scrutinized her kingdom. The sun, peeking over the horizon, kissed the wave tips and bobbing boats with a golden hue. She watched as it crawled towards the Aran Islands. Then solemnly, she lifted her mug in salutation, "Top of the mornin'. What a grand day to welcome home the Serpent's Medallion. It has been well away from these fair isles considering the hellish time we have had for centuries. Our hard-won freedoms have singed many an Irish soul, the lament seeping through our stories, poems and music. But today is a time for rejoicing. A cosmic cycle nears its completion."

She pulled herself up for a better view. "Here I sit on these blessed shores of the west coast of Ireland. Where else could one feel the magical presence of Celtic gods and goddesses, Druidic seers and bards, the Tuatha De Danaan, the Celtic Christian saints, and the aura of that phantom isle of Hy-Brasil, sitting cloaked off in the distance. Whether she knows it or not, the surname of the medallion's courier, has been well chosen - Talismann - how prophetic. Although we never met, I always held Nellie as family. What a tragic end to such a fine woman. But we all knew the price of being a Guardian. It could have been any one of us. Now it is my turn to participate in this grand drama." Rising, she headed towards the house. "No time for dawdling, my four guests will be here in a few hours."

Brigit (Cahill) O'Keefe had spent her entire seventy-two years in the Galway area. Her father was a well-known General Practitioner. At twenty she married Naill O'Keefe who also became a doctor, teaching at the University College Hospital located beside the university. The university was now known as the National University of Ireland, Galway. She had three pregnancies and two living children; a girl and a boy. At thirty-one she began her studies in Old and Middle Irish history, and by forty had a PhD, eventually teaching Celtic Studies at the same university as her husband. A widow of six years, her husband having died of cancer in 2006 at the age of seventy, she faced an inevitable move from her cherished bay a decision she hoped Fate would decide for her.

The four travelers departed Dublin about eight in the morning for an expected four hour drive to Galway Bay. So far, everything was going according to plan. Upon arrival in Dublin, Angi and Vette went to the Bawly Hotel, a short distance from the airport, to await the arrival of the others. In time, Wolfram appeared from Amsterdam and Dr. Andrew Sinclair from Edinburgh with two companions; Dana Norcross, a female associate from his history department at Edinburgh University who was a Celtic history expert and Dylan Gabriel, who he had hired as a driver. Few details were provided on these two companions. The meeting was brief. Andrew, because of prior commitments, had to return to Edinburgh. He would join them later. As expected, Vette had to bid her good-byes in Dublin to return to Canada, but vowed she'd return.

Angi and Dana sat in the back seat of the blue Peugeot SUV while Wolfram did map duty in the front with Dylan. Dylan's skill at exiting Dublin during the morning rush-hour spoke volumes. Their journey on the M6 motorway would take them westward to the outskirts of Galway. It was a clear day, the sun dancing across the green fields.

Still jet-lagged, Angi relaxed, trying to conserve her energies and ease the nausea which kept reoccurring. This being her first, and possibly last, trip to Ireland, she wanted to soak in every scene. She wasn't in the mood for much chit chat. The medallion had now become part of her. There were no untoward comments as she slipped through airport security systems. With some free time, she began to assess her new travel companions.

Dana was a slight woman, with dark brown hair, piercing eyes and a somewhat fragile personality. In her late forties, she was an associate professor at Edinburgh University. Symptoms of her recent divorce erupted in her occasional sarcastic comment about men. "The fact that her former husband was an American doesn't endear her to Wolfram and me," thought Angi. "Her anti-American jabs, cloaked in humor, are not appreciated. Let's hope she gets past this." Dana's English public school accent portrayed her posh school upbringing, a fact she imprinted on Angi in their initial conversation. From the little Angi could gather, Dana had been in Scotland for about ten years, having gone there from London with her American husband when he got a well-paying job with a technology company. With both jobs, even with the economic downturn, they lived well. Two surprises were that this was Dana's first trip to Ireland and she portrayed scant interest in the medallion. Angi got the impression that Andrew had not divulged much, so she followed suit.

Dylan, she knew, was more than a hired chauffeur. His silence and rapid action portrayed recent frontline experience, possibly military. A stocky individual, his hardened athletic physique, and alert mannerisms, to both traffic and his surroundings, conveyed a message of someone under strict orders. Conversation was terse and there was little humor in his frozen expression. Angi thought to herself, "I'll let Wolfram get a bead on Dylan. I'm sure he's been hand-picked by Andrew." Then she smiled, "Perhaps it is because of his surname. We could use an angel or two."

On the outskirts of Galway they stopped for directions to Brigit's house which, they were told, was about twenty kilometers west of the city centre in Inverin, a peaceful Gaeltacht village, where the main language was Irish. They had no trouble finding the stately white house with its large bay windows perched on a raised outcrop of land overlooking the bay. The wide driveway had gardens, trees and bushes on the right, raised flower beds in the front garden, and, to the left, a winding path which seemed to lead down to a secluded beach. The house, once exclusive, was losing its uniqueness as new housing developments encroached on the property. Sea gulls trumpeted their arrival.

Within seconds, Brigit, a stocky woman, with graying red hair dressed in casual slacks and a loose top, exited the front door to greet them. From Nellie's letters, Brigit immediately identified Angi who was the first to alight from the van. "Well, well, well, what a delight to welcome Nellie's granddaughter. Angi, my dear, I feel as if I've known you all your life. Nellie's letters were filled with your accomplishments. She loved you dearly. Welcome......a thousand welcomes to my home and this Sacred Isle," and she stepped forward and hugged Angi.

Angi was touched by Brigit's warmth, it was like coming home to a cherished aunt. Pulling herself away from the embrace, she turned to introduce her companions. "Brigit, this is Dana Norcross from Edinburgh University, Dylan Gabriel from Scotland, and Wolfram Stark from the United States," further details were either unknown or unnecessary as she had recently chatted with Brigit on the telephone in making the arrangements. With formalities over, they grabbed their bags and walked behind Brigit towards the house.

At the entrance, a slim, red-haired girl, about twelve, stepped out of the kitchen. "This is my granddaughter, Caitlin Hegarty, who is staying with me while her parents, both doctors, are in Dublin," said Brigit proudly.

The house was deceiving. From the outside it looked like an ordinary bungalow, but its back split design expanded its overall floor plan. The large double windows gave the interior a bright cottage appearance, the mixed furniture décor creating a relaxed atmosphere. Brigit provided a few comments on their new setting. "The house is over sixty years old. There are two bedrooms in the lower level for the men, and three on this level." Smiling, she continued, "Gentlemen, this is not a segregation of the sexes, just the type of accommodations."

Caitlin escorted Angi and Dana to their similar- sized modest bedrooms with en suite bathrooms and windows overlooking the bay, the billowing curtains disturbed by a warm sea breeze coming in from the Atlantic. Brigit went with Wolfram and Dylan to their rooms, which also had a bay view but were smaller with a shared bathroom. Once settled, Brigit invited her guests for refreshments on the sundeck. As they sat around a deck table enjoying a welcomed break, they got acquainted.

Angi watched Caitlin as she replenished the trays. Fascinated with her short copper-red hair, she remembered reading that red hair, a genetic mutation, existed in less than 4% of the world's population, the highest percentage found in Scotland and Ireland. Looking into Caitlin's hazel eyes, Angi contemplated, "Caitlin's a perfect candidate for the medallion. She's looks the part, was born in Ireland and likely speaks Gaelic. I'll tuck that away for later."

"This is a magnificent view," said Wolfram, looking out over the bay and the Aran Islands, "have you lived here long?"

"My husband and I renovated an existing house in the sixties, and chose the site for its view," replied Brigit.

"How has Galway faired in the recent economic downturn?" asked Wolfram with concern, having read about the Irish economy in a Dublin newspaper.

"They keep telling us that Galway is doing better than most. We're supposed to be the fastest growing city in Europe, and it is the third largest city in the Republic. I'm sure you encountered our summer traffic jam on your way in. There are still plenty of festivals and racing events during the summer which attract thousands. Obviously, someone has money but others are struggling. Galway keeps returning to its pre-occupation days of trade, commerce and making money, which should help us in these economic uncertainties."

Deciding to enter the conversation, Dana barged in on another tack, "Now that 'The Troubles' have passed life must be easier for everyone in Ireland."

Angi spotted Caitlin's worried look waiting for her grandmother's reply.

Brigit chose her words carefully. "Well, unfortunately, 'The Troubles' continue to haunt us, striking a major blow to our family in the nineties." Struggling to continue, she went on, "In 1993, my son of thirty-two, went to Northern Ireland to visit some old university friends. Unfortunately, they chose the wrong day to go to the Rising Sun Bar for drinks. That was the time of the Greysteel massacre. Eight civilians and others were shot, my son, badly wounded, died weeks later. The shooting was carried out by a small group calling themselves the Ulster Freedom Fighters, a loyalist paramilitary group of the IRA. My husband never got over the loss of his son and died of cancer over a decade later."

Dana blurted out, "Well, at least it wasn't the British who killed him."

Everyone froze.

Brigit response was crisp, "The IRA wouldn't have existed if it hadn't been for the British. As far as I'm concerned the occupation of Ireland was worse than the Black Plague. But let's speak no more of this," a command to change the topic.

Dana realized her blunder and shut down.

Angi held her fire. "How rude ....she's obviously brittle from her divorce but she doesn't need to take it out on everyone. Brigit handled it nobly, likely years of trying to be civil in dealing with such stupid comments. What's that old phrase, 'It is the conquerors who write the history books.' Such personal tragedies in our Western societies have been well sanitized in our history books. Imagine the hell my ancestors must have faced in the 1600s, caught up in insurmountable political and religious fanaticism which would take centuries to play out, the wounds still palpable in the 21st century. I have much to learn."

Desperate to shift direction yet wanting to say something about Ireland, Brigit pressed on, "For centuries, the Irish have endured much; a foreign occupation, a ponderous religion, famines, economic ups-and-downs, our citizens forced to flee to other countries and always this mystical climate of mist and drizzle and through it all, we have stubbornly survived. The Irish seem to have an inverse relationship with life; the worse fate throws at them the more we ratchet up our wit, words and song. We've watched the coming and going of a number of cultures and empires. It is no wonder so many are turning to our ancient, powerful and pagan past. Perhaps in completing some cosmic cycle, we'll rediscover our souls with our dignity intact." Glancing at her watch she announced, "Oh dear, look at the time. I need some private time with Angi. Can I leave you three in Caitlin's capable hands?"

Wolfram reacted. "I wonder Brigit, if I may accompany you both? I'll be glad to remain at a distance if you want to talk privately. Is that OK?"

Before Brigit could reply, Angi intervened. "Much water has poured under the bridge since my grandmother's death, Brigit. I would appreciate Wolfram's presence."

Brigit realized Nellie's death was likely not singular. Anyway, she thought, he's practically a Guardian, so responded, "No problem, Wolfram, come along." The three departed as Dana moved onto a lounge chair and

Dylan continued his lunchtime repast.

Dana felt out of place. "If I had known we were heading to Dr. Brigit O'Keefe's home I would have excused myself. She's got more credentials in Celtic culture than I have. She's known as an expert in the field, has written numerous books, and speaks Gaelic. After ten years I'm being surpassed in my own field by native Irish and Scots, many who speak Gaelic. I chose this academic specialty because I wanted to prove King Arthur was English, and enjoyed the limelight while it lasted. I was assured a senior university post until Andrew Sinclair appeared with his Scottish pedigree, international experience, academic credentials and he speaks several languages, including Gaelic. It is time to move on....but where; maybe London......or perhaps to something else? I wonder what skullduggery those three are up to, hell, who cares. Today, I'll soak up the sunshine and enjoy the sea breeze."

Brigit led the silent party along a well-worn, earthen path beside the house. They walked through flowering bushes to a shadowy enclosure with a circular well of large gray stones. Trickling water could be heard. The heavy treed canopy blocked out light and sound. One large tree, a hawthorn, commanded the site. Sunlight flickered through the leaves. Overhead the tree branches were decorated with rags, neckties, dolls and pictures. The air was cool, almost clammy. Angi's immediate reaction was, "How strange, it has an aura of timelessness. Maybe it is one of Ireland's sacred wells." Before she had time to ask, Brigit broke the silence.

"This was the second reason for buying this property. My grandmother and mother brought me here as a child. With all the upheavals my family felt this was the safest place to hide our gemstone, as rarely did the insurgents attack the sacred wells. Even the Catholic Church could not extinguish them so renamed them after female saints in recognition of the feminine principle."

"Brigit, what makes this place so special?" asked Angi.

"For generations we Irish identified certain places like this as 'thin places' where, we believe, the veil separating the physical world from the otherworld weakens. Thin places may be sacred wells, stone circles, old monasteries, places of natural beauty and, of course, the Hill of Tara. This concept goes back to the time of the Druids."

"What are the cloths for?" asked Angi, intrigued as she watched them flutter in the breeze.

"These are offerings, the cloths are called *clouties* by the Irish or *clooties* by the Scots, a slang word for rag which likely comes from the Gaeilge word *cluidin* meaning 'small covering'. My neighbors and others have free access to the well. The offerings are from many people over time."

Wolfram, taking the opportunity, shifted the discussion. "I saw your academic credentials on the study wall, Brigit; you have a PhD in Celtic

Studies. Does your daughter share your passion?"

"My daughter, a scientist, disowned her Celtic heritage years ago. She equates it in the same league as spiritualism. For this reason, I was training Caitlin to succeed me as the next Guardian."

As she answered their questions, Brigit circled the well three times clockwise. Stopping, she made an about face towards a stone wall hidden in the enclosure gloom. Above her head, she began to dislodge an inconspicuous black stone. Placing the stone on a small ledge, she reached into the opening and pulled out an oilskin bag. Undoing the tie, she retrieved a purple velvet bag, out of which she pulled a familiar gold and silver engraved box. From within the box she released a gemstone, identical in shape to the others, and held it up to catch the sunlight.

"Being Irish I would have preferred an emerald," said Brigit with a smile, "but this Golden Topaz was a perfect choice for our family. In my reading I learned that this gemstone attracts wealth, well-being and love, and is supposed to replace negativity with love and joyfulness, a quality I needed over the years. It is also known as the stone of true love and success. Now, Angi, is it possible for me to witness how the Serpent's Medallion receives my family gemstone as, I assume, it is unique?"

"Yes", replied Angi, receiving the Golden Topaz from Brigit and, taking a small plastic gem holder provided by Nat, she positioned the gemstone by one of its marquee tips and moved it close to the medallion. "I'm not sure what will happen as I've never personally held a gemstone like this for transfer but, I'll trust it'll do me no harm."

Within seconds, the center stone started vibrating, then the dancing sparks culminated in a single arc of light which lifted the exposed gemstone into the air towards the medallion, inserting it firmly into its rightful socket, and locking it in place.

Wolfram watched, "Just like a robotic-computer device, it recognizes each authentic gemstone and knows precisely its position in the medallion. It is likely set to reject substitutes. But when and by whom was this program designed? If the medallion is hundreds or even thousands of years old, it defies our current knowledge leaving us with overwhelming questions. I prefer predictability. This makes me uncomfortable. But I must press on with this quest if I ever hope to return to my life in Boston."

Speechless, Brigit whispered her first words, "Glory be to God........ How fantastic........what is it?........The rumors understated its power.......and it still awaits other gems. I can hardly believe what I've just witnessed. Thank you for allowing these tired old eyes this demonstration. The sacrifice was indeed warranted." Then, looking at the gemstone container she asked, "I suppose you want this wee box?"

"Yes," replied Angi, "for now we are collecting them in case they might be needed down the road."

Brigit returned the gold and silver box to its purple bag and handed it to Angi. She tucked the oilskin bag back into the stone safe, and placed the black stone firmly in place, tapping it and saying "Thank you for your protection." Turning, she explained, "We always give thanks for nature's blessings. Now, while there's time, let me try and answer your questions, for I'm sure you have many."

Wolfram responded, "Brigit, why did you call this the Serpent's Medallion?"

"It is called the Serpent's Medallion because it comes from the Dragon Lords of Anu, the Ring Lords, known to the Irish as the Tuantha De Danann."

Surprised, Angi asked, "Brigit, surely you are not referring to the Lord of the Rings saga? I thought that was fiction."

"Actually Angi, like so many books of fiction, there are often real facts hidden between the lines. The Ring Lords did exist, and it is this medallion which links these ancient people to the 21st Century. As a child I was told the medallion was left in this dimension, to herald *the coming times*. The Tuantha De Danann were known by many names; the Lords of Anu, the Black Sea Princes of Scythia, the Royal Scyths, the Good People, the Gentry, the Sidhe or the Tylwth Teg. Some say they were the neutral angels who were cast out of heaven after God banished Lucifer and the rebel angels to hell. Today, we dishonor their memory by referring to them as diminutive elves or fairies."

"Wow", thought Angi, "Mr Aucoin's, 'Lords of Anu' have finally surfaced." Overwhelmed, she responded to the possibility of Brigit's apparent comfort in revelations about Ireland's past, "Go on, Brigit, you are the first Guardian that seems to have any depth of knowledge about the medallion."

"To begin," asked Wolfram, "I'm assuming the Tuantha De Danann were not originally from Ireland, if so, where did they come from? When did they get here? And do they still exist?"

"Come, let us sit in this tree seat," said Brigit, directing them to a semicircular bench, beautifully carved from a fallen tree stump. Old markings, impossible to read, spoke of time and weathering.

Sitting with Wolfram and Angi on either side, Brigit continued, "It was said that the Tuantha De Danann came from the Black Sea, ruling Mesopotamia from the eighteenth to the sixteenth centuries B.C.E... They were considered the world's most noble race, alongside the early kings of Egypt. They settled in Ireland around 800 B.C.E... They were the oldest Ring culture in history, and in Ireland they were considered a race of god-men and women. One of the greatest Ring shrines still exists, you know it as Newgrange."

"I'm waiting for the Serpent connection," Wolfram asked, still focused on his original question.

"Well, the Tuantha De Danann were called the *Sumaire*, which in old Irish means 'dragon' or 'the coiled serpent'. In the past, the terms 'dragon' and 'serpent' were used interchangeably. It was said that the physician to the Tuantha De Danann was referred to as a 'Serpent', likely a title. Many cultures regarded the serpent as sacred, identifying it with wisdom and healing; the Sumerians, Egyptians, Israelites, Essenes (i.e. Therapeutae or the ascetic healing community) of Qumran, Vedic Hindus, Greeks and Romans, right down to our present time. The symbol of the central staff and serpent was thought to represent the spinal cord and the sensory nervous system with the two uppermost wings signifying the brain's lateral ventricular structures."

Wolfram pressed the point, "But why was this medallion called the 'Serpent's Medallion?'"

As Brigit spoke, Angi took another look at their newfound teacher. Brigit had a wise, gentle countenance, the years etched beautifully on her face. With few wrinkles, Angi deducted she had never smoked. She obviously loves teaching, possessing not only a depth of academic knowledge but that vanishing quality, spiritual depth. In this dreamlike setting ancient voices seemed to be speaking through this elder Guardian.

Brigit's voice echoed in the enclosure, "In time, the Druids, who arrived with the Tuantha De Danann, were given the medallion as their badge of healing. It was worn by the Arch Druid, a responsibility which required much training."

Angi, mulling over the new revelations, asked, "Brigit, I'm still struggling with the notion that the Tuantha De Danann are the wee folk or fairies in our children's books. How do you equate this with your version that these were a strong and powerful people?"

"I can understand your confusion, Angi, but this diminution of these people occurred in our era, mainly by political and religious people threatened by such facts. The Tuantha De Danann were far from small. The men stood six foot six and the women at six feet. They dressed in leather and woolen tartan clothes and were skilled with horses. They were fair, many with emerald eyes, just like yours, Angi, and were considered people of superior intelligence and artistic skill. As such, they were larger than mortals with an awe-inspiring radiance which explains why they were sometimes called '*the shining ones*'. It was said they evoked a sense of awe and respect."

"What happened to them?" asked Wolfram, still intrigued by this revised version of history.

"When a war between the Tuantha De Danann and mankind ended in a draw, the Fairies agreed to go underground, others say they went across the water, while mankind stayed on the surface of the earth," replied Brigit. "The unknown factor is what was meant by 'underground' or 'across the water'."

Now it was Angi's turn, "What you are saying, is that this medallion belongs to these fairy folk, an ancient people known as the Lords of Anu. Why then do I have it? What am I supposed to do with this when all the gemstones are in place? If this is some ancient technology, and you said that even the Druids needed training in handling it, who is going to train me, Brigit? At this point I'm both impressed and terrified."

"Angi, my dear, I'm not surprised you've been chosen to wear this medallion. My grandmother told me that your family, of the eight Sacred Gentry, possessed the highest genetic inheritance from this royal line. Not because your ancestor's name was Stewart, although that should not be dismissed, but because even by your generation, there must be a sufficient amount of the Dragon Lord genes to keep this sophisticated item in balance. That is a great honor."

Bewildered, Angi stared at Brigit and Wolfram. "A Dragon bloodline, that sounds ominous. Am I some kind of hybrid? We seem to be slipping into science fiction. It is no wonder no one in the family ever mentioned it, even if they knew."

"Angi, this is a lot to take in at once. The reason why it was never mentioned is that like so many families, after three hundred years, much of this information got lost. Angi, be proud of your heritage. Remember the sacrifice of your ancestors and the other seven families. They are counting on you to achieve this mission. The Guardians are still ready to assist you, however old we may be, and even give our lives if necessary. If all this is too confusing, remember your dear grandmother."

At that moment the image of her grandmother registered and calmed Angi. "I understand and will do my best. Thank you, Brigit for revealing this much to us. I hope this helps Wolfram and me in the days ahead," said Angi, with a cascading number of unanswered questions giving her a headache.

Not wanting to lose his chance, Wolfram aimed at one more mystery. "Brigit do you know anything about the blue stone in the center of the medallion?"

"It is likely one of the Blue Stones of Tara," replied Brigit, confidently. "Legend has it that there were a number of such stones from Atlantis. Perhaps you are aware of the recent book which argues that Ireland is a remnant of Atlantis. If so, then the blue stones may have originated here. That may explain another myth. Some say that the blue stones were given to Moses, and later brought to Ireland by Jeremiah when he accompanied the last Israelite princess after the sacking of Jerusalem by the Babylonians around 500 B.C.E... If so, then perhaps Jeremiah was returning the stones to their original home. Anyway, these are the blue stones which were used to establish the Druid Schools of Wisdom."

Wolfram couldn't hold back, "Angi, remember Nat's theories? We thought he was just theorizing. He may have been closer to the truth than we gave him credit. I hope one day I can tell him."

"We must get back, it is almost suppertime," replied Brigit, noting the shift in the shadows.

"A final question, Brigit," asked Angi. "By any chance do you know who has the original list of the eight couples?"

"I have the name of a Scottish Guardian who I have already contacted for you. She has the list. Her name is Fiona Stevenson and she lives in Scone, the old Scottish capital. Now Fiona is ninety-three, and the last member of her family. She is anxious to talk to you before her time runs out. Just for the record, my ancestors were Dermot and Grace O'Cregan."

As they turned to leave, Brigit added, "Angi, last night thinking of your arrival I remembered an old Irish prophecy. It is said that in this new century a great prophet, or prophetess, would arise in the west that would cause the Tree of Tara to blossom. Perhaps this is the purpose of the medallion. If so, I'd like to be on the Hill of Tara when you finally gather. In fact, I think it is imperative that all living Guardians be there with you to see the culmination of their family's sacrifice. Will you keep that in mind?"

"Brigit, Wolfram and I will do our best. We will need you with us for moral support for I suspect this journey will not be finalized until then. It would be nice if it is just the flowering of the Tree of Tara........but what else?" Regarding the prophecy she thought, "I'm no prophetess. My greatest hope is to return to nursing but these days I fear a Banshee may pop up. God knows how much time I have without chemotherapy."

As they exited the enclosure, Brigit commented, "We'll not discuss this with the others. If you need a further chat we can find a private corner. Before you leave in the morning I'll have some contact information and give you my cell phone number."

As they exited the grove, Wolfram spotted Dylan who had positioned himself at the side of the house giving him a strategic view of the area. "He's definitely on duty," thought Wolfram. Then aloud, giving Angi a familiar look, said, "I think I'll chat with Dylan regarding tomorrow's trip."

Another woman had appeared to help with the evening meal. It was a splendid Irish seafood feast; deep fried Celtic mushrooms, crab cakes, salmon rolls and a main casserole dish of sea scallops, shrimp, and crabmeat baked to a golden brown. With salads, bread and plenty of wine the group listened as

Brigit and Dana expounded on their knowledge of the Celtic world. Earlier negative feelings had been set aside for the evening.

Before retiring, Wolfram cornered Angi. "I believe Dylan is from some special military group with recent experience in the Middle East. Word is that our Antonino dropped off the radar in Boston, the street chatter indicating that his mob connections grew tired of his predilection for trouble. He was attracting too much heat."

"You don't suppose his relatives did us a favor?" asked Angi.

"Not likely. The British version of Home Security believes he's in Britain. By labeling him a potential terrorist, they hope to nab him before he has time to act. If he has learned anything, he'll avoid expensive cars, have a harder disguise to crack and, I expect, will be dogging our heels once we're in Scotland." Then with a smile and a wink he concluded, "Have a good night's sleep, Dragon lady."

Angi wasn't comfortable with her new title or even thinking about it. Before retiring she mused, "I thought life was complicated before, this is light years away. Maybe things will look better in the morning."

At midnight, the familiar apparition arrived and, once again, used a vibrating light over Angi's body. About to leave, she whispered "Welcome home, Angi. You are back on ancient ground. The next three stones will demand more but I'll be here to guide you." and with that she evaporated.

ɞ

Scotland, Inveresk: DunRoslin Castle

Having slipped into the twilight zone of Celtic magic and ancient gods and goddesses, Angi had few expectations, as earlier ones had long been dashed. It took all her energy to stay focused. As such, Dylan's off-the-cuff remark, "Andrew has connections," barely registered until they arrived back at the Dublin Airport to find a private jet waiting for their flight to Edinburgh. More surprises lay ahead.

In Edinburgh, Dylan picked up a silver, four-door Range Rover, and exiting the airport drove south bearing left on the A8, then right on the roundabout to the A720 to bypass Edinburgh. According to him, they were heading towards Musselburgh, 6 miles east of Edinburgh to the community of Inveresk where Andrew lived. At this point, Dana, delighted at being back in the U.K., began a lively repartee on their destination.

"Inveresk, located at the junction of the river Esk with the Firth of Forth, has been a favorite escape for Edinburgh gentry for generations. Recently, archeologists discovered two well-preserved alters to the Roman god Mithras. Over the centuries many armies have marched through the area. The village, a 19th century cottage development was created in front of large manor houses to shelter them from the noise and dirt of the main streets. When the cottages were demolished, their front walls became the garden walls of the mansions. The area was so highly regarded it was once known as 'the Montpellier of Scotland'." As she was completing this statement, Dylan swung the van between gray stone pillars, with '*DunRoslin*' chiseled distinctly on one, and entered a double-wide private driveway.

For a quarter of a mile they drove through a tree-lined road with manicured gardens on both sides. Then, the van approached an impressive, sculptured fountain in the center of a circular driveway near the main building. Parking the van under a portico, Angi alighted to find herself in front of a four-story, pinkish-gray, rough-cast castle with what appeared to be sandstone around the upper windows and turrets. Its storybook features included a rectangular tower, tall chimneys, semi-circular turrets and a coat-of-arms over the doorway. As Wolfram edged close to her while pulling their luggage out of the back of the van he whispered "My information said he was an Earl, a title he rarely used, but I didn't expect this." Before he had time to say more, Andrew exited the front door to greet his guests.

"I knew Dylan would get you here safely. He's off to drive Dana home. She lives nearby. Drop your luggage inside the door, my staff will take care of it for you." Angi, in awe, wasn't sure she was ready for such a social leap.

Andrew continued talking as he escorted them through the open doorway, "Welcome to *DunRoslin.* This place has been in my family for generations. Built in the 1600s, it has been renovated numerous times. The east wing is currently being updated so we'll keep to the center and west wings. DunRoslin sits on twenty acres overlooking the Esk River which gives us lots of privacy. There is fifteen to twenty staff, and as with any respectable castle, there are two resident ghosts; a 'Blue Lady' from the 1700s and a mischievous boy. I've never encountered either myself and no one has yet pegged their identities. With recent road changes, we are closer to the city and airport which is a bonus."

Andrew Sinclair was a disciplined man, observing strict dietary and fitness routines. Over six feet, he had a distinguished presence, his dark brown hair peppered with gray, and rimmed glasses gave him a professorial look. He walked with purpose striding through corridors as if on some urgent mission. He missed little, his piercing brown eyes scanning a room rapidly as if searching for some lost treasure. Possessing a mild Edinburgh professional class accent, his abrupt, bristly exterior disguised a quick wit and delight in a good laugh. The recent death of his wife of thirty years had left him restless.

They had three children; a son in business in London, and two married daughters, one in Edinburgh and the other in France. Only the daughter in France had children; two boys.

In his late fifties, Andrew had a notable reputation with an extensive network of contacts. For centuries, his family held prestigious Scottish credentials with direct ties to Rosslyn Castle, senior positions in the Knights Templar and military, advisors and ambassadors to kings and the Empire, and, in recent years, owners and directors of a number of British and international corporations. Money was plentiful and used with discretion.

Like his ancestors, Andrew, at seventeen, joined the Gordon Highlanders and advanced through the ranks to the position of Lieutenant Colonel. At thirty-seven, because of an injury acquired in the Middle East he retired from the military to pursue an academic career making good use of his family and military connections. He excelled in history and archeology, obtaining his PhD in the Scythian origin of the Scots as mentioned in the Arbroath Declaration of Independence. Currently, he was the Acting Head of the History Department at Edinburgh University, while the dean was on leave due to illness.

Irrespective of his military and academic achievements, Andrew longed for an extraordinary accomplishment, one that would bring honor to his heritage, Scotland or both. This was the reason he willingly joined two younger professors, Mandelthrope of Boston and O'Gratteney of Dublin, in their pursuit of a 17th century secret. He knew there were lots of secrets in the British Isles, some dating back centuries. So, he made time to search university sources, and contacted friends and acquaintances, especially those with private archives. Some months into the research, he received an invitation to a 'private' gathering of a secret society in Edinburgh. This powerful group of Scottish leaders confirmed the existence of an ancient lost treasure, one individual producing a faded sketch of a medallion. They agreed to help as long as they remained anonymous. So it was with great anticipation that Andrew welcomed Angi and Wolfram, for he was certain Angi possessed the tangible confirmation of this treasure.

The castle's entrance room had grand presence and little warmth. The coolness of the black and white floor tiles was ameliorated by the rose colored walls covered with commanding family portraits, tapestries, and a large tartan swathe. The carved wooden table with four uncomfortable matching chairs did little to improve the milieu. The space was designed as a temporary transition point.

As Angi and Wolfram set down their suitcases, a middle aged man, with a commanding presence appeared.

"I want you to meet Ian Fraser; he's my right hand here at DunRoslin. He rules this kingdom," said Andrew. Ian smiled, acknowledging his status.

"Ian, this is Angi Talismann from Canada and Wolfram Stark from the United States. As we discussed, I expect they will be our guests for some weeks."

Ian stepped forward and shook their hands, carefully assessing his new arrivals, and saying, "I will make sure your bags are placed in your rooms. I have an application for your cell phones to guide you around the castle."

Andrew, scarcely giving time for Ian's preliminary chat, continued, "Let's go to the Drawing Room on the next level where we can get better acquainted." He then turned and climbed rapidly up the white marble stairway, with its gray and gold carpet.

Following their host, Angi and Wolfram ascended the stairway taking an occasional glance at the family portraits framed in gold, some with similar features. Remembering the size of the exterior, Angi calculated, "I'll need a satellite navigational system in this place, even with Ian's map I'll likely get lost getting to breakfast."

The Drawing Room was another surprise. Some decorator, updating the interior had created a bright, modern setting with an air of relaxed luxury. A cream plasterwork ceiling was complimented by pale green walls trimmed with gold, elegant chandeliers, along with rose, mint and gold upholstered chairs and sofa and cherry-wood furniture. The pink-marble fireplace had an exquisite French clock trimmed in gold and the room was replete with costly ornaments. A small piano sat in one alcove and a round wooden inlayed cabinet in another. Huge windows, overlooking the entrance driveway and gardens, filled the room with light, several opened to admit an enchanting bouquet from well-placed bushes.

"If you don't mind, Angi, could you come to the window so I can examine this medallion in the sunlight? I didn't think it appropriate to ask this of you in a public place when we first met in Dublin," said Andrew.

Angi complied, pleased for the diversion from the challenges presented by her new living quarters.

Andrew said little as he inspected the medallion, but thought to himself, "It is an exact replica of the sketch................Three centuries have passed.......... this ancient relic has returned............. It is no accident............ I'll have to get word to the society as I'll need their help protecting this young woman. I'm sure she's aware of the mounting danger but we could be facing even more in the next phase." Then, turning calmly making no comment on his observations, he said, "Thanks, Angi. I'm curious, has there been any untoward activity of the medallion in recent days?"

"Only in its expected response to Brigit's gemstone," replied Angi, then realizing Andrew was unfamiliar with this, continued, "Each time a gemstone is placed near it, the center blue stone starts vibrating, then sparks appear around the edge which is followed by an electric arc which grasps the gemstone, places it in its rightful socket and locks it in place."

Wolfram added, "It is like a miniature computer but in saying that I realize this challenges our understanding of history. If correct, then hundreds, if not thousands of years ago, someone had a level of technical ability which we've assumed did not exist."

Seeming to momentarily ignore Wolfram's comment, Andrew, politely directed them to be seated, "Let's sit down, refreshments will be here shortly. Dinner's at seven."

Once seated, he continued, "Wolfram, I know you and Morgan have kindly kept me in the loop since Kevyn's accident but I realize much was avoided in our open communications. Now Angi, if you will be so kind, can you brief me from the time of your grandmother's attack? In that way I will be better prepared to help you with the next phase of this quest."

Without hesitation Wolfram and Angi proceeded with the update. For, before leaving Boston, Wolfram received a profile on Andrew from Gus's CIA contact. Thus, he was aware that Andrew was considered, in British circles as 'top drawer' with powerful contacts in the British government, military and even MI5. Knowing he would be in another country, Wolfram was pleased to have someone with such credentials on their side. He had conveyed this information privately to Angi as they waited for their Edinburgh flight. Angi covered the Canadian segment, leaving Wolfram to deal with the United States portion. As Wolfram concluded with the death of Morgan's wife, Andrew sat back.

"I'm sorry this turned out so badly for Morgan. While our contact in Edinburgh was brief, I liked the man, for all of his eccentricities. He had a brilliant mind and loved the Celtic world. He's had a key role in initiating this quest. Now, the last piece, what happened in Ireland?"

Angi and Wolfram described Brigit's comments on the medallion's history reinforcing Nat's earlier theories. While they chatted refreshments arrived and were devoured almost without thought. Around five, another individual appeared.

"Well, Andrew, these must be the guests you were expecting," said an elderly man in his seventies, walking cautiously with the aid of an ebony cane, his white hair crowning a broad face with a captivating grin.

"Indeed, old friend, come and meet Angi and Wolfram," said Andrew cheerily. "Angi and Wolfram, I'd like you to meet Bryce Roberts, who's also a guest at the castle."

Bryce limped slightly as he approached the three. "I'm glad you arrived safely. Dylan is a crack driver and has impeccable credentials in handling unexpected events."

Angi, analyzing his movements, thought, "His limping indicates he's either had a recent accident or surgery on that right knee. He's doing well but still in considerable pain."

As if reading her mind, Bryce commented, "I'm in from Cardiff for some knee surgery. I'm just back from rehab. Things are going well on that front." Then he zeroed in on a straight chair and sat down.

Angi liked this stranger, his friendly face and easy manner putting her at ease. She was getting use to the different accents but still struggling with the occasional word when spoken quickly.

Wolfram stepped forward to greet Bryce knowing, since Andrew said he might be there, that this friendly gentleman was far more than he seemed. This was Lord Lywillan, a rarely used title. He had a seat in the House of Lords, generations of family in top government jobs and was the past Vice Chancellor of Cardiff University. He had yet to convey this to Angi. Wolfram noted Bryce's keen observation of Angi's medallion which meant that Andrew had included him in the purpose of their visit. The question was, why?

They had little time to chat as Ian appeared to remind them that Angi and Wolfram had yet to get to their rooms to prepare for dinner. "With cocktails at 6:30, they will have just time to change before dinner," he stated.

"Yes, indeed," said Andrew. "We've got lots of time to get acquainted. I'll leave you in Ian's capable hands and see you at 6:30 in the Blue Room."

As Angi and Wolfram got up to leave, Wolfram glanced back to see Andrew and Bryce in an animated discussion. They followed Ian to the third floor of the west wing, through corridors of more family portraits. As they reached what was supposedly the bedroom wing of the castle, Angi estimated there were accommodations for about ten or more guests, perhaps more if additional rooms existed in the east wing. Wolfram's room was across the hall, and, she surmised, Bryce's was somewhere down the corridor. As promised, Ian provided them with the castle map App, pointing out areas to avoid and stating there were in-house telephones should they get lost. As Ian departed, and before heading to their respective rooms to unpack, Angi and Wolfram formed a pact to travel together, until they got their bearings.

Angi's room was a blend of old and new; expensive antique furniture with modern accessories. It was a large suite with a single bed, writing desk and chair, a curved bureau, a sofa and two upholstered chairs. A decorator had given the room a floral splash in the bedspread, drapes and window seat. More family pictures, this time in oval frames, graced the walls. A large modern bathroom opened off the bedroom. The windows overlooked the back sunken garden, where she noted a statue in a square fountain and a formal stream running the length of the garden. In the distance she got a glimpse of the Esk River, as well as a scattering of symmetrical flower beds, sloping lawns with shrubbery, and several well positioned benches. Noting the time, she unpacked and prepared for the evening meal.

Refreshed, Angi and Wolfram, with their castle map, struck out to find the Blue Room, supposedly adjacent to the Dining Room on the second floor. En route they passed the library, with its floor to ceiling shelves crammed with books, two computers visible in one corner, a rectangular table with stacks of books and documents, leather chairs and an alcove with stained glass windows, the evening sunlight creating miniature rainbows on the wood and carpeted floor. An adjacent room contained a distinguished desk and chair, more book cases and another computer. However tantalizing, they avoided opening a series of closed doors which held secret uses. The guide indicated the castle contained housekeeper and gardener quarters, a servant's hall, billiard room, gym, chapel, kitchen, laundry and storage spaces plus a wine cellar.

"I've a vague idea where the gym is located," said Wolfram, "and have Andrew's OK for us to use it. I'll meet you in the hall at 6 tomorrow morning and we can scout out its location. We'll likely get our exercise in finding it."

Earlier, Ian hinted at hidden chambers and secret staircases, necessities in past centuries. According to him, with the death of the Earl's wife, the east wing was being modernized with a future possibility of donating the estate to the Scottish National Trust. Apparently, the Sinclairs had a number of castles and residences, this was but one.

Eventually they reached their destination to find Andrew and Bryce ahead of them. Andrew looked up with a broad grin, "You are doing well, some guests get lost on their first few tries even with the map. What can I offer you both as a pre-dinner drink?" Angi and Wolfram opted to join Andrew and Bryce in a sherry, while Dylan, arriving at the same time, chose gin and tonic.

Andrew's opening statement was intended to calm concerns about talking about the medallion, "Bryce and Dylan have both been fully briefed on the medallion, so feel free to talk while you are here."

Wolfram wasn't so sure. While he had background profiles on Andrew and Bryce, he had nothing on Dylan. "I've got to get access to one of Andrew's computers in the morning to send a coded message to Josh for Gus's help. I'm uneasy not knowing who I'm dealing with. I trust Andrew and Bryce so it is likely not a major issue, just my predilection for detail especially with a killer on the loose."

Relaxing, the first, and rather unexpected, question came from Bryce, "Angi, I'm fascinated by names, can you tell me yours?"

An odd request, she thought, but complied, "It is Angela Jenesis Talismann."

"Interesting," replied Bryce, "was it your Canadian or American family who gave you the Jenesis name?"

"My father's family who lived in New York," replied Angi. "My parents were divorced and my mother died when I was a child. I had little contact with my American relatives. On the one occasion I visited them as a teenager, we never talked about it."

"Well, I'm sure you know, it is another form of Genesis," said Bryce as he glanced at Andrew.

Angi wondered why they were having this odd conversation replied casually, "I never thought much of it as I didn't like the name. You mean *Genesi*s like in the Old Testament?"

"Yes, the first book of the Old Testament. Genesis means '*a beginning*' and for some it means '*hope*'. So Angi, are you a beginning of hope for the world?"

"Odd" thought Angi. "Within days I've had Brigit talking about a prophetess and Bryce now mumbling something about a beginning and hope......... why do both statements rattle me? It is likely because I would like to tell them that I am just a courier of this medallion with little time for much else." But not wanting to expose her true feelings, she replied calmly, "Well, I think it was likely some family name which they insisted should be given to the first female child of their oldest son, nothing more," avoiding Bryce's question.

"That sounds logical," said Andrew with a smile and getting Ian's signal, continued, "I guess we'll have to leave it at that as dinner is ready."

The Dining Room was large, accustomed to grand celebrations. Its atmosphere was solemn elegance created by the dark mahogany furniture, wooden panels and huge paintings of battle scenes and family members in military garb relieved by the occasional female portrait from some past century. The setting was softened by the cream plasterwork ceiling, two large chandeliers, glistening brass and crystal, cream table linens and a large bouquet of flowers. The rectangular table sat in the center of the room on a thick green carpet, the chairs having matching green cushioned seats. Angi struggled to move her chair. Andrew positioned himself at the head of one end of the table with Dylan and Bryce on one side and Wolfram and Angi on the other. A cool breeze floated through the large windows.

Angi was amazed at how hungry she was and was looking forward to her first meal in Scotland. Along with a fine selection of wines, the meal consisted of asparagus soup, baked filet of salmon with Basmati rice, steamed vegetables with lemon and saffron sauce, and two dessert choices; apple pie and ice cream or brown sugar meringues with fresh lemon curd. The cheese board had crackers and oatcakes which arrived with coffee and tea. In the midst of such culinary delights and adamant conversation, the evening passed quickly. The medallion wasn't the center of conversation, but peripheral discussions had all to do with its existence. The dinner conversation took various routes according to the speaker. Wolfram began.

"Andrew, I realize that Brigit had little time to delve into the history of the dragon or serpent bloodline, but what fascinates me is that with all the historical material I've studied, little if anything has ever surfaced on the Scythians or this bloodline. So, either Brigit has an alternate version of history or there has been a deliberate obfuscation of this information."

"I suppose it is a bit of both," replied Andrew. "This alternate account is less known because it is very old and some people even today would prefer it remain lost in time. The dragon/serpent bloodline goes back thousands of years in what archeologists refer to as 'Before the Common Era (B.C.E.)'. Since our modern school system barely touches on the last five hundred years, there is an abysmal ignorance of ancient history. But symbols exist in our modern world. For example," picking up a green marble ornament from a nearby table, "take this Celtic Cross. Most associate it with our churches or cemetery markers, but it is actually a very old symbol. The cross within a circle was a graphic representation of kingship. The outer circle depicts a serpent clutching its own tail. The circle, sometimes called the *ouroboros,* has many meanings: wholeness, wisdom, totality of existence, infinity, the cyclical nature of the cosmos and seasons, as well as life and death. The Celtic cross had great significance to our ancestors for it was the original emblem of the Grail bloodline from the fourth millennium B.C.E.... It was also used by both the Druids and the Celtic Christian Church."

Angi, still struggling with Brigit's information, was fascinated by this new revelation. "Are you saying, Andrew, that the Celtic cross represents a royal bloodline that existed centuries before the fictional Medieval Grail stories? So, how far back are we talking?"

Andrew, delighted at the opportunity, continued, "This dynastic line existed thousands of years ago. It ran through the royal houses of Sumer and Israel, the pharaohs of Egypt, and down to Jesus. These special individuals were called the '*Purveyors of Light*' and were considered leaders of mankind. It may be of interest to you, Angi that this dynastic bloodline was matriarchal, through the females. It was this factor that the later patriarchal religious leaders feared. Since this is such a huge topic, I'll share some books with you while you are here. When you've had a chance to read them, we'll talk again."

"Thanks," said Wolfram, "I'll share these with Angi. She may have a

S. Robertson

definite interest in the topic," as he gave her a quick wink.

Ignoring Wolfram, Angi had her own question, "I wonder, Andrew, if you might clarify something for me. I thought the Celtic Christian Church was an earlier form of the Roman Catholic Church, but from my chat with Brigit, this may not be true."

Bryce picked up the challenge. "Well, Angi, you are not alone. Although a form of early Christianity entered Britain in the middle of the first century, there was no wide-scale conversion. At that time, life was based on druidic principles and many of the Britons maintained their old beliefs for a few more centuries. In 43 C.E., Roman records under Emperor Claudius cited Druidism and the Jews of Christos as being in Britain. The style of Christianity that came to Britain was Nazarene, followers of James the brother of Jesus. The Nazarenes favored the Old Testament, which was compatible with druidic thinking. Now it must be pointed out that the druidic order was not a religion, it was a way of life. However, because of this compatibility, when the same Roman Emperor decided to eliminate the Druids, he included the Nazarenes, stating that membership in either sect was a capital offence. With such a sentence, both groups melted into their communities. However, even after centuries of persecution, neither the Druids nor the Celtic Christian Church, a later version of the Nazarenes, were entirely eliminated. Both exist today although far removed from the modern Druidic examples you see in the media. As for the Church of Rome, it did not exist until the third century when Constantine, the Roman Emperor, adopted Christianity as the official religion of the Empire. He opted for one of many versions of Christianity which existed at that time. Centuries of religious wars followed to eliminate any opposition to this Roman version."

"From the little I know our ancestors paid a high price if they did not comply with the political or religious authorities of their day. Our generation knows little of this. I wonder if we would be as courageous under similar demands." Angi thought out loud.

"Indeed, Angi. Let's hope we don't have to face this again," replied Bryce. That old phrase holds true, '*those who do not learn from history are bound to repeat it.*' "

Wolfram, wanting to revisit another of Brigit's points, asked, "Andrew, what role did the Scythians play in this serpent lineage?"

Andrew was now on familiar ground, "As Brigit stated the Lords of Anu or the Royal Scyths were considered descendants of gods and goddesses, with special powers. So, it is not surprising that royal families in the ancient world wanted to intermarry with them. It was one such marriage of a Scythian prince and an Egyptian princess who landed in Ireland to become the ancestors of the royal families of Ireland, Scotland and Wales. I could talk

139

about this all night, but I'll leave it at that for this evening. I'll loan you a copy of my PhD thesis, it will give you some background for further questions and may put you to sleep."

Wolfram, realizing he was trying to get an injection of a mammoth amount of information, was glad to have Andrew streamline his search, so he pressed on, "Is there any possibility that these ancient cultures, thousands of years ago, possessed technology equivalent to what we have today?"

"Now you've hit on a tantalizing question which has puzzled many before you. My immediate answer is, yes, although it was likely very different from our modern version," replied Andrew. "Sadly, even with concrete evidence, many academics have dismissed the possibility or relegated it to mythology. Let's consider artificial light or electricity. Some believe that the ancient Egyptians possessed a form of artificial light because the interior of their tombs show no evidence of smoke from burning torches yet the artisans were able to do intricate paintings on the walls. In the Roman Empire there was mention of a golden lamp in one of Minerva's temples which was said to burn for a year at a time. And in the 4th century, Saint Augustine wrote about an ever-burning lamp which neither wind nor rain would extinguish. These are just three examples."

Then it was Bryce's turn. "I am sure you are also familiar with the Ark of the Covenant of the Hebrews which was thought to be a powerful electrical device. There are passages in the Old Testament which describe what appears to be an electrocution of those who mistakenly touched the Ark."

"That's right," said Angi, "I remember having an argument in Sunday school on that point only to have it dismissed by my teacher. And speaking of artificial light, I read that the Hopi in Arizona were supposed to have a generator for creating light out of some form of luminescent quartz. Apparently, friction produced by rapid rubbing made it glow in the dark. That was how they lit their sacred kivas."

"You see, if unknown artificial light existed, why not other technologies?" replied Andrew.

Now, Dylan, more relaxed, entered the fray, "Didn't I read about the discovery in an old Roman vessel in the Mediterranean which had a machine-like device that provided planetary information?"

"Yes, I read the same article," said Bryce. "That one got buried quickly after all we don't want our present achievements being undermined. And what about the scientific skills of the Arabs and Chinese, they even produced working robots. Or the many clocks found in museums which are mechanical devices."

Dylan added, "The arrival of engineers reviewing archeological sites has definitely introduced a different perspective. For instance, one engineer is arguing that a building near the Great Pyramid is a water-pumping station not a religious temple and another insists that the Great Pyramid is a power generator not a Pharaoh's tomb."

"You see," replied Andrew, "just sitting around this table we can identify unexplained ancient technologies. Imagine if we really studied the topic. Maybe it is time professionals other than archeologists reassess the ancient materials. We might make some fascinating discoveries. The sad truth is that with disasters, wars, epidemics, the fanatical actions of a few individuals plus the rigidity of academia, many scientific and technological facts have either been poorly labeled or lost. Just think of the loss to mankind in the burning of the Alexandrian library in Egypt, the destruction of Druidic books, and the burning of the South American Indian books and records. In summary, mankind has been its own worst enemy."

Angi, thinking of the medallion, asked, "So, if a piece of ancient technology survived would we not be endangering ourselves or society if we tried to activate it?" the ramification of her own question startled her.

Sensing her concern Andrew intervened, "I'm certain, Angi, that if such technology reappeared, it will be for a reason but will also come with guidance or let's hope so."

"That's comforting," thought Angi. "Let's hope it arrives soon, because we're just about to enter the final stage of this mission."

"Just one more question," asked Wolfram, "Brigit said the Tuantha De Danann went underground or across the sea. What does that mean to you?"

"Ah," said Bryce, "I wondered when that would surface. Well let me take a stab at it. There are a number of possibilities. Today, eminent scientists have not only confirmed the existence of parallel dimensions to our own but throughout history certain people may have known how to utilize gateways to access such dimensions. It was said that the Druids hid their magical treasures in another dimension, and the Knights Templar were supposed to have placed the Art of the Covenant in a similar place.

Underground is another possibility. Do you know there are people who believe that the earth is hollow, particularly at the poles, and that a more advanced civilization resides there? " Bryce stopped to see their reaction.

"That's a bit far fetched don't you think?" replied Wolfram. "If there's some giant hole in the North Pole how come orbiting satellites haven't found it?"

"Good question. I'm not saying I believe it, as personally I prefer the parallel dimension theory," replied Bryce. "But let's not rule it out."

"What about across the ocean?" asked Angi, anxious now to hear the full list of possibilities.

"When we're talking about the Tuantha De Danann we are in the time period of several hundred years before our first century. Since these people arrived by boat, they could just as easily leave the same way. But where would they go? I expect you are familiar with Hy-Brasil or the Fortunate Isle that exists off Ireland near Galway Bay?" said Bryce.

"No, Brigit didn't have time to get into that," replied Angi.

"Well, this island is cloaked in mist except for one day every seven years. Remember the Druids were experts at manipulating nature particularly fog and mist. Rumor has it that on this island there is a civilization a thousand years ahead of our own, where sonic and vibrational technology exists, and where all the citizens have great wealth. It was once thought to be Avalon where King Arthur sleeps." Bryce stopped again to let the information sink in. Then he continued.

"But perhaps the Tuantha De Danann sailed beyond this point. If so, a lost civilization may reappear with the melting of the Arctic ice shield. I'm sure there are many mysteries in North America that have yet to be discovered. So, there you have it, four possibilities. The Tuantha De Danann went somewhere. The question is whether we are prepared to believe in any of these rather outlandish options."

"Wow," thought Angi, "Here I sit with my comfortable old world being torn to shreds. What surprises me is that I'm not wanting to attack such wild theories." Instead, she craved more, "I sincerely hope that we can do this again. Obviously, there is much for me to learn."

"It will be our pleasure, Angi," replied Andrew. "But before we call it a night let's get back to two more practical matters. Did Brigit give you the name of a Scottish Guardian? If you have a name, perhaps we should get on to this first thing in the morning."

"I have the phone number of a lady in Scone who is in her nineties, so, you are right, we need to get to her as soon as possible," replied Angi.

"Fine, Wolfram and Angi, I've set up the computer in my office for you to use whenever you want. I have one in my bedroom and Bryce and Dylan can use the two in the library. If you need any assistance Dylan is our computer whiz. The phone in my office is at your disposal. Let's do some planning before we start phoning so we're all on the same song sheet."

"Agreed," said Angi and Wolfram in unison.

"Now, our next and more lethal matter, Antonino," said Andrew. "We know he's in Scotland from both government sources and street contacts. He's been trying to entice a couple of my university faculty into his viscous web but to no avail."

"So, you know his disguise and alias here in Scotland?" asked Wolfram.

"Partially, he's masquerading as an elderly professor and has, so far, cleverly escaped our nets. He may become more desperate when he gets wind of the medallion, which I'm sure is only a matter of time. For this reason we must move quickly."

Wolfram felt pressured to respond. "Like all predators, Antonino's clever at finding the weakest link in the chain, so, I hate to be blunt, but how can we be certain he has not infiltrated your staff? With the current economic climate he'll find someone as he flashes lots of cash incentive."

While Andrew should have been more incensed with this insinuation he calmly reacted, "I understand your concern, Wolfram. While the majority of my staff has been with the family for decades, nevertheless, I'll have Dylan recheck the lot especially new arrivals. Gus e-mailed me Antonino's latest photo so I'll have this circulated. Bryce and I will also work on extra security." What he did not divulge was that he had already contacted his secret society and expected results.

Reassured, Wolfram and Angi said their good-nights and, with their trusted maps, found their rooms.

Angi opted for a relaxing bath. After a half hour soak, she laid out her clothes, set her clock for the morning, and selected a book from the bookcase. While reading, an invisible presence arrived and proceeded to use an unseen vibrating light over Angi's entire body.

Angi sensed something. "I swear there's someone in the room. Oh help, not a ghost.......I don't need, nor do I want this." .... Hesitating, she thought, "Maybe the medallion is attracting unwanted forces. I wonder what would happen if I removed it. Who'd know, let's give it a try."

As she reached for the clasp at the back of her neck, her hands froze in mid air. Suddenly, within a bright light a vague image took the form of a tall female with flowing garments. Her voice, almost a whisper, said, "Angi, removing the medallion could kill you. This finely balanced instrument is unstable. You need all the gemstones before you can remove it."

Mesmerized, Angi asked. "Who in blazes are you?" Angi was amazed at her calmness.

"I'm Sirona," came the hushed reply. "I am a hologram sent to guide you through the next phase of your journey. My image will improve with the next gemstones." Unable to hold the pattern, before disappearing, she repeated her warning, now in a hollow tone, "Don't..... remove..... medallion!"

Trying to rationalize the vision, Angi said to herself," OK, perhaps I'm hallucinating or daydreaming, or have disrupted my subconscious. Whatever, I'd best heed the warning unless I'm suicidal."

Exhausted from travel and ongoing challenges to her reality, she placed the book on the side table, turned out the light and burrowed down between the sheets. Before dozing off a thought crossed her mind, "Imagine trying to explain any of this to my nursing colleagues. They'd escort me to the nearest psych ward" ....followed by a touch of melancholy .... "I wonder if I'll ever see my dear island again."

Wolfram's last act was to glance out of one of his bedroom windows which had a view of the entrance driveway. At that moment he witnessed two vans arriving, the front iron gates being locked, and eight individuals entering the castle. As he watched, two reappeared to take up position at the front gates. As he settled into bed he assessed the situation, "That was quick. It is clear, Andrew, and I expect Bryce, regard the medallion as an item of immense importance. Tomorrow I have to contact Josh."

ᛒ

Scotland: Antonino's Edinburgh Hideout

The pounding rain echoed his despondency. Irritated, Antonino sat looking out a second-rate hotel window drumming his fingers on the chipped window-sill. He chose an inferior lifestyle to maintain his new disguise. He cringed at his reflection in the mirror, the streaked gray hair, dark rimmed glasses and rumpled shirt and pants. "What a comedown," he said out loud. "Driving a second hand car is the ultimate insult. This better be worth it."

After days of effort, he had accomplished little. For the first time in his life he felt trapped with no one to manipulate. Negatives were popping up everywhere. His venture into Edinburgh University had accomplished nothing. "I've likely compromised my identity in trying to recruit one of those pompous university asses. Not only have four out of five turned me down, I've a feeling that miserable research assistant with the red hair and poppy eyes, was so spooked that he's already bleating to someone. On the other hand, he's a weakling and so terrified of life that's he's likely cowering in some library alcove unable to move. I left him with sufficient reason. If my mother's relatives had been more cooperative I'd have used a more permanent solution. I detest whimpering loose ends."

Antonino stiffened as he watched a police van drive into the hotel entrance. He chose his third floor, front room for that precise reason. As his eyes followed the van he calculated his escape. "Out the door and two steps to the stairs.........perfect. I'd be off in a flash." As the van careened back onto the busy street, he took a deep breath. He was unaccustomed to such jitteriness, he preferred being in charge.

For days, in contacting his mother's relatives he sensed a palpable uneasiness, and was keenly aware of their shallow excuses and deliberate attempts at ignoring him. He thought it might be due to the long reach of

Cosmo Scarpoli in Boston, as he was notorious for carrying out his threats. "By now he'll have word of my dismissal from the priesthood, that'll be enough to antagonize him. Considering the current economic climate in the USA, he'll have any number of takers for a contract. These days' contract killers come in all flavors; males and females, young and old. I'd be a fool to dismiss the possibility." But that wasn't entirely the reason. Earlier in the day a street addict presented another possibility.

Parking his car near the hotel, Antonino had to run to get out of the pouring rain. A few feet from the hotel entrance a young man stepped out in front of him, one he recognized as a panhandler at a nearby coffee shop. Antonino was surprised at his forwardness. The boy's guttural Scottish accent was difficult to follow.

"I've heard something about you that might be worth something ……… interested?" asked Jimmy, a thin, drenched teenager with gray sunken eyes and visible needle marks on both arms.

"What would you have of value to me?" replied Antonino, disgusted at the boy's lifestyle and fearing contamination even by being close to him.

"Well, I know the police are looking for you. I saw a photo they were flashing around near the coffee shop," replied Jimmy with a sly grin. "Now….. are you interested?"

"That might explain a lot," thought Antonino. "Perhaps the Boston police are faster then I thought. "OK, what price, how about ten pounds?"

"How about twenty, came the rapid response," Jimmy was gambling on quick financial gain to get out of the rain.

"You are pushing your luck, kid. I will give you ten and another ten if your information is worth it," replied Antonino, and to himself "I can't afford to alienate anyone right now; this kid could sell me to the highest bidder."

"Agreed," replied Jimmy, holding out his right hand.

Antonino peeled off a ten pound note and dropped it into the boy's outstretched wet hand.

"Well, it is all over the street. The police have you on what they call a Watch List as some kind of terrorist or being friendly with such undesirables. It is a younger photo but it is you. That won't make you popular in this place. I'd be looking for other digs if I were you."

For a moment Antonino wasn't sure whether to believe the boy or not. But the news could explain the uneasiness of his relatives. It is one thing to be a crook or even a killer, it is quite another to be running with terrorists. Thinking, "I should be flattered, if I wasn't so damned fed up with this water-soaked city. Who would be powerful enough to set this up……….Andrew Sinclair……….my God, he's no ordinary professor, he belongs to that posh Scottish family, the ones with castles and bags of money and power. The bastard has set me up. Even my relatives don't want any connection with a God-damn terrorist. I'm a sitting duck in this country with all those street cameras and the wonderful World Wide Web. This technology age is a real hazard to people like me. I'll have to keep a low profile."

"Where's the second ten?" demanded Jimmy, growing restless and chilly. "I earned it."

"Sure," replied Antonino pealing off another note and turning abruptly he dashed towards the front door of the hotel. Inside, he aimed straight for the elevator suspecting every glance as a potential police informer.

Still contemplating this latest news, he followed the rain drops as they streaked down the windowpane. "So, here I sit with a number of hounds on my tail. I must be mad. I've a good chance of being arrested for any number of reasons, or killed by my own relatives, and never seeing this damnable relic...........yet, it is like searching for a lost gold mine, with every step you are sure you are getting closer." As if fate was eaves dropping, at that moment the phone rang.

He cautiously picked up the receiver knowing few knew his new alias, Dante La Villa, or had his phone number. Relieved, he recognized the odd accent and post-smoking rattle of a middle-aged relative.

"Dante, this is your cousin Madge, I got that information you asked for. It is from a gossipy friend, so it is about 50% reliable. Take whatever fits. Apparently that American, Stark, is at the Sinclair castle in Inveresk, just a few miles from Edinburgh. He's there with, I think, another American, a female. The third person is a Lord or something. The older man has been in hospital and is recovering at the castle. But, something's afoot because they've suddenly increased their security, about six to ten well-trained security officers, maybe military. Getting near that place will be impossible. It is a huge building so even with a map you would be lost. The Internet is no help, this is not a tourist spot, it is a family home. Anyway, that's it. Put a good word in with your mother for me. Your family name carries weight even here in Scotland. I'll be in touch if I hear more."

A smile creased Antonino's narrow face as he hung up. "That's it! I'm a bloody genius..........a clever, intuitive genius.........I'm right on target. More security with Stark's arrival means someone in that damn castle has the relic. My Vatican source says it is likely a medallion with, what did she say, magical powers. I can already taste the sweetness of success. I'll take whatever comes ....gold, jewels, wealth and power........yes, all the stinking power I can get. I'll get even with those sons of bitches who crossed me over the years. Revenge will be delicious."

Nature had joined in his jubilation, the rain eased and he could see a speck of blue in the distance. "No time to waste. I've got two possible pawns; one at the university and another who used to work at the castle. Now that my goal's in sight I'll get generous. I'll offer 15,000 pounds up front, and 20,000 upon delivery of the relic. That should entice a greedy candidate." He whistled a familiar Italian ditty as he went about planning his next moves and contemplating his triumphant future.

THE CELTIC SERPENT

Chapter 8

Scotland: Scone

Rumbling thunder declared the day. A threatening rainstorm would haunt their Scone trip. Complications were setting in. Fiona Stevenson, their next Guardian, had informed them that in 1918 her family gemstone had been deposited at the Scone Palace Presbyterian Chapel and never retrieved. She would provide more details when they met.

The silver Range Rover with five passengers left the castle at 9am giving them plenty of time to navigate the morning commute for the fifty-four kilometer (thirty-four mile) drive. Andrew was now on map duty with Dylan leaving Angi, Dana, and Wolfram in the back seat. Skirting Edinburgh they eased onto the A90, crossed the Forth Bridge and headed north to Perth. Dark clouds hugged the hills with rumbling thunder in the distance.

Wolfram was more relaxed. Gus's phone call had given him a bead on Dylan. He was a commander of some crack British military unit trained to escort dignitaries through diplomatic quagmires. While Andrew used the service in some past mission, its presence at the castle remained a mystery. "I expect he's paying a hefty price for their services. Antonino is certainly a factor but is that all? I've handled plenty of antiques, admittedly, nothing quite like this medallion but still. I'll have to press this point with Andrew when we get back. Angi and I may be in more danger than I thought."

Angi wasn't thrilled with Dana's presence, but had no say in the matter. However, back on familiar ground, Dana's personality had changed for the better. "Perhaps Ireland was unfamiliar territory, or she was upset that her expertise was not needed, and she's still smarting from her divorce." As Angi settled back to take in the Scottish scenery, she partially listened to Dana's historical rendition of their next stop for, as she was discovering, she always had some valuable details.

In a semi-lecture tone Dana began, "First, there are two Scones; the old and the new. There's very little left of Old Scone, the village was demolished in the 1800s to create the new Scone. So we will be heading to the new site northeast of Perth, on the east bank of the river Tay and, some might argue, the geographical heart of Scotland. In the past Scone was the capital of Pictavia, the ancient kingdom of the Pictish king Kenneth 1 (d. 858) and the site of the 12th century abbey founded by Alexander 1 (d. 1124), but I'm getting ahead of myself. Since there's time I'll digress a bit to give you a more comprehensive picture.

Before the Common Era, legend has it that Scotland obtained its name from an Egyptian princess, Scota, who, exiled from Egypt, travelled by way of Spain, eventually arriving in Ireland. There her descendants became known as the Scoti. Some time later, the Scoti left Ireland and settled in Western Scotland. In the middle ages they established the kingdom of Dál Riata, a name long forgotten in most history books. Among the possessions Scota took from Egypt was a 152 kg sandstone block which had been used as a pillow by Jacob, you remember the story of Jacob's ladder in the Bible. This stone would become the seat on which the Kings of Dál Riata, and later the kings of Scotland, were enthroned. It is known as the Stone of Destiny or the Stone of Scone. Legends hold there is a direct connection between this stone and Lia Fáil, the coronation stone of the kings of Tara."

Angi was amazed at how often the Bible kept popping up, not that she was an expert on the subject. Recognizing another gap in her knowledge of history, she was pressed to ask, "Dana, I never heard of Dál Riata. This was a kingdom? Where was it and how long did it last?"

Glad to find someone listening, Dana continued. "Dál Riata, some say Dalriada, was a Gaelic over kingdom on the western coast of Scotland with some territory on the northeast coast of Ireland. In the late 6th and early 7th century it encompassed roughly what are now Argyll, Bute and Lochaber in Scotland and County Antrim in Ireland. During this time in history the kingships of Gaels and Picts underwent a process of gradual fusion, starting with Kenneth 1, (known as Kenneth MacAlpin) the last King of Dál Riata and rounded off in the reign of Constantine II. As late as the 730s, armies and fleets from Dál Riata were reported fighting alongside the Uí Néill, the kings of Ireland. Around the middle of the 8th century Dál Riata slipped from historic records. But enough on Dál Riata, our main interest is Scone.

When Kenneth 1st established the new kingdom of Alba (later called Scotland) old Scone became its historic capital. At one time Scotland itself was called the 'Kingdom of Scone'. In the Middle Ages Scone was an important royal centre, used as a royal residence and as the coronation site of the kingdom's monarchs. Around the royal site grew the town of Perth and the Abbey of Scone. In 1210, Scone's status was further enhanced when the Parliament of Scotland met there for the first time. This would continue until 1450.

The biggest change occurred near the end of the 13th century when King Edward I of England invaded Scotland and took the Abbey's coronation relics, the crown, scepter and the stone, to Westminster. Alexander III would be the last Scottish king crowned seated on the mystic stone. However, Scottish Monarchs, and those seeking to become Scottish Monarchs, continued to come to Scone to be crowned. These included Robert the Bruce in 1306, James IV in 1488 and Charles II in 1651, James Francis Edward Stuart (The Old Pretender), in 1716 and his son, Bonnie Prince Charlie (The Young Pretender) in 1745."

"I'm fascinated, why was the Stone of Scone so important to the Scots?" asked Angi trying to understand such traditions.

"A good question," replied Dana. "Well, unlike the English, Scotland's kings were crowned according to Gaelic tradition, on a coronation mound out in the open, not inside an abbey."

"So even when the Stone of Scone was removed, the site itself remained important to the Scottish people?" asked Angi.

"Yes, the Scone Abbey remained and flourished for over four hundred years until 1559. During the early days of the Protestant Reformation, the abbey was attacked by reformers and almost destroyed. There was some restoration in the coming centuries but, by then, it had lost its grandeur. In time the estate was passed from one noble family to another, eventually becoming the property of the Murrays whose descendants are still there. In the early 1800s, as I said, new Scone was created where the present Scone Palace resides. We'll see the palace today but will not be paying a call."

"Is the Stone of Scone still at Westminster?" asked Angi.

"It stayed at Westminster Abbey until 1996 when it was returned to Scotland. There was an eight month hiatus in 1950, when the Stone of Scone was removed by Scottish Nationalist students but later returned," replied Dana. "Afterwards, rumors circulated that copies had been made of the Stone, and that the returned Stone was not the original."

Wolfram interjected, "But I've heard that the Stone of Scone was never given to Edward 1st in the first place. The actual stone was hidden somewhere in Scotland. You are saying that the substitution only occurred in the last century. The Scots had lots of time to substitute the original stone before handing something over to Edward."

"That's been rumored for ages, but never proven," replied Dana. "Perhaps Andrew might enlighten us?" There was silence from the front seat even though everyone knew he was listening.

Dana finalized her narrative with, "Today at Moot Hill you will see a facsimile of the Stone of Scone at the chapel. Whatever existed at Westminster was returned to Edinburgh Castle where it remains along with the crown jewels of Scotland in the Crown Room."

Approaching Scone, Andrew, with maps in hand, started to give Dylan directions to their first stop on Abbey Road.

Fiona Stevenson lived on a street of large duplex gray stone houses, with identical low stone garden walls. Dylan eased the van between the pillared entrance the narrow space more suited to carts than cars. He parked in the small driveway near the walkway leading up to a side entrance. The four disembarked leaving Dylan with the van.

A middle-aged woman with gray hair and a somber face opened the door in response to the ringing of the front door bell. "Welcome. I'm Fiona's housekeeper, Audrey Babcock. At ninety-three, Fiona's not as agile as she would like, but fully alert. She has been waiting anxiously for your arrival." Looking past the four she asked, "Will the other gentleman be coming in?"

"No, we expect this will be a short visit," replied Andrew.

"Ah well, Fiona will insist on you having tea. I will make sure your friend is also accommodated," said Audrey as she escorted the party into the front hall.

They entered an elegant house of World War I vintage, a seven foot grandfather's clock announcing their arrival. To the left of the hall a winding stairway rose to the second floor while several rooms fanned off to the right. The rooms, in shadow, were filled with expensive antiques, tokens of several generations. Audrey beckoned them to the Sitting Room where a once tall, angular woman with white hair, balancing herself on a brown and silver cane, walked slowly to greet them. In a deep voice with a soft Scottish accent, Fiona welcomed her guests, "Finally....... the day has arrived. I was sure it would happen in my lifetime but feared it was fanciful thinking. Please come in and find a seat while Audrey gets us tea." Glancing towards Angi she said, "Brigit described you well, you are Angi."

"Yes," and Angi proceeded to do the introductions. "Fiona, this is Wolfram Stark from the United States, Andrew Sinclair and Dana Norcross from the University of Edinburgh. Dylan Gabriel, our fifth member, is in the van."

"Welcome to all of you." Looking at Andrew she continued, "It has been many years since I've entertained gentry in this house." Andrew shook her hand while the others proceeded to find comfortable chairs.

Fiona was the last living member of an illustrious family who once owned a furniture business in Perth. Her only sibling, a sister, had died at seventy in 1985. Fiona was married in 1938 and lost her husband, a Royal Air Force pilot, over Europe in 1942. There were no children and she never remarried. She became an English teacher and eventual Head Mistress of a girl's school in Perth, retiring at sixty-five. In her retirement she was renowned for her prized Brigadoon, hybrid tea roses and leadership in a number of charitable organizations.

Fiona, not wasting time, proceeded in an organized manner. "First, I have this list of names you requested." which she handed to Angi. "As I'm sure you've heard from the other Guardians, the reasons for the delegation of responsibilities by our ancestors in the 1600s have long been lost. So, I gladly relinquish this family responsibility to your safekeeping. Now, as a personal request, could you, Angi, come into the light so I may get a good look at the medallion? I expect all Guardians want to know what our families have been protecting for generations."

Angi got up from the huge upholstered chair and moved to where Fiona was sitting, under a deliberately placed bright lamp. But Angi discovered it wasn't just the medallion that Fiona wanted to examine.

After a few minutes Fiona commented. "Brigit was right you are indeed the perfect choice for this mission. Those emerald eyes are enchanting. Brigit and I had a grand chat on the phone after your visit. We're both positive about the outcome however long it takes." Then she turned to the medallion.

"It is exquisite, much more than I imagined. There are still three missing gemstones, one belonging to my family. Our gemstone remained in this house until World War I. In 1917, my mother was quite ill, and my sister and I were young children. When father was posted overseas he hired a housekeeper to care for us. Concerned about the safety of the gemstone and knowing the Murrays, he got permission to place the gemstone in a secure place in the Presbyterian Chapel. Why the chapel and not the Palace was never explained. He obviously planned on retrieving it after the war but, unfortunately, he died in the global flu epidemic. World War 1 was devastating for many families. After the war my mother was left to run the furniture business in Perth. She hired a manager, but ran the business behind the scenes. Sometime in the 1930s, the business was sold leaving my sister and I comfortably off but not wealthy as that was the time of the worldwide economic depression. My father left only this small piece of paper regarding the hiding place of the gemstone with the words "The *bairn* will guide you to the stone". Now in Scots *bairn* means 'child', but I have no idea what child, or whether this was some coded message. I wish I could be more helpful."

Angi, trying to remain positive asked, "Fiona, do you know what gemstone your family was guarding?"

"Indeed I do," was the quick reply. "It was an emerald, just like your eyes. As a young girl I loved the thought of guarding an emerald. Later I learned that an emerald is a healing stone, affecting the heart chakra. It is known to enhance spirituality and consciousness, stimulate mental abilities, and helps in attaining deeper meditation. I once thought every Guardian had a similar stone but now I see they are all different. I'd love to go with you to the chapel, but that's not possible. Nevertheless, like Brigit, I ask that whatever the outcome of this quest you will invite the Guardians to the final event. Brigit is certain it will be at the Hill of Tara. Since I have few remaining years, I pray you will find success in swift order." And with a smile she continued, "I'm a stubborn old woman and will fight to be there."

Angi admired Fiona's tenacity and determination. If possible, she would do her best to have the Guardians at their final stage, but already Fiona was presenting what appeared to be an insurmountable obstacle. She stored the papers in her large sac-like bag when Audrey arrived with tea, sandwiches and sweet breads. At this stage, Dylan joined the group. Relaxing they chatted about other things; their trip and Angi's grandmother.

Sitting quietly watching the proceedings, Dana was deep in thought, "Good God that damn thing is real. How many carats per stone, maybe two or three? A broad estimate of the gold and gems means that stupid looking pendant could be worth a fortune, added value, if you include the antique factor. What's all this about Guardians ....likely some Knights Templar jargon. I never understood that nonsense. But this medallion could be my ticket to fame. That American is obviously a courier, whatever that old woman thinks. This belongs to Britain."

As they prepared to leave, Angi asked, "Fiona, do you have any information on the two Guardians that you were in contact with over the years?"

"Unfortunately, the news is not good. Communications ceased on both fronts some years ago. Late in the sixties my Welsh Guardian, Morag Williams, stopped writing. I expect she died suddenly. I waited hoping that she might have passed the gemstone to a distant relative. All my inquiries failed. My second contact, Judith Gardiner of Mull was a descendant of the oldest couple, the Campbells. She lived into her eighties but she also stopped writing. From the beginning our ancestors knew this might happen and requested the families either pass the gemstone to a trusted relative or, failing that, take the gemstone to Iona. What little I know of the Iona location is a confusing partial comment from my father who said, 'It's not what it appears'.........I realize this seems little to go on but if you've come this far, don't give up."

About noon they said farewell to Fiona, their last sight of her was waving good bye from her walkway. Their next stop was Scone Palace Chapel. As the signs and Palace gateway loomed into sight Dana's unstoppable historic dialogue continued.

"Moot Hill, which is where we're headed, is quite unique. It is said to have been created from soil brought by Scottish clan chiefs from around the country to pay homage to their new king being crowned on the Stone of

Scone. Recently, two archeologists, using radiocarbon dating of an excavated item from the Moot Hill ditch pushed back the origins of this ancient site by a thousand years. It is like uncovering the 'birth certificate of Scotland'."

"In North America we talk about something being old when it is in the hundreds, here you talk about thousands of years. This difference seems more pronounced being here. I would like to thank you Dana for all this information, it is a great help," said Angi.

"Thanks, Angi," replied Dana, not accustomed to such gratitude.

Dylan parked near Moot Hill to let his passengers out as the continuing thunder and bending trees kept signaling an approaching storm. He took off to find a parking spot.

As the four walked up the steps toward the Mausoleum and Chapel, two peacocks strutted across the grounds, declaring their ownership of the property. Angi, Dana, Andrew and Wolfram stopped momentarily at the replica Stone of Scone, Angi and Wolfram seeing it for the first time. "It is not quite what I expected," thought Angi, "but then it is not like we have such stones in America as a comparison."

Next, they passed the Baptismal font, heading towards the chapel entrance where a man in a navy uniform stood waiting. The chapel was a small twin towered, pink stone building. The man smiled as Andrew approached.

"Welcome Andrew, it is a good day for your visit. The site's been booked for a major conference at the palace. Since the attendees are mainly from Perth, most will have visited the chapel and with the approaching storm will not be too willing to venture outside. I expect you'll have a free hand. As requested, I've opened the interior gate. Give me a cell call when you are finished. I will pop back in an hour."

"Thanks," replied Andrew, "It is hard to know how long this may take." As the caretaker left, he took charge. "Why don't Angi and Dana survey the inside while Wolfram and I look around the outer grounds. I am sure it is inside but it never hurts to be thorough. Give us a shout if you find anything."

The inside consisted of one large room with minimal furniture. Two walls were decorated; one with a pink and white, huge, marble memorial for the Murrays, the other, a smaller memorial with a Grecian urn. The Murray wall consisted of beautifully sculptured hovering angels, with two medieval knights in full amour standing guard over a kneeling knight reading the Bible. An altar stood in front of the memorial, draped in a gold cloth with two sets of brass candlesticks, one larger than the other. The sparse furniture consisted of a straight-backed wooden chair and bench against a stone wall. Dana broke the silence

"What are we looking for?"

"I'm not sure, something small, maybe in a leather or cloth bag. It is not likely larger than the palm of your hand. Fiona's father must have known this place well. Perhaps there's a hidden panel in all that sculpture. It has to be well hidden as decades of people haven't found it, or at least we hope not. Let's make a sweep and see if anything turns up. Fortunately, it is a small building."

"Agreed," said Dana. "We'll both tackle that sculptured wall, and then I'll go to the left while you take the right."

For the next half hour they searched poking their hands inside crevasses and corners pushing fingers into suspected trigger spots, testing various parts of the knight's armor and tapping wall stones for any hollow sound. Completing the agreed circle they came together with a look of discouragement.

"Nothing," said Dana. "This is really frustrating."

"Absolutely nothing," repeated Angi. "In addition, there's no child unless those cherubs up there can be classified as a *bairn*, but which one. Anyway we'd need a ladder to get up there. I think if the hiding place exists it is more accessible than that."

"Angi, I have to go. I need the toilet, too much tea at Fiona's. I expect we're done here. I'll be right back."

"Go on, I'll stay. Maybe Andrew and Wolfram will have better luck. There might be some sculpture or headstone outside with a child in it." Angi went and sat down on the wooden bench.

Alone, discouraged, she began to think, "Now what? After all the effort, without this sixth gemstone we're jinxed. I'll be left with this unbalanced medallion, unable to move on with my life and afraid of killing myself if I try to remove it." Lost in thought she didn't notice a small boy until he was right in front of her.

"Lo," came the cheery greeting as the boy tried to look into her face.

As she looked up she saw the cherub face of a young boy, about four, with a head of golden curls and dressed in a blue velvet suit with white lace cuffs. His accent was difficult but discernible. "He must be in some pageant at the palace," thought Angi. Not wanting to frighten him she replied, "Well, hello yourself. You are a real cutie. Are you lost?"

Looking puzzled, he didn't answer her question but asked his own "Do you know my Mama?"

"No, but perhaps it is best you stay with me and we will look for her together. How about that? What is your name?" asked Angi.

Proudly he declared. "Robbie Murray." Then wanting to continue talking he pressed her with another question. "This is my castle."

"So he does belong to the palace.........and he's a Murray," thought Angi. "You mean the big building across the road," she asked in reply?

"No, this castle," replied Robbie, dancing around in front of her.

"He's certainly a happy wee boy. What a charmer. I bet he's the apple of his parent's eye. Obviously, he's wandered off," thought Angi.

Robbie, pleased to have company, blurted out. "I have a secret place do you want to see it?"

"Why not," thought Angi. "I'll keep him occupied until the caretaker returns. He'll know where his mother is." "Sure," replied Angi, "show me."

Robbie, taking her hand pulled her towards the right side of the Murray memorial and, releasing his hand, squeezed into a small opening behind the armored knight.

Angi was surprised that even Robbie could get through the narrow slit. When he disappeared she called after him, "Robbie I am too big to get into your secret place. You'll have to tell me what's there." Concerned she thought, "I'll have to encourage him to get out of there."

With a mischievous smile Robbie peeked around the knight "I'll bring out the bag the man left. He told me you would come."

At that moment Angi remembered Fiona's father's note "The *bairn* ......is this the child? It is not possible, that was 1918. I must be day-dreaming." Then she asked out loud "Robbie. Why don't you come and show me what you have?"

Disappearing for a minute, Robbie reappeared with a soft leather bag. Raising it up to Angi he said, "For you."

Angi couldn't believe what she was looking at. Like Brigit's, inside the leather bag was the familiar purple velvet bag. She pulled it out, undid the tie and removed the expected silver engraved box. Gently lifting the lid, she saw the emerald. Then she rapidly closed the box, placed it back into the velvet bag and stashed it in her large handbag. The outer bag she offered to Robbie who had been standing quietly watching her every movement. "Thank you Robbie, this is exactly what I was looking for. Would you like this bag? " presenting him with the outer leather bag.

"Oh yes. Thank you," said Robbie and turned in delight to deposit his treasure behind the knight.

Sitting waiting for his reappearance Angi thought "How did he know to pass this to me? What did Fiona's father say to him..........but then, that's not possible.......it's a hundred years ago............. I better keep him close until I can get him back to his mother who must be sick with worry." But Robbie didn't reappear. She called and called .... "He's so quick, maybe there's another exit." ....Angi ran to the open doorway of the chapel arriving at the same time as Wolfram, Andrew and Dylan reached the same spot. "Have you seen a small boy in a blue velvet suit?" asked Angi.

"No," replied Wolfram. "He didn't come past us. But then we were talking so we might have missed him."

"I was just talking to him, he couldn't have gone far," replied Angi, in an

157

anxious voice.

"We'll take a look in back," said Wolfram. "You are sure he is not in there?"

"Yes, I've looked," replied Angi, concerned that the young boy was running free on such a large estate with a storm approaching.

She walked slowly to the Stone of Scone and sat facing the chapel, noting the return of the estate caretaker who joined the men at the back of the chapel.

"I've got a clear view of the area and will be able to see the boy if he appears," thought Angi, reassuring herself. At that moment a sound behind her drew her attention. Before she had a chance to turn a hard object struck her on the back of the head, and she crumbled to the ground. Falling, she gripped her handbag to protect the gemstone. Loosing consciousness, she was certain she heard a muffled scream.

What she couldn't see was when the hand violently jerked the medallion it responded with an electric charge that shot out and burnt the inside of the assailant's right hand. It was this scream which alerted the men who came running. When they arrived Dana was at Angi's side saying "Someone ran into the woods. I saw Angi fall as I came back from the toilet."

Dazed, blood running down the back of her neck, Angi forcefully grasped Wolfram's arm saying, "Take my bag...............guard it with your life."

Wolfram not understanding her plea, undid the purse zipper thinking Angi was asking him to find something to stop the bleeding. He spied the familiar purple velvet bag and abruptly closed the bag, draping it across his chest. "I understand, Angi. Everything's fine. We'll get you to the nearest hospital."

The van appeared and Dylan, arriving with a First Aid kit, placed a thick dressing over Angi's wound and expertly bandaged her head.

Andrew turned to the caretaker. "We will head to the Perth Hospital, it is the closest."

"Grab that stone it is likely the weapon," said Wolfram, his police instincts coming to the fore.

Dylan wrapped it in plastic and stored it in the First Aid bag.

"Can you stand?" asked Wolfram. "Dylan and I will help you to the van."

"I think so. I'm a bit dizzy but I can navigate," said Angi. She rose, grabbed their arms and pulled herself upright.

"Andrew, you go on. I'll lock up here," said the caretaker." I'll also alert security."

With her waning strength Angi turned to the caretaker, "What about Robbie? The wee boy needs his mother. Will you look for him?"

"My dear woman," replied the caretaker, "Robbie's our resident ghost.

He's seen by few but can be quite mischievous. He died in an accident in the 1800s."

As Angi limped toward the van she kept mumbling to herself, "A ghost.... I've been talking to a ghost.............so, Fiona's father also saw Robbie........ I'm really drifting into a psychic maze; first a woman from another dimension and now a ghost. What next?" As they reached the van the storm descended, rain coming down in sheets, bouncing off the street and van. The others scrambled to get inside. Angi, wedged between Dana and Wolfram in the back seat, took comfort in the steady drumming of the rain on the roof.

Wasting no time, Dylan, driving at top speed, ignoring the rain, got back onto A93, crossed the bridge, turned left on Tay Street, right on South Street, then onto Glasgow Road, before turning off at Rose Crescent into the Perth Royal Infirmary.

En route, Wolfram, grateful that Angi was slightly turned in his direction, noted the blue stone had been activated and was pulsating. "I hope this stops before we reach the hospital," he thought "or we'll have one hell of a time trying to explain it to the health workers." Within yards of the emergency entrance it ceased.

The next Angi knew she was being wheeled into an emergency treatment room. While Dylan and Dana waited in the hall, Andrew dealt with the paper work and Wolfram stayed with Angi. The attending physician was impressed with the First Aid as the bleeding had eased. Angi was examined for shock and four stitches applied to the wound. As a typical nurse she kept participating in the procedure describing her symptoms as, "I'm nauseated, dizzy and have a splitting headache." The physician prescribed a medication and had Angi moved to an ER holding bed while she waited for an x-ray. Wolfram tagged along, hoping that none of this activity would reactivate the blue stone. Concern mounted when the physician insisted that in light of the severity of the blow it would be advisable for Angi to stay overnight to check for any post-traumatic concussion or hematoma. This presented a dilemma.

Wolfram and Andrew conferred while Angi was getting her x-ray. "We can't leave Angi in this open area over night," said Wolfram. "If Antonino found her at Scone Palace, she will be an easy target. In addition, before arriving at the hospital the blue stone started pulsating. Dana didn't see it; she was looking out the window. But it could start again. This would complicate everything and the last thing we need is the media."

"That's to be avoided at all cost," replied Andrew, with a worried expression. "I'll make other arrangements. While there's security in the building we can't rely on them. We'll provide our own."

"I'll take the first shift," replied Wolfram.

"Good. Once this is set up I'll get Dylan to drive Dana and me back to

Inveresk. No need for all of us to hang around. You have my cell number. I will be back later with your replacement." With that Andrew hurried off to contact the hospital administrator.

Within the hour Andrew had a private room for Angi with a bathroom. Hospital security had been alerted. They were operating on the premise of another possible assault.

Following the x-ray, Angi was drowsy, her head hurt, and the nausea had returned. When the resident physician came in to check on her she received more medication and she asked for a white blood cell test. While her condition would normally not warrant such a test, the doctor knowing she was an ER supervisor and a friend of Andrew Sinclair, agreed. A lab technician appeared to draw blood. Foregoing food, Angi drank some fluid and drifted off to sleep.

Wolfram never left her bedside. He positioned himself as best as he could between two chairs. Andrew had arranged the delivery of a light meal for both which he thoroughly enjoyed; he was starving after the light tea with Fiona. Angi remained on liquids. When she went back to sleep he had plenty of time to think. "This has been one hellish journey for Angi; her grandmother's death and then bouncing from United States to Ireland and Scotland with a medallion which might erupt at any moment. What happens if we don't find the rest of the gemstones? Is Angi in any danger if we're unable to complete this quest? She's definitely a stoic, likely her nurse's training. But why the blood test? I'll ask later. Now to the critical issue, Antonino knew we would be at the chapel today. That means the castle is either bugged or we have a well-placed mole. Who? It has got to be someone with an inside track to our plans and discussions. Antonino's desperate so he's flashing big bucks. In today's world that could tempt anyone."

About eleven, Andrew pushed the door open with "How's our star patient?"

"Fine, she's been sleeping. The doctor and nurses keep checking her. She partially wakes and then dozes off again," replied Wolfram, reporting in an operative style.

At that moment a familiar voice was heard arriving with Dylan, "Hi Wolfram. I was hoping my return would be under happier circumstances. I am your replacement," replied Vette. "I got in this morning."

"My God it is good to see you Vette. I couldn't think of a better replacement. Angi will be delighted to see you. The doctor says she's doing fine and will likely be discharged in the morning," replied Wolfram. "I'll give you a quick briefing and introduce you to the resident physician, he's due any minute."

Leaving Andrew and Dylan with the sleeping Angi, Wolfram left the room with Vette. Just outside the door he said, "Vette, the blue stone started pulsating just before we reached the hospital. It has been quiet ever since but keep an eye on it and cover it with something if it recurs."

"Understood, that would create unwanted trouble," replied Vette.

"Come along I'll do the intros," said Wolfram.

As they returned to the room, before the men departed Vette said to Wolfram, "By the way, Morgan was my travelling companion. He's at the castle itching to talk to you. I better warn you, he's shaved off his beard and is dressed like a gentleman. According to him, this is his new life, as recent events have propelled him into maturity. I'll let you be the judge. We'll talk later."

"You are kidding........we are all together again. That's great," replied Wolfram with a smile. "I may have to get introduced to my old friend. I'm glad he's here. When times are tough it is good to be focused."

Even though they were mostly whispering, the commotion woke Angi. "I must be dreaming, is that you Vette?"

"Yes the one and only. I told you I'd be back; just like a bad penny. I am your night shift.......and believe me anyone getting in here will regret irritating me."

As the men turned to leave Wolfram looked at Angi saying, "I'll take care of this bag and return it in the morning."

"Thanks Wolfram. I'll not need it tonight," replied a drowsy Angi, grateful for Wolfram's trustworthiness.

Outside the door Dylan commented "It'd be an absolute idiot who'd pick a fight with Vette. I could use her on my team." Laughing, they departed.

Chapter 9

Scotland, Dunroslin Castle: The Grand Picture

By the next morning the storm had passed leaving nature to rejoice in the warmth of the summer sun. Angi, dressed and discharged, stood looking out the hospital window. Itching to get free, she relaxed as the medication was controlling her headache. Waiting she thought, "A hospital is no place to be stranded with an assailant on your tail. Of course, I'm well protected with my trusted bull dog," as she smiled and looked towards the doorway where Vette stood talking to the doctor.

The time had come. The attack on Angi had raised the stakes. Unless each member of the group was prepared to reveal all they knew the mission was in jeopardy. The question was how could they be open with a mole in their midst.

At 8:30 Wolfram and Dylan arrived to pick up Angi and Vette. Angi insisted on walking to the van without the aid of a wheelchair. Andrew had already arranged that she would see his personal physician in Edinburgh later in the week. "How is your head?" asked a sympathetic Wolfram.

"Still aching but I'm feeling better. A good rest does wonders. The doctor gave me some medication," she replied with a forced smile.

En route towards Edinburgh and Dunroslin Castle, Wolfram brought them up-to-date. "I don't need to tell you, we've got a problem. Antonino knew precisely where we would be yesterday and used it to his advantage. So, we think that he's either bugged the castle or there's someone on the inside, both unpleasant scenarios. Andrew moves quickly. When we left this morning a white van was arriving with a crew to scan the place for electronic bugs. As an added precaution he's stopped the renovations until further notice much to the consternation of the construction crew. The debugging process will take some time so they'll still be there when we get back."

"If there are no bugs, do you have any thoughts on who the mole might be?" asked Vette.

"None, but Dylan's team is working on that. What we know for sure is that Antonino knows about Angi and the medallion as before he was just chasing gemstones. That's the reason for the medallion grab at Scone."

As Dylan came to a stop in front of the castle, Ian appeared. "It is good to see you Angi, sorry about the attack. Your room has been scanned and is ready. Would you like anything to eat first?"

"No thanks, Ian, I'll wait until lunch but I'm sure Vette would like something."

"Fine, Vette, come with me," said Ian. "Wolfram will go with Angi. We're on orders that you are not to be alone even in the castle."

"Understood, I don't want a repeat of yesterday," said Angi and turning said, "Thanks Vette for doing the night shift. We'll chat later. I'll rest up before lunch. I expect you'll want a bit of shut eye yourself."

"Talk to you later, Angi," replied Vette, and walking off with Ian she could be heard saying "I'll take whatever you have to offer Ian, I'm famished."

By 11:45 Angi and Vette entered the dining room to greet Wolfram, Morgan, Dylan, Andrew and Bryce. Angi headed straight towards the listless looking stranger next to Wolfram.

Extending her hand she said, "I expect you are Morgan? I am delighted to finally meet you."

Morgan, having rehearsed what he would say to Angi over and over on his flight from the United States, replied, "Well, to be honest, Angi, I have been carrying one hell of a load of guilt over the attack on your grandmother. This, in addition to not releasing my wife earlier from an unhappy marriage, will haunt me for the rest of my life. Both outcomes may have been prevented if I had been more careful in your grandmother's case and more considerate in regard to my wife. I'm truly sorry, Angi."

"Morgan, you are not responsible for the sick mind of a person like Antonino. Actually, as much as I miss my dear grandmother, I believe we have all been chosen for different roles in this quest. Unknown to us, a cosmic clock reached the bewitching hour of *the coming times*, an event set in motion centuries ago. If it wasn't my grandmother, another event would have triggered the process and targeted another Guardian. Morgan, I am sorry about your wife's death, she did not deserve that either. What you may not know is, if we had waited any longer the gemstones might never have been found. As it stands we have few leads on the last two."

"I hope you are feeling better?" said Morgan.

"Yes, the headache has stopped which is good," replied Angi.

Wolfram then stepped in and asked, "Speaking of yesterday, Angi, can you tell us how you managed to get Fiona's gemstone when we had so little to go on. I suppose you are going to tell us it was the ghost."

"As strange as it seems, yes," replied Angi with a smile. "Somehow, Robbie Murray, a four year old ghost from the 1800s, knew what I was looking for and pulled the bag out from behind the Murray memorial. We'll never know if Fiona's father knew Robbie and gave him some instructions or not. But it happened. I'm still having difficulty believing he was a ghost. I could feel the warmth of his chubby hand as he pulled me toward his hiding place."

"Did you think the medallion helped you see Robbie?" asked Vette, intrigued with the continuing array of unusual events.

"I think this medallion has many strange properties," replied Angi. "For instance, it allowed me to see a woman who stepped into my bedroom from another dimension."

The revelation stunned the group. "Come again," said Wolfram. "When did that happen?" Thinking it just occurred, "Maybe it is the blow on your head."

"No, I know what you are thinking. This woman appeared on the first night at the castle. That evening, I started thinking, what if we never find all the gemstones? It was a daunting thought to be permanently attached to this unknown piece of ancient technology for the rest of my life. So, I contemplated removing the medallion. Anyway, as I reached for the clasp an invisible force paralyzed my movements. Within seconds a mist-like image began to appear, fuzzy at first and then a barely discernible figure emerged. Her face was never clear." What Angi didn't say was that she was certain she heard harp music just before the arrival of the mist.

"Are you sure it wasn't one of our resident ghosts?" asked Andrew.

"Andrew, this individual did not come close to matching the description of your resident ghost. As best as I can describe, this was a tall woman wearing flowing garments. She introduced herself as Sirona, the voice much clearer than the image. She stated she was a hologram from another dimension with no other details. Future visits were revealed as she indicated her image would improve with the addition of the final gemstones. In her right hand she held a pulsating device which she claimed was being used to keep my chakras in balance. She actually used it during her visit. The overall impression I had was that she was concerned about the instability of the medallion which had been inactive for centuries. Her assignment was to keep the instrument stable while guiding me through the final stages of whatever lies ahead."

"That might explain the vibrating of the central blue stone en route to the hospital," replied Wolfram. "Thank God it stopped or we would have had some explaining to do. I expect the assailant, in grabbing the medallion upset this fine balance. In so doing, he must have received an electric shock or burn to the hand. That was likely the scream we heard. It wasn't clear whether it was male or female. But we should keep an eye open for anyone with a bad burn on their hand," a statement directed towards Andrew, Bryce and Dylan. At that point Ian arrived to announce lunch.

As the group took their seats at the table, Andrew was last to arrive, placing an old book in front of Angi. He opened it to a listing of Celtic gods and goddesses, pointing to one specific name. "I thought the name sounded familiar. You will see that Sirona is a Celtic deity, her emblem was the snake and she's associated with healing, now isn't that a coincidence." As the book was circulated, Andrew asked, "Angi how tall was Sirona?"

"I was sitting on top of my bed, but I would say she was about five to six inches taller than me," replied Angi.

"You mean she's over six feet tall. She's a hologram from what dimension? How did you get in contact with a Celtic goddess? How come you never mentioned it before?" asked Vette, the questions tumbling out.

"I said nothing as I was unsure what had occurred. To tell you the truth I didn't know what it was. At first, I thought I might be overtired or it was a side effect of the medallion. But after yesterday's chat with a ghost, I now want company if any more weird things are about to happen. While my grandmother may have been comfortable in this Celtic world, I was brought up in a modern scientific one, which negates any such foolishness. I'm still uncomfortable talking about these two events even now."

"So, what you have just been telling us is that in the past two weeks you have been talking to a Celtic goddess from another dimension and a ghost from the 1800s. Wow, this is absolutely fantastic!" replied Morgan. "I thought this only existed in books or to a few mystics in past centuries."

"See Angi, this should be happening to Morgan. He'd be right in his element." said Andrew, trying to relieve Angi's anxiety. "What else did Sirona say?"

"She stated over and over not to remove the medallion until all the gemstones were in place, otherwise it might kill me," said Angi in a matter-of-fact tone.

"That's just great. You mean that madman yesterday could have killed you if that clasp wasn't so tight?" said Wolfram, in an irritated voice.

"Not a pleasant thought," replied Angi, "but yes."

"Is there anything else you can tell us about the visit?" asked Andrew wanting a full account.

"The image kept sputtering in and out. Before it finally disappeared Sirona said that she would be back to guide me, so I'm expecting a return visit or visits. Andrew, what do you think or am I just hallucinating?"

"As strange as this seems, I think it is all due to the medallion and that you may actually be in touch with an ancient Celtic goddess," replied

Andrew. "Your description of Sirona could easily fit the Tuatha De Danaan. They were tall with fair hair and some were known to have green eyes. As Bryce said earlier, scientists today have admitted to other dimensions and we know the Druids and the Knight Templars knew and used such knowledge. I'll need more time to absorb this, but basically I believe you." In reflection he thought, "I'll definitely have to contact the others, this is the sign we were waiting for."

"OK, since this is revelation time, perhaps I can get an answer to another issue. Angi, sorry to pry, but can you tell me why you asked for that blood test in the hospital. The doctor seemed hesitant but went along with it. Why?" asked Wolfram.

"I guess it is time to mention this as well. Just before I got the news of my grandmother's attack, I had been diagnosed with leukemia. Since my annual vacation was due I planned on discussing the implications for Gran and myself when I got home. That never happened."

"This is certainly a day for surprises. Was there any doubt in the diagnosis?" asked Wolfram. "It certainly explains your detachment and apparent reluctance to get involved in this quest."

"There's no doubt. It had been checked a number of times by experts at the medical center. I have the reports back home," replied Angi, realizing how distant that world now seemed from this Scottish dining room. She continued, "As a final act for my grandmother, I wanted to hand over the medallion in Boston to the other Guardians. Then I planned on returning home to make my final arrangements. I had no intention of having chemotherapy. To tell you the truth, I was relieved when forced to travel overseas as it reduced any unpleasant arguments with my family doctor over my decision. By the time I got back home it would be too late. So, while in hospital I thought I'd recheck my white blood count. I suppose I expected another confirmation of the diagnosis. To my surprise the test indicated my white blood count was normal. The change can only be attributed to the medallion. Anyway, as far as I'm concerned I've been given a second chance and feel rejuvenated except, of course, for this bang on the head."

Not wanting to be negative but compelled to say something, Vette responded hesitantly, "I don't want to be a killjoy, but maybe your disease is just in remission."

"True, but I'm sticking to the premise that my constitution has changed for the better. The nausea I've been attributing to my disease may be my body reacting to the power of this ancient relic. I'll know for sure when we add the next gemstone. Andrew, Wolfram said that you agreed to store the silver gemstone boxes in your safe. If you can get the Scone box, I'll be glad to demonstrate how the medallion reacts to each gemstone. The process should be of interest to those who have never seen it before. By the way, as Fiona said, the Scone gemstone is an emerald."

Andrew, becoming more cautious, replied. "At this point let's move to the library as it may be the safest place in the castle." Understanding his concern, the group followed him down the hall. In the library they circled a large table to watch the demonstration.

From his adjacent office, Andrew retrieved the familiar purple velvet bag from his safe and handed it to Angi.

Angi removed the silver engraved box from the velvet bag, and opening the lid, described to those not familiar with it the unique internal mechanism for securing the gemstone. Then using Zak's holder she inserted the tip of the gemstone and placed it next to the medallion. Within seconds, the blue stone awoke and the expected process was witnessed by the group including the electrical arc and insertion of the gemstone. Andrew, Bryce, Dylan and Morgan reacted as expected.

"Absolutely amazing," replied Andrew. "You are right Wolfram, it performs like a miniature computer. A sensor program must be activated to identify each genuine gemstone and move it into its rightful slot. Each stone must be in a specific place to perform properly. The last two gemstones are critical."

While Bryce and Dylan remained speechless, Morgan reacted. "Wolfram, I could never have envisioned anything like this from our first discussion of your grandmother's gemstone. I've never heard of such a relic in anything I've read but that doesn't exclude the possibility. The craftsmanship of the medallion and the storage boxes speak of great care generations apart. This was definitely a prized item. Having said that, I realize I'm in conflict with most of my academic colleagues who would not support any belief that such technology existed centuries ago. I'll need time to adjust to this."

"Is that it, Angi," asked Andrew. "I do not want to hurry you but I feel there is much we need to cover this afternoon."

"Yes, that's all from me," said Angi, aiming for a comfortable chair in an alcove near the stained glass windows. The exertion had tired her.

Seizing the opportunity, Wolfram waded in. "OK, then Andrew perhaps we might lay some other cards on the table. I know that Dylan and his team have this place locked down. I also know that Dylan's team has been trained for top government security work. While I'm not underestimating Antonino's capabilities, is this not excessive security for the medallion, or am I missing something?"

"I wish the security was as air tight as you think, Wolfram, but having received a negative result from the bugging scan, we now face the daunting possibility of having an internal spy. You are also intelligent enough to know that if the house staff check comes up dry then somehow it must be someone in this room."

Startled, they all looked at each other.

"That's impossible," replied an irritated Wolfram. "Surely the seven of us are above suspicion."

"Take it easy, Wolfram," replied Dylan. "Remember you told me that Antonino hired someone to hack into O'Gratteney's computer, right?"

"Right.......sorry........As far as I'm concerned this foursome," pointing to Angi, Vette, Morgan and himself, "are exempt. But I understand, go ahead."

"So, once we've covered the staff we'll be moving onto the computers and cell phones.........likely later this afternoon. Is everyone OK with that?" said Dylan.

In unison they replied, "Sure."

"The electronic route is a real possibility," replied Angi, inwardly pleased with Wolfram's vote of confidence. "We're indeed an odd foursome," she thought "but one I'm growing rather fond of."

"Now let's address Wolfram's question about the security," said Andrew, while concerned about the in-house mole, said to himself, "We'll have to risk it." Then glancing at Bryce, he started, "Bryce and I belong to several organizations....."

"Secret organizations, I expect," said Wolfram.

"Very well, one or two are secret but the others are well known, or were. Andrew, Dylan and I are members of the still existing ancient order of Knights Templar."

"I'll ask later..........go on," said Wolfram.

"Let's be seated, this could take some time," Andrew continued. "To understand our motives we need to step back in time to Atlantis. Volumes have been written on the topic with many theories as to its location. The Antarctic, South America, Bermuda, different parts of the Mediterranean, Spain, the Canary Islands, and northern Europe are but a few of the possibilities."

"Those are the key ones," said Bryce, "but most fail to meet the criteria that Atlantis was suppose to exist in an area where a chain of islands allowed easy access to America. The only possible locations that meet that criterion are Ireland, Scotland and some Scandinavian countries. This has been proposed by a number of authors including a recent Swedish geographer who argues that Ireland perfectly matches the measurements and other details provided by Plato."

"So, if we are standing on pieces of Atlantis, what, in your opinion, happened to it?" asked Morgan.

Andrew now interceded, "As described in ancient writing, myths and legends, Atlantis was destroyed by a celestial visitation or, as recorded in one account, hit by the thunderbolts of Zeus, which resulted in immense earthquakes. This left the island in tatters with major parts submerged below the sea."

"And the thunderbolts of Zeus were?" asked Angi.

"Possibly a single or double comet, or even a meteorite shower which, according to some accounts first appeared in the east, or north-east, in the sign of Aquarius. Gradually, as a heavenly omen, it crossed the sky in an east-west pattern, until the final catastrophe occurred in the sign of Orion, perhaps at the rising of Sirius, a star which follows Orion," replied Andrew as he continued the account.

"But surely, other than Plato's account, there must be more tangible evidence of such an event. Is there?" asked Morgan, his academic mind struggling with a topic which was denied vehemently by the academic community.

"Admittedly, it may seem limited, but there is evidence. Here in Scotland there are a number of ancient stones (i.e. the Golspie, Brodie, Elgin, Dyce and Logie) which depict people and animals running from a major disaster. In Sweden, there are fields of minute glass pearls that form when meteorites explode in the atmosphere. The suddenness of the event in the northern part of the planet has also been revealed in the stomach content of extinct animals like the mammoth which barely had time to digest its food. Plato said it occurred in a single day and night. This comet attack was supposed to be accompanied by electric storms, falling masses of rock, stones and other material, and accompanied by inundations and rains. As you would expect, it resulted in a long period of intense cold."

"Was the climate change due entirely to the volcano ash?" asked Angi.

"That was one of the causes, but it was also due to the effects of the enormous weight which the celestial body deposited on the earth. This resulted in 5 ¼ days being added to the previous calendar year of 360 days. By the law of gravitation the planet had to enlarge its orbit which reduced the strength of the sun. This 5 ¼ days has been a puzzle to academics ever since."

"You are absolutely right. I've often wondered why some old civilizations had two calendars; one at 360 days and another at 365. The old argument was that one was a lunar calendar and the other solar, but no one provided as logical an answer as you have," said Morgan.

"Was that all that happened?" asked Wolfram, fascinated at another revision of history.

"Not quite. Another affect of this shift was the alteration of the earth's axis, at the Poles, creating its present acute angle. The climatic effects took time to be felt, but the axis alteration was felt immediately particularly in those areas which lie within or near the present Arctic Circle; Siberia, Northern Russia, Northern Norway, Greenland, Canada, and less so in Scotland, the Scottish Isles and Iceland. This is what the Scandinavian sagas called the 'Great Winter', which forced many people to seek new homes or die of starvation. Beasts died and crops failed."

"That would explain some of the massive migrations of people recorded in the textbooks," said Morgan. "But if we accept the usual timeframe for Atlantis, then we're talking thousands of years in the past. Or are we?"

Andrew responded, "The timing of the destruction of Atlantis is the greatest problem. A good number of writers place the disaster at 13,000, 9,000 or even 6,000 years B.C.E... But, there are others, admittedly few, who argue that it happened closer to our time, in the 1300s B.C.E... A number of sources support this later date. The Scottish Golspie Stone records a disaster in this region of only 3,300 years ago. The other is the Sothic Cycle of the Egyptians, a system based on the movement of the star Sirius which dates from 1,322 B.C.E.. It is said that this cycle was the first to use the 365 ¼ years which marked the post-catastrophe shift in celestial movements. 5 ¼ days were added to the stellar year. These five additional days in many ancient societies were regarded with dread and became a time of public mourning when everything stopped and the temples were filled. There are books on that far shelf if you wish to explore this further. What I am saying is that Atlantis existed and was destroyed much closer to our time than we thought."

"Fine, lets agree on that, but why is it relevant to our situation and in particular this medallion?" asked Angi

"Because that blue stone in the center of the medallion is from Atlantis and Bryce and I believe the medallion may be from the same source," replied Andrew glancing at Bryce. "These Blue Stones were referred to in old texts as the Blue Apples or the Grapes of Eschol. It was thought they possessed supernatural powers and were capable of opening some 'gate'."

"You are talking about more than one gate?" asked Vette

"How many is unknown. But we do believe we have one in this medallion. The age and activity of the medallion points to Atlantis," replied Andrew.

"I am interested in your comment that it can open a gate, what gate?" asked Angi.

"Ah, that's the question," relied Bryce. "In light of Brigit's comment that, once the gemstones are in place, we will be gathering on the Hill of Tara, I will make a guess that a gate exists somewhere at Tara. After all, Tara is supposed to be a remnant of Atlantis, where the Druids and the kings of Ireland held sway. Any further details are tantalizing unknown."

"I'm still uneasy as to where this is going but let's continue. If we accept the medallion came from Atlantis, then I assume you are about to tell us that

171

somehow it remained in these parts, except for the past 350 year gap when half the gemstones were sent to America. Is that correct?" asked Angi.

"Yes and no," replied Bryce. "Some say the Druids came from Atlantis and there are legends that support that premise. They likely had the medallion after the disaster but fearing another inundation, they removed all priceless objects to safety, and some think it was to Egypt. Perhaps this will be confirmed when the records of Atlantis are found beneath the paws of the Sphinx."

"I'll let that one go for now.........too tempting," said Morgan. "Then how did the medallion get back to Ireland and Scotland?"

"Irish legends say that the Blue Stones of Atlantis were eventually given to Moses and taken to Jerusalem which means that they must have first been in Egypt. Centuries passed, and in 585 B.C.E... when Jerusalem fell to the Babylonians, Jeremiah the prophet arrived in Ireland with the surviving member of the House of David, a princess named Tamar from which the name of Tara is derived. In addition to the Blue Stones he is supposed to have rescued many of the Temple treasures. It was said that he used the blue stones to establish the Druid Schools of Wisdom," said Andrew

"I can't believe how many times the Bible keeps popping up. You'd almost think it was a historic code book," said Angi. "So, if I understand it, the Druids came from Atlantis, the Blue Stones were sent to Egypt for safekeeping, and centuries later the circle is completed by Jeremiah."

"That pretty well sums it up," replied Andrew.

"So, Nat was right," said Wolfram, "the gemstones in this medallion are similar to those listed on the breastplate of the High Priest of Jerusalem. Do you think there's any connection?"

"I'm not sure," replied Andrew. "What may happen, and this is strictly a personal opinion, is that the medallion works in combination with the breastplate crystals creating a perfect communication channel with the other dimension. Since Angi is already in contact with this dimension, the medallion must be able to work independently, thus making it the primary piece of equipment."

"So, where does this leave us?" asked Dylan, keenly following the discussion up to that point.

"It leaves us with a long list of questions," replied Andrew. "However, we now have a conduit to more information in you Angi and when Sirona next appears would you ask her the following three questions; Can she guide us to the last two gemstones? What and where is the final stage if and when we have all the gemstones? Can she give you instructions on how to operate the medallion or proof of its power? That's enough for now."

"I'll ask the questions and report back if she agrees to answer them," answered Angi, glad to have more specific instructions. "But, I don't believe Wolfram's question has been answered. Why have you hired so much security?"

Andrew was hoping to avoid this so early in the game but knew Angi and Wolfram were not easily diverted.

Taking a few seconds to select his words, he began. "It didn't take us long to realize that the medallion matched the ancient records of one of the secret societies we belong to. I actually saw a faint drawing. We were aware of *"the coming times"* prophesy, that it was expected in this century, but the pieces didn't come together until you appeared Angi with that medallion. It was definitely confirmed today when we saw the gemstone inserted. Whether you four understand it or not, you have been selected not only for this unusual quest but possibly to take humanity to the next level." He stopped to let that sink in.

"Oh, not again," replied Angi, in almost a lament. "Brigit's comment about me being a prophetess was unnerving enough but now you've taken it one step further. While I've gone along with this venture, I'm not prepared to think that I'm going to be responsible for saving humanity. That's too scary. It is way out of my range of possibilities. I'd prefer to think I'm just a courier."

"I agree with Angi," was Wolfram's rapid reply. "I'm here trying to function after a major car accident and in no way feel qualified for any such undertaking. I'm out."

"Well, if these two are out, I'm definitely out," said Morgan. "I don't mind being part of the foursome, but I'm no hero. In fact I'd argue the very opposite. You can't be referring to me."

"I've been delighted to be part of this venture, in fact I'd love to travel further with this group, but no way would I consider myself qualified to save humanity. I like manageable projects, numbers I can handle. Count me out," was Vette's response.

Bryce watching the four, smiled. "I'd have been disappointed if any of you thought you were qualified for such a task. In a world of overinflated egos I'm amazed the cosmos found you four. We would not expect you to handle this alone. We represent several organizations which are standing by to support and protect you. Two of these organizations have international roots. We are all walking into the unknown. Angi is just one step ahead as she wears the medallion. Angi remember I asked you about your name. Through our many sources we've discovered you have several royal genetic links and your Jenesis name was chosen because you are the 'beginning' of something. To answer your question, Wolfram, the degree of security is because we believe we are protecting something valuable, powerful and magical. We hoped to release this information in small doses but perhaps it is best it is out in the open. Don't negate it entirely. For now let's stay focused and get the gemstones. Can you agree to that?" said Bryce, trying to relieve their visible anxiety.

"OK, let's set this grand scheme aside for now. We'll stay on course and see what follows," replied Angi.

"Good. That's sounds fair. We'll speak no more of this unless we are pressed. Just know that you are well supported whatever transpires," confirmed Andrew.

"Then, to ease my nerves, can we return to our previous discussion. Since Atlantis is a topic I've shunned, can you tell me anything about it?" asked Morgan. "Andrew, I'll chat with you later as to how you have remained in the academic community knowing all this without destroying your career."

"Sure, but Morgan this will have to be a capsulated version," answered Andrew, glad for the diversion. "Atlantis, as you may or may not know was an island civilization. It had a large empire, ruling over countries as far as Egypt and Libya (the ancient name for Africa), and in Europe as far as Tyrrhenia (an ancient Greek name for the Etruscans). Plato wrote that the society was highly civilized, possessing outstanding arts and crafts, roamed the seas with ships and merchandise, had advanced science and even possessed the secret of flight. Their gods and goddesses, ordinary citizens elevated in legends, had technically advanced weapons of war which we are only now rediscovering. Many societies, including the Egyptians, Greeks and South Americans, kept saying that the tenets of their civilization came from a northern motherland, but this was ignored. However, like so many societies, Atlantis became debased, avaricious and corrupt. They were in the midst of a major war with several countries when destruction arrived from the skies. Survivors fled, some to the remaining pieces of their island, while others scattered to both sides of the Atlantic and into the Mediterranean. The destruction, according to Plato, left the sea beyond the Pillars of Heracles impassable and impenetrable because of the quantity of mud in the way, caused by the subsidence of the island. If Plato was aware of this, or it was still fresh in his time, then it speaks of a time closer to our own era. Anyway, as the centuries passed many groups of people kept returning to their ancient motherland, descendants, I would argue, of Atlantis."

"I was wondering, do you think our current fixation on disaster movies has anything to do with this cosmic disaster?" asked Vette.

"I wouldn't dismiss the connection," replied Andrew. "We're not alone in this fixation. May I remind you that numerous societies, some now in ruins, built impressive monuments and buildings to study the skies. Please feel free to explore this library there's plenty of information on all these topics. But, for a moment, we must not forget our emissary, Antonino."

This was Dylan's entry, "Someone gave, and is giving, Antonino details of our plans. So far, all our search efforts have produced nothing. We've ruled out the construction workers and are focusing inward. In the meantime our priority is Angi's safety. So, I must insist Angi that you have one of us with you at all times. I have also posted a guard in the corridor outside your bedroom."

"Thanks Dylan. I appreciate all your efforts," said Angi. "If Vette's not available I'll recruit any one of you, including you Morgan."

Morgan was glad to be included but prayed Angi would seek out the more experienced members.

As a closing directive Andrew said, "We must also assume that if we are unable to identify the culprit, then we can expect more trouble in the next two trips. Report anything suspicious, the smallest detail," and he turned and left the library with Bryce and Dylan.

Angi, Vette, Wolfram and Morgan looked at each other not knowing what to say. Angi broke the ice. "Let's leave what Andrew said until we've all had a chance to chew on it. I'm pleased that we're together. I like small steps. If Sirona appears I'll try and get answers to the questions."

"I totally agree," said Wolfram eyeing a comfortable chair. "We keep absorbing so much new information along with colliding into the occasional Celtic goddess and ghost that it is a lot to absorb. Let's tackle Andrew's bookcase and see what tomorrow brings." Silence filled the room as each tried to grasp the unthinkable possibilities which might lie ahead.

Chapter 10

DunRoslin Castle: Angi's Bedroom

That evening, alone in her room, Angi found the waiting nerve racking. She had retired early to await Sirona's arrival, not convinced it would even happen. "After all it was a mere suggestion," she reminded herself. Silence created room for questions; "Would she appear? Would the added gemstone make a difference? Why didn't she just come and retrieve the medallion? Surely they, whoever they were, could create similar gemstones or did the original stones hold some special magic?"

By 9:15pm, growing restless, she rose and began alternating between staring out the window and pacing. Annoyed, she demanded of herself, "Get a book and relax." She picked up a book and settled into a comfortable chair but couldn't concentrate as every sound diverted her attention.

Around 10pm, as darkness set in, she heard faint harp music. "There it is again. It must be Sirona's call signal.......a nice touch," she thought. With no preliminaries, Sirona appeared instantly in front of her, this time more distinctly. Angi wondered, "How does she judge the landing, a miscalculation could land her in the closet............ah, I know, she targets the medallion."

Confidently, Sirona greeted Angi, "There, I told you things would improve with the next gemstone. It is good to be back. I've missed the old place. Women's clothing has certainly improved since my last visit."

"Welcome," replied Angi, still adjusting to pop-in guests from another dimension. "Women's fashions have changed many times since the 1600s, which I assume was the time of your last house call. It is nice to see you again, Sirona, our last get-together was a bit fuzzy. By the way, are you the Sirona listed as a Celtic goddess in our books?" Angi was curious as to how she'd reply.

"I suppose that's what they'd call me. I never thought of myself in such lofty terms," replied Sirona. "Prior to the Romans when we had centuries of peaceful communications, I expect they had several names. I've never paid much attention. As with you, I state my name and assume that's the one recorded, but then there have been different languages over the centuries. For the past 2000 years my visits have been few and shrouded in danger so I'm surprised a name survived at all."

"How did you visit if the gemstones had all been removed from the medallion?" asked Angi.

"What you may not know is that the gemstones can be extracted and reinserted quite easily. So, when the Guardians, female Druids or later 'sacred gentry', wanted to chat they just reinserted the gemstones. Thankfully, those difficult times are over, but it will take time to reestablish the old linkages."

"You are saying the gemstones can be extracted as easily as they are inserted?" asked an amazed Angi.

"Yes, the process has likely been lost over the past centuries. I'll show you later. First we need to get the medallion fully operational." At that point, Sirona began to look around. In graceful movements she touched items, opened a book, looked out the window, inspected the bathroom and finally sat on a chair, her long legs stretching out into the room. "It is small but definitely an improvement. Is this where you sleep? I'm not sure whether this castle existed when I was last here, but it looks familiar."

"Yes, this is where I sleep," replied Angi, becoming relaxed in Sirona's company. "She speaks flawless English," thought Angi. "I wonder what I'd have done if she spoke Gaelic or some other foreign language?" With that in mind she asked, "I expect English is not the language of your homeland? Your command of the language is very good," said Angi, realizing she knew practically nothing of Sirona's world.

"I adapt," replied a confident Sirona. "I spoke Gaelic with the Druids, and later an earlier form of English in the 1600s. Knowing I was on travel assignment for your time I.... what's that phrase, oh yes......... I brushed up on your language, the idioms are fascinating. I also scanned the Canadian east coast where you grew up. How am I doing?" she said, with a slight grin.

"Not bad. You remind me of an old school friend," replied Angi. "Thanks for the consideration. I'd have been a dead loss if you spoke otherwise. I've a passing ability in French and Spanish but little else. So, now that we can communicate, let's clarify what lies ahead; how often will you appear and what is your role?" Angi's old administrative had clicked into action.

Sirona's arrival had confirmed Angi's earlier assessment. She was taller. Angi had to crane her head to talk to her. With a better image, Angi noted Sirona's pale, impeccable skin, platinum hair worn in a single braid down her back, and her graceful, slim physique. "It is nice to see someone else with emerald eyes," she thought. "Maybe there are more like me after all. Her outfit seems like a uniform, the blue flowing pants and silver tunic is accentuated by what appears to be three purpose-built pieces of jewelry; a pin on her left shoulder of a snake curled around a ruby stone, a watch-like band on her left wrist with flashing lights, and a gold ring with unusual lettering on her right index finger. She seems friendly enough, but be prepared for the unexpected. After all, she's from another dimension and you are judging her on this world's standards."

Sirona, wasting no time, proceeded, "Angi, we're moving into a critical phase so we'll need to meet more frequently. It is complicated, so my main task is to help you work with the medallion."

"Any idea how long this might take?" asked Angi.

Sirona hesitated, then responded, "Well, the Druids took twenty years for their basic training and, the one chosen to wear the medallion, had to have at least that much time again of proven experience. On that scale, it could take forty years as you judge time."

Angi gasped, "I'll be an old woman by then. Any chance of a quick version?" growing disheartened at the enormity of the task ahead.

"I've already considered that. We'll focus on some basic steps. But to do this we'll still need up to three to four hours every night for training. Even at that you will know enough to avoid trouble and achieve, what might be regarded in your world as magic. But it is not magic. Your actions must be based on scientific principles."

"But that schedule will cut into my normal sleep time," replied Angi, knowing she did poorly deprived of sleep.

"It would if I didn't intercede," replied Sirona. "Each night before you retire, I will use this vibrating instrument so your body will register a full night's sleep. In that way, you'll remain healthy. I'm under strict orders on that point."

"Sometime I'd like to discuss that vibrating device," said Angi, who kept wondering if it was permanently attached to Sirona's hand. "Does this mean you can juggle time?"

"In our world we measure time differently. Time is an illusion which can be manipulated. It is rather odd that you make such an issue of it," replied Sirona.

Her response triggered another obvious question in Angi's mind, "Speaking of time, if you've appeared to Guardians at least 2000 years ago, or even before that, how old are you anyway?"

"I suppose, using this world's calculation, I could be thousands of years old. But don't be too impressed, we age just like you," replied Sirona

"I recall an old phrase I once read which stated that a hundred or a thousand years of our time was but one of the gods. Would we call you an immortal?" asked Angi trying to grasp the reality of talking to someone of such vintage who looked about her own age.

179

"I suppose..........but," looking oddly at Angi, "you are also immortal, just different. As I said before, time is an illusion."

"Now that's a topic I'd love to explore," replied Angi....... "I know, later."

"Much later.......We have extensive training ahead and need lots of privacy, so it is best your colleagues know as little as possible about these sessions," said Sirona in a firm manner.

"That might be difficult," thought Angi, knowing Vette in the next room, her elephant ears sooner or later detecting that Angi was talking to someone. "I'll do my best. But what happens if someone knocks on the door and tries to enter," thinking of the security guard posted in the hall.

"That won't happen because when I'm here the door will be sealed," replied Sirona. "If they persist, I can easily leave."

"Neat," thought Angi. "She almost anticipates my questions........that saves time." But still wanting to clarify the situation, she pressed on, "Before we begin is there anything I should know about your hologram, although I admit, you look almost real?"

"I do have some time limits and other restraints. I'll let you know if anything turns up. I thought the harp music would alert you to my arrival or that I've entered the room and have, for some reason, chosen to be invisible."

"Ah, invisibility, that's a neat trick. I'll eventually get used to you popping in and out however hard it is to understand. I'm glad to see you as I want to learn more about this medallion. After all it is frustrating to be attached to an ancient piece of technology and know so little about it. I'm a quick learner so let's get started." Then she remembered the questions. "Oh, I almost forgot, my colleagues would like answers to three questions. Is that OK with you?"

"Sure, ask away," replied Sirona in a relaxed mood.

"First, can you guide us to the last two gemstones?"

"It is imperative you locate the gemstones yourself. My directive is to train you in working with the medallion to prevent any major mishaps. However, as you become more proficient I am hoping it will facilitate your efforts."

"Fair enough," replied Angi, and thought, "she sounds confident, that's a good sign." She then proceeded to the next question. "Is the location of the final stage of this quest the Hill of Tara? If not should we be considering another site?"

"It is at Tara. I'm hoping by then you will be sufficiently trained to open the gate. This invisible gate hasn't been disturbed in centuries, so it may present some unexpected problems. It has to be opened from your dimension as that is where it was sealed shut."

"So there is a gate at Tara?" replied Angi. "Are there any others?

"Yes, quite a few, but this is a key one," replied Sirona, reporting as if it was common knowledge.

"Let's leave the others for now, I can only handle so much," replied Angi. "My last question is whether you can give my colleagues proof of the medallion's powers? So far, the electrical properties of the medallion have been impressive, but they were hoping to have some sign of its actual powers," and realizing this seemed as if they were questioning the very purpose of the quest, she went on. "I suppose it is a question of whether this is just an odd piece of ancient electrical technology or something else."

This time Sirona wasn't so quick to respond. "I understand their concern. However, it all depends on how well we do with the training. When you are ready, I'll be able to give a more precise answer. It may take weeks."

"Fine, in that case let's begin," said Angi, contemplating how she would report back to her colleagues by saying enough but not too much.

"Angi, before we get into the practical training, we first need to explore your understanding of the world around you. Let me digress a bit. Centuries ago your world separated the spiritual and the scientific, which is not the case in other worlds. In the early days of your ancient empires the temples were centers of learning where spiritual and scientific education and practices existed as one. As societies weakened, scientific knowledge was lost and ritual, controlled by priests, dominated the civilizations. In the last 2000 years this separation has been reinforced time and time again; religious leaders condemning scientific advancement and scientists regarding spiritual beliefs and ritual as belonging to the dimwitted. Only now are there signs of the two coming together. So, not wanting to confuse you, I'll maintain this separation. We'll start with the spiritual.

Some of your philosophers and religious leaders envision the physical world as an illusion, created by your mind, senses and thoughts. Even when you are awake, you exist in a level of consciousness which the Australian Aboriginal people call 'Dreamtime'. In their culture, every person is a dream-child that exists before they are born and after death. To them the past, present and future coexist. Dreaming governs every aspect of life which must be lived in harmony with nature."

"That's fascinating," replied Angi, "my grandmother held such views and was known for her accurate predictions on the past, present and future. I regret not having enough time to discuss this with her before she died. People came to her with their problems and their dreams. I wasn't so gifted."

"You are if you gave it a chance to blossom," replied Sirona. "Everyone has the ability, it has just been negated in your society as something evil. This precious gift has been allowed to wither from neglect. Your grandmother's abilities were not surprising for your ancestors were carefully chosen to assure us of your birth at this time. But let's stay on course........ Thoughts shape your entire world and each person's thoughts are unique. For this reason no two people think identically no matter how hard they try. So, the world you see around you is an illusion. It is only as real as your mind, senses and thoughts think it is."

"That sounds like something I once read which said that we were but bit players in some play or movie. While watching the movie, the characters seem real as our senses become entwined with the story, but in the end the movie is nothing more than an illusion. So, we are but actors or actresses performing inside some gigantic illusion."

"That's true. Let's look at it in another way. Just think of a stage magician who is a master illusionist. Once you have an explanation of the illusion you realize that your senses have been tricked into believing the impossible."

"OK, if I accept this is an illusion, then what does that have to do with the medallion?" asked Angi. "I'm a practical person."

Undaunted, Sirona continued, "Fine, then you need to know that the secret of any illusion is to see beyond its boundaries to the bigger picture."

"And what is the bigger picture? Are you telling me that the director of this gigantic illusion is God?"

"As I recall, your world has had many titles for this supreme spirit, we refer to it as "the Law of One". And before you ask, that is a vast topic which is out of our discussion range."

In thought, Angi contemplated, "I suppose, we'd have done better with a single concept. It is not from lack of trying but it never seems to stick for long. It certainly would have saved us centuries of warfare."

Sirona determined to continue, pressed on, "It is important for you to know this as I will be pulling you beyond the illusion so you can work with the medallion's powers."

"So you are implying that we've limited our true potential by refusing to look beyond this veil of illusion? Perhaps our own philosophers and religious leaders have been telling us this for generations and we've refused to grasp the meaning."

"Most people resist change. Comfortable with their own version of the universe, they do not want to think, and some fear, what may lie beyond their senses. A fortunate few with extra sensory abilities already see beyond the veil. But slowly this invisible world is emerging as your scientists venture into the outer limits of your universe."

"What makes you think our scientists are reaching such limits?" asked Angi, not convinced she was comfortable with this world of illusion.

"That's a good opener to the scientific view. For years the human body has been regarded by your scientists as a complex machine, with surgery, drugs and other therapies used to fix some failing part. The universe was regarded in much the same way, and fixing it followed a similar mechanistic approach. By ignoring the spiritual and energetic fields of all living matter, healing options have not only been limited but the planet has been ravaged without due regard for its living properties. But this mechanistic approach is fading as scientists discover nature's unifying layers of energy. Some physicists have already come to the conclusion that matter is nothing more than frozen energy."

Surprised, Angi asked, "You mean that I'm frozen energy? I liked the illusion idea better."

"The physical body is the frozen part. You are actually made up of several layers of energy functioning at different vibrations. Some say the physical part is frozen light.........is that easier to accept?" Not waiting for an answer, she continued, "In fact, there are some who describe your entire world as a gigantic real-time hologram."

"That does it! ....You just shot me at warp speed beyond my comfort zone. I'm feeling as if I've stumbled into a course on philosophic quantum physics, one I didn't even register for. ....You are telling me that I'm a frozen glob of energy existing inside a gigantic hologram. To complicate this further, I'm sitting here talking to you, a hologram from another dimension .... now that's weird.......... actually it is beyond weird." Irritated, she continued, "Isn't this a bit much to drop on me in the first lesson. We don't propel our students into the end zone on the first lesson, why are you doing this to me?"

Taken aback by Angi's abrupt reaction, Sirona responded, "Good on you, Angi........ I had to test the boundaries. You absorb quite a bit before exploding. But now I know you will react and tell me off. I hate when someone just sits passively accepting all I dish out and later I find they understood practically nothing. We have little time and this is too important........ I need you to tell me whenever I've gone too far or to fast. Agreed?"

Warmed by her candor, Angi responded, "Agreed," and thought, "Well that's a plus. We should get along just fine if I don't drown first."

"I know this crash course is introducing concepts which may never have surfaced before," said Sirona, feeling sympathy for her young student. "Would you like a break?"

"No, I'm not that fragile. Press on, but could we backtrack to the energy layers, at least I've heard of them. The seven Chakras, the aura, and the spiritual, mental, emotional and etheric bodies were mentioned when I took yoga classes. Keep in mind my knowledge is miniscule. I'm also aware that our aboriginal peoples and Eastern cultures have followed these principles for generations."

"Yes, they persisted in their belief that humans were not machines but multidimensional entities constructed from the same subatomic building blocks as the rest of the universe. They knew that layers of energy existed in equilibrium with higher energy dimensions, that consciousness was a higher form of that energy, and that the physical body was a temporary, all be it frozen, shell needed for learning. However, no matter how much they voiced such thoughts your western nations ignored them or at worse belittled them."

"Sirona, can you be more specific? If I accept, in principle, that the universe is either an illusion or a multi-dimensional energy field, then how does this affect the use of the medallion's powers?"

"Very well, both views, spiritual or scientific, say in different words that the world around you is not solid but made up of energy which can be affected by your senses and thoughts. So, from this point, be careful what you wish or think, because each energy layer contains information that can be tapped, understood and even manipulated if properly approached. By manipulating the layers, disease can be prevented, or identified weeks in advance of its appearance in the physical body. As these subtle energies are unraveled your world will discover new means of measuring the energies and make better use of 'alternative' healing methods. I know this because in my world it is the alternative healing methods which dominate, while the surgical/chemical approach has the least prominence."

"The reverse?" said Angi's, fascinated at what this opposite world might look like.

"Yes, just think of it, with our approach there is less trauma to the human body and better long-term outcomes. The body doesn't age as quickly because individuals have their own sound and electronic devices to adjust their energy levels. We never allow disease to get established in the body," responded Sirona, as if selling a more effective health option.

"What about accidents," asked Angi, "surely they exist?"

"They do, even with the best methods of prevention, but even when surgery is required, we have devices which speed up healing by working with the different energy levels. No one is ill for any length of time. I expect we will have grand talks about this, but............not now," smiling at the eagerness of her student.

"Imagine what this could mean," thought Angi. "I need to make a list. In this first session I've enough topics for a university program." Then out loud she said, "Sure, I understand............. let's push on," But her mind couldn't stop thinking of the possibilities such change might bring. "Imagine preventing disease from happening.........cancer, infections, immune diseases... what would it do to our huge, costly health industry? The change would be catastrophic to some ....I'd love to see this other system." Then she charged herself, "Angi, get back on track, you are dreaming, now that is a good one, it seems I'm always dreaming.......... Wow, I will have to get my head around this, it is a bit intimidating."

Noting Angi's far away look Sirona thought it was time to shift gears, "To help you understand these energy levels, let's look at the easiest one, the etheric. Place your hands together, and then gradually pull them apart," said Sirona, as she demonstrated what she was asking Angi to do.

Angi complied.

"Do you feel a tingling or pressure sensation when you pull your hands apart? Now, if you partially close your eyes you may see a haze around the fingers and hands, something like a heat haze," said Sirona, giving Angi time to respond.

Excited, Angi reacted, "Heh, you are right. I can feel the energy and can see a colorless haze. So that's the etheric energy layer. Is that the 'aura'?"

"The etheric level is part of the aura. The aura, has seven colors, and is often described as a field of subtle, luminous energy surrounding a person or object. The aura in spiritually advanced individuals is often depicted as a halo," continued Sirona, "examples exist in some of your old paintings."

"I thought that was the imagination of the artist," as she continued to test the etheric energy of her hands. "OK, now that we've seen one layer, show me the rest," asked Angi, ready for the next demonstration.

"That's a bit more complicated. However, for you I can momentarily shift your vision so that you can see the other energy levels. Would you like that?"

"Great, go ahead.......I'm ready," replied an enthusiastic Angi.

Sirona, using the vibrating device made several passes over Angi's eyes and stepped away. "How's that?" she asked.

Momentarily, Angi's world exploded in light and vibrating energy. She waved her hands in front of her face to observe the flowing bands of energy. When she turned to look at Sirona she was overwhelmed by a blinding light. Caught in a moment of awe, Angi whispered, "How sad we can't all see this with our own eyes." And with that it faded. "Sirona you mentioned that our scientists have begun to open this door of energy, what tells you this is happening?"

"There are several encouraging signs. Crystal research has introduced computers, lasers and holographic technologies. Diagnostic tools have appeared, such as Computerized Axial Tomography (CAT) scans which combine computer technology and x-ray, and the Magnetic Resonance Imaging (MRI) scans which produce photos of the human body based on their reaction to high intensity magnetic fields. Others are using high-frequency magnetic fields to treat rheumatoid and degenerative arthritis, electrical currents to enhance the cancer-killing effects of chemotherapy, electrical techniques to switch off cell replication to destroy tumors and electrical stimulators to relieve pain and to accelerate the healing of bone fractures."

"What about Reiki or what some call Therapeutic Touch? These seem to operate on this principle of energy," asked Angi, who once considered such training.

"They are the beginning of a new wave of healers but their training needs to be augmented with advanced scientific principles for more effective results," said Sirona.

"I'm beginning to feel slightly drained. In a single evening you've turned my world upside down. The world I thought was real is either an illusion or layers of energy which can be identified and manipulated. I'm either frozen energy or frozen light, which is still a bit hard to accept. However, I'm beginning to see the connection with the medallion. I'm aware that the medallion's gemstones have been selected to affect different chakras. Is that it in a nutshell?" asked Angi.

"You certainly are a quick learner, Angi. You've taken a giant step. I am aware challenging your well established views can be threatening. But your openness to new ideas is impressive. Do not get discouraged nor be surprised that by morning you start doubting much of this. I'll keep repeating it in the days ahead. Now let's begin the practical application of this information. First I will get you to use your hands to manipulate the energy, and then later I will make you do it entirely with your mind." Looking at a box of tissues on Angi's table, she pulled one out and said, "Let us see if you can move this light object from the desk to the center of your bed. Concentrate on the item, force the energy through your fingertips, lift the tissue in the air and guide it towards the bed. The medallion will enhance your efforts."

The first, second and third attempts failed........the tissue barely rose, then it rose and fell abruptly, then it rose and landed on the floor. Frustrated, Angi remarked, "This is harder than I thought. What am I doing wrong?"

"Nothing," was the gentle voice of her instructor. "You are still not comfortable with these new concepts and your own abilities. Compare it to your early nursing days.........does that work?"

"Oh, that's indelibly etched on my brain..........understood......... practice makes perfect, or some such mantra," as Angi continued to move the object.

"We'll stay with this simple task until it's mastered, then we'll move to heavier objects," said Sirona. The rest of the night was filled with a repeated sound of "Again....... again........again."

Four nights passed as Sirona, a tough drill master, worked with Angi in moving items from the desk to the center of the bed, each task demanding more skill. If one could see into the room one would encounter various objects floating in the air with Angi apparently talking to herself, because only she had the benefit of the medallion.

Concluding the fourth night, Sirona decided it was time to test Angi's progress. "Angi, tomorrow you have a medical appointment. Your head wound has had a few days to heal but, taking a small device from her pocket, she examined the area through the dressing to record a before and after image. I want you to concentrate on the back of your head, visualize the wound, and begin to heal the area by working with the energy fields."

"Well, this is more my speed. Wound care I know." Angi thought of a former patient with a similar injury, and placing her hands over the back of her head, began. After some minutes she opened her eyes. "Now, can you take another photo, as I believe that is a miniature camera you took out of your pocket?"

Sirona smiled. "You are clever. Yes, it takes photos and does a lot more," and she looked at Angi waiting for the expected response.

"I know..........we'll talk about it later," said Angi, and thought, "I'll have to book more time with Sirona. There's so much to learn.........I wonder if I'll live long enough. It is like discovering an ancient treasure trove with an English speaking guide ....what could be better than that? It'll be tough sledding under her tutelage, but I prefer that."

Smiling, Sirona checked the results. "Very good, Angi," and not revealing her findings she turned and asked, "I want you to register the physician's comments tomorrow but say nothing. Whatever occurs, do not think we are ready to reveal much to your colleagues. You'll need a lot more training. This is a first test. We are making progress. See you tomorrow night," and after the usual routine scanning she disappeared.

℞

Angi reported back to her colleagues the answers to the first two questions, and said they would have to wait on the last one. She was pleased no one pressed her for more details. But Sirona had not taken into account the castle's inquisitive nature. Within days everyone knew that Angi's light was not extinguished until after two in the morning, a change from her previous routine. No one asked why, as they knew.

When Andrew's personal physician removed the dressing and examined Angi's head wound, he hesitated and asked, "When did this accident occur?"

He went to his desk to check his records and returned to Angi. "I've never seen a wound heal like this. There's practically no evidence anything happened yet the ER report is clear that you had a critical injury a few days ago requiring stitches. I'll remove the stitches but there's no need for another dressing or appointment." Puzzled, he asked, "Angi, do you have a history of healing quickly?"

"No," replied Angi, wanting desperately to relieve his perplexed expression. Elated at her progress, she could hardly contain her excitement, but held her silence. "No time to get too exuberant," she thought, "you are still a novice."

Fortunately, the others were preoccupied; the mole in their midst had not been unearthed no matter how many times they checked and rechecked the records and electronic devices, and plans for Iona were well underway.

Angi knew she had little time to dwell on her accomplishments for much would be expected of her at Iona. On the trip back to the castle a thought registered "Sirona knew. She wanted me to hear it from a physician in this dimension. I wonder what other surprises she has in store."

Scotland: Iona

Preparations for Iona had hit a frenzied pace. The road ahead was plagued with suspense. As the group focused in on the last two gemstones, they knew Antonino would be getting desperate.

Former Guardians, contacted to see if they remembered anything about the Iona hiding place, had nothing to contribute. Passing the gemstone onto a trusted relative was, they thought, their only directive. Several Iona experts were contacted by Andrew to see if they knew of a secret hiding place on the Island but this too came up blank.

Edginess hung over their inability to uncover the mole. Planning continued with trepidation assuming every detail was being transmitted to Antonino. The police, having missed their chance to arrest him, reported he had vanished. While word on the street was that he was not getting a warm reception from his underworld contacts, the police knew with the incentive being offered he was bound to find someone. So, for greater control, it was decided that a small group would travel to Iona by helicopter. Andrew would make the arrangements. Because Iona was a popular tourist site, the flight would begin at DunRoslin at 4:30 in the morning, allowing four hours to get to the island, complete their search and, hopefully, find the gemstone. "We'll have to be damn lucky to find anything in that short of time," said Andrew, growing restive.

For days everyone was busy scanning the Internet, checking Andrew's library materials and reviewing maps. Large maps covered the library table and several reference books lay open as the group tried to determine where someone, with three hundred year foresight, would pick a hiding place for the gemstones. Before the trip they gathered in the library to review their findings.

The weather was hot and humid, two open windows providing little relief. The group, so absorbed in their research, kept wiping beads of perspiration from their upper lips and foreheads. No one complained about the discomfort. While Angi and Vette sat on large leather chairs wading through books, Wolfram and Andrew manned the computers, leaving Morgan and Bryce scanning maps and old drawings of Iona.

"There's so much history to consider," said Morgan. "We'll need to go back further than the Christian era after all there are some items on the Island which go back to the Druids. Maybe there's some special significance to the hidden place, like a stone circle, an ancient cairn, a statue or a building."

"Now that you mention it Morgan, the old Gaelic name for Iona was *Innis nan Druidhneach* which translates as the 'Island of the Druids'. I've also heard it called the 'Sacred Isle of the Druids'. Apparently, Iona was a primary seat of learning for the Celtic Druid Magi," replied Andrew.

"Is that the source of its name?" asked Vette.

"Well, the name HY or I, by which Iona was generally known, is said to signify the sacred Isle of the Eye," replied Andrew.

"You mean like the Eye of Horus of the Egyptians?" asked Morgan.

"As you know, the Eye was an ancient symbol of life, understanding, and vitality related to sacred matters. It also represented Druidic wisdom and knowledge."

"But why was this particular island so sacred to the Druids and Celtic Christians?" asked Angi.

Bryce responded. "It may go back further than the history we know. Tradition says that there was once a city of sacred reputation on Iona, adorned with fine buildings and temples, a seat of learning visited by students from all parts of the world. Its present village, called Threld, means in the Gaelic, "*great city*" and the remains of stone circles and menhirs testify to its considerable antiquity. The original island is said to have had a colonnade of 360 engraved stones of which only two have survived. The 360 stones were thought to have had an astronomical significance and date from a period prior to the change in the calendar which we talked about before. The one surviving stone on Iona is called the Maclean's Cross. This stone has been carved out of a block of solid granite, stands eleven feet in height above ground, and its engraved figures are so worn they could be pre-Christian."

"Are you implying this island might have been an important religious centre of Atlantis, a place of high learning which was destroyed in the comet attack?" asked Wolfram.

"Possibly," replied Bryce. "It may have been this subconscious awareness which compelled the Druids and Celtic Christians to maintain a sacred presence on the site."

"Or, perhaps the Druids were continuing a legacy which they already knew," interjected Morgan. "It is argued that the Druids were a much older group than the historians give them credit. The Celts also called Iona a '*thin place*' where the material and spiritual worlds were separated by the thinnest of veils."

"Brigit talked about '*thin spaces*' when we were in Ireland," replied Angi.

"Well, thin spaces or Atlantis roots, it means that Iona possessed a mysterious something unique to other islands. But sticking to recorded history, there is another factor which may have significance. While most regard Iona's history as beginning about 563 C.E. with the monk St. Columba (also known as Colm Cille), there is evidence that there were monks there long before that. As you may know, Druid priests converted to the Christian faith forming a monastic order, an earlier Celtic Christian order, known as the Culdees (Coli Dei), which means 'servants of the Lord of God,' " said Andrew.

"Yes, I read about that in your books here in the library. What happened to the Culdees?" asked Angi.

"As expected, they established Celtic Christian churches in former Druid centers, with Iona being their chief seat. Being followers of the Old Testament, they were said to be connected to the Church of James, the Essenes, and the Gnostics. When the Roman church decided to get rid of any opposition, the Gnostic groups were their earliest targets. It took some time before the Celtic Christians were under attack, but it finally happened. At that time, the Culdees melted into existing Christian groups, some of their beliefs and symbols rising to the surface in later centuries."

"I'm sure you read that the Culdee's favorite symbol was the dove, which is still evident on Iona today," replied Bryce.

This prompted Vette to ask, "Isn't the dove a feminine symbol?"

"Fascinating," replied Angi, "it is said that in this century feminine spirituality will become essential to our survival because it is focused on the heart. Maybe this has already begun on Iona."

"That should create a royal battle with the males who favor a patriarchal religious hierarchy," replied Vette.

"Now, that's a topic we could chew on for days," said Wolfram with a broad grin, "but not today. However, Andrew, I'm assuming you've mentioned the Culdees because there may be some symbol, like the dove, which could lead us to the secret hiding place?"

"Yes and no," was Andrew's reply. "What I'm trying to point out is that we have a number of possibilities and, regrettably, we do not know what the original planners had in mind back in the 1600s. You will note that while we have the names of the original families, we do not know the leader of this carefully organized secret enterprise. Was it someone different from the chosen gentry? Someone went to a lot of effort and cost to have those miniature boxes made in Europe and assemble the couples in Scotland. I expect this is the same person, or persons, who financed the four couples who immigrated to the new world. If we knew this person or persons we might have a better fix on the site. Without that, we're speculating. So let's see what we have."

Angi began. "We have three buildings of significance; the Iona abbey, the nunnery and St. Oran's chapel and cemetery. Very little of the original monastery built by St. Columba in the 6th century, survives. In 1203, a Benedictine abbey was built and, while it came under attack by the Vikings in the middle ages, it continued until the Reformation when the building was demolished and left in ruins. It wasn't until the 20th century that the abbey was restored."

"Do we have any idea what the pre-restoration building might have looked like?" asked Wolfram.

"Here's a printout," said Morgan, who picked it out of a pile of papers on the table. "The abbey doesn't look too promising. In the 1600s, the medallion planners would know of the Reformation attacks and would not risk exposing the gemstones either to the elements or further attack."

"Nevertheless, Lord George MacLeod must have had these plans in the 1930s. Let's hold onto them, just in case," said Wolfram. "What's the next one?"

Morgan responded, "The nunnery, which was also destroyed at the Reformation and was never restored. It remains as it did in the 1700s. However, since the gemstones were left to females to guard, this could be the site, but, unfortunately it is open to the elements."

"It doesn't rule out a hidden chamber," interjected Angi.

"I don't suppose we have any detailed drawings of the nunnery?" asked Wolfram.

"No, we've searched the Internet and books, there is nothing. At best we have drawings of what it might have looked like on the outside," replied Morgan, pulling out another piece of paper.

"Let's go with that. It might have some use," said Wolfram "What's the third option".

"That's the chapel and cemetery. Both sit at the end of the Street of the Dead, and the chapel is regarded as the oldest standing building on Iona," reported Morgan.

"Why the Street of the Dead?" asked Vette.

"The name originated from the practice of medieval pilgrims walking along the street from the abbey to the chapel leading to the cemetery. The cemetery was an ancient royal burial ground, called in the Gaelic "*Reilig Odhrain*" (English: Oran's burial place or cemetery). It is said to have contained the graves of 48 Scottish, 8 Norwegian, and 4 Irish kings and possibly rulers from Dal Riata and France. As such, it may have been an important burial place long before the recorded 9th to 11th centuries."

"What about the graves, maybe one king stands out?" asked Angi.

"Unfortunately," replied Morgan, "none of the graves are identifiable, the inscriptions were worn away by the 17th century. So it is unlikely the 17th century planners would have considered this option, they would be looking for something more substantial."

"Nevertheless, let's look around when we get there just in case something stands out. The Internet videos didn't give us much," replied Angi.

"What about the chapel," asked Wolfram, realizing the options were dwindling?

Andrew reentered the discussion, "St. Oran's chapel has an interesting history. Some say it was built by Columba and others say it was there before he arrived. Irrespective of this unrecorded account, some ruin was restored in the 12th century when the Benedictine abbey was built. It is simple and unadorned except for an elaborate tomb-recess built into the south wall in the 1400s said to be for the MacDonalds, the Lords of the Isles. The exterior is of stone, with a beautifully carved Norman arch over the entrance. It is a good possibility."

"There's an interesting side story about this place," said Angi. "Apparently, in 1098 when the Norse King Magnus Barelegs entered the chapel with intent on plunder, he recoiled, shaken and ordered that none should enter. He never revealed what he saw or what caused such fear. Any chance we might rattle some ancient ghost?"

"There's quite a few tales about this place," replied Andrew, "even one that someone was buried alive when it was constructed."

"It is well known that conquering societies build their religious buildings on top of temples or sacred places of their enemies. So, this chapel may have been built over a pagan center. We'll know if a raging ghost appears from some ancient time period. While I'd love the possibility, I think it would hamper our search," said Morgan with a chuckle.

"What about the tomb?" asked Angi "Any chance it might be 'something else'. Remember what Fiona said 'It is not what it appears'."

"Good point," replied Wolfram, showing a decided interest. "I'll bring up a larger photo on the computers and let's take a look."

Using both computers the video and still photos were reviewed several times.

"It could be," said Andrew "but if it is not what it seems, then it begs the question, what would trigger a secret opening? We could play with the design and stones for days and come up with nothing. Let me check with an old colleague to see if there are any more details about this tomb." He went to his study, and closed the door to make a call. The others waited proposing various opinions as to how a secret compartment might be opened.

"That wasn't much help," was Andrew's returning comment. "As expected, there are no plans. In fact it is only thought to be MacDonald's tomb based on its design. If this is the site, then we face another obstacle. We need to unlock the secret chamber without damaging a stone or decoration. No destruction will be tolerated."

"That's a tough order, but understandable," replied Wolfram.

"I know this has not been mentioned, but for a moment, let's look at St. Martin's Cross, it has been standing there for centuries," said Bryce, "It does have longevity."

"Already checked," replied Wolfram. "It is solid. In addition, someone would have had to create a hidden chamber large enough for a number of boxes, however small. I can't see it happening. Look at the cross on the computer, it is pretty stark. But it doesn't rule out something in the vicinity."

"That might be difficult as there are path stones in the vicinity. But still, would the early planners risk leaving it so exposed. I don't think so. It has got to have some protection from the elements or someone accidently opening it," replied Andrew,

"So, what are we left with?" asked Angi.

"It looks like the nunnery, the chapel, the cemetery or, remotely, near St. Martin's Cross. We have to narrow it down quickly as we have little time. Basically, as I see it, our chances are slim to zero.........we'll need a miracle," replied Wolfram, turning towards Angi.

"Don't look at me. I'm no miracle worker. I told you Sirona said that she could not help us, we have to find the gemstones ourselves. I admit, she keeps saying I'll be ready for this trip.........which is more confidence than I have. It is some stretch to think I am going to be much help. Remember I told you the Druids took forty years...........what have I had, two weeks max." And with emphasis she continued, "I'm a pure novice. The best option, as I see it, is to have another ghost pop up."

"Angi, in fairness, should we hold off for a later date?" asked Andrew, aware that they were placing a great deal of pressure on her.

"Sirona is certain we'll have the gemstones before the next full moon which is five days from now. On that vote of confidence, let's go.......if, by some miracle we find the secret chamber, maybe there'll be two boxes and our search will be over."

"Good, I'll proceed with the final arrangements. Be ready for an early rise on Wednesday morning. Dylan will not be coming, but two of his crew will accompany us on the helicopter. The helicopter comes with a four member crew; a pilot, co-pilot and backup. By my calculation there will be twelve of us; four crew, two of Dylan's men and six of us."

"Six, is Bryce coming with us?" asked Angi.

"No, Dana will be coming along," replied Andrew.

"Why?" asked Wolfram. "Now that Morgan's here do we need Dana? I've got no beef with Dana, just trying to reduce the odds."

"This will be her last trip. She's never been to Iona and before Morgan arrived I promised her that she could travel with us if Iona was confirmed on our agenda."

"Fine, a dozen it will be. Vette and I will stick to Angi like glue, which leaves Morgan and Dana with you. Do you expect Dylan's team to accompany us on the island?"

"I'll leave that to Dylan. If we can land close enough to the abbey and chapel, they may stay with the helicopter. It is unclear whether the helicopter needs to refuel at Mull before we head back. If so, the crew may do this while we're searching the place. Such details will be confirmed within the hour. We'll review all of this again just before take off. Right-O.........talk to you soon," and he was off.

"Let's pray for clear weather. I don't relish scrambling over old rocks in the fog or rain. How about the rest of you, is there anything else we should be thinking about?" asked Angi.

"Yah, I'd like to know what Antonino and his sidekick have up their sleeves," replied Vette. "We've got this trip tightly organized, assuming we'll hit pay dirt and find one or more gemstones. But I'm certain by the time we embark on Wednesday Antonino will have been well informed. If he thinks there's little chance of finding the last gemstone, he'll strike. Angi, if we find a gemstone it might be prudent to insert it immediately into the medallion. What do you think?"

"Why, do you think that'll increase the medallion's powers?" asked Angi.

"It helped the last time. With more gemstones the medallion is bound to be more powerful and provide a more potent electric jolt. Of course, this will only be needed if Wolfram and I have been decommissioned. I always like a backup plan," replied Vette.

"That's a good idea, Vette," replied Wolfram.

"No problem. I'll do it. In the meantime I'll keep working with Sirona to prepare for the trip," was Angi's confident reply.

On Wednesday, everyone was ready by 4am. In the dim morning light a navy blue and white four-bladed twin-engine helicopter landed on the castle's side lawn. The interior had seating for nineteen plus storage. Wolfram watched from his bedroom window as Dylan and his team stored supplies aboard. "I suppose that's food and backup supplies considering we'll be travelling for hours. Andrew doesn't want us stopping off for lunch. By their congeniality, Dylan's men know the helicopter crew. That's Andrew's trademark, every detail considered. I've never travelled in a helicopter before, this'll be a first."

They took off at one minute past 4:30. Once airborne, Andrew opened one picnic container prepared by his staff and passed around snack boxes for everyone. A coffee thermos appeared and everyone enjoyed a light breakfast. It had been agreed, in light of the departure hour, that they would eat en route. As they travelled west and slightly north, Andrew, Dana and the crew took turns pointing out key Scottish sights. They watched the rising sun rays warm the land to a magnificent day. They were high enough to get a clear view of the geography and the distant sea. The two hours passed with an apparent relaxed group of travelers heading to Iona, but underneath was the lingering threat there was a Judas on board. Just off the south-west tip of Mull, across the Firth of Lorn from the coast of Scotland, the helicopter veered towards Iona. Approaching Iona they could see its sandy beaches, rock-strewn meadows, turquoise waters and the stately abbey. Of some concern was a thick fog hugging the shoreline. Before they had a chance to ask, the pilot commented, "That fog will dissipate once the sun gets up but it might delay the morning ferry from Mull. Do not worry, it is fine where we are scheduled to land." Within minutes the helicopter came to a smooth landing within 500 yards of the abbey.

"Andrew must have pulled some mighty strings for this," thought Angi. "We'd never have managed these trips without him."

Once the eight disembarked, the helicopter took off for refueling in Mull. It would return within the hour.

Stepping onto the soil of Iona, Angi felt a powerful sensation she had never experienced before. "This must come from centuries of sacred worship which has seeped into every grain of this hallowed soil. We must tread gently so as not to disturb such spiritual presence. It is no wonder so many have been attracted to this sacred isle in this corner of the world."

As planned, the eight members; two groups of three and one of two, set out to investigate the three possible sites. St. Martin's Cross was quickly eliminated as there did not seem to be any possible area which was not exposed to visitors or the elements. They then headed towards the nunnery.

They spent a half hour climbing up and over the ruins, carefully looking at every crevice and unusual outcrop. Nothing was evident but it was not dismissed.

Next was Oran's chapel and cemetery. A quick walk around the cemetery eliminated it as in keeping with the Internet description, the existing headstones were badly worn, some were non existent, and specific kings could not be identified. This left the chapel.

While Dana, Morgan, Andrew and Colin, one of Dylan's men, circled the exterior of the stone building, Angi, Wolfram, Vette and Matt, Dylan's next in command, went inside. The tomb still seemed the best option but there was nothing to aid them in their search. Angi, Wolfram, and Vette carefully felt every segment of the tomb's sculptured outline, and pressed each rectangular stone in the center. Angi, looking at what appeared to be an animal in the right hand design asked, "What do you think this might have been when originally sculptured, a lion, a dog or a lamb?"

"Likely a lion, as it is a common royal symbol. But since its features are so worn, it is hard to say. By any chance does it move if you fiddle with it?" asked Wolfram.

"Not a fraction, I had some hope this would be the key," replied Angi, and stepping back observed, "You know, I agree with the others, this doesn't look like a tomb, it is too small, but then what do I know about medieval tombs."

Wolfram, glancing at his watch, turned saying, "An hour has already passed. If there's anything you can do Angi, now's the time."

At that moment, Angi heard harp music but Sirona didn't appear. "Ah, she's doing her invisible act," she said to herself, "likely checking on how I perform." Then she heard a whispered command.

"Angi, go outside the chapel and address Nature as I taught you. Command the fog to assist you. Visualize what you want it to do and manipulate the energies."

Angi turned abruptly. The others sensing something was afoot, followed her back into the open. She positioned herself about twenty-five feet from the chapel. Wolfram and Vette stood a few feet behind her to give her space while the others moved further back and stood waiting.

Raising her arms, Angi, giving herself courage, thought, "Here goes.........I pray this works........I'm not entirely comfortable doing this." Looking out towards the shore, she commanded in a loud voice, "Fog, come forth. You were here when the gemstones were hidden, once, maybe twice, in the past. We need your help. Which building should we explore?" Angi closed her eyes to work with the energies. Not a word was spoken, the silence disturbed only by the whistling wind and the circling seagulls.

After a few minutes, Angi squinted wondering, "Has anything happened?" The fog stood firm.

Sirona's second command came more abruptly. "Angi, concentrate, this isn't child's play. You are trying to move a strong force of Nature. Command the medallion to help you in your request." Sirona knew this was a key test for Angi she had to control the power of the medallion.

Angi held the medallion with her left hand and raising her right arm, repeated the command, this time more forcefully. She waited and opened her eyes when she heard a whispered gasp from Vette.

To her amazement the fog had moved over the bank and in a single wall was progressing towards the buildings. First, the nunnery seemed to be the target, and then the fog moved towards the chapel. About fifty yards from the chapel, a portion of the fog separated from the main bank and floated over the top of the building, forming a halo.

Morgan whispered to those standing near "That's what they said the Druids could do. It was said they could command the mist and fog to protect their warriors or to confuse their enemies. I thought that was a fairy tale."

Still in awe, Angi, as if familiar with such phenomenon, said out loud, "Thanks for your help." At that moment, as if acknowledging her gratitude, the fog retreated back to the shoreline.

As she lowered her arm she heard Sirona's voice, "Good work, Angi, but it is not over yet. You have more to do inside."

Smiling, Angi turned to an amazed group of companions and said, "Well, we've identified the building .... How's our time, Wolfram?"

"We've got twenty-five minutes," and realizing the limitation of space inside the building asked, "Perhaps we should keep the number going inside to six." With no argument, Dylan's team assumed duty at the entrance.

Sirona slipped by invisibly and stood against a far wall to watch. While forbidden to interfere, she was determined to be present to see what happened.

Convinced the hidden chamber was at or near the tomb, Angi stood in front of it and raised her arms, more assured now of what to do. This time she kept the words to herself as she asked for assistance.

The group waited in anticipation. When nothing happened, Angi, growing uncertain, repeated her request.

Minutes passed.............still nothing.

Just as Angi was about to try a third time, a loud click broke the spell. From a corner of the room a lit glass votive candle broke from its position in a round metal stand, rose in the air, floated toward the tomb enclosure, and stopped in front of a center rectangular stone of the tomb. Acknowledging the signal, Angi stepped forward and pressed the stone with her right hand. She felt an infinitesimal movement. Then the candle moved to a diagonal stone and stopped. Again Angi obeyed by pressing the stone. In a series of seven random steps Angi followed the candle, with each stone showing increased movement. As she pressed the final stone the candle rose in the air and returned to its place in the metal stand. Still with her hand on the stone, Angi voiced a "Thanks for the help," and waited.

Within seconds the stones, forming a zigzag pattern, swerved inward revealing a small enclosure. On the top of a wooden storage shelf, covered with dust and cobwebs, were eight slots prepared centuries ago for their expected treasures. One was filled with a familiar purple bag. Angi stepped in and retrieved the bag. Returning to the chapel room, she opened the bag to discover the familiar engraved box. Opening the box she found another gemstone.

Unable to contain her silence, Vette whispered, "It is a ruby."

"Yes", whispered Angi. "Isn't it beautiful?" The rich red color of the gemstone glittered in the light. "The ruby is a noble stone which gathers and amplifies energy bringing spiritual wisdom, knowledge and wealth. I once read it could assist in changing ones world ....now isn't that a surprise." Remembering her agreement, she pulled out her small holding device, and placing the gemstone next to the medallion, the gemstone was quietly received. For the first time Angi felt a surge of energy. She reinserted the box into the purple bag and passed it to Vette who rapidly stored it in her knapsack. At that moment a mechanical sound was heard like wheels turning, and the wall began to close, the tomb rectangular stones reforming into a tightly knit pattern as if nothing had happened.

Remaining invisible, Sirona smiled. "You did it, Angi! You are a fantastic student. See you later," and she was gone.

"This may never have been a tomb," said Morgan from the back of the room. "It was likely a hiding place for the monks."

Suddenly, Andrew glanced at his watch, "It is 8:35am. Let's get out of here. I am relieved we were able to accomplish this mission without disturbing anything."

Exiting the chapel the group saw the helicopter was already revving up. They partially ran towards the plane, and were in the air within minutes. Looking down they saw a few early church goers to the regular morning service surprised to see a helicopter taking off.

Angi glanced out the window in time to see the fog dissipate. "It is as if it stood waiting to be summoned," she thought. "It is an example of nature's living cells which we ignore or insult with our ruthless activities. So much to learn................" She suddenly felt drained and sank into the leather seat. She craved peace and rest. But at that moment she looked up to see the three smiling faces of Wolfram, Vette and Morgan.

"You are absolutely amazing," said Wolfram, in admiration of all that she had accomplished. "Rest, let me know whatever you need."

"I'm speechless," said Vette, "this journey is an ever-ending basket of wonders. You deserve a rest, old friend."

"Angi, you've carried me into the stratosphere. I never thought such ancient miracles could be reawakened in my lifetime. My deepest thanks," said Morgan.

As Angi positioned herself with a pillow and blanket she reviewed the day's activities, "I wonder if I've graduated to another level? I'll ask Sirona when next we meet........................ Life is truly amazing. Imagine the grand chats Gran and I could have had about all this. They say when one door closes, another opens. Here I am in Scotland on a mysterious journey with a group of strangers, and three companions who are becoming closer than family. Who'd have guessed.........." weary, she dozed off. As she slept, her friends kept watch.

It was a half hour into the flight before anyone thought of eating. Andrew opened the second food hamper and distributed refreshments. Everyone chatted about topics other than Iona as they needed time to assess the events of the morning. There remained an underlying expectation that Antonino had yet to pounce, and they were facing the dawning realization that the last gemstone might never be found.

Chapter 11

Scotland, Musselburgh: Antonino Meets the Mole

At four minutes to midnight, Antonino eased his rented green Peugeot car into an unlit area near the Promenade within sight of the Quay Complex in Musselburgh on the Firth of Forth. It had taken him fifteen minutes to drive from Edinburgh. The Quay was a recognizable and a good meeting spot for someone unfamiliar with the town. His contact would be coming from Inveresk. A light evening fog swirled around the car. The meeting was set for fifteen minutes past midnight when it was assumed the place would be quiet. The tapping of his fingers on the steering wheel was the only sign of anxiety.

To calm himself, he began assessing his situation. "At last, I'm going to hold the medallion ....it'll be all mine," as he savored the possibility. "This caper has cost me a pretty penny. Not only the travel and ancillary payments in Ireland, Canada and the United States but this last vulture demanded 20,000 pounds up front and another upon delivery. But it is worth it. Imagine getting someone so close to the font who provided regular reports on every step of their plans. I've stuck it to that pompous Sinclair who thought he had me pinned down. Too bad the medallion wasn't grabbed at Scone, but then again, its value has increased with the addition of another gemstone." Taking time he visualized his future, "This medallion will make me a fortune. I've got two contenders already salivating at getting their hands on it. I'll find two more to raise the stakes. Then I'll head for warmer climates. I could finalize the deal from some beach. I deserve an easier life. Just wait and see what I do to those Vatican demi-gods. They'll regret ditching me." Growing irritated he checked his watch using a small pen light which he pulled from his shirt pocket. "Damn it, our meeting time was fifteen minutes ago. I'm the one who had the longest drive."

At 12:30 when a police car appeared he ducked down onto the seat. "Don't need that aggravation," he thought. The police car slowed, it appeared they were checking the license plate. No alerts, so they moved on, to Antonino's relief.

12:45 came and went. Antonino's agitation was growing more profound. "What the hell happened? I didn't expect this...........you don't suppose it has all been uncovered and I am a sitting duck. Perhaps I'm in the wrong spot......... maybe I misunderstood and should be closer to The Quay. But that wasn't our agreement. I wrote it down to be sure. No, it is not me it is that idiot I am working with. I prefer pawns that are afraid of me, this one's afraid of nothing."

Three minutes to one he was about to call it quits. "I can't sit here all night. Maybe I should have used the cell phone.........but we'd agreed that unless it was an emergency all traceable communications would be avoided." Chuckling to himself he said "After all, these cursed phones can be hacked.........I should know."

At 1:10 a black Volkswagan Touareg SUV pulled up behind him, much to Antonino's relief. "It is about time!" He reached down and tucked a stuffed envelope of money under his right leg. "I'll make sure I have the medallion in my hand before I fork this over, I'm no fool." Then looking up he thought, "That's an odd jacket, likely a British thing." He continued to watch the familiar figure in dark clothing walk rapidly towards his car.

The car door opened and his contact slipped into the side bucket seat.

"Sorry to keep you waiting I got held up with a long distance phone call."

"No matter, have you got the medallion?" asked Antonino, trying to show as little irritation as he was capable of.

"Ah, there's been a slight change in plans," was the cold reply.

"Just a minute, you haven't got the crust to ask for more money. You've been well paid. I expected a delivery tonight." Then realizing he might be overreacting, he pulled back and asked, "Is there news of the last gemstone?" Then a cold shiver crept up his spine accompanied by a sickening feeling in his stomach. "Did I misjudge this silver-tongued snake?" He waited to see how his question would be answered.

"Not quite," was the reply. Glancing out the window for possible witnesses, seeing none, his contact whipped out a nine millimeter pistol with a designer silencer from the left hand pocket of the odd jacket.

"What the hell...........you double crossing bastard!" came Antonino's panicked reaction. Scrambling, his instincts triggered an immediate desire to bargain his way out of the situation, and asked, "All right, how about another 20,000 pounds?"

In a sarcastic tone the reply came, "You haven't enough money for this. I've just seen what this medallion can do. It has powers you could never have imagined. If what I have witnessed at Iona is a glimpse of its capabilities, I shall be famous. This medallion will make me rich beyond my wildest dreams. I'm not about to share this with anyone ....it is mine.......I am confiscating this for myself," came the menacing reply.

"But you said that only the woman, what was her name,.....yah, Angi, ...only she could operate this medallion............what changed that?" replied Antonino, still gambling for time.

"If that dimwit can operate the medallion, so can I. It is likely a simple learning curve. It looked relatively easy."

At this point, Antonino reached under the car seat to retrieve a knife he had hidden as a backup, never expecting it would be needed. His long fingers reached the object, but it slipped from his grasp.

"Don't try anything, Dante. I am fully aware you have had a string of corpses in your wake with this caper alone. So, farewell.........Thanks for the treasure." Two muffled shots hit Antonino in the head and chest............the well placed accuracy was intended to kill.

Antonino's last thought before slumping across the steering wheel was "I should never have trusted................"

The killer didn't leave immediately but poked around the body until the envelope was discovered. "No point in leaving this behind." Stashing the envelope in one pocket and the gun in the other, the figure again checked the surroundings, scurried to the SUV and drove off.

Around three in the morning the police, noting the parked car with an apparent occupant, found the body.

&

Scotland, DunRoslin Castle: Exposing the Mole

It was five in the morning when, by chance, Wolfram looked out of his bedroom window to see a police car, lights flashing, enter the castle gates. He strained to see what was happening at the front entrance but didn't have a clear view. The police car didn't leave. Knowing she would be awake he dialed Angi on his cell phone. "Something's up, a police car just arrived and they're staying. Let's gather in my room in ten minutes. I'll call Morgan if you get Vette."

"Right," replied a sleepy Angi. "Any thought on what it might be?"

"No, but I expect we'll know soon. Maybe Antonino planned to be at Iona and drowned or something. To be so lucky," was Wolfram's immediate assessment.

"Not likely. If anything, he's planning an attack on the castle with armored knights on horses," replied Angi. "See yah in ten," was her sleepy reply.

When the four gathered they tried to imagine what the police would be doing at the castle at 6 in the morning. It had to be serious. Maybe it was something personal to do with Andrew, or someone else, but their gut feeling was that it had to do with the medallion. With no further information, they proceeded with their normal routine and headed to the gym. They had finally convinced Morgan it was good for him.

"I'll see if Andrew is around and join you in a few minutes," said Wolfram, heading towards the library and office.

Minutes later he appeared in the gym with a perplexed look on his face.

"What's up?" asked an inquisitive Vette.

"Andrew is upset about something......in fact, I haven't seen him so upset. It seems he's planning a group meeting sometime this morning, using the large open room in the east wing, the one that's been under construction."

"Is it for everyone involved in the quest?" asked Angi. Before Wolfram had time to respond, she continued, "If so, why? He didn't tell you?" wondering why Andrew had suddenly become uncommunicative.

"No, he's tight-lipped. He's definitely rattled. We need to be prepared for something big. By the way, he wants to speak to you, Angi, when you are finished here. Maybe you'll get more out of him. I'm certain the police are still in the building. Dylan's also gone silent, a bad sign."

"I'm off. I can't stand the suspense," said Angi.

Twenty minutes later she returned. The three waited. "Well, this is a surprise. Andrew wants me to announce at ten this morning, at the meeting you spoke of Wolfram that we will be ceasing operations and we, that's the four of us, will be heading home tomorrow morning."

"Wow, that was sudden," replied Vette.

"Yah, there was no sign of that yesterday. Do you think we've upset him? He's such a nice guy, any thoughts on what it might be," reflected Morgan.

"He gave no hint, in fact he was rather abrupt, not his usual demeanor," replied Angi, with a puzzled expression.

"I think this announcement is a ploy," said Wolfram, diverting the focus from them. "Andrew doesn't act like this. Whatever happened, he and likely Bryce and Dylan, need to flush out the mole. It is the mole they are after. So the mole has done something and, because he can't rule out any of us, he's upped the barrier."

"Good God, do you think he suspects one of us," asked Vette. "I should go up there and bop him on the nose for such evil thoughts."

"Vette, I understand your reaction but let's face it we tried every possible avenue and could not unearth the mole, which means he or she is damn clever or we're missing some obvious point. I keep thinking the answer is staring us in the face," replied Wolfram.

"OK, so we'll go to the meeting and I'll make the announcement as if I'm oblivious of what might be afoot. Let's hope it works," replied Angi, "otherwise we'll be heading home tomorrow morning. I hope it also unearths what's created this storm."

"Angi, be on your guard, you could be the target." warned Wolfram.

"Right, I've got the medallion and that's what Antonino's after," acknowledged Angi, having long realized the medallion had become a target for the unscrupulous.

Breakfast was eaten with little of the usual chatter. Andrew and Dylan were unavailable, but Bryce was pleasant enough.

At 9:45am they made their way to the east wing. The unfinished room on the ground floor which the workmen left had been hastily prepared for the meeting. Forlornly, at one end of the room were three chairs. There were no other seating arrangements. The four friends watched as household staff, Dylan's men, Bryce and Dana arrived and stood listlessly waiting. Finally, Andrew appeared and made his way toward the four. In the rush to attend the meeting one person in the room had mistakenly put on the odd jacket of the previous night.

As Andrew approached, Wolfram whispered to Angi. "I'm certain the police have been posted at the two doors."

Andrew, with a forced smile said as he approached Wolfram and Angi. "I'd like the two of you to come with me to the front. Vette and Morgan, can you join the others."

Vette taking Morgan's arm, responding as if her feelings had been hurt, said "Come on Morgan, it is clear we are not wanted."

The stage was set. Turning to Angi, Andrew spoke formally, "I'll announce that you have something to say and then you proceed as we discussed." Angi and Wolfram sat down leaving a side chair for Andrew. Angi would be in the middle.

"I understand. Go ahead," came the crisp response from Angi.

Andrew, projecting his voice, began, "I know you are wondering why I've asked everyone to come together this morning. I want to thank each and every one of you for all your effort in the past weeks, some of you going beyond the call of duty. For that reason, I wanted everyone to hear an important announcement from Angi." On cue, Angi stood up as Andrew sat down.

Angi looked out on a group of faces that had become friends on a rather strange journey. With mixed feelings she proceeded, "I would also like to thank each one of you for all your kindness and assistance to me and my three companions since we've arrived in Scotland. This has been an unbelievable quest, one we could never have imagined even months ago. However, we have come to a dead end. As you may know, we have no clue to the final gemstone and cannot keep imposing on Andrew. So, with regret, it has been decided that the four of us will be leaving to return to North America tomorrow morning. If and when something turns up we'll revise our plans. Once again, our deepest thanks." hesitating, she stepped back but remained standing.

A hush fell on the assembled group, several glancing at one another not wanting to believe this exciting interlude was over. Ian was the first to speak. "Well, I'm truly sorry to hear this, you were making such progress."

Matt, one of Dylan's senior team members spoke, "I'm also sorry. I know I speak for our team, we had such high hopes we would see this to the end."

As they were speaking, a member in the front row suddenly stepped forward directly in front of Angi. The room went silent when a pistol was pulled from a jacket pocket and pointed into Angi's face.

In a shrill voice, Dana said, "So, just like that, you God damn Americans are going to take the medallion back home. It is not yours, it is mine."

In disbelief, Andrew spoke, "Dana ....you? Why?"

"Never mind.......Pass it over miss goody two shoes," yelled Dana, as she held out her right hand, the gun rigidly grasped in her left.

A chill engulfed Angi as she said to herself, "I'm on my own...... must use what Sirona has taught me..........first, a shield against a bullet ....can't use my hands." ......Surprising herself, Angi created an invisible shield around her body. "There, that's done.... ....next? ....I could heat up the metal on the gun.........God, it is hard to concentrate with a gun stuck in your face."

"Time's up.............I'll shoot and take the medallion if that's what you want," snarled Dana. Angi remained irritatingly still. Suddenly, Dana felt the warmth of the metal which steadily grew hotter. "You damn witch!" In a panic, her dark eyes riveted on Angi she started to squirm when the metal began to burn her hand.

The instant Dana relaxed her grip, Angi's arm snapped upward causing the gun to fly into the air, stopping and hanging precariously about ten feet above the assembly.

Dylan and Wolfram reacted. Dana was instantly pinned to the floor. Together, they pulled a restrained Dana to her feet fighting and cursing. The local police were summoned. Three officers arrived and handcuffed Dana.

Andrew stepped towards her. "Why, Dana, I trusted you?"

"As if you care......I needed the money. My divorce diminished my lifestyle, and you stole my position at the university," replied Dana still struggling.

"I did no such thing, you were never on the list," interjected Andrew.

"Who cares," was the sarcastic reply. "I'm no fool. When I realized the value of the medallion, I wasn't about to pass it over to that bastard Dante for any amount of money."

"You killed Antonino? The police thought the shooting was a professional job. Where did you learn about guns?" asked Andrew.

"My x-husband, an American, was a gun fanatic. I knew your Antonino as Dante La Villa. I should get a reward for ridding the world of such scum."

Angi turned on her saying, "You are the one who hit me on the head at Scone. You could have killed me." She was incensed at Dana's ruthlessness and her own stupidity in ignoring her intuition.

"Too bad I didn't. Maybe then that damn medallion wouldn't have attacked me." Raising her right hand she said, "See this scar, that's what I got for my trouble. It is good I am left handed," replied a defiant Dana.

"Take her away," said a disgusted Andrew.

The incident had almost passed when Sirona arrived, alerted by the spike in the medallion's monitoring device.

Angi did not hear the harp music in the midst of all the commotion.

Seeing the gun floating in the air, Sirona smiled and said to herself, "Fantastic, Angi. All on your own.........now that is a step forward."

But Dana wasn't going quietly. In leaving she yelled, with vengeance, "You diabolical witch............Don't think you are free of me. I'm going to spill everything to the media. If I can't have that God damn medallion then no one will have peace. You'll never get to Tara."

At this moment Angi spotted Sirona, invisible to the others.

"While I can't interfere in helping you find the gemstones, I've got no restrictions in dealing with this chatterbox." With an adjustment of her hand device she flashed a bright light in front of Dana's face.

Dana blinked, a sign that subconsciously the flash registered.

"What did you do?" asked Angi.

Sirona replied, "Dana will have only a garbled memory of the medallion, and nothing of its magical properties. She will remember killing Antonino over an antique relic which is all that matters."

"Angi who are you talking to?" whispered Vette who had come to her side. Then she answered herself, "Oh, Sirona........."

"Yes, I'll explain later. I'm glad this fracas is over," said Angi, and to herself "and the shield wasn't tested......not sure it would have stopped a bullet......I'll need more training on that one."

As two police officers escorted Dana out of the building, a third, the apparent leader, stood talking to Dylan and Wolfram. Then Wolfram, with a plastic bag in hand, asked with a rye grin, "Ah, Angi, I wonder if you might retrieve the flying gun," as his eyes looked upward.

"Oh, I almost forgot." Angi raised her arm and the gun gently descended falling into the open bag.

Looking at Andrew the policeman said, "I won't even ask. I'll need to fudge this in my report. I'll request silence from the other two. If this gets out I'll be filling out papers for the next ten months or be committed to a mental hospital. Thankfully we've got the killer and the weapon. Let's hope that's enough," and he left shaking his head.

"What about Dana," asked Andrew? "She could be trouble."

Angi stepped closer to Andrew saying "That won't happen, Andrew, I'll fill you in later."

At this point the room was alive with chatter. Angi turned to ask, "Andrew, before everyone disperses, should we revise our earlier announcement or are the four of us still on flights back home tomorrow morning?"

"Right O.........definitely another announcement," came the happier reply. Andrew made two attempts at 'May we have your attention,' before the noise abated. In a more relaxed tone, he began, "I suppose there's little need to explain the theatrics, but I'll do it anyway. Early this morning the police arrived to inform us that Antonino, who some of you knew, had been murdered in Musselburgh. The killing had all the earmarks of a professional job, so we suspected anyone familiar with guns. Dana was not on that list. We gambled that this morning's ploy might force the mole in our midst to act, which it did. I'm grateful no one got hurt." Turning he added, "Believe me, Angi, I'm sorry you became the target."

"Alls well that ends well, they say," replied Angi. "No problem Andrew, remember I had the medallion on my side."

Andrew, having a captive audience, went on, "So, we are revising our previous statement. We have not given up on our search, our four special guests will be staying on but, it is true, we haven't a single clue to the whereabouts of the last gemstone. This will be our immediate focus."

The relief in the room was palpable. Smiles were everywhere. One of Dylan's men enthusiastic voice could be heard saying, "Yes......onward and upward!" Caught up in a shared journey none wanted it to end but in victory. It had become a magical trip. Their relationships had melded, each growing aware of their need for each other. Whatever lay ahead they would do it together. Dana's threat had solidified their feelings, a positive outcome to an unpleasant event.

Vette stepped forward and smiled. "I understand Andrew......this was not an easy call. Let's move on and, as they say over here, 'have a cup tea' or something. I'm famished."

"Me too, I could eat a horse," said Morgan. "In addition, we should be jubilant that Antonino is no longer haunting our footsteps."

Ian had heard the comments and stepped towards Andrew, "Sir, I think we deserve an early lunch, one with extra sustenance. What do you think?"

"An excellent idea, Ian, let's have a huge spread for everyone. We need a day off, time to relax and recuperate. There's plenty of time for the quest."

With that they joined a jubilant crowd heading back to the main castle.

Sirona smiling, thought, "Time to leave. It is good to have these two annoying obstacles out of the way. Time is imperative, although I'd never say that to Angi. The gates have to be opened, and soon. We're almost there."

&

DunRoslin Castle: The Last Gemstone

Forty-eight hours had passed with little headway. Whether Margaret Caldwell, the last descendant of James and Morag Morgan had passed the gemstone onto a relative remained a mystery. Andrew and Bryce contacted members of known and secret organizations, putting out feelers regarding possible relatives or some word of a secret gemstone. Wolfram and Angi worked the computers checking ancestry lists, while Morgan and Vette scoured the Edinburgh University library archives.

On a sunny Friday afternoon, Angi, Wolfram, Morgan, Vette, Andrew, and Bryce gathered in the castle library to discuss their progress. A gentle breeze cascaded through open windows and, patches of color danced around the room when the sun touched the stained glass windows. Everyone was in a relaxed mood.

With a broad smile Morgan began, "You don't suppose that Sirona could be wrong in suggesting we'll have the last gemstone by the full moon? I'm sure you know that's tonight."

"Bite your tongue, Morgan," snapped Vette. "You could be opening a hornet's nest.....if Sirona can be wrong with this, then what else? Not a positive for Tara."

"Just kidding," chuckled Morgan. "But now that we've kicked the door open have any of you considered what it might mean to travel into another dimension?"

"Why," asked Wolfram, "do you know something we don't?"

Morgan weighed his words carefully. "Well, most Celtic tales regarding the fairy folk, if that is what Sirona is, seem to infer there is a major time difference between our two worlds; as much as a hundredfold."

"What do you mean?" asked Vette.

"If the tales are true, it could mean one day of their time could be a hundred years of ours. In other words if we step into this other dimension we might be gone for centuries," replied Morgan, wanting to get this off his chest.

"Well, that's a kicker," said Vette, and looking at the others asked, "Is there any way we can be sure?"

"Maybe these were garbled tales told to discourage such travel," answered Angi. "After all, there are those in power that would discourage such interactions. But if the Druids and older civilizations used such gates in the past we would have to assume that this time factor wasn't an issue. Maybe I could run this past Sirona tonight."

"Good idea," replied Wolfram. "I expect we'll have quite a few questions for her before we blast through the Tara gate. But this whole discussion is rather premature or pointless if we don't find the last gemstone. By the way, Angi, how's the training going, or are you allowed to talk about it."

"At the beginning Sirona asked me not to discuss it, and I'll stick to that. However, in general, the sessions are getting increasingly complex. I thought nurses' training was difficult, this tops it tenfold. Sirona expects me to grasp new principles in spirituality and science in order to manipulate the forces around us. It is easy to slip back into our current world thinking, believe me. She keeps saying that I need to be more proficient by the time we reach Tara.........if I live that long."

The others smiled as this was Angi's first frustrated assessment on her learning curve under a tutor from another dimension.

She went on, "This is not easy, no matter how clever and easy magic appears in the movies. When spirituality and science are combined it creates a different world. I best stop there," realizing she still wanted to share more with her friends.

Andrew responded, "I speak for all of us, Angi, I hope there comes a time when you can divulge more. From my perspective it certainly looks like magic, but I also know that you are likely demonstrating forgotten skills from the past, which only a few enlightened masters even know about today."

"And believe me, Andrew, I'm a neophyte. There's part of me that is looking forward to learning more and another part that is terrified as to what that might bring," replied Angi, expressing her true feelings for the first time.

Wolfram itching to get back on tract said, "So, leaving these tempting discussions aside, can we discuss what we have, if anything, on the last gemstone?"

Andrew began, "Bryce and I have been in contact with a number of key people in Scotland, Wales and Ireland. These people can be trusted as we do not want to attract unwanted attention, we've had enough of that. Two individuals thought there might be a distant relative whom they are pursuing. The Caldwell woman was in her nineties when she died and had few known friends or family. We can only hope something turns up ....but all we have is hope. Any luck on the Internet or university?"

"We're in the same boat," replied Angi, "nothing. We tracked a number of Caldwell family charts but came up dry. Morgan and Vette found a James Morgan, but this turned out to be a later date than our man of the 1600s. Anyway, this line ended at the first World War."

"I feared this and am surprised it only involved one gemstone," replied Andrew. When family lines die out, unless family heirlooms and records are passed on to some library or museum, the information vanishes. But a secret of this magnitude would never be lightly discarded, but...." hesitating, "if she died suddenly it might be lingering in some lawyer's safe."

"We're within hours of the full moon," said Wolfram, "and it looks like we have not much to go on."

Angi responded, "I hear you, Wolfram, but until I learn otherwise I'm sticking with Sirona's prediction."

"All right, but maybe there's something we've missed?" asked Wolfram, growing frustrated with their blocked progress. "Can anyone think of another avenue?"

Before anyone could reply, Ian appeared saying, "Sir, a woman has arrived unexpectedly by taxi from the airport. She insists on speaking to Lord Lywillan, stating it is in regard to his urgent request."

"Cool.........is this the miracle we've been waiting for?" asked Vette.

"By all means," replied Bryce, "escort her to the Drawing Room, it is larger. If, as I suspect, this is in regard to the gemstone then it is something we all need to hear."

As Ian left, the group moved along the corridor to the Drawing Room in silent anticipation.

Within minutes a well dressed woman in an expensive mix of blue tones, entered the room with Ian. Unflustered by the number in the room, she scanned the group seeking her contact. In her late sixties, she had a single white streak of hair over her right eyebrow in contrast to her dark gray hair. Her manner portrayed an individual accustomed to being in charge. Ian escorted her directly to Bryce, standing near the entrance.

"Morag Williams this is Lord Lywillan," said Ian in his best managerial style.

Ignoring the others, Morag focused on Bryce and speaking in a similar Welsh accent, said, "It is truly with regret that I've taken this long to get here. I did not receive your summons until a week ago, when it reached me while I was on a business trip in Hong Kong. At first, I wasn't sure it had anything to do with the gemstone left in my care some years ago. After several discrete phone calls this was confirmed. Then I had to change my plans and fly back

211

to Wales where the gemstone was stored, and fly onto Scotland."

Smiling broadly, Bryce responded, "You have no idea how welcome you are. By any chance do you have the gemstone with you?"

"Indeed I do," replied Morag as she opened her beige travel bag and pulled out a familiar purple bag.

Everyone smiled..........but was it a true gemstone?

Angi stepped forward. "Morag, my name is Angi Talismann," reaching out to shake Morag's hand. "This bag is very familiar to us and I am praying it contains an engraved box."

"Indeed it does. The box is almost as beautiful as the stone." Then feeling she needed to explain her role, Morag continued. "I came by this by chance. Margaret was a distant cousin. When she became ill with cancer, for some unknown reason, she called me. I expect she had investigated the remaining family members and decided I was her best candidate. By the time I got to her she was very ill and was able only to stress the secrecy of the gemstone and that it belonged to some ancient medallion."

"This is the medallion," said Angi, giving Morag a good look at the pendant around her neck.

"My word," said Morag, taking time to examine the medallion. "It is certainly unusual and looks ancient. This gemstone will fit perfectly into that vacant slot." At that moment she opened the box which housed an exquisite diamond that glittered in the sunlight.

"Wow!" said Angi, staring at the largest diamond she had ever seen. "It is no wonder the diamond is considered 'the king of the crystals'. It is supposed to activate the crown chakra, connecting the intellect and higher knowledge, and increasing spiritual awareness. This definitely crowns the collection."

"Then I'm delighted to have been the courier of such an exquisite gemstone. My dear mother should be here, as she always said our family was not only descendants of James and Morag Morgan, but also of the Druid Seer, Imergin who lived at the time of the Romans. While another branch of the family was the Guardian of the gemstone, our family knew we shared the honor of something both ancient and powerful. But after so many centuries doubts occurred that this was just a pipe dream. But here I stand as a witness to its reality. Being the last of my family, it is good this is happening now. Completing my mission, I must go. I'm expected in London for an important business meeting this evening. Your secret is secure with me. All the best, whatever lies ahead." and with that Morag turned to leave.

"I'll accompany you to the door," said Bryce. "I assume the taxi is still waiting. Once again, our sincere thanks for all your effort. Can I reimburse you for your trip cancellation?"

"That is most kind, but not necessary. I accepted this responsibility with all of its duties. Money is not an issue," replied Morag, as she and Bryce left.

Angi looking at the diamond asked, "Andrew, would you like to invite Dylan to the installation of the final gemstone as he's been part of this journey?"

"Good idea, Angi. I'll see if he would like a few of his team to come along as well. I'll also ask Ian en route," and he was off.

When everyone was assembled, Angi pulled the small holder from her pocket and retrieved the diamond from the engraved case. Placing it near the medallion the others waited for the expected reaction, never tiring of the spectacle; the sparks dancing around the blue stone, an arc of light reaching out and grasping the diamond, and inserting it in the last slot. But the last gemstone had an additional show. The vibrations of the center blue stone did not stop; the pulsations continued rotating from pale to dark sapphire blue. Then, in sequence, each gemstone lit up, as if the blue stone was orchestrating a countdown. A rainbow of colors danced around the room as the sequence continued for seven rounds, the power of the medallion growing with each cycle. Then it stopped.

The burst of energy caused Angi's knees to buckle.

Seeing her stagger, Wolfram stepped forward and helped her to the nearest chair.

Silence gripped the room as the group tried to grasp the enormity of what had happened.

"What was that?" asked Dylan.

"I've always thought this medallion was a sophisticated computer, and this sequencing is like one starting up. I'm certain if we had extrasensory hearing that there would be a quiet hum as this machine has been fully activated with the arrival of the last crystal," replied Wolfram.

"I think you are right, Wolfram," said Andrew. "And how are you doing, Angi?"

Before Angi had a chance to reply Sirona bounced into the room, this time visible to all. Gasps and startled responses were heard from various individuals.

Standing at her full height, she smiled and said, "Now that's what I was waiting for. Finally the medallion is whole again. You have no idea how much we've longed for this day." Noting the startled expression on the faces in the group she proceeded to ease the tension. Taking a relaxed approach, she continued, "While Angi and I are acquainted, I best introduce myself to each one of you. Perhaps Angi you could do the honors."

"I'd be glad to," replied Angi, pleased to share this relationship with her friends.

For the next hour Sirona and Angi made the rounds, moving from one person to another. The reactions varied. Some were amazed at Sirona's height, some checked the technology, and others were just enthralled at meeting such a distinguished individual from another dimension. This was a momentous event in their lives. They knew that from this point they could never again deny the reality of certain ancient tales.

Relaxing, members had boundless questions. The first off the mark was Wolfram. "I'm curious, we understand you are a hologram. How long can you stay in this form?"

"Now that the medallion has been fully activated, I can stay much longer but still have some limits. I need to judge my time but that's no problem. In the days ahead we will be spending time together as I prepare you for the trip through the Tara gate. While this will be a new and exhilarating experience for you, it is my responsibility to be sure you can manage the journey."

Responding to her reply, Wolfram pressed on, "I'm amazed. If you are a hologram, then it is obvious there is a great deal we have yet to learn about holograms."

Sirona glanced at Angi before speaking, knowing that there was much she would need to convey to the group in time. "Later we'll discuss our advanced techniques and technologies, but first we need to plan for Tara. When we finally meet at the Tara gate you will see that I will be as real as you," as she smiled at Angi.

"Now that we have all the gemstones," asked Andrew, "when do you think we should be at Tara? I expect it may take some time for us to prepare."

"In your calendar, this is the first of July. I expect we will need to be at Tara by the first of the next month. Is that possible?" asked Sirona.

"That depends on what is needed," replied Andrew.

"Basically, each person must make a personal choice to go through the gate. That will be your first task. I would also ask that the remaining Guardians come to Tara as they should see the gate even if they may not want to go through it. Of course there are many logistics in getting everyone on site."

Concerned, Angi asked, "Sirona, several of the Guardians are quite old, will that not be a problem for them?"

"Their physical age is not the problem, but their ability to cope with change is critical. If they come here first, then I will be able to assess their endurance."

"Fine, we'll contact them at once," replied Angi.

"So we're heading to Tara at last," said Morgan, with a wide grin.

"Yes," replied Sirona, warming to the group of enthusiasts. "But remember the gate has been neglected for centuries which could present some unexpected surprises."

"That seems to be par for the course," replied Andrew. "But I expect the majority of us are looking forward to this leap into the future."

"I must go. I'll return this evening for our regular training session, Angi. I'll be intensifying the program." and as quickly as she appeared she was gone.

"Oh great," thought Angi. "I thought the program was already intense. Sirona's trying to cram forty years of training into weeks. Now I am scared. I'm facing a locked, invisible, ancient gate which can only be opened with magic.........God help me."

Chapter 12

DunRoslin Castle: Preparing for Tara

The countdown had begun. A month was all too short. It took days to firm up a plan considering the logistics of getting people to DunRoslin and then on to Tara, restarting the east wing renovations, hiring more staff, and pressing Sirona for more details on the Gate of Tara. The question, still unanswered, was how many would risk the leap into the unknown.

As with other tourist sites, arrangements, mid-summer, had to be made for everything to be completed prior to the morning arrival of employees or tourists, a complex operation in light of the popularity of the Hill of Tara.

At DunRoslin, Tara operations shifted to the large room in the east wing which had been set up with tables, computers, overhead projectors and display boards. Large maps of Tara and its surrounds were referred to regarding transportation and the positioning of everyone on the hill. The high ceiling and cathedral windows of the room provided a bright setting, enhanced by days of sunshine, a steady breeze and Ian's supply of refreshments.

Until confirmed, arrangements had to focus on twenty-one going through the gate; Angi, Wolfram, Vette, Morgan, Andrew, Bryce, the other Guardians (one each from the USA, Australia, New Zealand, Ireland and Scotland), Wolfram's grandfather, plus Dylan and his eight member team.

Andrew, Bryce and Dylan worked feverishly to hire a private jet to transport everyone from Edinburgh to Dublin, and to have a tourist bus at the Dublin airport for the trip to Tara, all difficult on such short notice.

The other Guardians had been contacted and, while they wished to be at Tara, they remained noncommittal about gate travel. Their arrival at DunRoslin was set for ten days prior to August 1st, allowing time for the completion of the east wing renovations, getting acquainted with Sirona, and preparation for the trip to Tara.

Sirona arrived each morning for the Tara planning sessions and returned again in the evenings for Angi's training.

Angi was grateful for Sirona's magical gift of time manipulation as sleep was becoming a scarce commodity. Her day began at 5am with meditation, followed by an hour at the gym. After that, the rest of the day was monopolized with Tara preparations, and training, which had become more complicated as they neared their goal. She rarely got to bed before three in the morning.

Sirona continued answering the many questions from the group and began preparing them for gate travel, the first step being to assess their physical limitations. One morning, standing regally in their midst she asked, "As I recall, Angi, your friends wanted a demonstration of the medallion's power and earlier I waved this aside."

"That's right," replied Angi, having forgotten.

Before Sirona had a chance to proceed, Wolfram interceded, "Actually Sirona that may not be needed as in the past few weeks we've had several impressive demonstrations. But then, I expect this was just the tip of the medallion's powers, right?"

"Indeed," said Sirona glancing at Angi, "the medallion has layers of scientific wonders. In the brief time we have before Tara we will barely tap its marvels. However, today, with Angi's help, I would like to show you another facet of this instrument. Wolfram, would you please come forward?"

Wolfram rose from a nearby chair and, limped towards Sirona not knowing what to expect.

Sirona took the pulsating instrument in her hand and moved it gently over his entire body saying, "It appears, except for some old wounds, that your left hip and leg are your main physical problems. Is that correct?"

"Basically," replied Wolfram, reluctant to discuss his handicap, "I've generally recovered from my car accident but this hip and leg remain a daily scourge. When informed there was no medical solution, I've forced myself to do daily exercises to strengthen whatever remains."

Then, turning, Sirona said, "Angi, I would like you to place your hands on Wolfram's left hip and knee. Using the healing methods I've taught you, I want you, with the aid of the medallion, to restore his physical body."

Angi moved to Wolfram's left side and placed her hands as instructed. She closed her eyes to concentrate on the energies which she knew had to be rearranged for healing. Determined to help her friend, she took her time.

No one spoke as they watched and waited in anticipation. Only the flapping of a distant window blind disturbed the scene.

After ten minutes, Angi stepped back, saying, "Wolfram, I hope that made a difference?"

Wolfram, not wanting to believe the unbelievable, hesitated, then stepped forward gently on his affected leg. When the usual stabbing pain did not greet him, he gingerly took a second step............then more ....then he walked with increased abandon taking several quick steps. Then, totally out of character, he began dancing around the room. In his joyful exuberance he exclaimed, "My God, Angi, you did it! ....The pain, that cursed, stabbing, damnable, pain, is gone............ I've been freed from a debilitating hell." Overjoyed he turned and gave her a bear hug. "Thanks, a million times thanks. I do not give a damn whether it is the medallion or not. If you hadn't appeared in my life I'd never have had this unbelievable journey or my life back." And ignoring the rest he kept gliding about the room unrestrained in his joy.

Angi, caught off guard, was delighted at his response.

"Now that's a happy customer," laughed Sirona.

A smile erupted on all faces as this was the first time they had seen Wolfram so elated. Morgan was the only one in the room who had known happier times.

"We're not through," said Sirona. "Bryce, I would like you to now come along? I know your right knee is still in its healing stage, but we might as well get this attended to as well."

Angi performed a similar but shorter healing procedure on Bryce's knee.

As Bryce walked about without his cane, he smiled "My dearest thanks Angi. I couldn't see myself limping through that gate on a cane. I concur with Wolfram, without your presence this quest would never have happened. At my age this has been a glorious adventure and it is not over yet."

"Good, that seems to have taken care of the apparent physical issues," said Sirona, looking around the room. "Next, I need to check each one of you to make sure you are in balance." And with that she made her rounds placing her vibrating instrument on each shoulder. As she finalized Andrew's assessment, she stepped back, "Angi, I believe we have one more client. This time I would like you to place your hand on Andrew's Third Eye as a general healing is needed." Looking at Andrew she continued, "This is a very old wound which has grown tentacles."

Angi took fifteen minutes this time. Finishing, she looked into Andrew's face, someone she had grown to respect, and said, "Andrew, I hope that gives you some relief," unsure of his precise physical ailment.

Andrew lifted his shoulders, and then raised both arms well above his head and stretched. Smiling he responded, "Fantastic, Angi. I haven't been able to do that in decades. I too was apprehensive about Tara, as I felt my old wounds would jeopardize my effectiveness. Angi, you have brought sunshine into my world, and the greatest quest this Scottish heart could ever have imagined."

Having stopped moving while Andrew was being healed, Wolfram asked Sirona, "What is the difference between your flashing hand instrument and

Angi's medallion? Could you have done the same thing?"

"Not quite. My instrument allows me to assess and rebalance your energy fields but it is not programmed to correct a major illness. Angi possesses a unique genetic makeup which is enhanced by the medallion. As you can see the medallion has a number of specially selected and cut gemstones. Multiple gemstones in combination with the blue stone of Atlantis function like a grid to amplify the energetic potential of a single gemstone to achieve a very powerful healing. The healer, using prescribed techniques, is able to focus and stream the energies in a manner similar to what is possible with what you call a laser."

"Is that the reason Aboriginal shaman throughout the world use quartz crystals in their healing practices?" asked Morgan, continuously impressed with the unfolding revelations of their journey.

"That's right," replied Sirona. "Using quartz crystals, they are able to rebalance and cleanse the blockages in the chakras. But Angi is able to extend this healing process to resolve a major illness and achieve permanent healing."

"Are you implying that crystals can function as some kind of thought-energy amplifiers and operate at some magnetic-electric level?" asked Andrew, trying to grasp the enormity of what Sirona was suggesting.

"That's it," responded Sirona surprised at Andrew's quick understanding. "Many substances and membranes within the human body function like liquid crystals, something you are just discovering. Reducing the process to its simplest form, the quartz crystals, aided by a trained healer, provide a resonance effect on the human crystalline structures, and thereby achieve the intended healing."

"Imagine what this could do for our health industry," commented Bryce.

"That was my thinking exactly," was Angi's instant response. "But can you imagine the resistance. But reducing the need for surgical or chemical intervention would be a precious gift to humanity."

We'll definitely talk about this again. But for now, I just want you to know that everyone in the room is ready for Tara," said Sirona. "A few days before we depart when I know precisely who will be stepping through the gate, I'll recheck you as an extra precaution."

"Whew, I'm glad that's over," said Vette. "I'd have been ticked off if I hadn't qualified. But I wonder Sirona if you might help me with a nagging concern."

"Certainly Vette, what is it?" asked Sirona, growing fond of her newly discovered team of adventurers.

"Well, if everyone in your world is as tall as you then I'm going to feel like a Hobbit in the Lord of the Rings movie."

"What's a Hobbit?" asked Sirona.

220

"Oh, a diminutive individual in comparison to those around them," replied Vette. "It is a character in a recent movie here on earth. Anyway, can you tell me I will not be the only one my size in your world? Be assured whatever you say will not deter me from going, I just want to know what I'll be facing."

"I share Vette's concern," piped up Morgan having had similar thoughts.

Sirona grinned suddenly realizing the problem, "Be assured you won't be alone. While the majority of my people are about my height or taller, we do have others who are more your height. Remember, over the centuries there have been humans who have come through the gates and stayed. You'll meet them when you get there. I'll make sure of that."

Morgan, relieved, pressed another point, "Sirona, I wonder if you might clarify the time difference between our two worlds? Some say centuries could pass in this world to one day in yours. Could this happen to us?"

"Ah, yes, the time factor, I thought that might turn up. Well, admittedly we regard time differently. However, on this occasion I'm under strict orders. If you decide to step through the gate, you will be gone precisely three months, and that is your calendar not ours."

"Sorry to be persistent," continued Morgan, "if you didn't have this strict order, would the gap exist as I stated?"

"No, but some variation may occur, more days than centuries. Our two calendars are not identical. However, there are other dimensions where the time variation could be quite different."

"Oh great........more dimensions." was Wolfram's surprised response. "For now I'd prefer to stick to one at a time."

"Agreed, we've enough to deal with on this first journey," replied Sirona.

"Did I detect an imperative on the opening of this gate?" asked Angi.

"You don't miss much, Angi. I guess it is time I explain the urgency. In past centuries the gates allowed a free flow of energy between our worlds. Because of this, when too much negative energy built up on either side we could reduce the dangerous overload. But, for almost two thousand years the gates have been shut and our worlds are reaching a critical mass of negative energy. Unless we relieve the overload both our worlds could be in jeopardy."

"So, opening the Gate of Tara is some kind of release valve," responded Andrew, suddenly grasping the practical significance of the medallion and the Tara gate.

"Yes, there will be other gates to open but Tara is the principle one. While you may know Tara as an ancient Druid site, or even the capital of the Tuatha De Danann, which is true, its real importance is that it was the central gate of Atlantis. Thousands of years ago Tara was a place of inestimable wealth with palaces, golden temples, marble halls, and many harpists. It was not only known as the entrance to the otherworld, it was also the place where aging was retarded for humans. It was a joyous site, a place of plenty, and one in which people from around the world came for guidance in spiritual and scientific advancement. A faint remnant of this glorious past remains in the five ancient roads which converge at Tara. The concentric ring on the site was a universal symbol for the gate. For these reasons, up until the 12th century the kings of Ireland continued to be crowned there, absorbing the powerful vibrations which lingered in its soil. The opening of the Gate of Tara will release a gigantic wave of healing energy into both our worlds. We have our finest scientists ready to act should this energy burst produce any untoward side effects, but all calculations point to a positive outcome."

"Isn't that amazing," said Morgan. "I just read that some Irish archeologist has discovered an enormous egg-shaped temple underneath the Hill of Tara. Was that a coincidence?"

"The timing of this discovery is coincidental but also important," replied Sirona.

Morgan continued, "Sirona, why was the gate closed in the first place?"

"In the first century when the Roman empire declared war on the Druids, their control of the gates in this corner of the world was not only threatened but there was a growing fear as to what the Romans would do with such technology. After much deliberation between our two worlds, it was decided the gate would be closed temporarily. No one envisioned two thousand years. But closing the Tara gate triggered the closure of all the other earthly gates. That was also the time when the medallion's gemstones were disassembled and passed onto female Druids, which continued right up to the present day. To make sure the site was not disturbed Tara was cursed by the Druids, with an edict of excommunication on all who continued to dwell there. This resulted in the place being deserted and eventually falling into ruin."

Angi, suddenly thought of something, "Will the gate be in the open or covered in some way?"

"That's another problem unique to Tara. In the past all gates were either in temples, mountains, or underground which protected them. When the comets hit Atlantis, the temple at Tara was destroyed. While we were able to save the gate it remained exposed. In past centuries that wasn't a problem, but today's population growth makes this a real concern which will need a temporary remedy."

"Speaking of Tara, Sirona, if there are numerous monuments spread over the hill, where precisely will we be congregating?" asked Andrew. "I am guessing that since the granite Lia Fail or the Stone of Destiny was said to be one of the four treasures brought to Ireland by the Tuatha De Danann, it may be one possibility."

"As they say, Andrew, you are 'spot on'," replied Sirona with a smile, "however, because Lia Fail was moved from its original place at the entrance to the Mound of the Hostages, we've had to revise our calculations. It is likely not serious, and the new location might be easier in the long run, but still it adds an extra wrinkle."

"I'm confused," interjected Vette, "I thought the Stone of Destiny was in Scotland. Are there two?"

"Good point, Vette," interjected Bryce, "If we accept the accounts in Scotland and Ireland there are either two, one is real and the other a fake or there's another story. According to the records, the Lia Fail, in Ireland, was supposed to have left Tara in the sixth century when the High King of Ireland, Murtagh MacErc, loaned it to his brother, Fergus, for his coronation in Scotland. But not long after the coronation Fergus perished in a storm and, it was said, the stone stayed in Scotland. But this story is now regarded as a fable, and, according to the Irish, the stone never left the country."

"So, the Irish stone is the real one?" asked Vette, looking at Sirona.

"Actually," replied Sirona, "the true Lia Fail or Stone of Destiny was sent through the gate when the Druids sealed it shut. They did not want the Romans getting a hold of this magical stone. It will be returned after we get the gate up and running again. There are other magical treasures which will also be returned, but only to their rightful heirs. Both tales were encouraged to remind the people of their true inheritance. Actually, the stone which is now referred to as the Lia Fail is the pillar needed for opening the gate. It was once a magnificently engraved standing stone with a gold cap. Over the centuries the gold and lettering disappeared, so I will have to give Angi precise instructions where to place her hand, a demarcation which was more pronounced in the past."

"Is it possible, Sirona, for you to give us a picture of what we might expect at Tara?" asked Wolfram. Others nodded in agreement.

"As you wish," replied Sirona, bringing up the Lia Fail stone on the large screen, "As you can see, the Lia Fail stone sits on an oval hilltop enclosure of Tara, called the Forradh or Royal Seat. There we will gather. You will be arriving by bus from the Dublin airport sometime before 5am in the morning, and make your way to the crest of the hill. There you will stand in a semi-circle, about twenty feet behind Angi who will be positioned at the Lia Fail. If all goes well, at 5:30 Angi will place her right hand on the Lia Fail, leaving her left hand to command the elements. It is imperative that the medallion is fully exposed. Then Angi, in both Gaelic and English, will command the release of the Gate of Tara. The spell, though powerful, may take several tries."

"Have you any idea how long this might take?" asked Andrew.

"That's hard to predict," replied Sirona. "I understand we have about three hours, and Andrew, you mentioned we might be able to stretch this by telling people that the site is being used as a movie location for the morning. That would help if you can manage it."

"I'll work on that, and will make sure there are chairs for the Guardians as we can't expect them to stand for an indefinite period of time," said Andrew continuing to fine tune their plans.

Sirona then, displaying a more serious tone, said, "There is one essential point that I must insist upon."

"What's that?" asked Wolfram.

"Whatever happens, none of you must go to Angi's aid...........no one," the last two words coming out forcefully as she looked around the room. "Don't make a move no matter what happens. She is the only one protected by the medallion. I don't want to lose any of you. Is that clear?"

"That sounds ominous," replied Angi. "Can you elaborate, as I'll be front and centre to whatever nature may offer," growing uneasy.

"Expect lightening bolts directed at the Lia Fail, and likely rain and wind," replied Sirona. "This spell is powerful and has been undisturbed for centuries. The originators intended to block easy access."

Angi continued, "If we're successful in breaking the spell, can you tell us what the gate looks like?"

"It is truly spectacular," replied Sirona remembering it from the past. "It is a large circular golden snake biting its tail, about 9.14 meters (30 feet) in circumference. The inner part will look like a glistening sheet of water but it is actually flowing energy."

"The golden snake!" thought Angi, "....it keeps reappearing."

Sirona continued, "If all goes well, I will walk through the veil with a group of individuals from our dimension. The number will depend on how many of you plan to return with us through the gate. To ease your first trip, each person from this world will have an escort who speaks your language. And before you ask, the journey takes a few minutes."

"It is customary when entering another culture to be forearmed regarding their culture and protocols, will these escorts provide us with such?" asked Andrew.

"Yes, this will be their role especially as you will be there for such a short time."

"Will speaking Gaelic be of any value in your world?" asked Andrew,

"It may help you understand some phrases, but a conversation will be difficult. Like you, our language has evolved over time, but I expect those who speak Gaelic will progress faster in communicating in our world," confirmed Sirona.

"When we get back I must get Brigit or Andrew to advise me on Gaelic language studies," thought Angi.

"For my inquisitive nature," asked Vette, "where has the gate been for the past two thousand years?"

"It has been at the Hill of Tara, just locked in another time zone. There was never any danger that someone would bump into it."

"Sirona, by any chance do we have a back up plan should we run into problems at Tara?" asked Wolfram.

"Good point," replied Sirona. "Let's agree that if there's no response after seven tries, I will get Angi to contact me. I can appear as I am now and we will reassess the situation. But I honestly don't believe this will be needed."

"Fine, then it is agreed, while some of us will go through the gate, arrangements will be in place for others to return to Edinburgh," said Andrew still working on the travel plans. "Another point, Sirona, how are you going to block any intruders while all this is going on?"

Sirona, taking a few minutes, finally responded, "Angi and I will travel to the site the night before and set up markers in a hundred yard radius around the site. When Angi places her hand on the pillar, it will activate an invisible but effective force field which will block any intruder."

".......and prevent us from leaving," mumbled Dylan with a glance at his team.

Sirona saw the glance and responded, "You are not trapped, Dylan. All Angi has to do is release her hand from the pillar and press the blue stone. The force field will dissolve instantly."

"What happens to the force field when we leave the site?" asked Wolfram.

"It will dissolve when Angi and I step through the gate."

Dylan thinking of Sirona's earlier comment asked, "By the way, if you can zap Angi to Tara the day before, why can't you do the same for the rest of us?" thinking of all the hassle they had gone through in making travel arrangements.

"It is feasible with Angi because she is wearing the medallion." And foreseeing the next question, continued, "It would not help to remove Angi's medallion to achieve your transfer as it works on her genetic makeup, which can't be duplicated."

"I expect that such DNA programming is common with your technology," asked Andrew?

"Yes, nowadays our technology is tailored to the individual," replied Sirona.

"That's a sure way to reduce thievery," replied Wolfram. "By the way do we have a firm date for our return?"

"I thought Samhain, Oct 31st, would be a good day. It is the old Celtic New Year," replied Sirona. "This was always regarded as the time when the veil separating our worlds was at its weakest, and the atmosphere is filled with magic."

"Returning to earth on October 31st we could encounter cool weather. We may need warmer clothing?" replied Andrew.

"I'll attend to that," replied Sirona.

"Another question on the gate, I don't suppose we're going to leave the gate exposed?" asked Wolfram. "That's a busy tourist site and a gate like this sitting out in the open will be an overnight sensation for the media."

"My people will cloak the gate when Angi and I step through it, as we will be the last to leave," said Sirona.

"Cloaked, but if it is just cloaked is it not still there?" asked Vette.

"A good point, Vette, but in this instance our technology will make it inaccessible. It is somewhat complicated but be assured we won't leave an exposed gate, particularly this one. But it begs the question that we will need a more permanent solution when we get back," replied Sirona.

"I know we'll go over this again, but could you tell us what to expect when we enter your world," asked Angi, realizing they still had little knowledge as to what Sirona's world looked like.

"Certainly," replied Sirona. "You will enter a marble temple where dignitaries will be waiting. Once the formal welcoming ceremony is over, you will be escorted to your quarters, which will be nearby. Your escorts will stay with you until you get oriented. Also, while you are with us you won't age. If you wish, we can also recalibrate your age."

"I expect the young folk will not be interested, but Bryce and I might take you up on the offer," said Andrew with a grin.

Then Sirona shifted the discussion, saying, "The other Guardians will be here in a few days. I'm looking forward to meeting them as elders are well respected in our world."

"I am curious, what constitutes an elder in your world?" asked Morgan. "If you live thousands of years, when do you reach old age?"

This was the first time the topic of age registered with the rest of the group. They waited to see how Sirona would address the question.

"As I mentioned before, we do age, it just takes longer. You will see older individuals in our world who are our leaders. We rely on them for their years of wisdom and experience." Then aware of their increasing anxiety about the challenges ahead, she continued, "I understand you must be experiencing both excitement and anxiety over the last stage of the quest, after all, I am asking you to trust me, a complete stranger and a hologram from another dimension. Be assured we want and need this as much as you. We are prepared to help you rebalance your world and improve the lives of your people. The Golden Age of your myths is true. And since cosmic cycles recur, you are at the entrance of another Golden Age, although the transition may have its birthing pains."

It was Angi's turn to speak. "Sirona, my grandmother always said that life was full of mystery. Little did I realize how much until now. In a matter of weeks the comfortable world I knew has been turned upside down as we slipped into what seemed to be a world of magic and science fiction while trying to cope with a killer stalking our every move. One item would have been enough. I am grateful, for your guidance into a whole new world in which I have learned to manipulate the energies of this world. As I see it, this unique band of adventurers have come a long way since we first met, and having come this far I'm sure we want to see this through. I expect the destiny of everyone present in this room was written on some ancient scroll generations ago. As such, we owe it to our ancestors to fulfill this prophecy. It is our duty to press on to Tara and whatever awaits us beyond."

The response from the group was unanimous. While more questions continued to surface, the group would continue their march in unison towards Tara.

ะ

Ireland: The Hill of Tara

The day finally arrived. In keeping with the solemnity of the occasion, everyone was up and silently boarding the bus by three in the morning, using the time for their own council. Each one carried an identical travel bag, those going through the gate having carefully considered every item.

The Guardians took a while to adapt to Sirona, and she gracefully waited until they felt comfortable in her presence. Wolfram's grandparents were overjoyed at his renewed health and couldn't stop thanking Angi. In the end, the Guardians decided to delay their gate travel, leaving the pioneer trip to the original team. So it came to pass that twelve would step through the gate; Angi, Wolfram, Morgan, Vette, Andrew, Bryce, Dylan and five members of his team, the others remaining behind to manage the transportation for the return trip.

With clear skies the flight to Dublin took the expected twenty-six minutes where, upon landing, the group made their way to a waiting bus for the short trip northwest to the Hill of Tara. Andrew's preliminary arrangements gave them easy access to the site, and in the dim morning light they scrambled out of the bus. Those returning left their travel bags with the bus driver, another hand-picked individual known to Dylan. He would remain with the bus, knowing that if all went according to plan, he would be driving a smaller party back to the airport. Wasting little time, the group headed directly towards the hilltop Royal Seat and the Lia Fail stone each one wearing a bright yellow waterproof poncho and hood, in readiness for the expected rain.

Nature sensed the significance of the day. Birds flitted and danced around the group boisterous in their morning song. A gentle breeze bent the bushes and grasses with a scent of roses in the air. Sunrise was still an hour away but the increasing light and cloudless sky provided a perfect setting for the event.

It was 4:50am when they reached their destination. As they looked around, some for the first time, they grasped Tara's importance as the hilltop provided a commanding view of much of Ireland. Then, taking note of their respective positions, like professional actors and actresses they assumed their places for the drama.

At precisely 5:25am, Angi passed her travel bag to Vette, made sure the medallion was positioned securely on top of her yellow poncho, and placed her right hand firmly into the indentation on the stone pillar as stipulated by Sirona. At that moment a swishing sound circled the hill.

"I expect that's the force field," said Dylan, as one of his team reached out to test its presence, nodding a confirmation to Dylan.

Angi, turning briefly to make sure everyone was in position, some standing and the Guardians sitting, raised her left hand. In a loud commanding voice, said,

First in Gaelic; "In ainm na Breataine Hermes, ordú mé go raibh an Gheata na Teamhrach a chur ar ais!"

Then in English; "In the name of the Great Hermes, I command that the Gate of Tara be restored!"

Andrew glanced at Bryce, both recognizing the name of Hermes from former organizational ceremonies.

Morgan, looking straight ahead, commented, "Now that's interesting. I once read that Hermes was considered the primary god of the Druids."

No one responded.

Nothing happened with the first command, except a few birds taking flight in the distance. Nature's former noisiness had given way to a hushed anticipation.

Just as the second command seemed to draw a blank, a dark cloud appeared out of nowhere and hung above their heads, in stark contrast to the crystal blue sky in all directions.

"Where did that come from?" whispered Vette, surprised by her own edginess.

Angi's third command seemed to aggravate the cloud which started rumbling as if a storm was eminent. At this point the medallion came alive, a rainbow of colors flashing from the gemstones, orchestrated by the blue stone of Atlantis.

Her fourth command brought a more violent reaction. The cloud darkened, the thunder increased in intensity, and lightening spit forth from the cloud. As the storm intensified, a powerful lightning bolt struck near the Lai Fail, cracking one of the rectangular stones within inches of Angi's feet, leaving a burning scent in the air.

"Here we go," was a comment heard within the group.

Standing firm, Angi made a fifth and louder command which aggravated the situation even more. The hill was covered in a shroud of blackness as three lightning bolts struck the ground at different points near the standing stone and Angi.

The only reaction within the group was the clinching of jaw muscles or hands.

Angi, feeling the storm around her, continued, her voice rising above the noise with a sixth command,

"In ainm na Breataine Hermes, ordú mé go raibh an Gheata na Teamhrach a chur ar ais!"

"In the name of the Great Hermes, I command that the Gate of Tara be restored!"

This resulted in more rolling thunder and two intense lightning strikes, one smashing another rectangular stone, the second chipping the base of the Lai Fail. But this seemed to exhaust its protest. A calmness followed as a heavy mist enveloped the entire Hill of Tara, so thick that each member could barely see the yellow ponchos of those standing or sitting nearby. The mist remained for about twelve minutes, soaking their protective ponchos and clothes and dripping down the Lia Fail. Angi had to strengthen her hand pressure to avoid it slipping from the prescribed spot.

Not knowing what to expect the group stood firm, waiting.

Then, a swirling breeze arrived starting at their feet. As the gusts ascended up the pillar it dried their clothes, and disbursed both the mist and the cloud. And, just as Sirona had described, floating in the air inches from the ground with no visible supports was a magnificent circular object, a foot-wide golden metallic snake glimmering in the morning sun, the watery centre alive with energy and light. Even though expected, its splendor and mute grandeur were overpowering.

"The unbelievable has arrived," whispered Morgan. "Before us sits the door to another world. Andrew, is that lettering on the golden snake, Gaelic?"

"Not the Gaelic I know," replied Andrew.

As they finished speaking, Sirona stepped through the silvery veil and strode triumphantly towards Angi, who had not stirred from her position at the Lia Fail.

"Congratulations, Angi, You did it!" said a confident and relaxed Sirona.

Angi, having taken every ounce of courage to withstand the lightning strikes was still glued to the spot. As Sirona approached she thought, "I'm glad I didn't need seven rounds of that bombardment. This magical stuff is not for the faint of heart. Am I ever glad to see Sirona, she does look different in the flesh.........or is this a high definition hologram. Whatever.........I'll go with whatever fits." Slowly releasing her hand from the Lia Fail she stepped forward to greet Sirona with, "Words can hardly describe this magnificent object that hangs before us."

"It is indeed stupendous," replied a jubilant Sirona as she turned to admire the gate. "It is wonderful to see it again."

At that moment eleven other similarly dressed, tall, companions, male and female, stepped through the veil. Sirona signaled the earthly members to come forth.

Passing their yellow ponchos to Matt, Dylan's second in command, the group went to meet their escorts. Sirona did the introductions as both groups assessed each other for the first time. Angi retrieved her travel bag from Vette, placing the strap across her chest.

Sirona then announced, "I think we should get started."

As agreed, the sequence for travel through the gate was to be Dylan and two of his team, followed in order by Andrew, Bryce, Morgan, Vette, Wolfram, Dylan's other three officers, and finally Angi and Sirona."

While the others began to assemble for their exit through the gate, Wolfram turned to bid farewell to his grandparents.

Tyloar reached out to hug his grandson saying, "My boy, this is indeed an auspicious occasion, a beginning of something incredible. Take care and know your grandmother and I, and the other Guardians, will be standing right here on Oct 31st to welcome you back."

Wolfram then turned to his grandmother and said, "Do not be upset Gran, I will be back. Our destiny has been written in the stars." Giving her a warm hug, he turned quickly, and walked towards the gate. Not looking back he stated in a loud voice, "See you on the other side Angi," and stepped through the veil with his escort.

Angi and Sirona went to bid farewell to those they were leaving behind with Sirona preceding Angi. Brigit stood last in line. As Angi pulled away from hugging her, Brigit gasped, "Angi look! Didn't I tell you the old Irish prophecies had substance."

Angi turned to find the entire Hill of Tara covered in a blanket of white flowers as far as the eye could see. "Oh my, how beautiful.........it must have been the energy release that Sirona spoke of. Brigit, you were right, but I'm still uncomfortable with being a prophetess."

"Never mind, child, it likely has an entirely different meaning in this modern world. My dear, you have brought joy to Ireland, giving us a glimpse of our glorious past and possible future. What more could one ask." Smiling she kissed Angi on the cheek. "Be assured we will be waiting to hear of your adventures and to know how we can help."

As they were saying their goodbyes, the others, in order, had been stepping through the gate. It was now time for Angi and Sirona. They walked together towards the gate, turned momentarily to wave farewell with Angi's parting comment, "See you in October!" Then, turning, she, like the others, placed her left hand on Sirona's right forearm, and stepped through the gate. At that instance, there was a whirling vacuum-like sound as the gate disappeared and the force field dissolved.

The small group remained for a few moments staring out over the familiar Hill and Tara landscape, now resplendent in its white mantle. Then quietly Dylan's men picked up the folding chairs and the group retreated towards their waiting bus. But the hill was not entirely empty.

Invisible to the naked eye in rows stood the spirits of those who had guarded the medallion over the centuries, silent witnesses to the sacred prophecy which had just unfolded. In a far corner stood the spirits of the Druid Seer, Imergin and his students.

"After two thousand years life on this planet is about to return to its former glory. I told you the prophecy would be fulfilled," said Imergin.

"Does this mean our job is done?" asked a senior student.

"Not quite. I think it would be wise for us to linger awhile until we are sure our descendants are firmly established in their new roles. There will be much resistance to the changes ahead. We will greet them again on Samhain. But for today, let us savor the glorious awakening of our precious Hill of Tara."

The End

www.ingramcontent.com/pod-product-compliance
Lightning Source LLC
Chambersburg PA
CBHW080726020726
47503CB00010B/2812